THE SHADOW OF THE NORTHERN LIGHTS

Satu Rämö is a bestselling Finnish-born crime author who has lived in Iceland for the past twenty years. Her Nordic crime *Hildur* series has sold over one million copies worldwide and has been a bestseller in Finland, Iceland, Sweden and Germany. A TV adaptation will premiere in 2026 and the series has also been adapted for the stage. Satu has also published numerous bestselling, prize-winning non-fiction titles in her native Finland.

She lives with her Icelandic husband and two children in the small town of Ísafjörður in northwest Iceland.

THE SHADOW OF THE NORTHERN LIGHTS

Secrets hide in the darkness

SATU RÄMÖ

Translated by Kristian London

ZAFFRE

First published as Jakob by Werner Söderström Ltd in 2023
Published in the English language by arrangement with
Bonnier Rights Finland, Helsinki, Finland

First published in the UK in 2025 by
ZAFFRE
An imprint of Bonnier Books UK
5th Floor, HYLO, 105 Bunhill Row,
London, EC1Y 8LZ

A CIP catalogue record for this book is
available from the British Library.

ISBN: 978-1-80418-843-9

Also available as an ebook and an audiobook

1 3 5 7 9 10 8 6 4 2

Typeset by IDSUK (Data Connection) Ltd
Printed and bound in Great Britain by Clays Ltd, Elcograf S.p.A.

FSC www.fsc.org
MIX
Paper | Supporting
responsible forestry
FSC® C018072

The authorised representative in the EEA is Bonnier Books
UK (Ireland) Limited.
Registered office address: Floor 3, Block 3, Miesian Plaza,
Dublin 2, D02 Y754, Ireland
compliance@bonnierbooks.ie
www.bonnierbooks.co.uk

The WSOY Literary Foundation supported the writing of this book.
The poems on pages 61 and 128 are from the book *Jólin koma* by Jóhannes úr Kötlum (1932).

For my mother, 1957–2023

Ísafjörður
Hólmavík
Dalvík
Stykkishólmur
Grundarfjörður
ISLANTI
Reykjavík
Hveragerði
Selfoss
Keflavík

Come to me
I'll take care of you
Protect you
Come lie down

Come to Me
Lyrics: Björk Guðmundsdóttir (1993)

BEFORE

Chapter 1

Äkäslompolo, June 1988

'I don' wanna.'

The youngest of the three boys swatted away a few mosquitos and stared at his older cousin and his cousin's friend back on land.

The older boys were the same age, the same height, and inseparable. At a distance, the only way to tell them apart was their hair colour: one had very dark hair, almost black, the other, sandy brown.

Although high summer was right around the corner, the water was cool. The sun was blazing from a cloudless sky; the birds were singing. The five-year-old boy's hands picked at the legs of his swimming trunks. He was nervous.

The three boys had planned the day's adventures together. They'd snacked on Swedish pancakes at the youngest boy's house. They'd slapped down Uno cards and joked. The bigger boys had told the younger one about a cool game you could only play if you hadn't started school yet. The idea of being able to do something older kids couldn't intrigued the five-year-old, and the slow summer day suddenly took an exciting turn. The boys had slipped their suntanned feet into trainers, pulled down the ball caps with the visors flipped up at just the right angle, and set off bicycling toward the local beach.

At the lake, the game had escalated to the point where pulling out was no longer an option.

'Go on, go! The treasure's there at the bottom,' the black-haired boy said for the umpteenth time.

The bigger boys had been priming the younger one all afternoon with a story about a boat that had gone down in the lake years before. There'd been three gold door handles on the old vessel, and they were still there at the bottom of the lake.

The legend had riled up all three boys.

Now the water reached up to the youngest boy's knees. The black-haired boy shot his friend a look: *Come on, help me out*. The sandy-haired boy at his side nodded encouragingly and shouted:

'It's not much further. Count ten steps and you'll be really close! I mean, hot!'

The boy in the water lowered his chin to his chest and eyed the boys on shore from under his brows. His tiny upper teeth, or the two that still dangled loosely from the gums, gnawed on his lower lip.

'Right on, Mikael! Just keep going!'

The shout of encouragement from the dark-haired boy prompted the five-year-old to take a few steps backward in the water. Now it reached up to his scrawny thighs. He was covered in goosebumps.

'Am I there yet?' he asked tentatively. It was hard to say whether the shrillness of his voice was caused by fear or the freezing water.

The chatter of cheerful voices and the *ting* of bicycle bells carried from the nearby road. The bicycles didn't turn toward the beach. After they passed, silence fell again.

'Why do I have to get it?' the five-year-old asked, his previous question still unanswered.

'Only little kids are allowed to get it. Big kids can't. That's what the legend says,' the boy's black-haired cousin said convincingly.

His sandy-haired friend continued: 'You're really close. In just a sec you'll be able to dive down and get the first one and show us.'

Defiance flashed in the younger boy's eyes. 'You guys can look at it, but it's mine, since I'm the one getting it. Finders keepers! That's what you guys said!'

The black-haired boy placed his hands on his hips and said with a ten-year-old's confidence: 'We know that. It's yours.'

The words persuaded his younger cousin to turn back to the lake. Sharp, narrow shoulder blades protruded from the smaller boy's back as he slowly made his way deeper. His steps were short, his body rocked lightly from side to side as he tried to maintain his balance. Inch by inch, the water reached higher. Now it was up to his elbows.

The sun shimmered on the lake. Somewhere in the distance, thunder rumbled. The rain clouds and stormfront weren't close, but the explosive sound echoed for miles.

A couple more steps, and the boy's feet wouldn't be able to reach the bottom.

'He doesn't know how to swim yet,' the boy with black hair chuckled to his friend.

There was a faint plop. As if a pebble had been carefully dropped into the water from just above the surface.

The mood shifted lightning fast. All joy evaporated from the game. The black-haired boy's body tensed. His forehead furrowed; his palms clenched into fists. His heart was beating in his throat. He tasted metal. 'Holy crap, he believed us,' he gasped.

A panicked guffaw escaped his friend's lips and then the laughter caught in his throat. The banter that had floated lightly between the older boys turned to huffing and panting as they dashed into the lake.

The friends dove and raked the lake bed with their hands.

They surfaced and urgently sucked in air until their lungs were bursting.

It was in vain. The younger cousin was gone.

Exhausted, the two older boys scrambled back to shore. They scooped up their clothes and threw them on, eyes avoiding the five-year-old's bunched-up sweats and the T-shirt on the sand. They grabbed their bikes, leaving the smallest one behind. Their feet caught in their pedals as they frantically rode to the edge of the nearby woods, legs on fire. They glanced around like a flock of songbirds scanning their surroundings. Had anyone seen them? Had there been anyone else on the road?

But all they detected was the soft silence of a summer afternoon. The wind rustled in the treetops. A squirrel scurried up the trunk of a nearby spruce, claws scratching exuberantly.

The black-haired boy lay belly down on the springy ground. He felt like someone was walking on top of him. His body was lurching strangely. The damp of the forest mingled with the cold sweat that had beaded up on his skin, penetrating his lightweight clothes. He was cold.

At his side, his sandy-haired friend retched. Between the deep heaves, he kept saying: 'We can never tell anyone about this. Ever!'

NOW

Chapter 2

Ísafjörður, October 2021

Detective Hildur Rúnarsdóttir felt the short hair tickling her cheek. She smelled watermelon shampoo. She squeezed hard, felt the broad shoulders beneath the heavy parka.

Her little sister. Björk Holm.

Hildur savoured the name, still trying to get used to it. Not that it was new: her little sister had been Björk Holm much longer than she'd been Björk Rúnarsdóttir. Her last name had changed to Holm when she moved to the Faroe Islands. Holm had been the girls' aunt Hulda's married name, and she kept it after her divorce.

Hildur kept hugging her sister. She knew she couldn't draw out the departure any longer, but she didn't want to let go. It would have been much easier to rip off the plaster and drop Björk off at the airport entrance, then drive back to her job at Ísafjörður's tiny police department.

But somehow Hildur hadn't been able to. She and Björk had been separated for over two decades, and every moment apart since reuniting a year and a half ago had been excruciating. After a long search, Hildur had finally found her little sister in the Faroes.

Björk had been shocked to discover she and Rósa had another sister, and that Hulda, whom she thought of as a foster mother, was actually her aunt. She knew her biological mother was dead, but she'd never discussed the matter in any depth with Hulda. She'd actually never discussed anything in any depth with Hulda: Hulda had been a quiet woman, lost in her own world.

But Björk didn't for an instant doubt the truthfulness of Hildur's account. The trust between them had been immediate. Hildur could still remember what Björk had said that first day, as she made them coffee:

'You feel so familiar.'

The impression had been mutual. Finding each other after such a long time had felt incredible.

That's how it is with some people: the space between two opened minds is bridged in the blink of an eye. Right after those first words, it felt as if the other one had always been there. They'd talked for days at the big table in Björk's kitchen about all that had happened. Hildur had shared everything she'd discovered about their past, and Björk had reciprocated with her own memories.

Childhood in the Faroes had been hard on Björk and Rósa. Hulda had looked after the sisters but been emotionally aloof. Quiet and reserved. Apparently, dementia had set in early, for as the sisters approached their teen years, Hulda completely lost her ability to manage. The girls had been forced to be independent at a young age. The two of them had done the shopping, the cooking, and the housework. But they hadn't had a curfew, and no one had asked where they were going or with whom.

Hildur had seen plenty of similar cases in her work as a police officer. In addition to serving as the local detective, she headed up the missing children's unit. Most of the kids had run away from child protection services. The fact that Hildur's own sisters had been neglected and forced to grow up far too young was an ironic twist of fate.

Björk had been so young when she and Rósa were sent away to the Faroes that she had very few concrete recollections of her time in Iceland. The earliest childhood memories generally form about the age of three. Björk had been six when tragedy struck. She'd said she'd sometimes caught flashes of being in the dark, rumbling back seat of a car, but she hadn't been able to place things in the correct chronological order or connect them to other events. Evidently, the memory traces had disappeared. Going to live among strangers and having to learn a new language had no doubt further confused whatever few images remained.

Hulda had never told the girls the truth about their mother or anything about their past in Iceland. And now it was too late to ask questions: Hulda had died early that year. Since her passing, Björk had decided to move back to Iceland. She'd said she wanted to be closer to Hildur and now that Hulda was gone, there was nothing keeping her in the Faroes.

Over the past year, Björk had repeatedly shared with Hildur that their meeting had nudged things into motion. She'd decided the time had come to make her plans reality; otherwise, they'd remain dreams forever. Björk had spent the entirety of her adult life running a sheep farm in the Faroes, but now she'd sold the sheep, closed up the house, and moved to Iceland and began putting her nursing degree to work. She didn't have a permanent job yet but believed it wouldn't be long. She spoke Icelandic, and there was a shortage of health care workers in the country. Just now she was filling in at the central hospital in Reykjavík. Temps were in particular demand during the vacation season.

Hildur had learned that when Björk wasn't working, she crocheted and kickboxed, devoured crime novels, and watched every possible police procedural on television. Björk had been incredibly interested in Hildur's work. That felt nice.

There were two doors in the rear wall of Ísafjörður's tiny airport. Arriving passengers entered the terminal through the southern door, while the northern one was for departing travellers. But Björk wasn't flying home; she'd come to the airport to rent a car.

During the pandemic, rental agencies had sold off much of their fleets, but now that Covid restrictions had gradually faded into history, travel was picking up again. As the Christmas season approached, agencies tried to keep whatever remained of their fleets rented as efficiently as possible, which meant moving cars between locations. That had suited Björk, whose own vehicle was currently in the garage.

'It would have been amazing to spend more time here, but I promised to work. There are a lot of shifts available right now.'

Hildur understood. Björk and Hildur were similar in that regard: it didn't make much difference what days they worked, because there was no one waiting at home.

'So we're set for Easter, then?' Björk asked. A vertical line appeared between her brows. Hildur had noticed it formed any time Björk was concentrating on something.

Hildur nodded firmly. For Icelanders, the long Easter vacation was the much-anticipated highlight of the spring. That was when families flew off on package trips to the Canary Islands or Florida or holed up at a relative's cabin to eat giant chocolate eggs and read the riddle found inside. Hildur and Björk had decided they'd fly to the Faroe Islands with Aunt Tinna. Björk would show them around, and they'd visit Hulda's gravesite.

Hildur noticed it was a little past two. The light would be fading soon. It would be best for Björk to hit the road, so she'd make it through the mountains before darkness fell.

Hildur felt the imaginary knot in her chest constrict. The familiar anxiety, the oppressive sensation she'd been feeling for a few days now, was tightening its grip. That could only mean one thing:

circumstances in her immediate environment were taking shape in a way that meant something bad was about to happen. Her toes were cold. She ought to have worn her winter boots instead of her running shoes. She rose onto her tiptoes a few times to get the blood circulating again.

Björk reached down for the backpack at her feet and threw it over her shoulder.

Hildur knew she ought to hold her tongue, but she couldn't stop herself from musing: 'I wonder how Rósa's doing?'

The smile on Björk's face evaporated. She nervously twirled the rental keys in her hand and glanced to the side, then adjusted her backpack and answered with firmly pinched lips:

'That topic is off limits, and you know it.'

Chapter 3

Hildur stood there watching as Björk crossed the windswept car park to her rental car. The airport was on a gorgeous but impractical site, at the foot of a mountain thrusting into the fjord. North of the runway was the sea, with the fjord's narrow mouth opening into the Atlantic. To the west and east rose steep, flat-topped mountains. Flying from the fjords to the capital could be an uncertain prospect; flights often had to be cancelled due to wind or fog.

Hildur was frustrated with herself for ending the pleasant visit on a sour note by raising the forbidden topic. She and Björk had grown close since that first encounter in the Faroes. But Björk refused to discuss Rósa. That had been her one condition when she and Hildur had decided to get reacquainted. Hildur had agreed to it. What else could she do? Björk had threatened to cut ties with Hildur if she insisted on pressing the matter. So Rósa remained a mystery.

Instead, Hildur had tried to make whatever discreet inquiries she could. She'd looked at every public source of information with no success. Rósa had no social media presence under her own name. Hildur couldn't find a phone number for her, and the Faroese address register indicated she still lived at the house owned by Björk, but Hildur had seen neither hide nor hair of her other sister during her visit to the islands.

Hildur had initially considered doing more digging. She could have used her police contacts to fish for more information. She had reached for her phone more than once, but each time she had pressed the cancel icon and slipped the phone back in her pocket. She didn't want to risk Björk learning about her sleuthing attempts. The Faroe Islands were even smaller than Iceland, and rumours presumably spread like wildfire. Hildur had to restrain herself from further inquiries. It was hard, but for the time being it was the only option.

Hildur climbed into Brenda, her trusty, rust-hemmed Toyota Land Cruiser. The vehicle had been named for the grass-skirted doll swaying on the dash, given to Hildur long ago by a grateful hitchhiker.

Hildur exhaled air onto the cold windscreen and used her forefinger to trace wave-like patterns on the fogged glass. The waves gradually shrank and eventually faded.

She bit her lower lip and tried to shake off the creeping anxiety. She tried to evade the feeling every time. But resisting was pointless. The angst wasn't going anywhere, and she knew it. Hildur had felt a variety of constricting sensations in her throat and chest since early adolescence. Serious traffic accidents, homicides, and other human catastrophes didn't come to Hildur as a surprise. She always knew several days beforehand. The hardest thing wasn't being able to prevent the misfortune from happening, because Hildur never knew where it would take place or who the victims would be. The gift – or maybe the curse – of seeing had been passed down to her through her maternal lineage. Her great-grandmother Hrafntinna had once been Iceland's most famous seer, capable of telling stories about the future and offering advice to those who sought it. Some measure of this gift had come down to Hildur. Hildur knew she wasn't nearly as skilled as Hrafntinna; only drops of foresight had drizzled down to her.

Hildur knew too much and at the same time too little.

The angst was an oppressive feeling, but Hildur had grown used to it over the years. Exercise usually helped.

She was considering going for a run now; she'd come prepared in her running gear. All she had to do was pull on the reflective vest she kept in Brenda's cargo space. The thought of jogging down the road to the base of the fjord and past the stables cheered her.

Just then Hildur's phone rang. A quick glance at the screen dampened her spirits again. It was her boss, Jónas Ingimarsson.

Hildur had been dismayed to learn that of all possible candidates, Jónas had been named police chief of Ísafjörður after the former chief, Elísabet Baldursdóttir, had moved to Reykjavík.

Hildur answered in a neutral voice: 'What is it?'

She heard a loud grunt at the other end. 'What's got your goat? Or is that the problem – you need a little butting?'

Jónas guffawed until overcome by a powerful coughing fit.

Hildur seethed. She had the urge to let fly with an equally crude retort but snapped her mouth shut. Her boss was an idiot. There was no point losing her temper over it. That would just encourage him. She left a lingering pause before continuing in an overly friendly voice: 'What's up, pal?'

'Get your arse back here to the station, on the double.'

Jónas was his usual irritable self on this December day. He'd retired on a disability pension from the Reykjavík police department a couple of years earlier due to chronic hip pain, but apparently he'd grown bored of the pensioner's life or found better pain meds. When the position of Ísafjörður police chief had opened up last autumn, he'd been the only applicant. Jónas had always spoken disparagingly of rural life, but the position and especially the salary appeared to have won out over the horrors of living in a small town.

Hildur knew she'd have got the job if she'd applied for it. But she didn't want the responsibility of a supervisory position. She wanted to be out in the field, investigating crimes. She had no interest in answering to other people or their behaviour. She was happiest performing duties she could carry out independently.

But when she learned who her new boss was, she'd been shocked. Of all the people in the world, Jónas. It had felt like a punishment.

'What's going on?'

'Get a move on, sister! I want you to twirl through the station for some instructions, then take yourself down to the harbour.'

Twirl through? Jónas spoke of his office as if it were a strip club. Well, he'd spent plenty of time at those establishments. When Hildur spent a few years working in Reykjavík as a rookie before moving back to her hometown, she'd ended up in the same department as Jónas. From their very first shift together, it was clear Jónas was a redneck who worshipped his musclebound reflection and looked down on everyone except his white male colleagues.

Strip clubs had been legal in Reykjavík at the time, and on more than one occasion Jónas had boasted in the break room about having conducted 'in-depth fieldwork' before letting out a belly-laugh. One day, Hildur had retorted there probably weren't many women who were willing to take off their clothes for him for free. That had shut him up.

Rumours of Jónas's violent behaviour toward his wife had reinforced Hildur's view of his nastiness. The wife had finally got wise and called it quits. She was in a new relationship now, with a consultant who worked at the Ministry of the Interior.

'Jakob's already on his way to the harbour to make arrangements for your departure. You'll meet him there.'

Hildur pressed the phone to her ear to hear more clearly. She was getting the sense a run wasn't in the cards today. 'Departure where?'

'To the salmon farm,' Jónas snapped. 'A diver feeding the fish found a body in the water.'

Chapter 4

'Daginn!'

Junior detective Jakob Johanson's loud greeting was swallowed up by the thick blanket of snow. The white mantle had dulled the sharp steel contours of the Eimskip containers.

The soft yellow streetlamps cast a spectral glow over the harbour yard. An old man in a blood-spattered apron looked out the window to see what had caused the sudden commotion outside his little fish shop.

Hildur returned Jakob's greeting with a wave and slammed the driver's door. It didn't close. Hildur opened it and slammed it again, this time harder. Brenda required a firm touch sometimes.

Hildur nodded at the fishmonger. On the rare occasions she made herself a home-cooked meal, this is where she bought the ingredients. Fresh-caught fish tasted heavenly fried in butter. But just now the thought of fish made her nauseous.

Jónas had brought Hildur up to date at the police station. She knew what awaited her and Jakob offshore.

Her first instinct had been that an accident had taken place at sea. But no fishing boats had been involved in accidents recently, or at least none had been reported. Winter swimming had exploded in popularity: maybe someone had swum out too far, exhausted themselves, and died? Or maybe an intoxicated individual had fallen in the water and drowned, and the powerful marine currents had carried the corpse out into the fjord? The sea didn't freeze in the winter, and nearly every town and village had a deep-basined fishing harbour. Occasionally, some unlucky soul ventured too close to the edge, slipped, and fell in.

But the facts listed by Jónas had precluded any possibility of an accident.

The individual whose remains were found at the fish farm hadn't spent his final moments swimming anywhere. His body dangled from the netting encircling the salmon pen, and the fish had already nibbled at it, making it unrecognisable.

The afternoon light was fading. It was the darkest time of year.

Working out on the pitch-black sea would be difficult, but they couldn't wait for light. Hildur and Jónas had agreed the body needed to be pulled out of the water immediately. They couldn't even afford to wait for the technical team to arrive from Reykjavík. They would have to conduct the preliminary forensic examination now, while they still had a body to examine. The diver had seen the salmon eagerly nipping at the limbs of the deceased. The variation from the usual industrial food was presumably an unexpected feast for the fish.

Hildur and Jakob climbed into the little boat whose captain had agreed to take them out. Jakob sat at Hildur's side against the cabin wall. There wouldn't have been room for anyone else on board. The captain introduced himself as Einar. Hildur had never met him; he must have been a recent transplant to the fjord. Einar pulled down his wool beanie and started up the motor. He opened a ventilation flap to allow fresh air into the cabin for the three of them.

'It's a fifteen-minute trip. Life vests are in the boxes under you,' Einar growled, nodding at the bench. He slipped some snus under his upper lip and turned his attention to steering the boat.

Hildur filled Jakob in. He stroked his stubbled chin as he listened, eyes glued to the floor.

The police usually used a search-and-rescue boat or coast guard vessel for marine gigs, but there didn't happen to be any in Ísafjörður harbour just now. Einar's tin can had been the only vessel available at short notice. Apparently, he owned a small company that took tourists on boat excursions in the summer. In the winter he did a little fishing.

After Hildur had relayed the necessary information to Jakob, the detectives sat in silence, staring out through the small window.

Hildur was grateful to have Jakob with her. They'd met when Jakob, who was studying at the Police University College in Finland, had come to Iceland to do his internship at the Ísafjörður police station. The pandemic had messed up everyone's plans, and Jakob's internship kept being extended. Now it was officially over. But Jakob hadn't been eager to return to Finland immediately. No doubt his relationship with his live-in girlfriend, the ravishing yarn-shop owner Guðrún, had played a role in his reluctance. Besides, Jakob said he enjoyed working at the small police station in Ísafjörður. His duties were varied: mediating arguments between sheep farmers, monitoring traffic, and keeping the peace on the stretch of street that ran between the town's two bars on weekend nights.

Although Jakob wasn't a citizen of Iceland and therefore couldn't be hired by the department, he could still do the work if his partner was a trained officer. It was hard convincing Icelandic police officers to work the country's remote towns, which left an opening for a Finn without his final credentials. This was fortunate for Hildur, because working with Jakob was a dream: he was calm, dedicated his complete focus to the task at hand, and knew how to get along with people. Hildur could rely on him.

'Who owns the fish farm?' Jakob asked, once they made it out of the harbour.

The boat was rocking but not badly. The wind wasn't strong, probably under eight metres a second, Hildur guessed.

Hildur told Jakob about the world conquest of Norwegian fish farms. The company that owned the salmon farm in Ísafjörður owned similar outfits around Europe.

As Norway tightened its laws, the country's salmon farming companies had begun searching for new locations abroad. Several had established fish farms and processing plants in Iceland's coastal villages. The pens couldn't be plonked down in the open sea; the currents were too strong. But the country's eastern and western fjords were sheltered as well as deep enough to allow for the necessary circulation. In addition to its geographic advantages, Iceland had lax environmental regulations that made it a desirable location for fish farming.

'The salmon are raised to adulthood in the pens, then transported to the slaughterhouse to be killed. Usually, the farm and slaughterhouse are owned by the same company,' Hildur explained.

It was impossible to live in town without understanding the basics of fish farming. New fish farm openings were constantly reported in the news. The environmental movement, business interests, and local politicians were in perpetual conflict over this development. Local debate had been particularly intense lately, as the fish farm off the shores of Ísafjörður had recently expanded.

'Sounds familiar,' Jakob said. 'There was a lot of debate about fish farms in Norway when I lived there, and some of the companies behaved pretty shamelessly.'

Hildur knew all about Jakob's connections to Norway. Jakob was presently engaged in a searing custody battle with his Norwegian ex-wife, Lena, who was doing everything she could to keep Jakob from seeing his son Matias.

'The salmon eggs are fertilised with the sperm of a masculinised female. In that instance, the fish that hatch are exclusively female. Another way is to produce salmon with three chromosomes, in which case they're sterile.'

Hildur tried to maintain a poker face, despite the fact that the unexpected report on the reproduction of fish seemed to deliver unintended comedy.

'Don't forget, I was a biologist in my former life,' Jakob said. Hildur grunted at this, but her teasing didn't seem to bother Jakob. 'Could this somehow be related to shady activities in the industry? Maybe the victim was an environmental activist someone wanted to get rid of?'

Hildur pondered. An environmental activist who'd been killed in some small town? On the other hand, why not? Less plausible things happened all the time all over the world.

'Let's see where the clues lead us. If we find any, that is.'

Warning lights circled the pens, alerting boats to the farm's presence. The lights flashing in the gloom drew near. Einar slowed and cut the engine as he pulled up next to the farm's maintenance vessel. Jakob tossed the gear bag he'd brought to the vessel's deck and extended a hand to help Hildur cross from boat to boat.

'I can do it myself if you just move out of the way!' Hildur said. She built up speed, sprang into a long leap, and thudded down on the deck.

Jakob spread his arms in feigned offence, but his crooked smile gave him away. Jakob knew Hildur: she had little use for gallant gestures and no need for anyone to open doors for her.

Einar raised a hand in farewell and started chugging back to town. Hildur and Jakob would hitch a ride back to the harbour on the maintenance vessel.

Hildur turned to the bearded stranger on the vessel's deck and introduced herself and Jakob. 'Are you the one who made the call?' she asked.

The worker was wearing heavy winter coveralls and a wool cap with ear flaps. His huge gloves turned his hands into small shovels, and his sturdy boots had spiked soles. Hildur recognised the model; she had a pair too. They made it possible to walk on the slickest ice without falling.

He gave a flustered nod and extended one of his massive hands: 'Valgeir Óskarsson. You can just call me Cook. I cooked on fishing boats for years, until I got tired of being at sea. These days I work here, maintaining the pens. I feed the fish and make sure everything's as it should be . . .' He explained he checked on the fish and the feeding system regularly. There were no other employees on site. Cook spoke a lot and fast.

He's probably still in a state of shock, Hildur reflected and suggested they step inside and sit while they talked.

Cook got himself a water bottle from the cooler and handed bottles to Jakob and Hildur too. The captain of the maintenance vessel said hello and indicated he hadn't left the bridge since they'd pulled out of harbour.

Cook took a long swig of water, removed his hat, and raked his hand through his cropped hair as Hildur started the conversation. Jakob's Icelandic had improved so much over the past year that Hildur could speak the local language, confident Jakob would understand.

'I came in for my shift this morning. First, I checked the feeding equipment, then I changed into my diving gear and had a look at things below the surface.'

'What time was this?' Hildur asked.

'We headed out from the harbour before noon, so . . .' Cook said, glancing at the captain as if seeking confirmation.

The captain scratched his head thoughtfully: 'It couldn't have been much past one.'

Cook explained each dive took about half an hour. That was enough time to assess the condition of the fish. 'Viruses, bacteria, and parasites can cause all sorts of diseases. We remove any fish that are sick or dead,' Cook said, before falling silent.

Hildur nodded, urging him to continue. But Cook's movements showed he was closing up. He wrapped his arms around himself and looked at his feet.

'Tell me about when you noticed the body,' Hildur said encouragingly. She was trying to get him to describe the moment in his own words.

'I'll have to drop my head underwater for a second, as the saying goes,' Cook replied.

He shut his eyes and sank into his thoughts. Hildur gave him time to concentrate. The sound of the sea carried inside, the occasional splashes punctuating the gentle lapping of the waves. The reality of Icelandic blue-collar work scented the boat's interior with sweat, pipe tobacco, strong coffee, and the sea.

'It's dark underwater, so you don't see everything right away,' Cook began. He'd nearly finished his rounds when he caught a strange shape in the beam of his spotlight. 'I aimed my light at it. At first, I thought it was plastic rubbish. Sometimes the wind blows hay bale wraps out to sea. I was probably about two metres away before I realised that wasn't what I was looking at.'

The body wasn't very deep. It was floating upright at the edge of the pen. Cook hadn't seen any weights on the feet, but he was sure they were there; that's the only way the body could have stayed in that position.

Hildur considered what she'd just heard and glanced at her watch. Eighteen hours would pass before it was light again. They couldn't afford to wait that long.

'Listen, Cook. We really need your help now,' she said, glancing at the diving gear hanging on the wall.

Cook's face went even whiter. He'd presumably guessed what Hildur was about to say.

'It was ghastly. The body was totally naked. Face half gone, the limbs on one side partially eaten . . .'

Hildur assured Cook he wouldn't have to look any more closely at the body. All they needed was for him to free it and help lift it to the surface. She and Jakob would hoist the body aboard and take it from there.

Cook grunted loudly and stood. 'I guess I can't refuse. If you want to be the bishop, you're going to have to take a beating.'

Hildur liked Cook's way of speaking in old sayings. This one was based on a twelfth-century bishop who'd had to earn his status in paganism-riddled Iceland through hard work. He'd toiled and put himself through a lot of pain to promote the power of the Catholic church.

'It'll all work out somehow,' Hildur said. She and Jakob began pulling on white hazmat suits and disposable gloves. They'd be touching the body once it was retrieved from the sea, and protective gear helped minimise avoidable contamination.

After getting into his diving gear, Cook perched on the edge of the boat and somersaulted backwards into the water.

The captain had emerged from his place at the control board and now stood behind Hildur and Jakob.

'Did you notice anything unusual when you were piloting out?' Hildur asked without taking her eyes off the surface of the water.

The captain leaned a hand against the exterior wall of the cabin. 'Nothing out of the ordinary. The harbour was quiet, the way it always is that time of day in December.' The cargo and fishing boats that had pulled into harbour early that morning had already headed back out to sea.

Hildur knew it was possible to reach the fish pens from nearby villages too: she and Jakob would have to talk to all harbourmasters in the vicinity as soon as possible and review the CCTV footage from the harbours. Someone might have seen something.

'I wonder if the murder happened here?' Jakob said, as if reading her mind. 'Or maybe the victim was killed somewhere else and then the body was hidden here?' He shrugged his shoulders and rocked back and forth. The movement helped him stay warm on the frigid sea.

'One thing at a time,' Hildur said. She wanted to put the brakes on hypotheticals. They knew nothing yet. No doubt their examination of the body would reveal something.

A moment later, they saw movement in the water. Jakob aimed a powerful spotlight at the sea. There was a slosh as the surface broke and Cook appeared, a big pale blob under his left arm. Hildur could see the horrified look behind his diving mask.

Once Hildur had a grip on the corpse, Jakob handed the light to the captain and helped her lift the body to the tarp they'd spread out on the deck.

As Hildur studied the body, the sounds around her faded. All she could hear was her breath, her heartbeat. She had an acrid taste in her mouth. She turned away from the bloated corpse, took a deep breath, then turned back for a closer look.

She'd never seen anything like it before. She knew the body had been badly eaten by fish, but she hadn't expected to see what she saw protruding between its shoulder blades.

'This was left here on purpose for us to find,' she choked out. 'It's as if it had been put on display.'

The torso was pierced by two big metal objects reminiscent of giant fishhooks. Lengths of yellow rope were tied to the hooks; Cook had severed them under the surface to free the body. The ankles were bound with the same rope; a twelve-kilo kettlebell hanging from them had kept the body upright in the water.

'Someone seriously wanted to express their views on fish farming,' Jakob said. Then he hustled over to the side of the boat and retched. Hildur gulped air furiously and forced herself to breathe through her mouth so the smell wouldn't set her stomach churning.

Hildur knew people had strong views on fish farming. Environmentalists were opposed; they accused the farms of polluting the surroundings. Most residents of small towns supported the fish farms because they offered employment and brought new neighbours to remote fjords. Some locals were unhappy the profits from fish farms went to international conglomerates instead of Icelanders. Hildur had read opinion pieces on the topic and articles about county council meetings in the paper. She'd have to reread them, just to be sure she hadn't missed anything. She also remembered having seen sharp-tongued posts on social media. She didn't use the socials herself, but she had to follow them because of her work and hadn't been struck by anything particularly violent. A handful of smaller demonstrations had been held around the country, but they'd all been peaceful.

It felt unbelievable that a mangled body had just been found. Was the victim an activist? The representative of some company? Presumably they'd know soon.

And then there was a third option too: the dead person had nothing at all to do with fish farming. He'd been killed for some other reason and then transported here.

That seems like a far-fetched alternative, Hildur reflected as she eyed the corpse.

She tried to make sense of the details she was seeing, to gather as many observations as possible to formulate some theoretical chain of events. But there was one impression that crowded out all others: that of a half-eaten worm dangling from a pair of hooks.

Chapter 5

Oslo, Summer 2012

Jakob put on his sunglasses and took Lena's hand, then they started off down the narrow street toward the park.

The hot July sun had been blazing down on Oslo for weeks. One could feel the warmth radiating from the brick walls of the city's buildings. Today was supposed to be one of the hottest days of summer, and Lena was wearing a short white sundress that swung as she walked. Jakob loved the sight.

He glanced at the woman on his arm and smiled. He couldn't be happier. He was holding hands with the most beautiful woman in the city and felt invincible.

The way they'd met earlier that summer had felt like a miracle. It was as if they were destined to be together. Jakob hadn't believed it was possible to fall instantly in love except in films. But he'd had to change his mind when it happened to him. He'd seen a blonde woman in a red dress reading a tourist-agency map at the Budapest train station. Lena had drawn him to her like a magnet. When she looked up from the map and glanced in Jakob's direction, that was it. They'd stood there staring at each other, and when neither turned away, they'd burst into laughter. After a week of shared bliss, Jakob had moved in with Lena in Oslo. His work meant they'd have to spend some time in Finland that autumn. But once that was done, they'd planned on coming back to Norway for good.

Today Lena had brought him west of downtown Oslo; she'd wanted to show him Frogner Park. Jakob had seen pictures of the park's statues but had never been there in person.

They passed the car park. To the left, there was a playground designed to look like miniature red-roofed castles. Lena and Jakob instinctively stopped to watch the waist-high children scale the jungle gyms and thunder across the wooden bridges. Jakob hoped Lena was thinking the same thing he was: that maybe someday, they, too . . .

He'd instantly felt foolish. He and Lena had just met, and he was already dreaming of having children together. He gave Lena's hand a firmer squeeze, and they started walking again.

So he was a fool in love. What was he supposed to do about that?

Frogner featured over two hundred statues by the Norwegian sculptor Gustav Vigeland. Jakob and Lena crossed the bridge leading to the heart of the park, and Jakob recognised the statue of the angry boy from postcards.

'Come on; I want to show you the *Wheel of Life*,' Lena said, stroking Jakob's man bun.

Goddammit, how is it possible to feel like this? Jakob thought to himself.

He was perfectly aware he didn't deserve such happiness. The panicked pinprick in his gut was the past reminding him of its presence. No. Jakob refused to let the thought take shape. He just wanted to enjoy the moment now, revel into Lena's presence.

As they made their way toward the far end of the park, they passed the *Monolith*, a twenty-metre-tall sculpture of a hundred human figures entwined in each other. A little further on, they came to a wheel-shaped sculpture of four adults and three children in a ring.

'A lot of people think this is the most boring statue here, but it's my favourite,' Lena explained. 'Vigeland said it was technically the most challenging to execute.' They slowly circled the *Wheel of Life* as Jakob listened. 'I like the way it underscores the brevity of the journey between birth and death.' Lena's raspy voice set Jakob's innards quivering.

They turned around and started back the way they'd come, walking as one.

Jakob spotted an espresso truck at the edge of the park. A sign on it advertised cold drinks.

'Should we get some iced coffee?' Jakob said. The sun was beating down on his bare skin, and he was sweating more than ever after the short walk. Chilled coffee sounded tempting.

Lena stopped in her tracks and turned to Jakob. 'But coffee isn't supposed to be drunk cold.'

'Well, you have a normal one, then. I want iced coffee,' Jakob whispered, leaning in to press his lips to Lena's bare shoulder.

She continued to the truck to order their drinks, and Jakob sat on a bench to wait. He let his eyes linger on the artworks. The sculptures of people of all ages contorted in a variety of positions, evoking the full range of human emotions: sadness, anger, love, longing. All aspects of life visible at a glance. The visit to the park had made an impression on him.

Lena walked up and held out one of two identical cups.

Jakob took one and found himself confused. It was warm.

He looked at it, then at Lena. 'Um, I wanted iced—'

Before he could finish, Lena cut him off. Jakob was startled by the hardness of her smile. Her lips were smiling, but her eyes weren't. 'Coffee is supposed to be drunk hot.'

Lena sat down close to Jakob but not right next to him. The gap she left felt like a chasm just then, and the cup felt burning hot in Jakob's hand.

He squeezed it harder than he should have.

Chapter 6

Ísafjörður, December 2021

A paring knife jutted from the thickest part of the slab of grey meat. Cinnamon and sugar were mixed in a one-to-ten ratio in the deep crystal vase. Hildur took the knife, cut a generous slice of *lifrarpylsa* sausage, and crumbled it into her steaming helping of rice porridge. Then she sprinkled half a teaspoon of cinnamon sugar over her sausage-porridge stew.

Hildur's aunt, Tinna Atladóttir, had Hildur over for dinner every Monday. Today Tinna had made a simple, nostalgic Christmas dish. The *lifrarpylsa* she was serving was made of sheep's liver and other organs stuffed in a sheep's stomach. It was easy to tell the difference between traditional *lifrarpylsa* and the industrially produced supermarket variety, which was too dense in texture. Tender, homemade sweetmeat sausage wasn't easy to find these days. There weren't many who still knew how to make it, since it was inexpensive to buy vacuum-packed off the shelf.

Tinna served herself a big helping of porridge. 'Ívar likes to make sausage in the wintertime. He came by yesterday. He hung up my Christmas curtains too.'

Hildur topped her serving with a splash of whole milk and glanced at the kitchen window. Tinna had been using the same Christmas curtains since Hildur had moved in with her aunt following her parents' deaths. Red-cheeked elves, bells and green Christmas trees alternated across the white cloth. Red, belled tassels dangled from either end of the valance, setting the curtain tinkling when the air stirred. A beautiful home was a priority for Tinna. She arranged tchotchkes on the shelves and changed the curtains according to the seasons, despite living alone in her big house and having lost her sight years ago.

Over the past year, Ívar had been coming up increasingly often in conversations with her aunt. Although it sounded like he visited almost every day, Hildur had yet to meet him. She was happy Tinna had the company. Although they spoke on the phone nearly every day, Hildur only visited her aunt once a week.

'When am I going to meet this mystery man?'

Hildur knew Ívar was an aluminium plant maintenance man. His work demanded he make the rounds of Iceland's coastal villages and towns where the facilities were located. Smelting aluminium was an expensive undertaking, and if any part of the process wasn't operating at maximum efficiency, losses could mount quickly.

'He's on the road so much . . .' The red Christmas wax-cloth tablecloth squeaked as Tinna pushed the porridge pot toward Hildur and changed the subject: 'Did Björk make it home all right yesterday?'

Hildur knew there was no getting up from the table if she didn't take a second helping. She reached for the wooden spoon and half filled her floral-patterned bowl.

'The road was in good shape, and she made it to the highway before the blizzard hit.'

Hildur was happy she'd found Björk while Tinna was still alive. Björk and Hildur had spent a lot of time at their aunt's over the past couple of days. The three of them shared a strong bond.

'Has Björk had any luck getting a job?'

Hildur shook her head. 'She still hasn't found anything permanent. But she seems satisfied with the temp work. It leaves her more time for hobbies. She gets paid so well for evening and night shifts that she makes enough to pay the rent even if she's just working part-time.'

Tinna asked Hildur to describe Björk's home in old-town Reykjavík. She wanted to hear about it every time they met. Hildur felt that sharing the details of her younger sister's life brought her closer to Björk too. The easy conversation did a little to raise Hildur's spirits.

The oppressive periods that had afflicted Hildur since childhood eased when she and Tinna discussed ordinary family matters. Her angst was replaced by lightness, even joy. Nevertheless, it wasn't as if Hildur transformed into some ambassador of positivity. The unpleasant episodes weren't likely to ever disappear completely. She still felt like she was splitting into too many pieces, as if she were in too many places at once.

'I wonder what happened to Rósa?' Tinna asked with a sigh. 'Do you suppose she's even alive?'

Hildur set her spoon down at five o'clock on the rim of her empty bowl. Tinna had asked the same question every time the two of them had seen each other since Björk had re-entered their lives. She asked it despite understanding there was no answer.

'There's no way to know.'

Tinna nodded glumly, then cleared the bowls and set them in the sink. She ran some lukewarm water over them and left them to soak. Hildur knew Tinna preferred to turn on the dishwasher late at night so she could listen to the soothing rumble as she fell asleep.

'I'm so excited about our trip to the Faroe Islands,' Tinna said, taking a floral dishtowel from the hook and drying her hands on it.

'Hopefully, it will already be spring and green at Eastertime,' Hildur said. She'd been thinking she'd buy Tinna a new suitcase for Christmas.

Just then her phone pinged. Tinna used film theme tunes for her ringtone, but Hildur's phone was still set to the default settings. She stepped into the entryway, pulled the phone from the pocket of her oilcloth coat, and glanced at the screen. The message was from Jónas.

Hildur was supposed to have had half a day off. The trip out to the salmon pen had meant a late night; it had been after midnight by the time they finally got the body sent to Reykjavík. Jakob had promised to handle the paperwork related to the case. And two days ago, Hildur had worked almost around the clock to find a child who'd run away from a youth home.

Hildur read the message:

Fish bait update. I don't think this lump of lava has ever seen anything like this before.

Chapter 7

Rural Iceland, December 2021

That morning the clouds had been silver, but they'd darkened as the hours passed. Now they didn't even have silver linings. The charcoal mass hung so low that the drizzle that had been coming down all morning would be turning into a downpour. It was only a matter of time.

Today had been the small ones' time to go. The owner had no use for them, and their presence was no longer of use to anyone. The loading had gone smoothly once the bigger ones had been moved aside. The red taillights of the slaughterhouse truck had grown fainter and fainter until they eventually vanished in the fog. The earth underfoot felt soft. The truck had dug deep grooves in the soil at the gate to the muddy pasture. Before long they would fill with rain.

Lift the upper electric wire, step over the bottom one, close the gate, and make for the bigger pasture.

The waterlogged soil gave with every step. Heavy boots and a heavy mood slowed the feet. There was nothing pleasant about the assignment at hand, but feelings were of no consequence just now.

The wind was in the north-east, the valley's most brutal direction. The two lines of dun-coloured mountains formed a tunnel, and when the wind rose in the highlands and blew from the north-east, it plunged through the narrow gap at full force, stirring everything it came across.

The horses had turned away from it. They stood side by side in a row, heads lowered. The wind barrelled into their backsides and snatched at their tails, fanning them out.

A few turned to look as the visitor approached from the front. Their gazes licked the ground along which their foals had just been loaded into the truck. Their heads remained lowered to keep the wind out of their ears. The big herd looked apathetic, dejected. Whiskers grazed the ground, nuzzling for nonexistent grass. The animals wouldn't be fed until evening.

Work first, then dinner.

A stall of boards and metal pipes had been jerry-rigged in the middle of the pasture. The structure rocked in the strong wind. The squeak of the box's gate hinges was gut-piercing, even for those not particularly sensitive to sounds. This noise was an exception. The opening of the gate, the squeak, the closing of the gate. It was nauseating, even after countless times hearing it.

An eight-inch line drawn on the flank in red marker made it easy to spot the right horses. White paint was used on the brown and black horses. These symbols would last fifty days, after which they'd be shaved off and the coats of the new group of horses would be marked.

Take the nearest horse by the halter.

Halters and bridles weren't usually used on free-ranging horses, but the halters made these individuals easier to catch. Even a strong, tall human wouldn't stand a chance against a beast weighing several hundred kilograms that decided to balk.

The horse stretched out its neck and dug in its hooves. The resistance proved superficial. The animal gave in quickly, because it knew struggling would do no good. A way with horses helped – as did an electric whip if one was willing to use it. One lash generally sufficed. Horses were fast learners.

The other horses watched. Fear flashed in their eyes, followed by relief that it wasn't their turn.

Or am I imagining things?

Horses seemed intelligent, but did they possess the same sort of consciousness as humans? Who knew? Pondering the question wasn't going to do any good.

Open the stall gate. Lead the horse into the restraint box. Tie it firmly to the wall.

Wiry fingers tightened the lead, then tugged it to make sure the knot held. The rope had to be taut to keep the horse's neck as still as possible.

The wind picked up, and the rain that had just begun falling came down harder. Luckily, the restraint box had been built in a way that left the north-easterly behind their backs.

Close the gate. Open the bag of supplies.

'Just stand still, and this will be over soon,' the low voice said soothingly.

And then the long, thick cannula sank through the horse's coat and into its jugular, and the warm fluid started flowing into the canister.

Chapter 8

Ísafjörður, December 2021

Declension of masculine nouns in four cases, using the indefinite form of 'horse' as an example: *hestur*, *hest*, *hesti*, *hests*. Jakob jotted down notes in his notebook and tried to remember how to tell masculine forms from the other two genders. How did 'horse' decline in the single definite form? Then he had to do it over again for the plural. On top of that, verbs, tenses and adjective inflections. Luckily the language had a lot of similarities with Nynorsk, which Jakob had studied while living in Norway. But in Nynorsk there had been no need to differentiate between masculine and feminine forms when inflecting adjectives. That had accelerated mastering the grammar.

Jakob let out a deep sigh, pushed his chair back from his desk, and rubbed his stiff neck. He'd been at his textbooks for hours.

As part of the process of applying for citizenship, Jakob would have to demonstrate fluency in Icelandic. For immigrants from the Nordic countries, Iceland required three years of residency, no criminal record, and passing a language proficiency exam. Jakob had a little under a year left before he could take the test. He'd decided to dedicate all possible free time to learning the language so his performance on the exam wouldn't stand in the way of his being awarded citizenship.

Guðrún was a good teacher. She'd glued Post-its around the house marked with the Icelandic terms for furniture and foodstuffs. And she helped Jakob apply what he'd studied in practice.

For the past year, they'd had a deal: they would communicate exclusively in Icelandic on their weekends off. It had been surprisingly hard at first. Jakob had been embarrassed by the way he'd sounded like a two-year-old when trying to explain what he wanted for breakfast. It hadn't fazed Guðrún; she'd taken it as a game. Jakob could still remember how delicious she'd looked at the fridge door in her little silk nightshirt, quizzing him on the correct pronunciation of the words for milk, cheese, bread and skyr.

Jakob had made the acquaintance of part-time flight attendant Guðrún on a domestic flight from Reykjavík to Ísafjörður a couple of autumns back. In classic Icelandic style, Guðrún had multiple jobs. When she wasn't working in the skies, she ran a yarn shop she owned in Ísafjörður or subbed at the local daycare centre. Jakob still couldn't believe his luck. He found it incredible that after all these years he'd met someone like Guðrún, with whom life was fun, easy and passionate. Jakob felt calm in her company. Guðrún had no interest in bossing around anyone, including Jakob. That was amazing.

He glanced at his watch. He had five minutes before it would be time to call Matias.

Matias would be turning seven soon. Jakob didn't even want to think about what a large chunk of those seven years he'd been forced to keep his distance from his child.

For most of that time, his ex-wife Lena had been denouncing Jakob to anyone who would listen, especially the social workers. She'd succeeded in engineering for herself sole custody of Matias. The decision handed down by the Norwegian courts clearly stated that Jakob had a right to see his son, but Lena had come up with a constant stream of excuses to prevent the meetings from taking place. One day Matias had a bad cold, the next time he had a stomach bug or a bad headache. By some ruse Lena had managed to get doctor's notes to support her stories.

After moving to Iceland, Jakob had begun executing the plan he'd been mulling over for ages. He'd decided to fight for his rights and his child. With the help of his Norwegian lawyer, Jakob had turned to the courts to enforce his visitation rights, but then Covid had thrown the courts' schedules and his plans into turmoil. The courts were trying to work through the backlog of cases, and Jakob's day hadn't come.

And now it never would.

Two months earlier, Lena had called to inform Jakob that she and Matias would be moving to Finland. Her current partner, Filip, who had built up a lengthy career working in the mining and petroleum industries, had landed a good position at a mine in western Lapland. When Lena's boss at the hotel heard about Filip's new position, she'd offered Lena the opportunity to run the hospitality chain's Finnish operations.

Jakob snorted. *Finland, and northern Finland to boot.*

Lena had never liked Finland. She'd always denounced everything related to Jakob's background. Jakob had spent much of his childhood and adolescence in Lapland, near the Seven Fells region of Äkäslompolo. He'd tried to show Lena around the area, but she couldn't have been less interested. She'd just complained about the mosquitos and cursed the long distances. It was an extraordinary coincidence that Lena's new husband's work had brought her back to Finland, with a position of her own, no less. The coincidence was so extraordinary there was no way it could have been a coincidence. When Jakob heard the news, he'd been positive Lena had somehow manipulated events simply to torment him.

She'd succeeded.

Jakob had been on the verge of a nervous breakdown during the call. The news had exploded in his consciousness like a bomb. He'd felt the panic ooze into his body and spill into his limbs like cold, liquid metal. Jakob had hired a good lawyer in Norway and had carefully prepared his case. Doing so had consumed enormous amounts of time and money. And just when the court was supposed to take it up, he'd had to rethink his strategy.

When hope died, *sisu* stepped in. Jakob had tapped into this legendary Finnish grit and refused to give in. He'd decided to carry out his plan, no matter how hard it was to do so. He'd got a new lawyer, told him the whole story, and brought a case to the district court in Rovaniemi. His attorney had guessed the hearing would be scheduled for December or in the new year. Jakob had waited on tenterhooks for updates on the timing.

When the clock struck six in Iceland and eight in Finland, Jakob brought up Lena's contact info on Skype and pressed the videocall icon. He'd have about half an hour to talk with his son before it was time for Matias to go to bed.

After several rings, his call was finally answered. Jakob pulled himself together and set his smartphone in the stand on the kitchen table. Matias appeared, his face filling the shaky shot. His son was holding the phone himself. Jakob was pleased. This meant he wouldn't have to talk with Lena at all.

'Hi, Matias. How are you?'

The boy swivelled his head from side to side and made funny faces. Jakob laughed.

'We had swimming at school today.'

'Did you get the flippers I sent?' Jakob asked. He'd sent his son swimming gear as a pre-Christmas present.

Matias nodded happily and shifted the phone so Jakob could see the swim bag on his bed.

Jakob's eyes hoovered up details. The familiar *Diary of a Wimpy Kid* poster and pictures of Messi hung on the walls. A PlayStation and its cables took up half the bookcase, and clothes were strewn across the floor in heartwarming heaps.

A pang of deep longing struck Jakob's soul. He'd have loved to clean his son's room. Organised the socks and extended to the bookshelf. He'd have given anything to be more present in his son's life.

But Jakob didn't want to show the misery caused by his longing. He didn't want Matias to feel like he was caught in thc middle – and by no means wanted Matias to feel any guilt about seeing each other so rarely. It wasn't Matias's fault.

They talked about swimming lessons and school. Jakob asked Matias what he'd eaten for dinner and what time he had to get up for school the next morning. Matias replied cheerfully. It felt good to see his son in such a buoyant mood. There was still a bond between them.

'I miss you so much,' Jakob said.

He instantly regretted it. He realised Lena had appeared in Matias's bedroom and heard him. Her cold voice carried into Jakob's little kitchen and echoed frostily from the walls.

'Matias, it's time for bed. Can you hand me the phone, please?'

Matias turned first to his mother, then back to his father, a confused look on his face. 'But it's not that late yet.'

'Yes, it is,' Lena said, snatching the phone out of her son's hand. 'Put on your PJs and brush your teeth.'

Jakob said goodbye to Matias, even though the boy was already gone. Hopefully Matias heard him. He was peeved by Lena's helicoptering. But after years of experience, it no longer came as a surprise.

'Did you have to take the phone from him?' Jakob asked in a firm voice. He had stopped speaking amiably or accommodatingly to Lena long ago, because it had never done any good.

'We have to go,' she said icily, looking at Jakob yet somehow a little past the camera.

Jakob was prepared for the call to end. His next call with Matias wasn't scheduled for the upcoming weekend but the following one, and he reminded Lena of this.

'Oh, right. That's not going to work.' Lena's voice was matter-of-fact, almost indifferent. As if she were laconically reporting on the weather.

Jakob asked why.

'We'll be in Rovaniemi.'

'But we have an agreement. You can't just change it without consulting me. I'm sure you understand that your constant excuses won't look very good in the eyes of the court. I have a record of every single one of your attempts at sabotage,' Jakob said in an overly steady voice.

Lena shifted her gaze to the right and stared Jakob dead in the eye. Jakob felt a shiver run up his spine.

She tilted her head and looked at Jakob as if he wasn't capable of understanding basic facts. 'Listen, I couldn't care less. I think you're going to have much bigger fish to fry after the court date than a single postponed phone call.'

And then she hung up.

Chapter 9

Hildur had driven from Tinna's straight to work, and when she walked in the first task Jónas had assigned her was making a pot of coffee. The boss still hadn't learned to use the coffee maker.

The station's utterly unremarkable coffee mugs made Hildur wistful. Hildur thought about Beta, who'd filled the break room cupboards with big, sturdy mugs sporting the names of political parties, athletic associations and companies. It had been Beta's way of signalling she was the whole community's police chief and wouldn't act as the spokeswoman for any one stakeholder. When Beta and her husband had divorced, Beta had moved to Reykjavík and taken the mugs with her. She must have figured Jónas wouldn't tolerate any reminders of his predecessor in his territory.

Jónas was the complete opposite of Beta. He accepted any and all invitations from prominent locals, no matter how insignificant the event. Beta had done her job and spent the rest of her time at home caring for her children. Beta had trusted Hildur and Jakob and given them free rein to do their jobs as they saw fit. Jónas, on the other hand, didn't do anything except interfere in trivial matters: the wording of reports, the frequency with which the department's vehicles were washed, the radio station they listened to at the office.

'What are you doing in there? Milking the cow?'

Jónas's grating voice reverberated from the station's sole conference room.

Hildur chewed her cheek. *What a loser.* She was supposed to do her work, then run around like a chicken with its wings cut off – or whatever the Finnish version of the saying was that she'd heard Jakob use. Hildur had the urge to cram a chicken down Jónas's throat.

Little straw hearts with red ribbons hung from the cupboard handles. Jakob had decorated the break room for Christmas to lift their spirits. If it weren't for Jakob, Hildur wouldn't have been able to work under Jónas.

Hildur walked into the conference room. It was coming up on nine o'clock. Jónas reached for his coffee mug and glanced critically at its contents but didn't comment. He cleared his throat and began going through his notes.

'It looks like this fish-farm case involves international narcotics trafficking.'

Hildur registered the enthusiasm in Jónas's voice. He was finally going to be able to investigate something bigger than a DUI. Apparently, her boss found this inspiring.

'This could be such a major case we have to think carefully who we can inform at this point.'

'I see. Is that why Jakob wasn't invited to this conclave?'

Jónas nodded. 'He doesn't have the credentials to act officially as a police officer yet. He can't be told everything.'

Hildur was flabbergasted. Jónas had never had a problem with Jakob's lack of official police status before. A sizable slice of the country's rural police force didn't have police training. Jónas clearly wanted to show who was in charge.

Jónas glanced at the documents in his hands. The victim's appearance and his tattoos' texts had led the technical investigators to conclude he wasn't an Icelander. Fortunately, it had been possible to take fingerprints from his fish-gnawed extremities.

'The international unit in Reykjavík searched for matches. It didn't take long before they had a hit. The victim is a twenty-three-year-old Slovenian, Luka Kopitar. He lived in in the capital, Ljubajana,' Jónas read.

'Ljubljana,' Hildur said.

Jónas shot his subordinate a quizzical look.

Hildur clarified: 'The capital of Slovenia is Ljubljana.'

Jónas took a sip of coffee and set his mug down with a bang. His irritation was evident in the wave-like movement of his eyebrows. 'Whatever. Somewhere in Eastern Europe. According to my information, a lot of Slovenians have been turning up in Reykjavík's narcotics markets lately. They probably have a new cell somewhere up here. Maybe Luka was involved.'

Hildur listened, intrigued. She hadn't heard anything about Slovenians, but she hadn't been involved in policing serious narcotics activity either.

'Slovenia doesn't have an embassy here, but I was able to determine Luka had been living in Iceland since the summer before last,' Jónas said. 'He worked at the Sel farm in Eyjafjörður. He had an Icelandic social security number, and the appropriate taxes and pension contributions had been withheld from his pay.'

So he was working legitmately, Hildur thought to herself as she jotted down the name of the farm. It sounded familiar somehow.

'Did he live alone?'

'Officially, yes, but you never know . . .' Jónas said, before falling silent.

The previous night on the fish farm's maintenance vessel, Hildur and Jakob had performed a basic forensic investigation. They'd photographed the location where the body was found and the body itself, taken fingerprints and DNA samples from the surface of the skin and under the nails – from the fingers and toes that were still present, that is. If they were lucky, they might find someone else's DNA under the fingernails. Because the victim had been naked and submerged in saltwater for some time, there was no way to get any fibre samples. The circumstances made it impossible to take footprints or gather other evidence from the scene. They still weren't sure whether he'd been killed at the fish farm or somewhere else.

They would also have to review the CCTV cameras of nearby harbours and make a list of the vessels that could have been at sea at the time the body had ended up there. The forensic pathologist could determine a more precise time of death and perhaps also the time the body ended up in the sea. The one thing that was plain as day was the body hadn't ended up at the fish farm by accident.

Hildur opened the laptop she'd brought with her and turned it so Jónas could see the screen. 'These pictures are from yesterday,' she said, zooming in so she and Jónas could see the details in the photos of the corpse.

Big iron hooks pierced either side of the torso. The hooks entered under the collarbone and exited just beneath the shoulder blade.

'We haven't had time to look into the source of the hooks,' Hildur said, adding that Jakob could start that right away, using the photos as reference. They'd left the hooks in the body. It would be better for Axlar-Hákon to have a look at them first.

Earlier that day, the remains had been delivered to the lone medical doctor in Iceland who performed forensic and pathological autopsies, Hákon Bjarnason – or Axlar-Hákon to those who knew him. The results would be ready within two working days at the earliest. The DNA tests might take longer. The forensic pathologist had been given his unique nickname during his student years, when he'd played the role of sixteenth-century Icelandic axe murderer and serial killer Axlar-Björn in a student production.

Jónas looked at Hildur from under his brows. 'Why don't I decide who's going to do what, since I'm in charge?'

Hildur swallowed her rising ire and responded with a nod. The less time she spent conversing with Jónas, the better things tended to go. She waited for him to continue.

Fine, so tell me what I'm supposed to do next. We don't have all night to wait around.

Jónas finished his coffee and pushed his mug to the middle of the table as if to signal someone else could clear it away and load it in the dishwasher. He rubbed his temples with his pinkies and eventually opened his mouth:

'While Axlar-Hákon is conducting the autopsy in Reykjavík, I want you and Jakob to head out to Sel. Try to find out as much as you can about the victim and his movements, but don't tell Jakob about the suspected narcotics link. I'll call the police up north and let them know you're coming to talk to people. I'll request the CCTV footage from the harbours and the victim's call data and start going through them.'

Hildur popped to her feet, knocking her knee painfully against the table leg. She swore under her breath. 'We'll head out first thing in the morning so we can make it through the trickiest stretch of road in daylight,' she grunted.

Hildur packed away her laptop, pulled on her winter coat, and strode out. The walk home only took a few minutes. The streetlamps and clusters of Christmas lights strung up in the windows created flashes of light in the dark town. The sky was black and cloudless, setting off the stars. Hildur and Jakob might even catch a glimpse of the sun during the drive tomorrow, up on the highland road.

Early December was the darkest time of year, the period when most people dreamed of shorter workdays. But Hildur didn't care much for Christmas. It was above all a family celebration, and aside from her Aunt Tinna, she hadn't had any family for decades. So she'd spent most Christmases at work, a tradition that would continue this year too. The notion that it might be time to try celebrating Christmas differently, maybe have Christmas dinner with Björk, intrigued Hildur but still felt odd. She wasn't used to holiday rituals.

Jónas's talk of a narcotics connection to Slovenia had put her in a strange mood. The information probably needed to be double-checked. Hildur couldn't help it: she didn't trust Jónas. She had to listen to herself and trust her gut.

There was no denying it. The eerie, searing sensation in her stomach could only mean one thing: the past wasn't done with her yet. Some serious misfortune was about to happen. Yesterday was merely the prelude to something bigger.

Chapter 10

Helsinki, Autumn 2012

The floor felt sticky underfoot. You could feel the squeak, but you couldn't hear it. Pantera was blasting so loudly from the speakers the bartender couldn't make out the customers even when they shouted their orders.

Jakob pointed at one of the taps behind the bar and raised two fingers.

The twentyish woman in a Metallica T-shirt winked and began filling two glasses with beer. Jakob noticed her tattooed arms. The artistry was beautiful; delicate vines trailed under her watch, across the back of her hand and down her fingers.

Jakob took the pints and wove his way through the crowd to the corner table. He and Lena had grabbed a bite and gone to the movies. On their way home to Jakob's flat, they'd decided to stop for beers in Kallio.

Jakob didn't go out much, but now and again he liked to let his hair down and drink till last orders or beyond. He didn't have to wake up early: he and Lena both had tomorrow off, and the only thing they had planned was Jakob's college buddy's kid's basketball game in the afternoon.

The evening had got off to a great start, but at the bar the vibe had chilled to freezing.

'A cold beer for my favourite woman,' Jakob said, giving Lena a winning smile.

Lena was facing Jakob, but she didn't react to his arrival in any way. She just stared straight ahead with a bored look on her face.

Jakob pulled out a chair and seated himself. He took a sip of beer and set down his glass. Lena's hand was on the table. Jakob tried to reach for it, but his bid for intimacy failed: Lena pulled back her hand.

'Don't even try it! I saw the dreamy look in your eyes when you smiled at Little Miss Tattoos.'

Jakob exhaled deeply and took a moment to study the structure of the bar's ceiling. There wasn't anything interesting to see there, but he couldn't look at Lena, because he didn't want to say anything that would make things worse. Maybe it would be best to be as up-front as possible?

'I wasn't looking at her. I love you. I don't have to dream about anyone else.'

Lena tossed her long blonde hair over her shoulder and narrowed her eyes at him.

Jakob felt the good mood that he'd been in all day pop like a punctured balloon. He knew there was really no point trying, but he did his best to choose his words carefully and sound as convincing as possible: 'It's kind of cute that you're jealous, but there's no reason to be.'

'I'm not sure I can believe you. I'm starting to think all men are liars.'

'I'm not lying,' Jakob insisted. He heard his voice growing louder. He didn't want to lose his temper.

Lena snorted and took a sip of her beer. She slammed the glass down with such force that the contents sloshed to the table.

'You know what? I hate this backward country. All we do is sit in smelly bars and go to the movies. I don't even know anyone here.'

Jakob eyed Lena at length and considered. Was she suffering from culture shock? Lena didn't speak Finnish. Jakob knew it could be hard to adjust to a new place if you didn't speak the language. He'd moved from country to country as a child due to his parents' careers. People said kids were adaptable and always made new friends. But it hadn't been easy. Jakob had frequently found himself standing alone during break time and being left out of birthday parties.

'We're going to that basketball game tomorrow. Mikko's wife Silja will be there. She's really nice. You guys might become friends,' he said encouragingly.

'Listen, you don't have to set me up with pity friends.' Lena narrowed her eyes again and eyed Jakob probingly. 'Or is Silja the whole reason we're going to the game? Have you two ever been involved?'

Jakob leaned in and attempted a conciliatory tone. But there was a little voice in his head that asked, why should he be conciliatory? He wasn't the one who'd started it.

'Do you want us to move to Norway right away?'

He raised his pint and tried to get Lena to toast their plans for a shared future.

Jakob was doing everything in his power to pretend like things were fine, but deep down he knew he was betraying Lena. He hadn't been able to tell her everything he should have. Jakob hated lying, but just now it felt like the only option.

'I could apply for a PhD programme in Oslo. I think I'd like living there. Norwegians are nice. That much I've noticed,' Jakob said, reaching across the table for Lena's hand again.

And once again, Lena yanked it back: 'So you can drool over Norwegian blondes, huh?'

She spun her pint glass between her hands, then without any warning picked it up and tossed her beer in Jakob's face. She staggered as she stood, but once she was on her feet she headed unsteadily for the door and disappeared into the night.

Jakob dried his face on his sleeve. He blinked hard a few times so the tears would wash the beer from his eyes. He felt an emptiness in his gut. Pain and self-pity weighed on him so heavily his shoulders ached.

But most of all, he was terrified to think what Lena would do to him if she ever found out about Regina.

Chapter 11

Ísafjörður–Súðavík, December 2021

Hildur sat in the idling car, staring straight ahead. She was waiting for Jakob, who was still inside packing for the drive. They lived in the same duplex, with Hildur in one unit and Jakob and Guðrún in the other.

A light gust sent up a puff of powdery snow. Across the yard, yellow Christmas lights flashed in the neighbours' spruce. There would be no Christmas knick-knacks in Hildur's windows this year; there never had been. She would go to Tinna's on the twenty-third to eat lutefisk and exchange gifts with her aunt. That had been her sole Christmas tradition as an adult.

She sat there gazing out the windscreen at her dreary front yard. When would she get around to changing the bulb over her front door? On the other hand, it wasn't as if there was any hurry. The lamp above Jakob's door worked and gave off enough light to illuminate the front yard. Besides, when Hildur was at home, she was either sleeping or watching TV. She didn't spend time in her yard, even in the summer.

Where the hell is Jakob? Hildur wondered. She was one of those people who didn't need much time to get ready. She'd already been for a morning run, showered and thrown her toothbrush and clothes for the short trip into a bag, poured coffee in the Thermos, grabbed a bag of small pastries, attached her surfboard to the rack on Brenda's roof, and warmed up the car. Hildur tapped the steering wheel with the fingers of her left hand and decided to call Ólafur Ragnarsson, or Óli, Ísafjörður's harbourmaster.

'Am I calling at a bad time?' Hildur asked. She could hear noise in the background.

'I'm just on my way to Patro. We have our harbourmasters' winter get-together today. Then we'll go for a long Christmas lunch, which means I won't be home until tomorrow.'

Patro was shorthand for Patreksfjörður, a small but busy fishing village in the southern Westfjords.

'Did you get a chance to look at that CCTV footage?' Hildur asked.

Óli replied that he'd reviewed the footage early that morning. He'd also received the footage from nearby harbours. 'But I already told Jónas.'

Hildur used her fingernail to scrape at some dirt on the rim of her steering wheel. Jónas hadn't passed on the information to her yet.

'To be honest, I don't really trust Jónas,' she said. 'That's why I wanted to call you directly and check.'

Óli's voice thickened. He'd presumably just lit a cigarette and was inhaling the smoke. 'I get it. He can be a lot.' Hildur heard Óli exhale the smoke from his mouth. 'There wasn't anything to see in the footage. It's saved for three days. Anything older is overwritten by newer footage.'

Hildur pondered. Cook had said he'd checked on the fish two days before finding the corpse. So if the cameras had captured anyone carrying a body, that footage would have still been visible during the review.

'There was one thing. I already told Jónas, but I'll tell you too,' Óli said. 'No footage was captured at Súðavík harbour that night or the night before. Apparently, the camera wasn't working. The harbourmaster promised to check it tomorrow.'

Jakob had climbed in the car during the call. The information about Súðavík piqued Hildur's interest, and she shared everything she'd just learned with Jakob, as well as the suspicions Jónas had voiced the previous day.

'Let's go straight out to the harbour in Súðavík. It's on the way,' Hildur said, steering Brenda onto the street.

After the roundabout, Hildur accelerated to fifty. At the base of the fjord, the speed limit rose to ninety. Hildur accelerated again. There was no immediate emergency, so she had to obey the speed limits.

'What's wrong with Jónas anyway?' Jakob asked, taking an unfinished sweater and a pair of knitting needles from a tote bag he'd carried out over his shoulder.

'I don't know. I guess he hopes he'll break open some massive crime involving the underworld and get to play the hero.'

A tanker truck was approaching in the opposite lane. Hildur turned off her high beams and steered closer to the right shoulder. Fifteen more minutes and they'd be in Súðavík.

'Lena spoiled my call with Matias, for a change,' Jakob said, adding that he couldn't wait for the hearing in Finland. He wanted to put an end to the nonsense. Regardless of the outcome, he craved clarity.

Hildur was happy to listen to Jakob's story and the metallic clink of the needles moving in his hands. Every few minutes he pulled more yarn from the tote on the floor.

'How can you knit without any light?'

Jakob grunted, once again reaching into the tote. 'I'm making the sleeve. This stage is so monotonous I don't need to see.'

After the tanker truck thundered past, Hildur switched back to her high beams. It was still dark out, but the snow-covered mountains were visible in the headlights. Hildur and Jakob were surrounded by stillness. The tanker truck was the only other vehicle they'd come across. They were solitary travellers in a desolate, wintry landscape.

Hildur dropped Brenda's speed to thirty and flicked the blinker to the left. Súðavík was a village of a few hundred residents on the sea.

'We've been here before,' Jakob said, indicating the houses on the slope to the right.

'Your first work assignment in Iceland,' Hildur recalled. The two of them had arrested a violent man who'd kidnapped his son from his ex-wife. The situation had ended happily, thanks to Jakob's skill at approaching people on their level.

They drove into the harbour: two warehouses, a small harbour basin, and not even a dozen boats. Óli had said there were two cameras, both of them trained on the harbour yard: they covered the area in front of the building, the loading bay, and the harbour basin itself. Evidently, there were no security cameras inside any of the structures.

They circled the building. Hildur could faintly hear the sea, but there were no waves. The water was calm. Some time had passed since the most recent winter storm. A raven croaked overhead. The fishy smell grew stronger. Every day, boats brought in fresh catches, hundreds of kilograms of cod and haddock, which were packed on ice, loaded onto trucks, and driven to Reykjavík to be sold.

Hildur eyed the old harbour building. In traditional Icelandic style, the roof was red and the walls were white. She and Jakob were using torches, for the harbour lights illuminated the boats and the piers, not the buildings.

Jakob stopped his beam under the gutter. 'I see some wires over there.'

Hildur walked closer. There was a small hole in the wall and a few wire-ends where a security camera used to be.

'It's been ripped out,' Hildur said. She walked to the far end of the building and looked up at about the height where the first camera had been. Same thing with the second one. There was no footage because there weren't any cameras. Apparently, no one had noticed the missing CCTV devices until Jónas had asked for the footage. Hildur figured no one around here thought anything bad would ever happen. People trusted each other, and if strangers showed up and acted suspiciously, they trusted someone would notice.

Hildur shifted her torches to get a better look, and then she spotted it: a plastic document protector rolled up in a tight scroll. It had been shoved into the hole left by the missing camera.

'Hey, Finn, come have a look. There's something here,' Hildur said. She asked Jakob to help her up. They didn't see any ladders in the vicinity, and they couldn't reach the scroll without something to stand on, so Jakob gave Hildur a boost.

What the hell is this? Hildur said to herself as she unrolled the sheet of paper inside the plastic:

Segja vil ég sögu
af sveinunum þeim,
sem brugðu sér hér forðum
á bæina heim.

Jakob pulled down his red beanie and looked as lost as an American tourist in an Icelandic fish shop. Hildur decided his Icelandic wasn't good enough yet. She translated the words into English: 'I'll tell you the tale of some lads who used to come to our farms.'

'I understood the poem, more or less . . . But it's just so weird.'

Hildur glanced at her colleague from under her brows and asked him to explain.

'I studied it for my Icelandic exam. I read that exact phrase in my Icelandic textbook a few days ago. It was the beginning of a poem. It had something to do with Christmas . . .'

Hildur took another look at the sheet of paper in her hand. The words were written in poem form: four lines that rhymed. She pulled a freezer bag out of her pocket – she always brought some along on work gigs – and slipped the piece of paper in. It would have to be checked for fingerprints.

A breeze blew off the sea and across the harbour yard. Hildur shivered.

She silently repeated the words to herself. And then she remembered. Of course she remembered! They were from a song that was sung in every Icelandic home and school at Christmas-time. The rollicking, major-key ditty told the story of thirteen Yule Lads who came down from the mountains before Christmas to play tricks on people and farm animals.

It looked like someone had come to Súðavík and removed the security cameras before transporting the body to the fish farm. And whoever that someone was had left a poem about the Yule Lads in the camera's place.

But why?

Chapter 12

Hildur clicked open the central console and took out two golf balls. The three-hour drive was taking its toll. Eyes on the road, she held the steering wheel in one hand and raised her backside a couple of inches. The balls slipped effortlessly under her buttocks. A small shift of the bum, and they were in place. She let her body sink onto her pelvis. The tension release felt amazing.

Hildur and Jakob had pondered the meaning of the rhyme for most of the drive. Someone knew once the body was found, the police would start reviewing CCTV footage from the harbours. Hildur would send in the sheet of paper and the document protector to be checked for fingerprints, but she suspected nothing would be found. Someone had gone through a lot of trouble to get her and Jakob to read the poem, and whoever that someone was had no doubt worn gloves. It was impossible to deduce anything about the perp from the text itself, because it had been typed on a computer. Maybe the forensics team in Reykjavík would be able to say something about the paper or printer that had been used, something Hildur couldn't detect with the naked eye.

When they reached the valley of Heydalur, Jakob pinned a tiny battery-powered reading lamp to his coat lapel. He explained he'd finished both sleeves and was now moving on to the body of the sweater. He'd start knitting it from the hem. It was still dim out, so the extra light was necessary as Jakob flipped back and forth between knit and purl stitches.

'Did you just put golf balls under your bum?' Jakob asked.

Hildur leaned back forcefully in her seat and pushed against the steering wheel with both hands to straighten her elbows. The movement kept her arms from going numb on long drives.

'Yup. But actually, I put them under my thighs at my physiotherapist's recommendation. My hamstrings get tight. The golf balls release the tension.'

Distances were long in the Westfjords, and the kilometres added up. It wasn't uncommon for a detective to spend most of the day in the car. Sitting on golf balls had helped reduce the tightness in the back of her legs.

Hildur and Jakob had left Ísafjörður around nine, and it was coming up on eleven thirty. Although it was the brightest hour of the day, light was scant. A heavy blanket of dark grey clouds had blown in from the sea. The ice- and snow-covered road winding through the highlands bled into the sky. It would have been impossible to see the route ahead without the reflective posts erected on either side of it. Hildur found driving through the incessant whiteness tiring, and they still had some way to go before their first pit stop.

The thought of lunch and a cup of coffee perked her up. 'Jakob, is there something wrong with the yarn? It keeps snapping, and you keep having to tie it.'

One of Jakob's eyebrows dropped lower than the other, and his eyes narrowed the tiniest bit. He reached into his knitting bag and pulled out a soft disc that reminded Hildur of a clump of freshly shorn wool.

'This is traditional Icelandic yarn. Are you saying you don't recognise it?' Jakob asked.

A several-minute-long monologue ensued. Plötulopi was a soft, unspun, single-stranded pre-yarn sold in disc-shaped bundles. It was tricky to knit, but the fibres were long, so it was easy to connect the ends of broken strands by rolling the strands together. Knitting with plötulopi required a deft touch. It broke immediately if you pulled too hard. Jakob explained he was knitting the sweater with double-strength plötulopi.

'This is a new pattern. Sigga gave it to me to test out.'

Everyone in town knew Sigga. She'd been knitting the colourful beanies and sweaters sold at the yarn shop for years, and she occasionally created sweater patterns too.

There was a crackle. Hildur gave the radio a couple of slaps. They'd come to the end of the highland road, and Brenda's radio was picking up the signal again. In the news broadcast, a volcanologist was discussing the chances of Fagradalsfjall erupting again in the near future. Fagradalsfjall was in southern Iceland, not far from Keflavík International Airport, and it had erupted the previous spring. The lava had flowed for months. The volcano wasn't active just now, but it could erupt again. The report was followed by a tense-voiced analyst pondering the retail success of the upcoming Christmas season. The news ended, and a beautiful acoustic guitar piece by the band Hraun began to play.

Hildur had listened to the song back in her student days. It had been the contestant in some international music competition, and the radio stations had played it nonstop. 'Ástarsaga úr fjöllunum' was a ballad set in the mountains. The lyrics were based on an old story in which a troll in love had waited for his beloved to arrive. Then the sun had come up, the way it always did in such stories. As trolls couldn't tolerate sunlight, the lovesick creature had turned to stone. For some reason, Hildur found the song about a heart beating deep inside the stone moving. She wiped the corner of her eye.

Only half an hour to go and they'd be in Hólmavík, where they'd stop for pizza. The village at the eastern edge of the Westfjords was the first settlement one came across when taking the northern road to Route 1, which circled the island. In winter, the northern road was the only way out of the Westfjords, as the southern one passed partially through steep mountains and was closed due to snowfall.

The sound of the phone ringing interrupted Hildur's dreams of pizza. She connected her phone to the car speakers through Bluetooth and replied.

'I've been trying to call you.' It was Axlar-Hákon, the forensic pathologist.

'You're on speakerphone. I'm with Jakob headed to the farm up north where the kid on your table used to work.'

The farm was owned by a married couple, and Hildur had reached the husband golfing in Spain. Naturally, he'd been shocked by his employee's death. The investigators hadn't been able to contact the victim's family in Slovenia yet.

Axlar-Hákon took the long way to get to his point. He'd done so for as long as Hildur had known him. He started off with generalities, then focused his story using detailed observations. He put together the puzzle by starting from the edges and gradually approaching the centre.

'Of course I'll send you the autopsy, the cause and manner of death, and the death certificate once all the documents are ready. It's going to take a while to get the results of the DNA analyses. I still have the body wide open here. Literally.'

Hildur wasn't fazed by the indelicate phrasing. She knew Axlar-Hákon was fundamentally a courteous man. He spoke respectfully of people and treated everyone, especially the dead, kindly. Axlar-Hákon had often noted he was the dead person's last conversation. The humour that peppered his speech was just his way of lightening a heavy subject.

'But I wanted to call, because there are at least two unusual things you ought to know.'

A sign at the edge of the road indicated they were approaching a settlement. Hildur slowed and turned left. She could already see the centre of the village.

'There's no water in the lungs. He didn't die by drowning. Several days have passed since he died, and at this point I can't say how many. I'm not sure I'll ever be able to give a very precise estimate.'

Hildur nodded as Axlar-Hákon spoke. His observations confirmed hers – Hildur had taken the body's temperature at the scene. It had been the same as that of the water, about seven degrees Celsius.

Axlar-Hákon paused before continuing: 'I also found four ten-gram cocaine pellets in the deceased's stomach.'

This was startling information. Darned Jónas had been on the right track after all! Drugs were involved. A quick calculation suggested narcotics worth almost half a million krona had been found in the deceased's stomach.

Questions ricocheted around Hildur's head. Was the Slovenian kid killed over drugs? But why only four pellets? Mules smuggling condom-wrapped narcotics in their stomachs usually transported more than that.

'One of the condoms had a hole at the edge, from which the drug entered the body. They haven't finished the blood work yet, so I don't dare give you a precise cause of death, but it's looking pretty likely he died of poisoning.'

Hildur shook her head. A dead drug mule in a fish-farm pen. 'But no one would take a risk like that over forty grams, would they? There were probably more pellets. The deceased must have passed some of them before he died,' she mused, mostly to herself.

Axlar-Hákon promised to get back to her as soon as he knew more, then ended the call.

Hildur pulled up outside a green wooden house and killed the engine. She looked at Jakob and asked him if he'd got the gist of the conversation.

Jakob thought for a moment. 'If this has something to do with drug trafficking, and someone wanted to get rid of the body, they should have dumped the body in the sea, not attached it to the pen and left it floating there. It's like it was left there to be found. That strikes me as odd.'

Hildur grabbed her phone from the stand and put it in her pocket. She climbed out of the car, stretched her limbs, plucked the golf balls from the seat, and slipped them in her pocket too.

'We still have four more hours before we get to the farm. I'm not driving another mile until I have something to eat.'

Hildur made sure her surfboard was still firmly attached to the roof. Then she locked Brenda's doors and started up the pizzeria's front stairs. Just as she was reaching for the door handle, she stopped: 'What did you just say about dumping the body in the sea?'

Jakob glanced at his colleague, a thoughtful look on his face: 'If this has something to do with drug trafficking . . .'

'No, after that.'

'It was left there to be found.'

Hildur opened the door, and she and Jakob stepped into a pizza-perfumed ambience.

'Exactly. Just like the note at Súðavík harbour.'

Hildur thought back to Rjómi, the soft, furry cat she'd had during her childhood. Rjómi used to bring home the songbirds and mice she hunted for show. She carried their carcasses into the entryway, sat behind them, and waited for praise.

'It's as if someone wants to show off what they're up to.'

Jakob took off his coat and hung it up. 'You mean they want to intimidate us?'

Hildur frowned. 'Or toy with us.'

Chapter 13

Asker, Winter 2014

Jakob was sitting in his armchair. A white burp rag lay over his shoulder, and a baby bottle was pinched between his thighs. Matias was resting in his father's lap, eyes closed and tiny fists clenched on his tummy. His delicate nostrils quivered like butterfly wings. He'd just eaten and been burped. Jakob's left arm ached, but he didn't dare move because his son had finally fallen asleep. He knew the next five minutes would determine whether the sleep lasted, and the smallest movement or sound would wake Matias. But if Matias were allowed to drift off without interruption, he would sleep for at least an hour or two, even if a balloon popped right next to him.

The living room window gave onto a view of wintry Asker. The snow had softened all contours, and the homes on the suburban street looked like gingerbread houses. Jakob liked living in this family-friendly neighbourhood west of Oslo. Lena's cousin had lived in the house before him and Lena. When she went abroad for a few years for a work assignment, Lena and Jakob had moved in as tenants. The cousin only charged them for electricity, heat and a small mortgage contribution. Lena and Jakob planned on renting for a couple of years while they saved a deposit for a home of their own.

They had each other, a beautiful home, a healthy child, and food in the refrigerator. Everything looked perfect, but even so, something felt off. Jakob knew why.

Lena still didn't know about Regina.

Jakob hadn't been able to cut ties with his ex-girlfriend. He'd taken on Regina as a protégée or ward over twenty years before. Initially they'd been friends, but over the years they'd grown closer. In their early twenties they'd started dating. Their first home had been a waterfront row house in Jyväskylä. A move to Helsinki had followed. Life had gone smoothly until they found out Regina was incapable of having children. The news had come as a big blow to her. She'd turned inward and cut herself off. There were better periods among the dark days, but gradually their shared life had turned from a romantic relationship into a sibling-like companionship.

Jakob still sent Regina caring text messages and emails asking her how she was doing and telling her he missed her and how busy he was. Lena was incredibly jealous, and although Jakob couldn't prove it, he was sure she secretly read his email. And so he'd opened a second email account for corresponding with Regina. He and his ex had also exchanged the occasional message via social media. But the idea of telling Regina about his Norwegian wife and newborn child felt impossible. At least now, with Regina having one of her bad spells, the revelation would come as too great a shock to her.

Jakob had built himself a cage he couldn't escape without smashing. He was painfully aware that one misstep would shatter everything.

Jakob had last seen Regina during a business trip to Helsinki a little before Matias's birth. He'd booked himself a hotel and signed in but hadn't so much as set foot in the room. He'd spent every night at Regina's place. Sex with Lena was a lot wilder, but the intimacy he felt with Regina was in a class of its own.

He was such a damn coward. Luckily, he had Matias, whose life he was responsible for and who was the best thing that had ever happened to him.

Lately, the responsibility had begun weighing on him, it was true. What if he failed at this, too, made a mistake? What if his son slipped from his arms . . .

Jakob forced himself to think about something else. He turned on the television and started watching a Norwegian quiz show. Jakob had already learned the language. Moving to a foreign country was nothing new for him; after all, he'd spent his childhood learning to pack his suitcase as his parents built their careers abroad: Sweden, Germany, Russia, China . . .

In a year or so, when Matias started daycare, Jakob would resume teaching biology and writing his dissertation. That's what he and Lena had agreed. Lena had returned to her job in an insurance company's finance department a couple of months after Matias was born. Matias had no trouble drinking from a bottle, so it had made sense for Lena, as the higher earner, to go back to work and for Jakob to stay home with the baby.

The second hand on the wall clock ticked ahead. Mornings felt endless, as did these quiet early afternoons. He'd tried to take Matias for a short walk in the stroller around noon, but the streets had been too snowy. After fifteen minutes of slogging through snowbanks, Jakob had given up and carried the stroller inside.

Jakob glanced at the clock. Exactly eight minutes had passed since Matias had dozed off. Now he was sleeping soundly. Jakob adjusted himself in the chair and stretched his arms, which had gone numb from holding his son.

The front door opened. Lena only worked a half-day on Mondays, and it was almost one thirty. Jakob wasn't surprised to hear loud cursing from the entryway instead of a greeting.

'The floor in here is swimming!'

Before Matias had drifted off, Jakob had texted Lena, warning her about the water on the entryway floor, which he would finish drying once the baby fell asleep. Lena had seen the message; the message said 'read' on his phone. She just always found a reason to get angry. It had been happening more and more often lately. The dishes had been put away the wrong way, the dishwasher was being filled in the wrong order, Matias was dressed in the wrong romper.

Lena stepped into the doorway, a storm cloud over her head. One hand was on her hip and the other was propped against the doorframe. She stared icily at Jakob.

'The entryway floor is a lake. The kitchen is a mess. What exactly have you been doing all day?'

Jakob knew attempting to discuss the matter would be pointless. Regardless of how he answered, Lena's attacks would grow increasingly ferocious.

'I tracked in some snow with the stroller. I didn't have time to finish drying the floor because I had to feed Matias. I was planning on cleaning it up once I got him in his crib.'

Lena sighed. She looked in Jakob's direction but a little past him, then turned on her heel. She looked at him that way all the time: sort of toward him, but without making eye contact.

A moment later there was clattering in the kitchen. Lena walked past the doorway again, this time with a rag. She waved the rag as if it were a victory flag and shot Jakob a scornful look. After drying the floor, she stopped in the doorway again: 'I know about Helsinki.'

Goddammit, Jakob swore to himself.

'My work computer looks just like your laptop. I took it to work by mistake the other day. I guess you forgot to log off Facebook Messenger.'

Lena stared frostily at Jakob and shook her head in disappointment. Then she said in a high, mewling voice: '*It was so nice spending the night with you again. I wish I were in your arms.*'

Jakob felt his guts freeze.

'Or something like that, is what the translation software spat out.' Lena's voice was quivering with rage. The wet rag made a loud slap as it landed at Jakob's feet.

'The heart emojis didn't need any translation!' Lena shouted, running into the kitchen.

Matias woke up and started whimpering, then wailing in bursts. Jakob tried rocking his son and did everything he could to keep himself together.

Jakob heard a cupboard open. There was an earsplitting crash as the first plate smashed against the floor.

'How can you go shove your junk inside someone else while I'm sitting here at home, about to give birth?'

Matias's wails had turned to shrieks. Something heavy broke and shattered. Jakob deduced the kitchen mirror had fallen and was no more.

Silence fell in the kitchen.

And then Jakob heard a low, dragging sound. Lena was probably sweeping. The shards tinkled as they dropped into the rubbish bin.

A moment later, Lena reappeared in the doorway. Her face was swollen from crying, but her voice was steady. She looked Jakob dead in the eye and said in a cold, calm voice: 'I hate you. I hate you more than anything in the world.'

Chapter 14

Eyjafjörður, December 2021

A few hours after stopping for pizza, Hildur and Jakob passed the village of Dalvík and continued up Eyjafjörður fjord. They had no trouble finding the farm, which was located a few kilometres beyond the centre: a big sign advertising Icelandic horse riding had been erected at the side of the road, and horses – at least a hundred full-grown animals – were grazing in the sizable, partially lit winter pasture beyond.

On the other side of the road, a smaller herd of yearlings stood in a pasture that sloped toward the sea. The spindly beasts had gathered around their hay. They'd be allowed to grow for another year or two before being put to work; horses weren't trained for riding until after their third winter.

The place seemed peaceful. A rusty old Subaru parked at the end of the stable was the only vehicle in sight.

Hildur and Jakob agreed to handle things according to their usual MO: Hildur would lead the way and do the talking, and Jakob would follow a few steps behind, keeping an eye out. A slender strip of light slicing across the snow indicated the lights inside the stable were on. Hildur pushed open the wooden door and knocked the toes of her shoes against the threshold before stepping in. The central aisle had just been swept. Most of the stalls were empty, but one held a tired-looking, big-bellied white horse munching on hay.

'Hello! Hello! Is anyone here?' Hildur called out as she looked around. The white horse stopped munching and took a second look at the newcomer. Apparently, it didn't find what it saw very interesting, because it immediately lowered its nose back into its hay and continued eating.

There was a faint thud at the other side of the stable. A door at the end of the passage opened, and a woman with short hair looked quizzically at her visitors.

'I'm Hildur Rúnarsdóttir from the Ísafjörður police. This is my partner Jakob Johanson,' Hildur said.

The woman approached, extended her hand, and introduced herself: 'Lisa Weber.' She spoke English with a German accent and said she worked on the farm.

Hildur switched into English and explained they were there to get some information about a man named Luka Kopitar. According to records, this was Luka's last official address. 'Did you know him?'

Lisa nodded, but the question seemed to confuse her. 'What do you mean, "did" . . . Did something happen to him?'

Hildur suggested they have a seat somewhere. Lisa led them into the back room. It looked the way horse farm breakrooms did: an old coffeemaker worn down by years of use, a side table stocked with a carton of UHT-pasteurised milk, a box of sugar and two open packages of biscuits. Helmets and baskets of riding gloves hung on one wall. A white stable cat purred in a glove basket on the floor. The opposite wall was festooned with ribbons and photos from Icelandic horse competitions. The room smelled of horse.

'I'd offer you coffee, but I'm out of filters. I won't have time to make it to the store until I've finished the evening chores.'

Hildur sat down across from Lisa. Jakob seated himself at the head of the table. Hildur began by simply relating that Luka had been found dead in the Westfjords. She didn't think it was necessary to share the details.

Lisa's entire body tensed, then, after a couple seconds her shoulders slumped, her jaw dropped, and her eyes went wide. Her surprise seemed genuine.

'I'm sorry. Were you two close?' Hildur reached into her pocket for her notepad and a chewed-up pencil.

Lisa shook her head and looked around distractedly, as if searching the walls for answers. 'We worked together. Luka is . . . I mean, Luka was pretty quiet, but nice and polite. He was already here when I came at the beginning of the year. He showed me the ropes.'

Lisa said the farm's sheep and horses kept them busy, except maybe in deepest winter. Lambs were born in the spring. Summer meant work in the fields, on top of the tourists who came to ride. Bringing the sheep down from the mountains took several weeks in the autumn.

'In the summer, Árni and María host a children's vacation home here. One of those places where kids from children's homes and foster homes can come stay for a little while. The first kids usually come in the spring and the last ones leave in the autumn.'

Hildur thought back to the sixteen-year-old caught drunk-driving near Ísafjörður the previous Easter. He'd had a little hash on him. It turned out he'd run off from Sel farm. Further investigation had revealed that running away from the Sel vacation home had become a common event over recent years, and many of the young fugitives had been victimised during their escapes. As head of the missing children's unit, Hildur had assembled a group of local police officers and social workers. Together they'd presented a few suggestions for improvements at Sel. The farm had committed to decreasing staff turnover. Employees had been promised two weeks' extra pay at the end of autumn as a commitment bonus if they worked at the farm for at least four months. The idea was to make it easier for the children to form trusting relationships with employees they'd come to know. The young people had begun contributing to light work; for instance, everyone who wanted had been assigned their own horse to care for. Thanks to the changes, the number of runaways had decreased. Hildur had considered it a significant victory. More restrictions hadn't been needed, but more caring.

'Were you involved in the child protection work here at Sel?' Hildur asked.

Lisa shook her head. 'Luka was. He would give the occasional grooming lesson and take the kids on short rides.'

She explained that during the summer the farm had well over a dozen workers. Things were quieter during the winter, as the only chores that needed doing were feeding the animals and shovelling the snow. She and Luka had been the only two employees this winter.

'What about the owners?' Hildur asked.

Lisa said they were mostly around in the summer and travelled the rest of the year. They were currently in Spain.

Hildur asked Lisa to tell her about Luka. How had he spent his free time? Did he have many visitors?

Lisa rolled up the sleeves of her sweater and lowered her hands to the coffee-stained table. 'Luka would spend his evenings playing PlayStation and strumming his guitar. Neither of us really went anywhere. We worked and lived here.'

'You must have some time off, though?'

Hildur was well aware that foreigners who came to Iceland to work at farms put in long hours without necessarily receiving a decent wage for their efforts, let alone vacation days. For many young people hungry for new experiences, room and board, and a chance to ride horses for free and live in Iceland was compensation enough. But it was a tricky situation. If employees weren't paid, they wouldn't accumulate a pension, and there was no security in case of an accident. Lisa seemed to guess what Hildur was thinking.

'I get paid every month. No one is shoving crumpled bills in my hand. My pay is deposited directly into my account,' she said, continuing that she had legally mandated days off, which she had to take.

The fact was, there simply wasn't much to do in the countryside. During the summer, the workers would go hiking together in the mountains that rose behind the farm, but in the winter the days were short and the weather miserable.

'On my days off I like to sleep in and watch TV. Luka usually went to meet his friends somewhere.'

Hildur shot a glance at Jakob. They didn't have a warrant, but if Lisa let them inside the house, they would certainly look around. 'Could I see Luka's quarters?'

Lisa stood and gestured for Hildur and Jakob to follow. They walked past the stall where the white horse was still munching on hay.

'Is it sick, or why is it inside?' Hildur asked as they passed the animal. 'It seems pretty plump to me.'

Lisa looked at Hildur in amusement. 'You mean Hekla? She's not fat; she's pregnant.'

'But horses usually foal in the spring,' Hildur said in confusion.

'I suppose,' Lisa said distractedly as she continued down the aisle. 'This is all really new to me. This is my first year here.'

Halfway down the central walkway they reached the mouth of an unlit passage. Lisa flicked on the light and told them to watch their heads. The ceiling was unusually low. A door at the far end led to the first floor of the main house.

'My room is down here. Luka's room is upstairs,' Lisa said, pointing at a narrow staircase. Hildur interpreted Lisa's hand movement as an invitation and started climbing the creaking stairs. Jakob followed her.

Hildur stepped from the landing into Luka's room. Jakob entered after her, pulling on a pair of disposable gloves. He started going through the belongings.

'See anything interesting?' Hildur asked, eyeing the closet's chaotic contents: riding trousers, sweaters, socks, and a heap of long johns. She sifted through the garments but didn't find anything interesting herself.

Jakob took photographs of Luka's desk and mumbled his findings: 'Coins, condoms, half-eaten bags of sweets.'

The bed was unmade, and a Stieg Larsson detective novel lay open on the nightstand. The only other pieces of furniture were a desk and a bed. There weren't even any curtains. There was no sign of personal effects. No passport, no wallet, no cell phone. They had vanished with Luka. The toothbrush was in the bathroom. That was odd. People who went on planned trips usually took their toothbrush with them.

'Hey, I think I found something,' Jakob said suddenly, lifting a metal box out of the only desk drawer. The lidless container held a stash of thousand- and five-thousand-króna bills and small freezer bags.

Jakob started counting the cash. Hildur took the box to check for any remaining contents. The freezer bags were empty, and there was nothing else in it.

'There's about two hundred thousand krónur here in small notes,' Jakob said.

Hildur let her gaze circle the spartan room. 'He was dealing drugs. We need to send these in for analysis,' she said, studying the box in her hands.

There was a loud creak, and Hildur jumped. She turned and saw Lisa standing in the doorway, eyeing them uncertainly.

'This doesn't necessarily have anything to do with anything. But I told you the owners are holidaying in Spain right now.' Lisa lowered her eyes to the floor. Her slender fingers tugged down the sleeves of her shirt. Her demeanour radiated discomfort.

'Even little details can be helpful. Tell us,' Hildur said encouragingly.

'Could you not say anything about this to our employers?'

Hildur didn't promise, but she looked warmly at the younger woman.

Lisa continued, saying the arrangement with her employers was that at least two people would be on site at all times. 'Six days ago, Luka told me something urgent came up and he had to leave to take care of some things. He seemed nervous.'

'Do you know where he went?' Jakob asked, rising to his feet. He'd been peering under the bed and the nightstand.

Lisa shifted her weight from foot to foot. 'He said he had to go to Copenhagen. He promised to bring me two bottles of wine from the duty-free and to feed the horses the whole week next week if I did his work while he was gone. I didn't think it would be an issue. It's so quiet here.' Luka had said he'd be back in three days. 'And he was.'

Lisa had got the wine bottles Luka had promised, and they'd watched two episodes of some German police procedural together.

'The weird thing was . . .' Lisa thought for a moment before continuing: '. . . that he disappeared again.'

'Disappeared again? What do you mean?' Hildur asked, looking Lisa square in the face.

'Luka had promised he'd do the stable chores the morning after he got back, so I didn't set an alarm. When I woke up around ten, the house was empty. The horses were in the pasture, waiting at the gate for their breakfast. Hekla was knocking against the walls of her stall; she was hungry. But there was no sign of Luka. It was like he'd suddenly disappeared. I haven't seen any sign of him since.'

Chapter 15

Horse pasture, December 2021

The plastic-wrapped sandwich tasted good. The tea was steaming in the cup holder. Lunch was from the nearby service station. Eating at roadside cafés or petrol stations was never an option; the stares were too much. A quick in and out was the only way to go, and it was easier during winter, since a big neck warmer made for a convenient mask.

Anyone who saw the face once remembered it forever. Its owner was an oddity, and a reprehensible one, and never allowed to forget either.

Time passed, but it didn't erase the memories.

The left side of the face had been badly burned years before. Hot oil had turned the smooth skin rough. It looked like massive fish scales or the pitted surface of some distant planet. No one had suggested a skin transplant.

And I was too young to know any better.

The face would be fixed later, once the money was together. First item of business was paying off the debt. There'd be opportunities later to travel to a clinic abroad for reconstructive surgery. It would take some time, but that was a detail. The goalposts were approaching, one tiny step, one horse at a time.

There were upsides to the work, too: no coworkers, plenty of fresh air and an excellent match between skills and job description.

Best of all, the horses didn't judge. They obeyed.

Chapter 16

Northern Iceland, December 2021

Hildur lifted the flowerpot on the front steps and found the key right where it was supposed to be.

The inn, converted from a former school, stood right off Route 1. Between the building and the road was a small car park with a self-service petrol station and space for two dozen cars. If there'd been any traffic, the noise would have doubtless carried into the rooms. But on this December night, the place was quiet. Hildur and Jakob would be able to get a good night's rest.

Hildur had to jiggle the key in the lock a few times before it caught. The door creaked open.

The roadside inn was one of those places in Iceland that was only open part of the year. Hundreds of thousands of tourists circled the island every summer, admiring the waterfalls, volcanic sand beaches, hot springs and volcanos. Lodgings were fully booked from June to September, but darkest winter meant almost no foreigners on the road this far from Reykjavík. Many hospitality-industry businesses closed their doors for the season.

But Hildur had spent the night at this establishment on many occasions and knew the owners. Travellers in need of lodging could stay outside the season proper if they called in advance to make arrangements.

The owners had come by to turn on the electric heaters, so it was pleasantly warm downstairs. The inn's location in the sparsely inhabited countryside meant either electric or oil heating. Most Icelanders had given up oil heaters during the oil crisis, and although electricity was inexpensive, electric heaters weren't usually kept on in unoccupied buildings for safety reasons.

Hildur put the water on to boil and pulled four packages of chicken-flavoured instant noodles from the shopping bag. Jakob had wanted something 'healthy' too. He'd said something about salad, but service stations didn't sell fresh produce in December. He'd found tinned corn and carrots in the canned goods aisle instead and was now plating them.

They ate in silence.

Hildur spooned some corn from the plate between her and Jakob and shoved the spoon straight into her mouth. Then she lifted her bowl to her lips and guzzled down the noodle broth. Loud slurps filled the kitchen. She set her bowl in the sink and watched Jakob use his spoon to fish for the last of the yellow kernels. Her Finnish colleague had always been reserved, but lately he'd seemed even quieter than usual. It looked like some time had passed since his last visit to the barber too. The furrow between his brows had deepened over the past few months. He seemed somehow haggard.

'Are you nervous about the hearing?'

Jakob shrugged, reached for his milk, and drained his glass in one swig. Hildur noticed the kitchen's floral wallpaper was splattered with grease and peeling at the edges. Even so, it lent the kitchen a comfortable, timeless ambience.

Jakob groaned and rubbed his face with his hands. 'Really damn nervous. The only thing I can control is my behaviour, and that's the thing I'm most worried about.'

Hildur thought she understood what Jakob was referring to. He'd told her Lena still had in her possession a video recording of the time he threw an apple at her. Lena had criticised Jakob's family thoroughly and at length, and when he finally lost his temper, he'd grabbed the half-eaten fruit from the table and chucked it at her. She'd prepared for the moment by recording it on her smartphone, then later used it against Jakob during the custody trial in Norway. It had been only one of the many manipulations Lena had conceived to shut Jakob out of their shared child's life. Hildur had often wondered what was wrong with Lena. Why was she so nasty? She didn't get it.

'All you have to do is stay calm. I'm sure she'll try to goad you into losing your temper.'

Jakob stood and moved over to the sink. He filled it with hot water, added a few squirts of dishwashing liquid, then took the sponge and started scrubbing the bowls. He handed the clean dishes to Hildur, who dried them on a threadbare gingham tea towel.

Hildur tried to cheer up her colleague. 'Luckily the hearing is in Finland. That's better than having it in Norway, right?'

Jakob rinsed the last plate under the hot water and passed it to Hildur. 'I've been thinking about that Luka . . .' he said, yanking the plug from the sink. He clearly wanted to change the subject. 'Luka brought drugs back from Denmark and disappeared with the cocaine pellets in his gut. Someone killed him but didn't take the drugs from his stomach. That doesn't make any sense.'

The same thing had occurred to Hildur. Mules generally didn't sell the drugs they smuggled into the country; they played a small part in a bigger scheme. They swallowed the pellets, defecated them, and delivered the goods to the agreed place, where the next person in line took possession of them.

But Luka's body had been dumped into the sea, drugs and all. If he was killed over the narcotics he'd been transporting, logic dictated the contraband would have been extracted from his stomach before his body was disposed of.

'Unless the murderer simply hadn't been able to cut into his abdomen,' Hildur reflected. Slicing into a corpse and rummaging through the innards was no mean feat. Few so-called tough guys were capable of doing it.

Jakob leaned against the counter and fiddled with the damp dish cloth. 'Those hooks piercing the body . . .'

He folded up the tea towel and set it to dry on the back of a lone chair. He said he'd called the four pork processing plants in Iceland and received confirmation for his suspicions. 'Luka was pierced with the hooks used to hang slaughtered pigs. I saw them all the time the summer I worked at a slaughterhouse in Forssa when I was young.'

Hildur listened to Jakob's report of his summer job as a butcher. The pig carcasses dangled from the hooks as they were moved down the line.

'All the slaughterhouses in the country use the same hooks. Which means tracing them will, for all practical purposes, be impossible. Besides, anyone can order the hooks online.'

So much for that, Hildur thought to herself. The steel hooks weren't going to be any use in advancing the investigation.

'Beer before bed?' she asked, taking two glasses from the cupboard.

Jakob got the bottles from the fridge, popped off their caps against the counter, and poured their contents into the glasses.

Hildur stretched out her shoulders and thought. Homicides were always senseless, but this case had an extraordinary number of curious details. The poem, the drugs in the stomach, the crumpled wad of cash at the horse farm.

She was hoping she'd be able to reach her contact in the narcotics unit by tomorrow morning. Jónas had said he'd get any information on possible Slovenian involvement in narcotics activity, but Hildur figured it might be best for her to move things along herself. She and Beta were close. Since moving to Reykjavík, Beta had been hired as acting head of the National Narcotics and Organised Crime Unit. Hildur had tried calling her as soon as they left the Sel farm but got a busy signal. Hildur had left a voicemail asking Beta to call back as soon as she could. The narcotics unit had the latest information on drug trafficking in Iceland and generally a pretty good idea of the main players and their subordinates. Maybe Luka was already on their radar? Maybe he'd made a lot of short trips to Europe or even further? They'd know soon enough.

Just then Hildur's phone pinged with an incoming message. When she glanced at the sender, she was disappointed: it was Jónas, not Beta. Hildur opened the message, read it, and replied that she and Jakob would be back at the station after noon the following day.

'What does the pain in the butt want?' Jakob asked, placing the empty bottles in the plastic crate next to the wall.

Jónas had requested and reviewed Luka's call data. For someone involved in the drug trade, Luka didn't communicate much via phone. He must have used one or more prepaid SIM cards, as his registered number had only received a few calls and text messages per week.

'Luka's phone was turned off eight days ago. That aligns with Lisa's statements. The instant he left the farm the first time, his phone was off.'

Hildur took a hairband from her wrist and twirled it in her fingers. What exactly had happened the night Luka had vanished?

Chapter 17

Seawater streamed down Hildur's face. The waves had been as spectacular as promised in the forecast: long, broad and symmetrical. It had been a rewarding morning, surfing in the cold light.

Hildur hadn't slept properly the previous night. She didn't suffer from insomnia often. Yes, she was plagued by occasional angst, but only when she was awake. Waking up between 3 and 4 a.m. was a less frequent torment. Lack of sleep muddied her thoughts and drizzled feelings of hopelessness over the following day. Sometimes, but not often, she was able to fall asleep again. Last night she'd woken before 3.30 a.m. Mind-numbing anxiety and worry over not getting enough sleep had prevented her from drifting off again until 5 a.m. Hildur felt drained, but the early-morning doze had prevented catastrophic exhaustion, and surfing had lifted her spirits.

She and Jakob had woken early and breakfasted at the service station in Hvammstangi before heading for the shores of Miðfjörður fjord. Jakob wasn't interested in joining Hildur in the waves, so he'd gone for a little walk down the dirt road.

Hildur loved the movement of the sea and the smell of the water. It was possible to read waves and currents, but only to a certain point. They always surprised you. With the sea, there was no way to explain everything or consistently make accurate predictions. The mystery and inexplicability were what made it so compelling. There was nowhere Hildur felt as free. When she paddled into the waves, responsibilities vanished, tormenting demons were silenced, problems ceased to exist, and no one could contact her.

She was sure surfing would have done Jakob some good, too, but maybe he got the same relief from knitting.

Board under her arm, she walked ashore. She licked a drop of saltwater from her lip as she turned to take one last look at the waves. The sand was black and the sea was rolling. The north wind pushed and pulled at the surfboard. She took a moment to listen to the movement of the waves: when they broke against the shore, there was a crash and a sigh. A hiss followed as the water drained through the small stones and back into the sea.

A shout from Jakob roused Hildur from her reverie. It was time to go.

She changed into dry clothes, shoved her neoprene suit into a black garbage bag, and started up Brenda. As she was turning from the car park onto the road, her phone rang. She was pleased to see it was Beta. The Bluetooth didn't connect, so Hildur reached for her phone and raised it to her ear.

'Sorry I couldn't call you right back,' Beta said. 'We had an overnight operation in Keflavík. I'm headed home to sleep. I've been awake for almost twenty-four hours.'

Beta sounded tired. She couldn't share details about the case under investigation, but she did reveal their unit had been monitoring international flights arriving from the west. The narcotics unit in Reykjavík had received a tip from abroad about an Argentinian group suspected of smuggling. Almost all traffic from South and Central America to Iceland was funnelled via the US or Canada. Direct flights from the metropolises of North America landed at Keflavík International Airport every day. Most arrived late at night or early in the morning, so their passengers could transfer to the morning flights to Europe.

'But they didn't show up,' Beta huffed. 'Apparently, they didn't board at the last minute.'

Tips needed confirming, and sometimes they proved wrong. It was all part of the job.

Hildur didn't want to prolong her weary colleague's bedtime, so she got down to business. Assuming Beta would be better informed about international criminal networks than she was, she explained about the corpse found at the fish farm with drugs in its stomach.

'His name didn't ring any bells, and he doesn't have a criminal record in Iceland. His only infractions in Slovenia were for speeding,' Hildur said.

There was a pause. Presumably Beta was thinking. 'There are a bunch of links to Croatia, Serbia and Poland, but nothing to Slovenia. And I've never heard the name before.'

Hildur heard Beta tapping at the keyboard.

'How are things going out west otherwise?' Beta asked. She and Hildur had commiserated so much over Jónas's naming as chief that they were bored of the topic.

'I've been wishing for a peaceful Christmas. But it doesn't look like my wish is going to come true.'

Beta grunted and said the situation sounded familiar: the upcoming holiday seemed to be luring all the weirdos out of their hiding places. Two days earlier, she and her team had raided a cannabis plantation next door to the country's biggest tomato farm, and yesterday they'd interrupted a guy shitting behind Hallgrímur church with his pants around his ankles. He turned out to be an exhibitionist who had a significant stash of illegal pills in his backpack.

Beta said she'd conduct a quick search of the narcotics unit database to see if Luka's name brought up anything. Hildur took a sip of coffee from her Thermos cup.

'Listen, there's nothing on him in the database.'

Dammit, Hildur silently cursed. 'How likely do you think it is a freelancer would smuggle drugs this way?'

Drugs were usually brought into the country in larger quantities. Whether you were transporting one hundred grams or five hundred grams, the chances of getting caught were the same. And in this case, no one knew how many cocaine pellets Luka had swallowed.

'Maybe he went to Copenhagen to buy enough for his personal use and planned to sell the rest in small amounts through private Facebook groups,' Beta said. 'Drug trafficking by micro players has increased by leaps and bounds since dealing moved from bars to social media.'

Maybe so, Hildur reflected. She knew digging up Luka's contact in a city the size of Copenhagen would be impossible unless his other phone turned up somewhere. That might lead them to the source. But the narcotics police in Copenhagen would ignore a query about forty grams of cocaine. That was a drop in the ocean for them.

'None of the micro dealers really order through the mail anymore; they pick up their purchases in person,' Beta explained.

Relying on postal delivery had grown difficult recently, as every individual package and letter went through a careful check at the post office's terminals. Apparently, it was easier for the dogs to sniff out five grams of speed in a brown envelope than a couple of hundred kilos of cocaine in a sealed, tightly packed shipping container. Small players had a greater chance of getting caught than criminals moving large amounts of money and drugs.

'If I hear from the field that a cocaine stash got lost in transit, I'll let you know. It won't take long for word to reach us if someone's looking for their missing drugs,' Beta concluded. And then she apologised and said she had to get home. Hildur thanked her and hung up.

Hildur liked Beta. They'd first met when Beta moved to Ísafjörður to assume the role of police chief. For the first year, Beta's then-husband had worked part time and looked after the kids, and Beta had had time to dedicate to her own interests after work. She and Hildur had gone to the gym and become solid workout partners. Beta had always been a no-nonsense straight-shooter who didn't kowtow to anyone. She'd trusted in her own competence, not social networks, which wasn't necessarily typical of those in her position. But it was probably why Hildur had always felt like she and Beta got along so well.

Although Hildur missed Beta, she was happy for her former boss. She had no doubt Beta's talents would be put to their best use in the service of the narcotics unit. Beta approached narcotics crimes and organised crime first and foremost through cash flows. There was no point dedicating resources to tracking down users; the important thing was finding out where the cash was and who it was flowing between and the identities of big players, the ones you didn't see on the street. Beta would no doubt hear if Luka had had any dealings with the criminal organisations that ran the drug trade in Iceland.

Hildur shared the most relevant details from the call with Jakob, who reacted with an uncharacteristic reticence. His only comments were a couple of *yeah*s and *oh*s. Hildur had decided it would be best to stop talking.

For the next hour they drove toward the Westfjords in silence. When the radio came back on, Hildur listened to the news and current affairs programmes. As Brenda wound her way through the remotest curves of a deep fjord, Hildur twisted the volume all the way down to mute the ear-scraping crackle.

And Jakob had just kept knitting. The sweater was a few centimetres longer than it had been since they'd stopped to surf.

'Your knitting is pretty manic,' Hildur said, to break the silence.

Jakob grunted and rubbed his beard with the back of his hand. 'It helps me focus.'

A sign at the side of the road said the next service station was ten kilometres away. The fuel gauge indicated they had enough petrol to get them back to Ísafjörður. The route was straight, the weather was good, and the road wasn't slippery.

Hildur stepped on the accelerator and drew a deep breath. 'Listen, Jakob.'

Brenda accelerated past one hundred kilometres an hour. That was a little over the speed limit, but this time Hildur didn't care. She knew the road and could see tens of kilometres into the distance. There was no oncoming traffic, and since it was winter there weren't even any sheep on the road, which you had to keep an eye out for in the summer.

Jakob had seemed tense the day before, but now he was as taut as a violin string.

'What's wrong?'

Jakob just turned to the passenger window and gazed out at the frost-covered fields.

The mood had turned awkward. It was unnerving to Hildur, because she and Jakob had been close since the day they met. He'd helped her get to the bottom of her family's deepest secrets, and up until recently, he'd talked openly about his son and difficult ex-wife. But something about his attitude had changed.

'Come on, tell me,' Hildur insisted.

Jakob took a breath and exhaled loudly through his nose. 'While you were surfing, I got a phone call. I have to go to Finland.'

So it's happening, Hildur thought to herself.

'My lawyer called. I'm supposed to be at the district court in Rovaniemi next week. I need to rehearse for the hearing on Friday. I know the timing is catastrophic—'

Hildur cut him off. 'It always is. I can handle the investigation by myself.'

Jakob started knitting faster. The clink was relentless as his hands moved the needles that wove the yarn. 'It shouldn't take more than a day. I'll fly back right after. I might have to wait several weeks for the decision.'

'I can get Gylfi to help me if necessary. Don't worry about that,' Hildur said. She and Gylfi had worked together before; he was one of the more experienced officers at the Ísafjörður station. 'Listen, Jakob. There's something I've been thinking about.'

Hildur considered whether to continue. She knew it might be wisest to keep her mouth shut and drop it, because Jakob had never raised the subject during their conversations. But her curiosity beat out her caution.

'I've always wondered about your parents. Could they be of any use in the trial? You've never talked about them. Is there a reason for that?'

Jakob slowly turned toward Hildur. She was startled by the look on his face. His pupils had shrunk, and the wrinkles around his eyes had deepened. His glower could have turned a bucket of water into ice cubes. He slid down deeper in his seat, pulled up his hood, and turned back to staring at the treeless landscape.

And then he growled: 'Stop right there. It's none of your business.'

Hildur was stunned by the aggressiveness of Jakob's reaction. What had just happened?

She didn't want to show how shocked she was, so she maintained a poker face and kept her eyes glued to the road. But she couldn't stop the shivers from running up her spine.

Something was off, and badly so.

Chapter 18

Grundarfjörður, West Iceland, December 2021

Rasta-haired Olga Ragnarsdóttir had ordered herself a non-alcoholic beer. Even a single serving of alcohol in the evening tended to keep her up at night, so if she only came for one, it was wisest to enjoy it alcohol-free. Olga crossed the packed pub with her filled pint glass, trying not to slosh her beverage.

The only free table in the little pub was at the back, next to the wall. Olga lowered her pint to the bar table. She pulled her phone from the pocket of her winter coat and glanced at the posts on her Facebook wall. She was disappointed she didn't see what she'd hoped to find there.

Five members of their group had been shooting photos in rural West Iceland that afternoon. Due to the delicacy of the assignment, they'd agreed to take the same precautions as in the past: if they got good material, they replied to a photo posted on Facebook with a red heart emoji. If they didn't, they replied with a like instead. It was critical they avoid direct contact after an assignment to ensure no one could track them down. Olga saw four blue thumbs-ups under today's photo. She added a fifth.

The day hadn't gone as well as she'd hoped. But it was impossible to succeed every time; she knew that. Luck had been on their side the week before. They'd got multiple photographs and forwarded them to their contacts. They'd just had worse luck today.

Olga slipped her phone in her pocket and started filling out the crossword someone had left on the table. After pondering a few clues, she reached for her pint and took another big swig. The pub was packed; the place was stifling.

By the time she was almost finished with her beer, Olga realised something was off.

She suddenly felt weak. That was odd. The beer was completely non-alcoholic, but it was as if she were drunk. She couldn't focus her eyes. Her legs were tingling, and she couldn't move them the way she ought to be able to. Olga took hold of the table's edge and tried to stand tall, but it was in vain. Her legs refused to obey. Her field of vision narrowed, and suddenly the people around her were swaying from side to side.

Maybe fresh air will help, she thought to herself, and quickly crossed the short distance to the front door. She grabbed the handle, pulled it, and exited. But after a few steps, she had to stop and lean her back against the building. The world was spinning faster and faster.

'Have one too many?' quipped a young man across the street. But he didn't break his stride and didn't wait for an answer.

Olga shook her head to indicate no. She struggled to stay awake. Was she having a stroke?

A figure stepped out from behind the pub and walked up to Olga and took her by the arm. Olga was filled with relief that this angel had appeared to help her. She let herself be supported. She tried to open her mouth to explain how she was feeling.

But then something bizarre happened. The person who'd hurried to help stepped aside, letting Olga fall to her face. Before Olga lost consciousness, she registered her saviour was carrying a burning candle. As her world dimmed, she caught a horrific whiff.

It was the stink of burning hair.

Chapter 19

Ísafjörður, December 2021

The loud metallic sound bulldozed into the cushy slumber Hildur had sunk into only a few hours before. It had been a rough night. She'd spun in the sheets for hours without falling asleep.

Her hand groped at the floor. Her fingertips touched a dust bunny, then a lone running sock . . . and at last her phone. The call was from an unknown number. It was only 6.30 a.m., so it couldn't have been an insurance salesperson or any of the countless survey companies that posed questions about random topics on their clients' behalf. Hildur answered with her full name.

The wind was howling at the other end, and the background noise drowned out the caller's clipped sentences.

It was Arnór Dagsson, police chief of Akranes and Hildur's old friend from her Reykjavík days. The small municipality on the west coast was located at the very tip of a peninsula. The wind never stopped blowing in Akranes.

'I'm sorry for calling so darn early, so I'll get right down to it. We're incredibly short-staffed. Every other officer has caught some winter bug. I got a call from Grundarfjörður an hour ago. An unusual case, and I could use your help.'

Great, Hildur thought to herself. *Just great*.

Jakob had set out for Reykjavík the evening before to catch today's flight to Finland. Hildur had her hands full. She'd sent in the sheet of paper they'd found at Súðavík harbour for fingerprint analysis, along with the currency and freezer bags from Luka's room. Today she'd planned on making the rounds of the homes near the harbour to ask for eyewitness statements. As of yet, she and Jakob hadn't found anything of use from the fish farm's security cameras, most of which had been trained on the feeding equipment. They'd also reviewed the footage from the transport companies' cameras, but they'd only covered the storage and loading areas of the harbour. Nothing out of the ordinary had come up there either.

Hildur turned on the nightstand lamp and rose to sitting in her bed. Arnór summarised the previous night's events in a few sentences. A woman in winter clothes had been found unconscious behind the sole pub in the village of Grundarfjörður. Her body temperature indicated she hadn't been outside many hours.

'Did she pass out?' Hildur asked. Hildur remembered at least two cases over the course of her policing career where excessive alcohol use had led to fatal unconsciousness in freezing weather. Both had been such senseless deaths.

'We're waiting for the results of the blood analysis.'

A dog-walker had found her lying in the snow and called the police. The local patrol had arrived within a few minutes and successfully shaken her awake. The confused woman had been transported to the medical clinic in the neighbouring town, which had a few beds.

'I'm calling because I need someone with experience to talk to her and possibly any patrons who were at the pub last night. And then there's one really disturbing detail: the woman's hair was burned.'

'Excuse me, what did you say? Is she badly injured?'

Hildur clambered to her feet and slipped into the brown plaid slippers waiting next to her bed. Jakob had given them to her for Christmas last year.

'Most of her hair was burned off, but her scalp wasn't damaged. She has a few centimetres of hair left.'

Weird, Hildur reflected. It sounded as if someone had lit the woman's hair on fire, then immediately put out the flames. Otherwise, they would have spread so fast they would have burned her whole head.

'I just called Jónas and explained the situation. He seems like a pretty, hmm, cantankerous guy . . .' Arnór said, choosing his words carefully.

Hildur walked into the kitchen as she replied that Arnór's guess would have won him the jackpot in the Eurolotto. She turned on the dimmest light over the counter and spooned coffee into the coffeemaker, phone pinched between her ear and her shoulder.

'Well, in any case. He said Ísafjörður could spare you for a day.'

The coffeemaker started up, and a moment later the aroma of fresh coffee wafted through the kitchen. Hildur opened the fridge for breakfast supplies and the cream, which she poured in her coffee. There was still half a tub of Skyr left. Hildur bent down and reached into the freezer for some of the crowberries she'd picked and frozen whole, then mixed them into the Skyr. Two fistfuls of oatmeal, and her gluey purple breakfast was ready for consumption.

'Tell me a little about the victim,' Hildur said.

Arnór wrapped the facts in a tight package. Woman in her early twenties. Has lived alone in Grundarfjörður a few years. Drops by the pub a few times a week to read the paper. Works at the day-care centre kitchen. Locals recognise her by her long dreadlocks. Animal rights activist.

'An animal rights activist. What do you mean?'

It took Arnór a moment to reply; he was presumably checking his notes. 'Involved in all sorts of animal welfare advancement.

Now that it's Christmas, apparently she's been going around from house to house almost every day collecting blankets for animal shelters in Reykjavík.'

Arnór gave Hildur the address of the clinic where the woman was recuperating. He promised to be in touch that evening and continue wherever Hildur left off.

'I wish this darn flu season would pass,' Arnór said heavily.

'I'll hit the road right away. I'll be there . . .' Hildur glanced at the clock on the wall and made a quick calculation, '. . . before noon.'

'Thanks a lot for helping out, Hildur. I'll send you a reindeer fillet for Christmas. I still have a lot of grade A meat in the freezer from the autumn hunt.'

This cheered Hildur. 'I almost want to say the pleasure is all mine, but that would be an exaggeration,' she said, before signing off.

Hildur downed a quick cup of coffee, poured the rest in the Thermos, and grabbed two bananas from the bunch to tide her over. She had a drive of almost five hours ahead of her on a snowy highland road, and she had no idea what she'd find waiting for her when she arrived.

Chapter 20

Stykkishólmur, December 2021

The fridge in the hallway was humming steadily. There was no one at the glass-walled cubicle, but two half-drunk cups of coffee, a pair of glasses, and a banana peel lay on the desk. Hildur called out and knocked on the reception desk window.

A moment later, an older woman in a grey cardigan appeared at its rear door. She was leaning on a cane and seemed to be having a hard time making it to her seat.

'Hildur Rúnarsdóttir. I'm a detective with the Westfjords police. The station in Akranes had their hands full, so they sent me. I'm here to see the woman who was brought in in the middle of the night.'

'I'm happy to see you. It was truly horrific. Iceland the best place on the planet? I'm starting to strongly doubt whether that's the truth. What is this world coming to?'

The woman continued muttering as she pulled her grey sweater more tightly around herself, then explained Olga Ragnarsdóttir had been delivered to the medical centre by ambulance around four o'clock that morning. Despite some apparent disorientation, she'd been conscious and able to speak.

'I could immediately smell she wasn't drunk. According to her, she'd had one non-alcoholic pint at the bar after a long day and then blacked out.'

The blood work had supported Olga's story. Hildur suspected someone had spiked her drink. The police occasionally came across suspected cases of spiking, especially on weekend nights in Reykjavík. Sudden bouts of nausea, memory loss, passing out in pub bathrooms. Often, although not always, the cases involved sexual violence and video recording. Hildur remembered a specific case particularly well. A young woman in her thirties had passed out at a house party, a male acquaintance had raped her, and his friend had recorded everything and uploaded the clip to some porn site. The men were charged and convicted, but it had been impossible to get the video taken down. The victim suffered a psychological collapse and ended her life on Route 1, throwing herself in front of a tanker truck transporting milk.

The receptionist seemed to read Hildur's mind. 'Nothing came up in the drug panel. Other substances are usually used to lace drinks, and they don't necessarily show up. The blood sample was sent to Reykjavík for more detailed analysis.'

The woman started to rise from her chair, but she seemed to be having such a tough time that Hildur said she'd find Room 3 on her own. She thanked the receptionist and started down the left-hand corridor. The right one would have led to the live-in unit for the elderly.

The mint-green corridor had been hung with posters asking DO YOU DRINK TOO MUCH? and ARE YOU EATING WELL? that advertised a support group for young mothers that met at the parish centre on Fridays.

The long drive had given Hildur the chance to speak to the police patrol that had responded to the late-night call about Olga. The most unusual detail had been the candle found in the snow next to her. Hildur had immediately called the pub and learned it was theirs: a candle had gone missing from one of the tables over the course of the evening. There were no CCTV cameras. It had been a busy night: in addition to the regulars, a lot of out-of-towners and tourists had been present. The owner and his wife had handled the shift alone and hadn't noticed anything out of the ordinary.

When Hildur reached Room 3, she knocked and tentatively opened the door. The long cotton curtains had been pulled back from the window, but the room was still dim.

A petite woman lay face up in the hospital bed. Her eyes were closed. As Hildur took a step closer, her boots squeaked against the floor. The woman opened her eyes and looked at Hildur in fright.

'I'm sorry. I don't mean to be creeping around,' Hildur said. She introduced herself and explained she'd come to talk about the previous night's events.

Olga rose slowly to sitting on the edge of her bed and took a sip of water from the glass on the table. Her hair – or what was left if it – looked crazy. The sides hung almost to her chin. But at the back, it was almost completely burnt off. The charred remnants of her dreadlocks had shrivelled to the top of her head like a wad of gum.

Olga asked Hildur to pass her the lightweight beanie that was on the coatrack. After she pulled it on, she looked at Hildur as if she was ready to talk.

'Could you tell me what happened yesterday? Why don't you start from when you arrived at the pub,' Hildur said, seating herself on a chair next to the wall. She leaned forward, elbows on thighs, and interlaced her fingers under her chin. She wanted to set as informal a mood as possible. This was just a preliminary conversation. Hildur wouldn't record it with her phone; she'd jot down some notes afterward. The police in Akranes would bring in Olga for a formal interrogation if doing so was deemed necessary. Hildur's sole purpose now was to find out what had occurred from Olga's perspective.

Olga coughed and began talking.

She worked at the kitchen of the daycare centre at the edge of the village. She also took some afternoon and evenings shifts at the local pool, and that's what she'd done yesterday. Olga clarified that she had to work two jobs to make ends meet. Hildur was familiar with the phenomenon: the recent rise in prices had made things even harder on those on a limited income. Olga's shifts included cleaning duties, so she hadn't finished until eleven or so.

'I live in the little wooden house next to the hostel. I was headed home when I changed my mind and decided to go for a beer.'

Olga had lived in Grundarfjörður for a long time, so she knew most locals. She explained she went to the pub fairly regularly and knew everyone who worked there.

'They were busy last night. It was a full house.'

Olga had ordered a pint and retreated to the back of the pub to enjoy it. She'd spent a little time browsing through her phone, then turned her attention to the crossword in a paper she'd found on the table.

'Did you talk to any of the other customers?'

Olga shook her head. She'd been so engrossed in the news that she hadn't paid much attention to the people around her. When she was almost finished with her beer, she'd started feeling so sick that she'd left.

Hildur made a mental note of the details. She'd write herself some notes as soon as she was out of Olga's presence. She didn't want to ruin the delicate moment by pulling out her pen and notepad.

'My plan was to go home to rest. But . . . but I never made it that far,' Olga said, bursting into tears. The clumps of hair visible under her beanie jiggled along with her shoulders.

Hildur stood and gave Olga an encouraging pat on the shoulder. 'We suspect someone spiked your drink. Did you step away from your glass at any point? To go to the bathroom or anything?'

Olga shook her head. Her eyes had been glued to her phone and the crossword puzzle. The pint had been right there next to her, but she hadn't been looking at it the whole time.

'Did anyone bump into you? Or did anything else happen that could have distracted you?'

Olga shook her head again.

'Do you happen to remember anyone sitting at any of the nearby tables? We're trying to find eyewitnesses.'

Olga took a tissue from the box on the table and blew her nose. She closed her eyes and appeared to think. 'There were some students right next to me. I was irritated by how loud they were being.'

'How do you know they were students?' Hildur asked.

Olga told Hildur about their shirts. The group had consisted of at least five young men, maybe more. They'd been speaking in some foreign language, presumably German, and had all been wearing matching hoodies. 'They were dark blue and said *Berlin* and *university*. That stuck in my mind, because Berlin is my favourite city. Last time I was there was last summer . . .' Olga seemed to sink into her memories. 'One of them tried to talk to me, but he was so incredibly drunk that I pretended not to hear when he said hello. He turned away.'

Hildur wanted to question the students from that table ASAP. She stood to leave. 'Try to get some rest. We'll keep you posted as to how the investigation is progressing.'

Olga nodded meekly and lay back down on her bed.

After exiting the health clinic, Hildur dictated what she remembered of Olga's story into her phone. She would write up a report when she got home. Then she drove along the winding coastal road that took half an hour to reach the village where the hostel was. The students Olga had mentioned had been out partying, so it was likely they'd spent the night in town. The hostel was the only wintertime lodging available on a student budget. Or of course they could have rented an Airbnb; there were several nearby. But Hildur had to start somewhere.

Hildur kicked both feet against the doorjamb to knock the snow from her boots and stepped into the hostel's reception area. A young woman was wiping down the tables and lighting candles.

She seemed to immediately know the group Hildur was talking about. She shook her head in apparent dissatisfaction. 'They showed up after midnight and kept drinking, even though we have quiet hours from 10 p.m. on.'

The other guests had complained about the late-night noise, and the boys had left a horrific mess in the lobby. The vacuuming alone had taken over an hour.

'Now those jerks are snoring away in the dormitory at the end of the hall,' the young woman said, waving her rag toward the hallway. 'Straight on that way.'

Hildur knocked loudly on the wooden door. When there was no answer, she knocked again, harder. 'Open up. Police,' she said in English.

That did the trick. There was a thud on the other side of the door, followed by a groan, and a moment later the door cracked open. A sleepy-looking kid of about twenty stood there, red hair sticking straight up. Hildur couldn't help but notice the powerful smell of alcohol.

The young man looked at Hildur in alarm. Evidently, the arrival of a police officer had thrown him into a tizzy.

'We're really sorry about last night. I guess we were being too loud. But come on, we didn't think the police—'

Hildur rubbed her forehead and turned away; the reek of stale booze was nauseating.

'That's not why I'm here. You guys were at the pub last night? I need some eyewitnesses. Could you come out here and talk?'

The boy grabbed a hoodie from somewhere behind the door and threw it on, then slipped his scrawny legs into some jeans. He looked relieved the police presence had nothing to do with the previous evening's carousing.

Hildur thrust her head into the room: 'I want the rest of you to put something on, too, and come to the lobby right away,' she said in a clear, resonant voice.

Before long, all five young Germans were sitting around one of the round tables in the lobby. They'd spent the autumn term in Iceland as exchange students, and once their finals were over, they'd set out to drive around the country. They weren't scheduled to fly back to Berlin until next week. Grundarfjörður had been their first stop, and they were so happy to be on break they'd pulled out all the stops.

'We could have probably skipped that last beer,' groaned the redhead, who'd introduced himself as Bruno. He took a sip from a cold bottle of orange soda.

Hildur explained why she was there.

'A woman with dreadlocks in a green coat,' Otto pondered audibly at Bruno's side. Otto cleaned his glasses with the hem of his shirt, looking thoughtful.

The boys had had a few pints at the pub. According to them, they hadn't been particularly intoxicated when they left. Back here at the hostel, they'd taken the beers they'd bought from the liquor store earlier that day out of the fridge and continued partying.

'I remember her,' Otto said. 'Kind of pretty with long dreads.'

Bruno guffawed and gave Otto a friendly slap on the back: 'Of course you remember her! You tried to talk to her, but she shut you down fast. She probably didn't even notice you!'

Otto blushed and adjusted his glasses. 'She was staring at her phone so hard she didn't even really look my way . . .' He seemed disappointed.

Hildur wondered whether he could have slipped a roofie into Olga's drink to get back at her for ignoring him. So she asked him.

'There's no way I would put anything in her drink!' Otto cried. 'Believe me!'

Otto explained his sister had been spiked at a club in Berlin once. He swore there's no way he'd ever do anything like that. He said he'd been at least a few feet away from Olga the whole time. The other boys confirmed his account.

'Did you notice anyone else in her company that evening?' Hildur asked. She knew sometimes people who'd suffered rejection could take it so badly they'd keep an eye out to see if anyone else succeeded where they failed. Comparing oneself to others was human, though few people cared to admit it.

Otto studied his cuticles, then looked up at Hildur: 'Yeah, some guy approached her table. Ordinary, pretty normal-sized guy. I noticed him, because it was so hot and crowded inside the pub and he left his coat and hood on the whole time.'

This caught Hildur's attention. She asked Otto to explain.

'I don't really know. He just had his hood on the whole time. I didn't see his face, because he never turned to face the room. I just saw his back. He was wearing a long coat, and he walked a little crooked. Or maybe he was just leaning against the table. I don't know.'

'About what time was this?'

Otto scratched his chin and pondered. They'd ordered their last beers a little before lights out, so maybe somewhere around 12.30 a.m.

Hildur took some notes on Otto's account and asked him to think back again. Even the tiniest detail could be of use.

'Did the guy with the hood order a drink? Are you sure you didn't see his face? Try to remember. Any information could be helpful.'

Otto tapped the tabletop with his fingers, then suddenly seemed to remember something.

'He was holding a lighter and kept fiddling with it. I noticed, because you couldn't smoke inside.'

Chapter 21

Ísafjörður, December 2021

Hildur had driven almost five hours straight to make it home from Grundarfjörður by evening. The effects of the long drive manifested as a stiffness in her shoulders and a need to clear her head. After arriving at Ísafjörður, she realised she hadn't eaten since breakfast. So first thing she stopped by the grill and picked up a few slices of pizza and a bag of salt and vinegar chips. She munched on this dinner at her computer while wrapping up the paperwork on the young woman who'd lost her hair.

Hildur proofread her report one last time and then uploaded it to LÖKE, the Icelandic police database. She texted Arnór in Akranes to inform him the notes on her conversation with Olga were available for review. Not long after, her phone pinged with an incoming message. Arnór's reply was succinct: a policewoman emoji and a thumbs up.

Just then, Hildur heard heavy footfalls from the corridor. It was 9.30 p.m. Who would be moving around the station at this hour? The patrol officers on duty sometimes dropped by for coffee and to shoot the shit, but they always travelled as a pair. Hildur rose from her chair and peered into the corridor.

She was surprised to see Jónas standing there, fiddling with a bunch of keys. Apparently, he was trying to find the one for his office. A faint whiff of alcohol mingled with the aromas of tobacco wafted through the air.

'Good evening, Jónas,' Hildur said from the doorway.

Jónas jumped, and his keys fell to the floor. He groaned as he bent down.

'What are you doing creeping around here this time of night?' he snapped.

'I was helping out Akranes and just got back. I came straight in to finish the paperwork.'

Hildur gave the short version of her day's excursion. Jónas nodded in approval and eventually managed to unlock his door. He explained he'd come in to fetch the satchel he'd forgotten, then continued, hand still on the door handle: 'Listen, I have to tell you something important while we're here.'

Hildur got the impression he was drunk.

'I've been invited to give a lecture in the US. The FBI Academy in Virginia wants a presentation on border controls in our little island nation. While I'm there, I'm also going to be participating in a panel on cooperation between law enforcement and parents to reduce alcohol use among minors. That's in Washington. One of the head honchos from Reykjavík was supposed to go but had to cancel. I promised to handle the presentations for him,' Jónas said, glancing at his watch. 'I'm taking the evening flight to New York tomorrow. I have a layover there. So, um, I'll see you in a little over a week. I'm sure you'll be fine. And Jakob will be back soon.'

Hildur was delighted by her boss's unexpected business trip. She was also amused. So Jónas *promised*, did he? Sure. Jónas loved pomposity and playing the bigshot, so it was unlikely anyone had had to flatter him to convince him to go. His upcoming absence was probably the best news she'd have this December.

Hildur returned to her desk and sat cross-legged on her chair. She rattled the mouse to wake up her computer. A thought had occurred to her. If possible, it was always important to double-check any information provided in a witness statement. You could never tell with people. Some spewed nonsense intentionally; some forgot details by accident.

She took another look at the report she'd just written. Olga had told Hildur that she'd spent the day working at the daycare centre kitchen, then pulled a shift at the pool before stopping by the pub. It was almost 10 p.m. now, so Hildur wouldn't get hold of anyone at the daycare centre, but most swimming pools in Iceland were open late.

The Grundarfjörður pool was a traditional public facility in a rural area: the changing rooms and showers were indoors, while the heated pools were out under the sky. Hildur had been there during one of her longer surfing trips in the area, washed the crust of sea salt from her skin and took a moment to relax in the steaming water before continuing on to the next surfing site.

Hildur checked the municipal website for the pool's phone number. In wintertime, the pool was open to the public for a couple of hours first thing in the morning and for a few evening hours. The daytime hours were reserved for schoolchildren. Few schools had their own pool, despite swimming being a mandatory subject in grade school and a national law requiring all Icelanders to know how to swim. And so schools used municipal public pools during the day.

After two rings, her call was answered by what sounded like a young man.

Hildur introduced herself. 'I'm calling about an ongoing investigation . . . I need to find out what time one of your lifeguards, Olga, left work last night?'

There was silence at the other end of the call. It was a common occurrence in such situations. People often felt nervous about talking to the police.

'Olga isn't suspected of anything. But I need to know what time she left work.'

The young man's voice was even more uncertain: 'Did you say yesterday?'

'Yes. She worked the evening shift last night, and according to my understanding, the lifeguards also handle the cleaning after the pool closes.'

'No. I mean yes, we clean after the pool closes. But . . .'

Hildur uncrossed her legs and let her feet drop to the floor. She pulled her chair closer to the desk and straightened her back. She focused on waiting for the young man to finish his sentence.

'. . . but no one was working here yesterday. We were closed for maintenance of the heated pools.'

Chapter 22

Äkäslompolo, summer 2016

The creature's body and the fragile wings attached to it quivered softly as it intently sucked blood. The proboscis was incredibly fine but stood out clearly against the sun-browned skin it had pierced. Jakob kept his eyes glued to the insect. When would its belly be full enough to quit? Did mosquitos feel full?

Just now he had time to think about all sorts of things.

He had the morning at the cabin to himself. With his left foot, he nudged the rocking chair into faster motion.

The wooden chair had belonged to Jakob's late grandmother. She'd explained how her mother had saved it from the house they'd feared the Germans would torch during the Lapland War. Jakob's great-grandmother and her family had taken the rocking chair and photographs and left everything else behind. As luck would have it, they'd been able to return to the house after the war. Äkäslompolo had been spared being burned to the ground.

Jakob remembered another story his grandmother had told him decades before: a German extermination squad had motorcycled into the village and strewn flammable material on the floors of a few homes, but fate had intervened. Two young men who'd stayed behind had seen what the Germans were up to and unleashed a barrage of gunfire at a barn to make a lot of noise. Alarmed by the possibility of serious resistance, the Germans had retreated.

Jakob's family's tiny cabin was still standing. It was one of the most important places in the world to him. It stood on a riverbank in the middle of a spruce wood. The current was weak, so Jakob had swum in the river even as a child. There was a lake a few kilometres away. The cottage had two beds. The little kitchenette was fitted out with a camp stove and a cold-water tap fed from the river during the warm months.

This is where Jakob had spent his childhood summers with his grandmother while his parents were travelling on business. It had always had a special place in Jakob's heart. His grandmother's estate was still waiting to be distributed, but anyone who knew where the key was could use the cabin. Jakob was really the only one who ever did.

Jakob and Lena had agreed to spend a few days of their Finland trip here and the rest of the time in Helsinki, which Lena didn't care for but found more palatable than Lapland. The endless bargaining. It frustrated Jakob. He'd known his plan of visiting the cabin was dead on arrival, but it had been a dream of his to show it to Matias. Introducing his son to this place had been his way of carrying on the family legacy. And two-year-old Matias had enjoyed himself. He'd toddled cheerfully across the lawn and been delighted by the conifer cones Jakob had heaped into pyramids for him. Kids that age were too young to form lasting memories, but bringing his son here had still felt important to Jakob.

Lena had spent most of the time at the cabin on her own. She'd gone for walks in the forest and talked on the phone with her Norwegian friends. During the day, Jakob and Lena went grocery shopping together and discussed practical matters related to Matias, but otherwise they barely spoke. Jakob slept at Matias's side, and Lena slept in the other bed. This was the path their life had taken over the past two years. To outside eyes, they seemed to live an ordinary existence, parenting a young child. But the truth was something else: they occupied the same space but lived apart from each other. It was all polite enough on the surface, but things roiled beneath and occasionally exploded. Lena had wanted to keep the family together despite Jakob's lying, but doing so had grown increasingly difficult. She was still angry with Jakob. She bossed him around and nagged about everything under the sun, from how long he took doing the grocery shopping to whom he was allowed to spend time with outside the home.

Of course, Jakob noticed how single-mindedly Lena was trying to control him. But he didn't have the heart to raise the issue. When something was heavy, shifting it was usually the last thing anyone wanted to do.

Jakob glanced at his arm. The mosquito was still sucking away.

He raised his other hand and brought it down hard. The blood spread across his palm like an ink stain. Amid the gory mush he made out a pair of legs. So much for that mosquito's life.

Just then, he heard a vehicle approaching outside. Lena was pulling up to the cabin. She lifted Matias out of the child seat and kicked the car door shut too forcefully.

'Hey,' said Jakob. He'd stepped out of the cabin and was picking at the grass that grew next to the front steps. He wiped the remains of the mosquito from his palm onto a tuft of grass.

Lena didn't offer any response as she walked inside. She set Matias down on the bed. He immediately reached for his stuffed animal and clasped it to his body. Lena took a small glass from the cupboard and greedily drank a glass of cold water. She put the empty glass in the sink, took the sunglasses from her forehead, and turned to Jakob. There was something in her gaze he couldn't quite read. The expression was friendly but somewhere deep down he caught a flash of indifference, perhaps arrogance.

'Listen, I've been thinking about something.'

Jakob was sure Lena was about to bring up Regina again. Lena's monologues about Regina always followed the same pattern: a steadily rising voice followed by smashing and breaking that came to a climax in outright screaming.

'I know this cabin means a lot to you. What do you say we skip Helsinki and you spend the rest of the vacation here? You could fix the place up a little. Matias and I could go back to Norway early and get ready for him to start daycare.'

Jakob was delighted by the offer. 'I do need to replace a couple of porch planks and paint the window frames.'

He'd be happy to spend a few days at the cabin doing odd jobs and enjoying the silence. It was going to be a busy autumn, and the rest and relaxation would do him good.

Lena grazed Jakob's cheek with her hand. The unexpected show of tenderness felt nice. 'Great. Then I'll see you in Oslo in a week.'

Chapter 23

Hveragerði, December 2021

Felix Karlsson's body ached. He was walking home from the local cross-fit studio with clipped, cautious steps, gym bag casually slung over his right shoulder. The veil of grey clouds hung low, concealing the mountains that rose behind Hveragerði.

His afternoon workout had been taxing. He'd warmed down and stretched properly. Even so, the physical exhaustion was almost unpleasant. Felix's local gym was small but top of the range. One of the country's best-known cross-fit pros trained there.

Felix worked out four times a week. He liked to take evening training a little easier so his body wouldn't be too stimulated afterward. Getting a good night's sleep was important. Felix had quit bingeing on beer the year before and started looking after his health. A solid night's rest, low-fat food and a lot of exercise. His core had tightened up, and his shoulders had broadened. His lean, firm body gave him confidence.

Felix had let himself go during his student years. His veterinary studies in Estonia had been so demanding he hadn't had time to exercise. Bars had been easy places to meet people, and he'd spent a little too much time in them. The move to Estonia had been necessary, because there was no veterinary training in Iceland. Felix had immediately returned to his homeland after graduating the summer before and got a temporary position as a municipal veterinarian. Finding work in his hometown had felt like a stroke of luck.

The thought of the upcoming evening put a smile on Felix's face. Get horizontal on the couch first thing, with a cold beer and a bowl of tuna pasta on the coffee table. He'd be meeting friends at the pub later; the local brewery had advertised the arrival of a fresh batch of its Christmas beer. But the limited-edition beverage wasn't Felix's only reason for wanting to go to the pub.

The most important motivation was his neighbour Anna. Anna's long red hair was almost always tied back in a big, loose braid that reached down to her lower back.

On a couple of occasions, Felix had gathered up his courage and concocted some lame excuse for a conversation before approaching Anna while she was walking her dog. Most recently he'd asked her for the time. She'd given him a mischievous smile and suggested he check the watch on his wrist.

Since that encounter, they'd exchanged lingering glances when they ran into each other at the grocery store or the heated pools at the pool. Today, Felix meant to find the guts to ask her out.

The wind picked up, and Felix turned his head sideways. A familiar eggy smell permeated the air. The sulfurous stench from the hot springs wafted into Hveragerði whenever the wind was in the north.

Felix crossed the street and approached the park. He'd cut through to get home faster. He was so engrossed in thinking about Anna from the brewery that he didn't notice the figure in dark clothing step out from behind the spruce hedge.

The figure approached Felix from behind, baseball bat poised to strike.

'Hey, buddy,' the figure said in a raspy voice, then drew a lungful of oxygen before bringing the bat down on Felix's head. There was a dull crunch as it made contact. A series of whacks followed rapidly.

Felix felt an explosive pain, but it wasn't long before the pain ended and the world went black.

Chapter 24

Beta was on her way to Hveragerði. When she reached the highlands, she adjusted the windscreen wipers: heavy snowflakes the size of ten-króna coins were slapping the glass with increasing speed. The weather in Reykjavík had been ordinary, the mundane drizzle and southern wind of most December days. Outside the city, the reality was something else. Clouds had gathered above the highlands, and the temperature had dropped below freezing.

Beta felt like she was finally getting a handle on normal life. After everything came crashing down with the divorce, she'd registered for introductory Spanish and tango classes. Her new hobbies had helped her pick herself up. This would be the second Christmas she and the kids spent in the Reykjavík neighbourhood of Fossvogur, and this winter their rowhouse had finally started to feel like home. She'd been fortunate enough to be approved for a mortgage that had allowed her to buy a spacious two-bedroom place for herself and the kids. Beta's ex-husband Óliver had purchased a unit at the far end of the row of attached homes. That made it easy for the kids to go back and forth between places every other week.

It was less than an hour's drive from central Reykjavík to Hveragerði, and the expansive Hellisheiði highlands separated the capital's townships from the village. Beta was driving a little under fifty kilometres an hour. Driving any faster up here wasn't wise. This road saw its share of fender benders and worse as commuters raced to their homes on the far side of the mountain. A badly mangled car had been placed at the side of the road to remind drivers that speeding could have fatal consequences.

Beta had set out driving as soon as the call came in. The local police in Selfoss had reached out to the technical investigation unit in Reykjavík for assistance. A man had been found beaten to death in a village park. Beta had been to Selfoss earlier that autumn to train the local officers on fighting organised crime. The police department didn't have its own detective at the moment, so Beta's assistance was required.

The snow stopped at the highest point of Hellisheiði. Only a thin layer of clouds remained in the sky, filtering the gentle rays of deep-winter light across the broad lava fields.

Beta was listening to a programme featuring old favourites on Icelandic public radio, Rás 1. One of Elly Vilhjálms's best-known songs, the one about a little bird, was playing just now. The song was heavy on the minor chords, but even so, as she listened Beta realised for the first time in ages she wasn't sad. The grief that had enmeshed her since the divorce had momentarily loosened its hold. It was an invigorating feeling.

Beta turned left at the big greenhouses, toward the centre of the village. Coming from Reykjavík, the park was to the right. The cordon established by the local police was visible from a distance. Beta pulled over at the side of the road and walked toward the plastic tape fluttering in the wind.

She introduced herself to the officers at the scene: 'Elísabet Baldursdóttir. Just call me Beta.'

The tall, solid-looking policeman introduced himself as Benedikt Viktorsson. His partner, Dóra Káradóttir, was about Beta's age.

'The guys from forensics are on their way. They should be here in about fifteen minutes,' Beta said.

Dóra and Benedikt explained they'd arrived at the scene about forty-five minutes before. A jogger running through the park had seen a man bleeding on the ground and immediately called the emergency services.

'She felt for a pulse while she was on the line with the dispatcher and didn't find one,' Dora reported. 'We confirmed he was dead when we arrived.'

'And no one else has touched the body?' Beta asked.

Both officers shook their heads. 'Except the doctor, who came by and pronounced him dead a little while ago,' Benedikt added.

Beta looked around. It was rare for anything like this to happen in a sleepy Icelandic village, and it wouldn't be long before curious onlookers started dribbling in. Fortunately, the area had been cordoned well, and the three of them could keep an eye out until the technical team showed up. After the forensic investigators finished their work, the body would be transported to Reykjavík.

Beta glanced at the sky. The clouds were grey but didn't appear weighed down by precipitation. Hopefully, it wouldn't start raining; that could easily destroy evidence.

'Can you tell me anything about the victim?' Beta asked, eyeing the man lying on his side on the wet, winter-grey grass.

Dóra explained that Felix Karlsson was well known in the area; he was the municipal veterinarian.

Benedikt, who was standing at her side, looked miserable. He added that Felix had been well liked in the village. 'He was active in the cross-fit community. As a matter of fact, I knew him pretty well. We trained together a lot. He and I almost always partnered up for two-person exercises. Felix was a real champ at chin-ups. He was . . . he was a really nice guy.'

Benedikt's voice cracked, and he fell silent and averted his gaze from the body.

Beta considered the situation. A popular young man beaten to death in broad daylight in a park sheltered from view by a few bushes. It sounded like a thorny case.

'Any word on eyewitnesses?'

The more energetic Dóra answered: 'Benedikt and I will make the rounds of nearby homes and talk to Felix's relatives and friends as soon as we're freed up here. The other patrol is delivering the news to his family.'

Beta didn't want to approach the body so as not to foul up any possible footprints. But even from a distance, she could see the big dent at the back of the victim's head and the gore spilling out of it. It's possible the body had taken more blows, but this was the only injury that was visible.

'You guys have any immediate thoughts about a weapon? That head looks like it was struck with a blunt object.'

Once again, Dóra hurried to answer first. 'I can't be sure, of course, but something did occur to me.'

Beta nodded, encouraging her to continue.

'One time I was investigating an assault out in the countryside. A pair of adult brothers had been making hay, and out of the blue one whacked the other in the head with a fencepost. The victim didn't die, but the head injury was pretty ugly,' Dóra said. She indicated the body on the ground. 'It looked exactly like that.'

Beta took a moment to think, then made a proposal: 'You two go and ask around about eyewitnesses. I can stay here and wait for the technical investigators. We can meet a little later at the station in Selfoss. If either of us learns anything, we call each other.' She handed the officers her business card.

A total of forty officers worked at the Southern Region police department. Reinforcements would arrive soon to lend Dóra and Benedikt a hand, but it was wisest to start talking to eyewitnesses as soon as possible.

Beta had another reason to get rid of the pair: she didn't want them to hear her next conversation. She pulled her phone from her pocket and brought up Hildur's number.

'I'm cutting to the chase. Remember the Christmas rhyme you mentioned last time we spoke?'

'Of course I remember,' Hildur replied, immediately adding it had been a false lead. She had just received word from Reykjavík that no prints had been found on the sheet of paper. As she'd presumed, whoever wrote it must have been wearing gloves.

'I'm sure this is like looking for a lost lamb in the fog, but one detail occurred to me.' Beta told Hildur about the dead veterinarian she was looking at and how he'd presumably been killed by some blunt object. The technical team would conduct a more precise analysis, but Beta said she was pretty sure she saw tiny slivers of wood at the site of the injury. 'That victim you found at the fish farm, wasn't the body skewered on hooks?'

Beta heard Hildur gasp. 'Goddammit, Beta! You probably haven't heard yet, but there's a woman recuperating at the Stykkishólmur health centre who was assaulted. Her hair was burned . . .' Hildur held a brief pause, '. . . with a candle.'

Beta closed her eyes. Her brain was being flooded with so much information that she needed some darkness to focus. The song was about the Yule Lads who came down from the mountains at Christmastime. Children set out shoes on the windowsill in the hope the Yule Lads would leave them a little present. Disobedient children found a potato in their shoe instead.

'The shoe show starts next week,' Beta said, reciting the poem from memory:

'The first of them was Sheep-Cote Clod,
he came stiff as wood
to prey upon the farmer's
sheep as far as he could.'

Beta remembered another Yule Lad from the poem, Meat Hook, who would use a long hook to steal the family's Christmas meat through the chimney, and Candle Beggar, who stole the children's candles on Christmas Eve.

Neither Hildur nor Beta immediately spoke. Then Hildur broke the silence: 'There are thirteen Yule Lads . . . which means if there's some sick game going on, there are going to be more victims.'

A shiver ran up Beta's spine. She'd been thinking the same thing.

'Listen, Hildur,' Beta began. She was going to need her former subordinate's assistance. Hildur had done superb work combining crumbs of information to discover the identity of a serial killer who'd plagued the country. She was a dogged detective. 'Is there any chance you could come down south tomorrow, even though it's the weekend? I think we're going to have to transfer the entire investigation to Reykjavík. I'm going to need your help.'

Chapter 25

Rural Iceland, December 2021

The horses stood side by side at the far edge of the corral. The sky echoed with the thunder of jets flying overhead. The airport was only about ten kilometres away. The horses seemed to have grown accustomed to the noise, as they just glanced up lazily before lowering their heads again.

Be sure to close the gate.

A person could get used to anything. All it took was time. It helped to be good at one's work. A busy week meant visiting twenty paddocks, and the miles added up, driving to the hidden farms. Those at the ends of narrow tracks, far from the highway circling the island. Iceland was a small country with a lot of winding roads.

The clients added up too: 215 of them, to be exact.

No, wait. There are 216 now.

A new one had reached out in November after buying the farm at Hrafnadalur when Bjarni moved into a nursing home.

There was no training for the job. One picked it up by observing and doing; for instance, by being mentored by a much older German who'd been in the field for ages and whose very name was nauseating. A loud gasbag who behaved condescendingly to everyone and kept fiddling with his expensive Rolex, as if to make sure everyone saw it. But Germany and Rolex Man had seemed like a stroke of luck for someone deeply in debt to the wrong people.

It was the first job that actually paid decently. A certain amount of blood had to be collected every month for the German's contacts. If one didn't reach the quota, the shortage was deducted from one's pay. Four years, and not short a single time. Practicality had beaten out some initial scepticism. The work was as easy as could be. A lot of horses and not many people with prying eyes.

Stop in front of the herd. Scan it from horse to horse.

There she is.

The little mare was pale grey from her ears to her hocks. She stood a little further back, between two bigger horses. She was low in the herd's hierarchy. The herd protected its members, but its weakest ones were protected last.

None of the horses had names, but this one was nicknamed Stjarna because of the large, symmetrical white star adorning her dainty head.

Hold Stjarna around the neck, slip the halter over her head.

Stjarna started breathing faster. She'd panicked the first time. Unfortunately, that meant disciplining her. Fortunately, once had been enough.

A scratch under the scruffy mane and a few words spoken in soothing tones. The impulse came to congratulate the mare on her fine belly, but Stjarna would be losing her foal soon.

Stjarna allowed herself to be led to the restraint box in the middle of the pasture. The little grey mare stepped in obediently and let herself to be tied to the wall. A short lead would ensure she didn't move.

Years of experience made it easy for sensitive fingers to find the right place on Stjarna's neck. The cannula was a little too big, but it had to be. Seven litres of blood was the minimum, and there was no way to get so much so fast with a fine needle.

Speed and efficiency were key to the operation: in and out without leaving a trace. Draw the blood, carefully pack the gear bag, and hand-truck the canisters back to the vehicle. Today's take was fifty litres.

Once the canisters were at the vehicle, the rest was easy. They didn't take long to load.

Lock the back, one last look at the pasture.

What was that?

A raven? No, it was too big to be a bird. A figure in a long grey winter coat was walking away from the pasture. Had they been watching? That was no good. The figure was higher up the slope and quickly disappeared from view.

Walk up the hill and through the gate. Scan the surroundings.

There was no sign of anyone outside the pasture. Snowcapped mountains rolled at the horizon, but there were no humans anywhere.

Maybe I imagined it?

And then the eye caught something of interest. The road wasn't deserted after all.

Chapter 26

Asker, Summer 2016

Jakob walked slowly down the street, a small backpack on his back. 'Song of the Finnish Veterans' had been playing in his head the whole journey home. It had been on the local radio station's playlist when he drove to the train station at Kolari, from where he'd continued via Helsinki to Oslo. A strange song choice for the hottest days of summer.

The lazy lilt of birds penetrated the male chorale echoing in his head. They weren't in any hurry in this heat. Early-summer mating concertos were a thing of the past. The birds had already paired off, and a new generation of chicks had hatched. The autumn migration wouldn't begin for a few weeks.

The corner of the backpack was pressing uncomfortably above his waist, so he adjusted it and tucked a few fugitive hairs from his bun behind his ears. He felt conflicted. On the one hand, he felt rested. After Lena and Matias left, he'd had all the peace and quiet he could hope for at the cabin; he'd relaxed and tended to his business.

His satisfaction had been temporary, though. An uneasiness had found him on the homeward journey, stalked up alongside him. He wasn't sure where it had come from. His discomfort had grown when his numerous attempts to reach Lena had failed.

Jakob had flown from Helsinki to Oslo, then taken the train from the airport to Asker. He'd tried calling several times from the train, but Lena hadn't picked up. She hadn't called him a single time over the past week. There was nothing particularly unusual about that; they didn't really text or call much when they were apart. But this time every one of his calls had gone to voicemail.

Their apple trees were laden with ripe fruit. *Those need to be picked before they fall and rot on the ground*, Jakob noted to himself. He glanced at the dark living room windows. The kitchen curtains were drawn shut, and it looked like the lights weren't on in there either. He tried to reassure himself that the evenings were bright and no one kept their lights on in the summer.

A cold sensation spread through Jakob's lungs as he glanced at the front yard. Everything looked the way it had before their vacation. Too much the way it had. Stopped. Matias's plastic tractor stood in the middle of the sandbox in exactly the same place it had been when they'd left for Finland.

Hands shaking, Jakob slipped the key into the lock. It turned effortlessly. He grunted in relief. What had he been thinking? That it wouldn't work anymore? That Lena had changed the locks in his absence?

Things hadn't been good between them for a few years now. Lena had never forgiven him. Jakob hadn't seen Regina since his last trip to Helsinki, before Matias was born. He'd written her an email so curt it was almost rude, informing her they couldn't communicate anymore. He'd cut off all contact, but that had done nothing to change things at home. Lena was as difficult, controlling and jealous as ever.

Sometimes Jakob felt as if she was intentionally trying to provoke him. He acknowledged his short temper and knew Lena was aware of it too. Now and again, he'd let himself get caught up in Lena's games and lost his temper. On a couple of occasions, he'd been whipped into a true rage. And at those moments, he'd done things he'd been ashamed of after the fact.

As soon as the door was open, Jakob registered something was off in the entryway. He leaned his backpack against the wall and removed his shoes. It took him a second to grasp what was wrong: the entryway was empty. There wasn't a single coat on the rack. The only shoes on the floor were his.

'Lena! Matias!' Jakob called out as he stepped into the hallway.

No response. The walk to the living room felt endless. When he got there, the sight from the doorway was a punch to the gut.

The room was empty except for one chair and one floor lamp. Even the art had been stripped from the walls.

Jakob ran to the bedroom. The same desolation greeted him there. He pulled the doors open one by one. Lena's wardrobes were empty. His were still filled with his clothes.

'Matias!'

Jakob's voice had risen to a shout. He ran into his son's room. It was empty too. Jakob's heart was galloping. He could barely breathe. Scrambling to the kitchen, he stubbed his toe on the wooden threshold, but his panic numbed any pain.

The kitchen was the only room where nothing seemed to be missing. But that was because the kitchen had been furnished when he and Lena had moved in.

A piece of paper torn out of a notebook had been left on the counter, between the dish brush and the grey dish towel. Jakob reached for it with clammy fingers.

Jakob. I've had enough. I can't trust you. I tried, but it's no use. I don't have any choice but to leave. I'm going to start over somewhere else. My attorney will be in touch about practical matters.

Empty the place of your belongings by the end of the month. The cleaners and new tenants are scheduled to come then.
Lena

Jakob had to support himself against the counter or he would have collapsed.

The curtains pulled across the kitchen window reminded him of the home life that had just come to the end of its road. He wrapped his finger around the pale fabric and tugged with all his strength. The curtains ripped and the rod fell to the floor, revealing a heartbreaking view of the front yard.

The plastic tractor was still there in the middle of the sandbox, looking forlorn.

Chapter 27

Reykjavík, December 2021

Very Christmassy, Hildur thought as she strode toward the police station in central Reykjavík. The winds had been favourable that morning, and she'd been able to fly from the fjords to the capital. As the plane descended, the captain had announced the temperature was four degrees Celsius. But the reading only told part of the truth. The island's humidity made the cold harsher than thermometer readings suggested.

This was the Reykjavík of Hildur's imaginings: a dark, bleak place. Summertime temperatures would occasionally pamper the city's residents, but usually the sun was cold. People hurried from place to place. This wasn't a town where you stopped to chat with acquaintances you happened to bump into on the street. A quick greeting was enough; longer conversations took place indoors.

Hildur passed a café where bossa nova rhythms wafted through an open window. Cactuses of various sizes lined the sills. Hildur smiled at the imported exoticism. Trendy cafés and restaurants with their display windows, neon signs and fanciful décor brought an elevating element the old city centre, which had been worn down by time's teeth.

Before long she arrived at her destination. A total of four hundred people worked at the four police stations located in greater Reykjavík. The largest stood on Hverfisgata, next to Hlemmur, which had once been the site of the city's main bus station. Nowadays people visiting the former bus terminal came for its cluster of dining establishments.

The Hverfisgata station wasn't big enough to house all its employees, so supplementary space had been procured at various sites around the old town. Hildur was on her way to the Narcotics and Organised Crime Unit to meet Beta.

Hildur stepped in through a door that resembled the entrances of the neighbouring residential building. A clanking elevator carried her to the fourth floor, where she stepped out and turned right. A discreet sign on the glass door stated office hours were from eight to four on weekdays, but there was no indication as to the nature of the office in question. Outsiders didn't need to know.

Through the glass, Hildur could see Beta approaching. The familiar cloud of curls bounced from side to side in time to her brisk stride. Beta opened the door with a broad smile, and she and Hildur exchanged air kisses. Months had passed since they'd seen each other in person, and Hildur had missed her former boss.

'Come in. I've prepared coffee for us in my office,' Beta said, striding ahead.

Tumi had received an unexpected and urgent phone call and would be joining them in a moment. Hildur took in Beta's enormous corner office. It was a clear upgrade from her workspace at the Ísafjörður police station. The huge window looked out onto the city. There was no real sea view, even though the Atlantic crashed into the shore only a few hundred metres away.

'You're doing well for yourself. Corner office and everything,' Hildur said, moving a laptop from a stack of folders to safety on a side table.

Beta grunted. 'You can even see the sea if you stand at the end of the desk and crane your neck really far to the left.'

She offered Hildur a seat in an armchair pulled up to the round coffee table.

'It's all the same administrative stuff. The higher-ups are closer, so there are more politics. I wish that weren't the case, but what can I do? It's a mandatory perk.'

Hildur updated Beta on Jónas's and Jakob's travels. The only development to report on the Luka investigation was the laboratory tests hadn't picked up any DNA other than the deceased's. Multiple fingerprints, including Luka's own, had been found on the currency discovered in his room. But fingerprint analysis indicated Luka was the only one to have handled the freezer bags.

Hildur took hold of the ornamental handle of the petite, decorative china coffee pot with her thumb and forefinger and shot Beta a quizzical look.

'Procured by the chief of police,' Beta said. 'Nothing I can do about it.'

Hildur poured milk into her coffee and downed half a cup in a single slurp. Beta offered her chocolate biscuits. Some things hadn't changed. Hildur selected a layered biscuit dipped in white chocolate from the plate.

She glanced out Beta's big window. Before the ten-plus-storey hotel went up across the street, it would have been possible to see all the way to Mount Esja across the bay.

The mountain was related to the case at hand. According to the Icelandic Christmas rhyme, the thirteen Yule Lads lived on or in Mount Esja. They came down to Reykjavík one at a time in December. Sometimes their mother, the child-eating ogress Grýla, came down among humans to hunt. Grýla was accompanied by a black, sharp-clawed Christmas cat that gobbled up anyone who hadn't put on clean new clothes for Christmas. Hildur was sure a

Christmas cat that mauled the thrifty was some greedy capitalist's dream come true.

'I've been giving myself a headache thinking about those Yule Lads,' Hildur said. 'We have three victims so far, and there are thirteen lads. Christmas is a little over two weeks away.'

Just then Tumi Jónasson entered. He didn't knock, of course, simply opened the door and filled the doorway with his massive frame. He spread his big hands and smiled broadly. 'The Westfjords' gift to the world! How are you?'

Hildur stood to give her former colleague a big hug. They patted each other heartily on the back before sitting down at the coffee table. Tumi led the national missing children's unit. He and Hildur had worked closely together during her time in Reykjavík, and he was the one who'd trained her to help children and adolescents in trouble. When the missing children's unit had been granted more funding, Hildur had been hired to head up operations for rural Iceland. The country's small size made it hard for police officers to specialise, because all the basic duties had to be tended to as well. And so Tumi occasionally worked on cases that didn't involve child protection.

Hildur was slated to return to the Westfjords on the afternoon flight, so she wanted to keep things moving. 'If this guy is hoping to get through the whole Yule Lad rhyme, he still has ten victims to go.'

Beta coughed and opened a folder on her desk. 'Which is exactly why we want you here.'

She spread a thick stack of documents across the table. Hildur reached for the papers and took a quick glance. Dozens of pages of reports, photographs of the assault victims, various maps and stills from CCTV cameras.

'Icelanders have been beating each other up since the 800s, when the original settlers landed here,' Beta said. 'Wrestling, fighting and revenge are elements of our national heritage that are showing no signs of going anywhere.'

Hildur had called the medical centre near Grundarfjörður and learned that Olga had suffered some complication. She was being intravenously administered a nonsteroidal anti-inflammatory. The woman whose hair had been burned was weak but on the mend.

'We need to talk to her again as soon as possible,' Hildur said. 'She claimed she went to the pub straight from a shift at the pool, but the pool was closed on the evening in question.'

'Interesting . . .' Beta remarked. 'She's a victim, though, not a suspect.'

'But she lied about the course of her evening. There has to be a reason, and we need to find out what that reason is,' Hildur insisted.

Beta promised either she or Tumi would go talk with Olga again.

Hildur searched the stack of documents for a familiar report: the one she herself had written on the victim found submerged in the salmon pen.

'I had a chat with our organised and habitual crime team. No one is sending out feelers about a missing cocaine shipment. As a matter of fact, very little cocaine is being brought into Iceland at the moment.' Beta added she was pretty sure the Slovenian had been working alone. Maybe Luka had gone partying abroad and bought the cocaine home for his personal use.

'Either that, or he bought as much as his bank account could handle and brought it to Iceland to sell,' Hildur mused. 'Maybe he needed money for something.'

People in Reykjavík's party circles were willing to pay three times more for cocaine than it cost in Denmark.

Beta ceded the floor to Tumi, who'd been following the conversation from the sidelines. 'When Beta showed me these folders, I almost had a heart attack.' He sat up straighter and scratched his neck, looking thoughtful. 'The incidents have more in common than those damn Yule Lads.'

Tumi took the papers and created a separate pile for each case, then set a fourth pile aside. 'I knew the Slovenian kid from my work with foster families. He arranged riding lessons for foster kids. We were in pretty frequent contact, actually. A really nice guy. He was also active in the local animal welfare association and other volunteer organisations. I did a little digging and discovered Olga was involved in similar organisations in West Iceland.'

Beta took a chocolate biscuit from the plate and broke it in half. She glanced at Tumi and asked about the cross-fit-loving veterinarian. Had Felix's professional dedication been to his customers or their animals?

Hildur knew right away what Beta was getting at. Distances were long, farms were large, and veterinarians were few. One of the duties municipal veterinarians were charged with was monitoring the condition of production animals. Not all farm owners were equally successful at meeting regulations. Some stinted out of frugality; others didn't have the energy to offer the proper care.

'The local cattle farmers thought of Felix as, in their words, "a real asshole".'

'So he refused to pander to their interests?' Hildur clarified.

'Something like that. The guy had balls,' Tumi conceded, reaching for the fourth stack of papers. 'I also reviewed all recent assaults and accidents where questions remained – at least all those that were reported to the police.'

Homicides were infrequent in Iceland, but assaults were relatively common. Hildur thought back to her Reykjavík years, and how on weekend nights in particular the fists and empty bottles flew fast and hard as drunken Icelanders fought it out on the city's streets. Domestic violence respected neither the day of the week nor the time of day. But those cases didn't end up in police files as often as public acts of violence.

'Then I sifted out the cases that somehow fit the Yule Lad rituals,' Tumi continued.

He'd found two. In one, a newspaper delivery person had found a woman in her early twenties who'd come home from the pub and passed out at the street-level door of her suburban Reykjavík apartment building. She'd been bleeding from the head.

'Someone had bashed her head against the entrance. There was blood and hair on the doorframe. Fortunately, it didn't result in anything worse than a mild concussion. At that building, the newspapers were still delivered inside, so help arrived in time and she didn't freeze to death.'

'Door Slammer,' Beta said. Hildur and Tumi nodded. This was the Yule Lad who liked slamming doors in the middle of the night to disturb sleepers.

The other case was a middle-aged man from Selfoss. He'd been walking home from work when he was struck by a car. By some miracle, he'd survived with a single broken bone.

'How does that case have anything do with the Yule Lads?' Hildur asked.

'Thanks to a smart cop,' Tumi replied. The report on the hit-and-run had been meticulously written. 'It included all sorts of details, including the fact that a package of hot dogs had been found in the victim's coat pocket that he claims not to have put there.'

Hildur strained to remember: 'Sausage Swiper.'

Tumi nodded slowly, then continued. 'Well, because by now you can probably guess the link between these cases, I won't keep you in suspense any longer.'

He told them the sausage man had worked as Felix's veterinary assistant in the neighbouring town. The woman victimised by the door slammer had connections to the UK-based Animal Welfare Institution. 'She has a blog where she talks about her year as an exchange student in England and how she became an animal rights activist during her time there.'

Tumi lowered the papers to the table. Now there were five stacks of papers.

'So some lunatic is playing at Yule Lads and attacking animal rights activists?' Hildur said. It sounded insane. But life could be senseless and irrational at times; Hildur had experienced that personally over recent years. 'Should we warn the public about the threat of violence?' she asked, despite knowing the answer.

Beta looked at the documents on her desk: 'I would tread very carefully there.'

The police didn't want to fan the flames of panic. Besides, they didn't know who to warn about what. There were a lot of people around the country who worked or volunteered on behalf of animal welfare.

The three of them reviewed the cases for over an hour. The only possible sighting of the perp was the scarf-swathed figure the German exchange student had seen at the pub in Grundarfjörður. There were no eyewitnesses in the other cases, and the acts hadn't been captured on a single security camera. The call data from Luka's, Olga's and Felix's phones had been compared without revealing any significant connection among them. They would have to get the call data for the latest two victims too. Beta had confirmed none of the victims belonged to any criminal circles, and none of their names had come up in connection with narcotics-related activities.

'Let's keep this to ourselves for now,' Beta said, looking from Hildur to Tumi. 'So we can do our work without distractions.'

Some police officers maintained regular contact with journalists in the hope of monetary rewards and other quid pro quos. The more people on the force who were aware of the common denominator, the greater the risk media interest would grow. The last thing they wanted to do was cause a panic.

Beta said she wouldn't be keeping any official records of their activities yet. 'Let's allow the local police to investigate the cases, and we'll conduct our own investigations on the side. For the time being at least, let's keep this off the books.'

The first step was talking to each victim and asking them about their animal rights work.

When the meeting was over, Hildur rode the elevator down to street level and started across the courtyard of the neighbouring hotel. She was making for the legendary pizza joint, De Vitos, on the corner.

It was pleasant watching the bustle from the window table when you didn't have to be part of it. The pizza was delectably soft at the centre and crisp at the edges. Piece by piece, it disappeared from Hildur's plate, and by the last piece she felt full. She rinsed the remnants from her mouth with an orange soda and burped in her fist. The sports watch at her wrist indicated she'd have time to visit her sister before the afternoon flight departed.

Chapter 28

Hildur climbed the front stairs and rapped on the red door. Björk had presumably observed her arrival from the kitchen window, because the door opened right away.

Björk said she'd come home from a night shift earlier that morning and was doing laundry. Folded bed linen waited on the couch to be put away. Hildur ran her hand across the coarse linen cloth.

'Aren't you tired?'

Björk shook her head. She couldn't fall sleep in the mornings. She had a day off tomorrow, so she'd sleep in then.

'Have a seat,' Björk said, turning on the gas stove. An afternoon snack had been set out on the table: thin, tightly rolled pancakes, rhubarb jam, whipped cream and a jar of syrup.

'When did you have time to make these?' Hildur asked, snatching one of the pancakes between her fingers like a cigar and chomping off half of it. Her teeth crunched on the sugar sprinkled inside. The pancakes were still warm. Hildur was full after her lunch at the pizzeria, but she couldn't resist the lure of the pancakes. She'd be able to get a few down.

'Looks like you've had your hands full at work lately,' Björk said, setting the cocoa jar and a pot of hot whole milk on the table. 'I've been following the news.'

'I've accrued a mind-blowing number of miles. I haven't been able to exercise. And I can tell it's making me cranky,' Hildur said, helping herself to another pancake.

A few days had passed since her most recent surfing excursion, and she hadn't made it out for a run or to the gym since late November.

She knew work wasn't the only factor, but she didn't want to trouble her sister with her angst. The weight in her chest had grown heavier by the day. She felt worse today than she had the day before. Hildur knew something would emerge somewhere soon that would bring about a permanent change in many people's lives.

'Are you in town for work?' Björk asked, pouring hot milk into two mugs. They were both coffee drinkers, but with pancakes one drank hot chocolate.

Hildur mixed cocoa powder into the hot milk. The teaspoon clinked as she swirled it around her mug. 'Yeah. I had a meeting that couldn't be handled remotely.'

Björk looked at her with interest. 'Does this have to do with the man who was found dead in the sea off Ísafjörður? I read about it in the news. Pretty gruesome . . .'

Hildur nodded as she chewed down her food. 'The case is being investigated in the Westfjords because the deceased was found in our jurisdiction. The police here in Reykjavík were interested in a few details, but as you know . . .'

Björk used her knife to slice herself a bite of rolled pancake, then stabbed it with her fork and popped it in her mouth. '. . . You can't say anything about it, I know, I know. Your work just seems so interesting.'

And then Björk launched into describing a new Swedish police procedural she'd found on a streaming platform. They chatted about books and television series for a moment. It felt nice having a conversation where the connection between the participants was more important than the topic. That sort of exchange didn't necessarily increase one's knowledge, but it banished loneliness, and that felt good. Is this what relationships were always like between siblings?

Björk poured more hot milk into the mugs. 'Is it hard? Seeing bodies, I mean? Do you ever get used to it?'

Hildur paused to think. She wasn't sure. Yes, you got used to it, but that didn't mean it was ever easy. The familiarity didn't necessarily alter your attitude toward it.

'If you're repeatedly faced with something hard, it feels bad every time. But the feeling passes more quickly with the fiftieth body than it does with the first one.'

Björk pondered this. She drizzled the sticky, thick syrup over her pancakes and wiped the rim of the jar clean with her finger. 'In that Swedish series, the detectives are always arguing over who gets to investigate which case. Is that how it is here too?'

Hildur was pleased that Björk was interested in her work. 'Well, not really. Whoever has time takes the case. Usually, it's investigated by the police department closest to the scene of the crime. But they don't always have the resources, and in those instances investigations can be transferred elsewhere.'

'Then there are joint briefings where the cases are discussed and everyone eats a bunch of donuts,' Björk said, then stood. It was time to go down to the basement and empty the washing machine.

Hildur glanced at the clock on the kitchen wall. She needed to get going. The airport was a couple of kilometres away, and she meant to walk. A taxi would have been the easy alternative, but she felt like she could use some fresh air.

She looked out the window. The sky was clouding over. Big snowflakes drifted down to the street and melted there. According to the forecast, the snowstorm was local and would pass before her four thirty flight.

Guilt gnawed at Hildur. In violation of her promise to Björk, she'd started digging up information on Rósa. She'd taken the first step yesterday almost by accident, when the Danish detective Mads Lund had called to discuss a seminar that was going to be held in Reykjavík. Hildur had met Lund in Copenhagen in early November at a pan-Nordic seminar on best practices for questioning under-age victims, suspects and eyewitnesses. The two of them had deepened their acquaintance after the official programme ended. Wrapped in chain-hotel sheets in the middle of the night, Hildur had promised to take responsibility for organising a follow-up seminar in Reykjavík in the spring, on the condition that 'Mikkelsen', as she'd playfully nicknamed Mads after the Danish movie star, agreed to participate.

'Yoohoo, where are you? Thinking about some man?' Björk asked.

Hildur started. She'd noticed during previous visits to Reykjavík that her sister's basement stairs creaked. She must have been so lost in thought that she hadn't even heard her sister return from the laundry room.

'Ha! No time for that at the moment. I was thinking about the passage of time. I should probably start making my way to the airport.'

During her walk, Hildur's thoughts returned to Mikkelsen. He'd said he'd be heading on a work trip to the Faroes soon, and mentioned he had good contacts there due in part to his family. On a whim, Hildur had raised the topic of Rósa. She'd fibbed that Rósa had something to do with some old, unsolved case she returned to now and again. Mikkelsen hadn't hemmed or hawed. Instead, he'd promised to get back to her if he learned anything. Hildur wasn't sure she wanted her hunch to be right this time. Because she'd begun to be nagged by the thought that she might hear something she wasn't prepared for yet.

Chapter 29

Downtown Oslo, Summer 2016

The beautiful summer day felt like a mockery. The sun was blazing down so brightly it hurt Jakob's eyes. Sweat dripped down his neck, making him even more uncomfortable. He strode onward.

The park was a couple of blocks from the train station. He and Lena were to meet near the playground. After three weeks of agonising silence, Lena had finally picked up when he called and agreed to see him.

His body struggled under the weight of the uncertainty and worry. More than anything else, Jakob wanted to see his son. He wanted to clear things up with Lena, who had abruptly emptied their home, ended the lease, and taken their child. She couldn't do that, dammit!

But apparently, she could do exactly that. The social workers hadn't given Jakob the time of day when he called and tried to explain what had happened. The embassy had shoved some lawyer's contact information in his fist. None of it helped. No one took his distress seriously. They simply sent him from agency to agency and spread their arms. What were they supposed to do? Jakob had called the solicitor, who'd given him two pieces of advice: start preparing for a custody battle, and don't contact Lena.

There was no way he couldn't contact Lena. She had Matias, and if he wanted to see his son, he had to try and see her. He'd tried to visit Matias at the daycare centre, but the staff had driven him off the premises and threatened to call the police. When

Jakob had tried to explain he was his son's other guardian, no one had showed the slightest interest. The staff had just looked at him as if he were some dangerous psychopath.

Jakob's steps slowed. He'd immediately recognised Lena, even though she was facing the other way. Her long blonde hair fell down her back, and the familiar bright red purse was at her side on the bench.

Jakob tried to calm himself by repeatedly clenching and unclenching his fists. He circled around to the front of the bench and took a few deep breaths, hoping to get the upper hand in the situation. That would only work if he didn't get angry. The second he lost his temper was the second he lost the game.

He stood in front of Lena, blocking the sun. She slowly lifted her sunglasses and looked at him. A faint smile had formed on her painted pink lips. But her eyes weren't smiling. They looked carefully made up too. Lena was wearing white high-waisted shorts and a sleeveless, lacy pink top unbuttoned so far down that her breasts would have slipped out if she'd leaned over the slightest bit.

Goddammit, Jakob thought to himself. He was furious that he both wanted her and hated her at the same time.

'What the fuck is this game you're trying to play?' Jakob's voice was quivering with rage.

He noticed the parents playing nearby with their children stop in their tracks. All eyes turned to him. But Jakob could no longer restrain himself. 'Where's Matias? What's wrong with you?'

Lena slipped her purse up to her right elbow, stood, and hissed at him between her teeth: 'Keep it down, for God's sake. Everyone's watching.'

Jakob looked around but didn't see Matias. 'Tell me! Where's Matias? Did something happen to him?'

Lena lowered her sunglasses from her forehead to her face and gave Jakob a cloying smile. 'He's over there playing ball with my friend,' she said, nodding toward some tall trees.

Jakob could feel his temper sizzling. He did his genuine best to keep his voice steady and not say anything that would escalate tensions. 'I want to see him.'

Lena laughed and shifted her head. Jakob realised she was looking past him. 'That's not possible right now. My solicitor will be in touch. We can agree on the details later.'

'Goddammit, Lena!'

Lena lifted her dainty chin and swept her hair over her left shoulder. 'Listen, sweetheart,' she said in a honeyed voice, 'You've never been concerned about anyone else's well-being but your own. I'm sure you still have other women. I don't trust you. You don't have anything to offer me anyway. I'm better off on my own. It would be best if you built yourself a new life somewhere else.'

Jakob tried to keep up with Lena's train of thought, but it was hard. He didn't understand anything she was saying anymore.

'Even an idiot can see you're trying to control me through our child,' Lena said. 'Well, it's not going to work.'

Jakob's jaw dropped, but he couldn't get a word out. His throat was dry, and his legs were suddenly so weak they were shaking. Nothing Lena was saying made any sense. This whole scene was like something out of a strange dream.

'That's not true! There's no one else!' Jakob raised his palms to his temples and forced himself to calm down. 'I just want to see Matias.' His voice had softened practically to a whisper.

Lena stood up straighter and clasped her purse more tightly to her body. 'This isn't about what you want or don't want. The only thing that matters now is Matias's well-being. You're not good for him. That's why I left. I brought him to safety. I should have had the courage to do it a lot sooner. As I said, don't call me anymore. My lawyer will be in touch. Why don't you go back to that Regina? You guys don't have to hide now. I couldn't care less what you do anymore.'

Lena swept a few loose strands of hair over her shoulders and took a sidestep to leave. Jakob saw her lips curl up in a small, supposedly apologetic smile. Her delicate nose was moving in time to her breathing. Her high-waisted shorts made her mid-section look deceptively slim. Confusing emotions ricocheted through Jakob's head.

The devil in a Barbie disguise.

That was his last thought before he raised his right hand, clenched it into a fist, built up speed, and swung. For a moment, Jakob wondered what it would have felt like had the blow connected. Blood would have spattered from Lena's face, streamed to her chin and under her collar.

But he'd missed.

Jakob lowered his hand.

He heard a panicked voice in the distance. Jakob saw a woman on a bench a few dozen metres away staring straight at him. The little boy at her side wasn't looking his way. Matias swung his little legs and kept his gaze firmly on the red ball in his lap. His face had tightened with tears.

Jakob felt the strength drain from his body. He collapsed to the bench and buried his face in his hands. Everything had gone wrong – and in the worst possible way.

Chapter 30

Tampere, August 2019

Jakob sat in the pub and drained his pint in honour of the good news. He'd been shopping for yarn on Ilmarinkatu when his phone had pinged, signalling an incoming email. The message had been from Iceland. For the first time in ages, he'd felt the thrill of joy. He'd got the Icelandic internship at the Westfjords police department through the Nordcop programme. The sender had succinctly signed the email *Beta*.

In the message, Jakob's new boss had inquired if he could possibly start as early as October. The department would help him find an apartment and provide him with the necessary equipment. His future partner would be detective Hildur Rúnarsdóttir. 'In rural departments, everyone does everything, so you'll be doing traffic duty, too, but mainly you'll be getting hands-on experience in detective work.'

Jakob had immediately answered, agreeing to everything and expressing his deep gratitude for the opportunity he'd been given.

Iceland sounded good.

Maybe things are finally looking up, Jakob reflected. Things had been extremely challenging over recent years. A long trudge down quicksand paths that had led him to an even darker place. His life had fallen off the rails once Lena had successfully schemed to get full custody of Matias.

Jakob had been granted a few monitored meetings a year and weekly videocalls. He'd been a poor foreigner in an unfamiliar country, so his chances of winning full or even shared custody of Matias had been minute. And he hadn't won. He'd lost, big time.

Maybe the outcome would have been different if he could have afforded a better solicitor.

In any event, following the loss, he'd flown back to Finland to lick his wounds. After several weeks of drinking, his heart had ached so badly he'd been afraid for his life. Shaking naked in bed, he realised he only had two options left to him: start over or die.

The Police College University had been the first step in the right direction. He'd wanted to get his life in order. He'd wanted to learn the rules underpinning a framework he could exist in without anyone getting the better of him or bossing him around. He admitted it: he'd wanted power, and as a police officer he'd have it.

There would have been other alternatives, and he'd considered all of them. A security guard could lord it over those he was guarding, but the pay was too low. A career in the military or as a mercenary were no longer options for a man his age. The one option left to him had been the police academy. So here he was, a police officer an internship short of graduating. And now he was about to fly to Iceland to complete said internship.

But a law enforcement career wasn't his only source of meaning these days. He'd learned to knit. Jakob's new hobby had become an important release for him. Repeating the same movement hundreds or thousands of times kept his nerves calm and his mood stable. Small mistakes lent the end product its uniqueness; big mistakes ruined it. The same applied to life: mistakes were inevitable, but you could control how many you made. Combined with his police training, his mastery of needles and yarn convinced him he was in control of his life.

Besides, doing handcrafts slowed his heartrate and lowered his blood pressure. He'd learned to identify when he was about to see red. His field of vision would narrow, his chest would swell, and little shivers like electric shocks would compel him to reach for anything within arm's reach. Lena's actions had roused the beast, and Jakob had had to learn to control it. The knitting had helped.

His strategy had worked.

When carrying out the detailed plan he'd drafted three years before, he knew he'd made the right choice. He was able to meet life on its terms. Since starting at the Police University College, he'd decided he'd stay candid and calm regardless of the circumstances.

He'd grow even stronger in Iceland, learn even more about knitting. Once the internship ended, he'd come back to Finland, graduate, and find a job as a police officer somewhere.

And then he'd reclaim custody of his child, no matter what it cost.

Chapter 31

Reykjanes, December 2021

Investigative reporter Hlín Jónsdóttir felt energised. That morning she'd finished a tax evasion story involving a major fishing company. When it broke next week and the truth was revealed about the enterprise that presented itself as a responsible, family-owned business, the resulting scandal would be huge.

The thought of the truth coming out put a smile on Hlín's face. She'd truly had a stroke of luck; she'd found an anonymous source in the company's inner circle.

But Hlín wasn't one to rest on her laurels. A journalist was only as good as her most recent story, which was why she was already working on a new one.

She leaned forward with her full weight. The valley before her was a windswept passage, a narrow gap where the wind always blew. It hummed in her ears and made her eyes water. She pressed ahead on short, strong steps.

Her thoughts turned to Luka, the young man who'd disappeared without a trace. She'd read in a police bulletin that he'd been found dead in a fish pen in the Westfjords. Hlín had been shocked to learn of his death. In the press release, the police had hinted that a drug overdose had played a role in it. She knew it was impossible to determine who used narcotics and who didn't based on appearances alone, but she still couldn't believe Luka was an addict.

Hlín turned her back to the wind and reached deep into the pocket of her winter coat for her cell phone. According to the map app, she had almost three kilometres to go before she'd reach her destination. She'd visited the area several times before, and each time she'd left her car at the side of the main road and walked the rest of the way. She wanted to remain as inconspicuous as possible. Hopefully, Luka's information was right and she'd see someone here today. The previous tip had been accurate, but on that occasion Hlín hadn't been able to approach the scene without risking exposure. This was a better location. She'd be able to observe the target from above. Her hand dropped to her big shoulder bag as if to ensure she still had her camera and lenses.

Hlín knew she should have called the police right away and shared what she knew about Luka, but her journalistic instincts had won out. Besides, Hlín was sure the information she had wouldn't have been any use to the police in their investigation. It was in no way related to drugs.

Or how would I know? I wouldn't, she silently corrected herself. Hlín decided she'd check out this tip, then call the police first thing tomorrow morning and report what she knew.

Hlín had bumped into Luka a few months earlier in Reykjavík, when their careers and chance had brought them together at the same restaurant table. The juicy shrimp cocktail had been the perfect starter. As they savoured their food, they'd begun chatting about fishing and discovered they got along well. A few beers and several hours later, Luka's tongue had loosened like a groom's trousers on his wedding night, and that's when he started to talk. Hlín had excused herself to the ladies' from time to time to type everything she heard into her mobile phone for later reference. A couple of days later, she and Luka had met a second time. He'd known Hlín worked as an investigative reporter at the newspaper *Timman* and said he was willing to give her information he and his network had collected if she'd keep her sources anonymous.

There were two sorts of horse farms in Iceland: the type where horses were raised for riding and the type where horses were raised for meat. The staff at the former trained riding horses, organised treks for tourists and gave riding lessons to children. At the latter, horses were raised to be eaten. Old horses were made into sausage, while foals provided tender steaks. But the price of horse meat was so low that it was difficult to make a profit from the business.

And so, some meat farms had begun selling the blood of pregnant mares to the pharmaceutical industry. The blood was a source of PMSG, a hormone administered to production animals like pigs and cows in the hope of increasing litter size. With the hormone therapies, sows gave birth to bigger broods. Trading in mares' blood took place in South America and Germany too.

Hlín knew all this. But Luka had been able to tell her more.

Blood collection was regulated by law. It wasn't supposed to cause the animal pain and the procedure was to be handled by a licenced veterinarian, with only small amounts of blood taken during defined periods. The local food safety authority was supposed to monitor the collection.

Judging by Luka's accounts, all parties were asleep at the wheel. A black market in mares' blood had emerged in Iceland alongside the legal trade. Horse farms that had a lot of gestating mares and sold their blood were called 'vampire farms'. The more gestating mares at a farm, the more blood was collected. So blood was also being collected from half-wild horses unused to being handled by humans. People spooked them. Because the hormone was only secreted during a specific early gestational period, vampire farms aborted the foetuses and immediately impregnated the mares again. There was no time to treat the animals gently or give them local anaesthesia; the idea was to quickly collect and sell as much blood as possible. The stories about foal factories and pregnant mares being tied up, beaten and forced to abort their foetuses had made the hairs on Hlín's neck stand up on end.

Luka had shown her video clips that provided evidence of the brutalities. The problem was they'd been recorded with mobile phones and were of such poor quality that it was impossible to make out any details. Hlín had envisioned a major story on the topic, and she'd be needing a lot of background material. The credibility of sources and the tips they provided had to be carefully double-checked.

Hlín had reached the corral. The wind was still blowing, but it didn't matter, because now she could lean against the wooden fence. She saw a figure in coveralls among the horses in the pasture. Finally! Her timing had been spot on! With a swift motion, she opened her shoulder bag and pulled out her camera. Focus, click. She meant to take as many shots as she could.

The individual in the pasture bustled around the horses like a magician. The massive beasts submitted as if bewitched. Hlín found something about the horse handler's demeanour chilling. Unnerving. Hlín took more photos. The limping figure led a horse to a restraint box in the middle of the pasture. A gangly young foal tried to follow its mother into the stall, but a small side lash of the handler's whip drove it off.

Hlín photographed everything she saw. She was both revolted by what she was witnessing and thrilled that she was catching it on camera. She finally had good photographic material.

She adjusted her camera's video settings and took a few more ten-second clips. Next she'd drive to the newspaper's offices in Reykjavík, record voiceovers, and begin cutting and editing the footage. Hlín turned away from the corral and started back toward her car.

She was so pumped up with adrenaline that she didn't notice the figure following her. The tailwind was sweeping Hlín down the road, and it was blowing so hard she didn't hear the figure walk up right behind her, raise a big cast-iron pan in the air, and bring it down full force on her skull. The thud was followed by the tinkle of shattering glass, as the camera and its telescopic lens fell to the icy ground.

Hlín dropped next to her instrument and lay there, as the wind began blanketing her with snow.

Chapter 32

Ísafjörður, December 2021

Tinna's kitchen smelled of browning sugar. Hildur's aunt stood as far from the pan as her frying stance allowed. As the mound of white crystals grew hot, it gradually began to melt at the edges. Hildur knew her aunt could sense the sugar's movements through her briskly moving spatula. Once it transformed into a simmering liquid, peeled boiled potatoes would be added to the brown paste and thoroughly swirled in the sweet sauce.

Hildur had replied to Tinna's earlier inquiries about what she wanted to eat, saying she'd love to have caramellised potatoes and lamb chops. The potatoes were labourious to prepare, but that didn't stop Tinna.

Aunt and niece had already shared what was going on in their lives and listened to the six thirty news. Hildur had also reported on Jakob's doings and her visit with Björk.

And then Hildur decided to broach a new subject delicately: 'Listen, Tinna.'

The movement in the frying pan stopped. Tinna shifted the pan off the burner and set the wooden spatula on the counter. She turned toward her niece.

'You can never tell Björk, but I did a little asking around about Rósa's past,' Hildur said. She told Tinna about the handsome Danish police officer with Faroese roots. 'I asked him to ask his contacts on my behalf.'

Hildur had been stunned by what she'd learned during Mikkelsen's call. Child protection services had paid frequent visits to Björk and Rósa's home when they were children. The records extended across several years and mentioned home visits, none of which had led to anything. Rósa had been only fourteen when the police caught her drunk driving for the first time. Despite her young age, the incident hadn't led to any interventions.

'The years passed, and more reports accumulated.'

By now, Tinna had seated herself at the table. She lowered both hands to it, as if seeking strength. 'What kind of reports?'

Hildur spoke about a long, sad list: numerous DUIs, possession of small amounts of narcotics, shoplifting and assaults, either as victim or perpetrator. In her early twenties, Rósa had served two years in prison for robbery.

'And then the reports came to a sudden end.'

Tinna's expression turned sorrowful as Hildur explained the Faroese police didn't have any information as to Rósa's present whereabouts. Officially she still resided at the farm Björk had once run. But there was no information as to where she actually lived, or if she was even alive anymore.

'Why didn't you ask these questions before?' Tinna's voice carried no hint of accusation or irritation. She was just wondering.

'I couldn't. I promised Björk I'd never mention Rósa again. An official request for information would have left traces in the system, and I don't personally know anyone who works for the police in the Faroes.'

Tinna stood, took hold of the spatula, shifted the pan back to the burner, and started stirring the sugar sauce so it wouldn't cool and congeal.

'So that's how things went. From bad to worse.' Tinna paused, then continued: 'Still, I don't suppose anyone can live in such a small country without being seen, or leaving no trace? I assume most people at least have a library card? And a speeding ticket or two?'

Hildur suspected there were two alternatives, and now she shared the theories she and Mikkelsen had come up with: 'Either she's hiding for a reason, or she's dead and the body hasn't been found yet.'

Tinna let out a deep sigh. 'Then that's how it is. Most shipwrecks happen just before the vessel reaches harbour.'

Silence fell. Tinna moved the spatula through the melted sugar; Hildur tore two sheets of paper towel from the roll. First, she folded each sheet in half, then she made a triangle of the left side and folded it back to the side. She placed the decorative napkin upright on the table. It looked like a sail. Tinna couldn't see the handsome effect, but Hildur didn't care. Sometimes it was nice to give others small surprises without them even realising.

Hildur offered to help her aunt with the potatoes.

'Nonsense. I'm doing this from start to finish. If you want something to do, you can open the post. It just arrived.'

Hildur left her aunt fussing at the stove and fetched the post from the entryway console. She started opening the stack of letters. The envelopes and ads ended up in the recycling basket. Although a sign on Tinna's mailbox refused junk mail, the advertisements kept pouring in. Hildur took the rest into the kitchen and pulled a stool under her bum.

'Property tax invoice from the county.'

Tinna knocked the spatula against the edge of the frying pan. 'It's paid automatically. Tear it up and throw it out.'

'A reminder to come in for breast cancer screening in mid-January. This says to make an appointment beforehand,' Hildur read. There was a phone number on the letter.

Tinna asked Hildur to make her a morning appointment. That's when she'd be most alert.

At the bottom of the pile was a postcard. It looked like any other tourist postcard sold at service stations and bookshops. The photos of Icelandic landscapes usually shared shelf space with plastic magnets and troll-themed bottle openers made in China.

Hildur took a second look at the card. The image was of Goðafoss waterfall in northern Iceland. The strong currents of the Skjálfandafljót river carried meltwater from Vatnajökull glacier to the northern Atlantic. At Goðafoss, the river dropped ten metres, forming a photogenic waterfall that sent droplets spraying.

'You've got a postcard of a waterfall.'

Tinna turned off the stove and moved the pan to an unused burner so the potatoes could cool a little before serving. She was smiling.

'That must be from Ívar. He sends postcards from his work trips, then reads them to me when he visits.'

How cute, Hildur thought to herself. 'Can I read it this time?'

Tinna nodded, rinsed the spatula, and left it in the sink. She deftly removed a serving spoon from the top drawer and set it next to the frying pan.

Hi there, Eye Candy,

Greetings from the north. I was doing some maintenance work out east and stopped for a swim in Egillstaðir on the way home. It's a beautiful little village with an impressive forest. We'll go together sometime. I'm sure you'd love it. It's a peaceful spot. I'll be taking the northern route back to the fjords.

I stopped for the night in Akureyri and bought you this postcard from the petrol station. We'll see which one makes it to you first, me or the card.
Hopefully me. I can't wait to see you again.
Yours, Ívar

'Hm, a walk in the woods,' Tinna mused as she put dinner on the table. She took the lamb chops from the oven and placed them in a serving dish, then set the caramellised potatoes down next to them. 'Ívar made it first, by the way,' she remarked. 'He came by this morning.'

'I'd love to meet this secret admirer of yours someday.'

Tinna said she'd be happy to introduce Ívar to Hildur and would have invited him to dinner that evening but he'd had other plans.

Again? Hildur thought to herself. Ívar's avoidance of her felt odd. Even when in Ísafjörður, he never visited Tinna while Hildur was there. 'Hm. What's he doing?'

Tinna wasn't completely sure. He was probably just taking it easy and hanging out at home. Apparently, Ívar needed to get his rest between jobs. 'He has a lot of trouble with his lower back. Driving exacerbates the pain.'

Hildur took the pitcher and poured herself and Tinna some of the deep-purple juice made from crowberries she'd picked the previous autumn. Then she plopped some potatoes on her plate. She drizzled a second spoonful of the sugar-butter sauce over her seven small potatoes. When she was cutting into her lamb chop, her hand suddenly stopped. What was it her aunt had just said? Lower back pain?

The delicious meal steamed in front of Hildur, but she couldn't focus on it. An uncertain but incredibly unpleasant thought had slunk into her mind. Hildur grounded both feet solidly on the floor. She did so whenever she had to focus her attention. She'd have to proceed cautiously.

'That's a beautiful gesture, sending those postcards,' she said.

A faint flush rose to Tinna's cheeks. She looked so happy. Hildur's thoughts felt particularly ugly when contrasted with Tinna's joy.

'Have you saved all the postcards he's sent you?'

'They're all in the entryway credenza.'

Hildur sang the meal's praises and tried to converse as naturally as possible. What she had to do next felt bad. But deep down, she knew she had no choice.

Chapter 33

The postcards were burning a hole in Hildur's parka pocket as she bounded up the stairs to the police station. While Tinna had filled the dishwasher, Hildur had quietly opened the credenza drawer and taken the cards with her.

The station's ceiling lights flickered on one by one. With Jakob gone, the whole of the narrow office was hers to use. And it clearly looked like it. The place was chaos. The paper piles on the desk just kept growing. The report on cooperation between the national child protection authorities and law enforcement from the perspective of foster children was far from finished. Hildur had promised to get it done by the end of February, after which the results would be reviewed during a training organised by the Ministry of Social Affairs. She could already tell some of her Christmas vacation would go to writing it.

But now everything else was going to have to wait. Hildur moved the stacks of paper and folders from her desk to Jakob's tidy half of the room. She gaped in disbelief at his pen holder; Jakob had arranged his pencils in order of length.

Hildur set the postcards down on her desk. She remembered where the crimes had taken place, but she double-checked the locations again from the case folders she'd been given by Beta and Tumi. Hildur used pins to mark every crime on the map that took up half the wall. Jakob had insisted it be hung in a prominent place, as it helped him get a sense of the locations of and distances between the curiously named places.

One in the Reykjavík area, one in Hveragerði, one in West Iceland, one in the northern fjords . . . Next to each pin Hildur stuck a Post-it with the date of the crime or as precise an estimate as possible. Once all the information was on the map, she stepped back to take in her handiwork.

The Slovenian who'd worked at the farm in northern Iceland was the first victim. Then the young woman who'd had her head slammed in the door, followed by the guy who'd been found with hot dogs in his pocket in Selfoss. Not long after, the roofie case in Grundarfjörður, West Iceland. That woman had lost her hair, and then a few days later the veterinarian in Hveragerði had lost his life.

If the perp was the same in all instances, he was jumping quickly from place to place. The moves were fast but not impossibly so, even for a lone perp. The distance between scenes was presumably traversed by a personal vehicle; public bus services were scant in the winter and not all villages had an airport.

Hildur's hands felt unpleasantly clammy. She wiped the sweat on her worn-out jeans and pulled on a pair of disposable gloves. She carefully slipped the rubber band off the stack of postcards and set them face up on her desk.

The postcards' motifs were familiar to most Icelanders. Hildur's gloved fingers tingled. It happened anytime she sensed she'd stumbled across something significant. She compared the postcards' landscapes to the locations she'd marked on the map. Some appeared to match geographically, or at least close enough.

The island of Hrisey was near the horse farm where Luka had worked. Hallgrímur's church was Reykjavík's most photographed building, and one of the victims had been assaulted in the capital. Snæfellsnes was a popular postcard theme. Thousands of book lovers visited it every year. In *Journey to the Centre of the Earth*, the book written by Jules Verne, the adventure began from the glacier's peak. Snæfellsnes was less than an hour from Grundarfjörður, where the young woman had been knocked out by roofies.

They only had one eyewitness sighting, and an unclear one at that: one of the exchange students had seen someone from the back who'd favoured one leg and lingered near the victim inside the pub. The remark about the limp had steered her attention to Ívar, who had a bad back and thus presumably a crooked gait. The bad back alone probably wouldn't have been enough to catch Hildur's attention, but Ívar had avoided her for so long that he'd started to pique her interest. Why did he want to stay hidden?

There were dozens of postcards, many more than there were crime scenes. Ívar had sent them from around the country. But what did that prove? Hundreds of thousands of people sent and received postcards every year. Hildur took the cards that matched crime scenes and set the others aside. She flipped over the cards she was holding and set them down on the desk. She went through each card again one by one. In every case, the message was more or less identical: lamenting how much he missed Tinna, greetings from the road, and hopes for a rapid reunion.

Hildur focused on the postmarks. She held a card away from her eyes to bring the faint mark into focus. *Dang it, I need to get glasses*, she silently lamented.

Hildur shivered. The postcards featuring landscapes near the December crime scenes had been postmarked in December. But the order was wrong. Maybe her suspicions were misplaced after all. Maybe her instincts had been off this time.

Dammit, Hildur swore to herself. She'd remembered something. Maybe her instincts hadn't been off after all. Rural postboxes were generally emptied less frequently than urban ones. The mail could wait for days in a red mailbox before it was emptied and a card picked up to be postmarked and delivered.

All the cards had been written in the same hand. She would have to take a closer look at Ívar's background, get permission to review his phone data, and go through all the security camera footage near every scene again. She'd have to get more precise information on Ívar's movements. Hildur was perfectly aware that none of this clearly marked Ívar as the perp, but the postcards and his bad back had made her uneasy.

When Ívar had come into Tinna's life a year before, Tinna's mood had appeared to improve greatly. She'd been happy since then, and Hildur had no desire to rob her aunt of that joy. She'd just have to grit her teeth and do what she had to do.

But as she brought up Beta's number, a detail began to nag at her. It had struck her in passing earlier, but now it returned in sharper focus. She eyed the postcard of Hrisey that lay on the desk.

The Slovenian's workplace was located nearby; Luka lived in North Iceland.

So why was his body found in Hildur's hometown, in the remote Westfjords? Had Ívar transported it here?

Chapter 34

Hildur ordered two strong coffees with room for cream and two chocolate-covered wheat buns. Jakob's partner Guðrún had reserved the window table for them. When Hildur had returned from Reykjavík a couple of days before, Guðrún had been working the flight. She'd seemed worried. She'd wanted to talk with Hildur about Jakob. The two of them had made a coffee date at the local bakery.

The establishment's café was empty in the mornings. Frantic customers selected their buns and sandwiches from the display case and turned right around, some headed to work, some back home. The tables would fill with hungry diners at lunchtime, but that was hours away.

'I don't get how you and Jakob can eat these same pastries day in, day out. Is it some police thing?'

Hildur chuckled and glanced at the woman sitting across from her. The wet snow had dampened Guðrún's hair and streaked her mascara. Hildur didn't find it at all surprising that Jakob had fallen for Guðrún at first sight. She had an inexplicable glamour. Even with mascara running down her cheeks and hair dripping, she looked somehow polished. 'Would you rather have a roll? She just put some ham-and-cheese sandwiches in the case.'

Guðrún waved away the suggestion and dug into her bun with gusto.

'What's new?' Hildur asked, breaking off a piece of her pastry. She couldn't help but notice the concern in Guðrún's eyes.

'The usual Christmas stress,' Guðrún said, looking out at the street.

She was busy at the shop, and the mills were out of yarn. She said business was particularly good this Christmas and lamented she couldn't keep her shelves stocked with yarn to sell. 'And the mill is rattling with orders. Their shelves are empty too.'

Demand for Icelandic Lopi had exploded during the pandemic and hadn't slowed since. Most of the yarn went to buyers in Germany, Finland and Sweden.

'I'm having to sell foreign yarn this Christmas. I ordered a ridiculously big shipment of yarn with the upcoming spring in mind. But apparently, I can't guarantee top-up orders. They're selling all they can shear.'

Hildur and Guðrún chatted about sheep and knitting. Evidently, Jakob's knitting frenzy had intensified to the point that he and Guðrún had dedicated one of the spacious wardrobes in their shared home exclusively to his yarn collection and unfinished sweaters. Hildur noted the way Guðrún's face shone when she talked about Jakob. By all signs, things were still going well for the two of them.

There was a lull in the conversation. Hildur used her forefinger to fish the crumbs that had fallen to the table and pop them in her mouth. Guðrún gripped her coffee mug in both hands and looked out into the darkness.

'I'm worried about him. We haven't spoken in a couple of days now.'

So Hildur wasn't the only one whose calls to Jakob had gone answered. She'd tried to call him the day before to ask how things were going.

Guðrún took a yellow scrunchie from her wrist and heaped her hair into a loose bun on top of her head. 'When I tried this morning, the call didn't even go through. His phone was off. Jakob always replies to my texts, but now he isn't even seeing them. I've also reached out to him through social media, but those messages haven't been going through since yesterday either. Have you heard anything from him?'

Hildur shook her head. She'd last spoken with Jakob the morning of the day he'd flown to Finland. 'Maybe he's skiing up in the fells somewhere where there's no network coverage?' she suggested, despite knowing Jakob would have mentioned such an excursion beforehand.

Hildur proposed a second cup. Guðrún nodded gratefully. When Hildur returned to the table with the refills, Guðrún was browsing through her phone.

'Still nothing. The hearing's tomorrow. I was hoping to find out how he's feeling. Jakob isn't the best at talking about what's going on with him.'

Guðrún said Jakob had been even quieter than usual before his departure for Finland. She'd tried to get him to open up about the feelings sparked by his upcoming hearing, but Jakob had refused to talk.

'It can be a little hard with him sometimes. He can suddenly close up and stop talking,' Guðrún said, popping the last of her bun in her mouth. 'It gets on my nerves.'

'Maybe it's a Finnish thing,' Hildur replied, trying to inject a little humour into the moment.

Guðrún raised her eyebrows dramatically, then relaxed her facial muscles. Her lips pursed prettily. 'He usually falls into a funk without any warning. Our personalities are pretty different.'

The women finished their coffee and chatted a moment longer. They promised to keep each other informed if either heard from Jakob.

'I'm sure he'll be in touch soon,' Hildur said, trying to put on a brave face. She stacked their empty plates and wiped the crumbs from the table.

'I'm not. I've come to learn over the years that he's as unpredictable as the Icelandic weather. You never know in the morning what you're going to get in the evening.'

The two women said their goodbyes outside the bakery. Guðrún headed left toward her yarn shop, while Hildur continued straight on toward the station. She reflected on Jakob and Guðrún. Hildur was more convinced than ever that she had no interest in a permanent life companion. If she had someone at home to whom she was supposed to report how she was feeling every day and what was going on at any given moment, she'd probably be crazier than she already was.

Hildur had just stepped through the station's street-level doors when her phone rang. It was Beta.

'I thought our phone conference didn't start for another hour. Are you calling about Ívar?' Hildur asked. She'd discussed Ívar with Beta the day before. At first Beta had taken a dubious stance on Hildur's postcard theory, but after hearing the whole story about the postmarks and the way the postcards matched the locations of the crimes, her curiosity had been piqued.

Beta sounded out of breath. She was speaking in clipped, simple sentences. 'No. We haven't got that far yet.'

'Is this about Olga?' Tumi had gone to talk with Olga again and ask about her inaccurate account about her shift at the pool.

'Stop interrupting. Let me finish,' Beta said. 'A sixth victim was found in Reykjanes early this morning. A milkman saw a woman lying in the road. She's alive but suffering from serious hypothermia. She's being treated at the hospital as we speak. We won't be able to talk to her until tomorrow at the earliest.'

'What happened to her?' Hildur asked.

'Someone whacked her over the head with a frying pan. A cast-iron pan was found at her side.'

Beta was about to say something, but Hildur cut in: 'Stubby.'

Stubby was the shortest of the Yule Lads. A cute little bearded fellow who roamed from house to house at Christmastime, licking dirty frying pans.

Beta grunted and continued, voice quivering, that that wasn't the worst of it. 'You know her. It's Hlín Jónsdóttir. The reporter.'

Hlín and Hildur had been friends for years. Hlín used to live in Ísafjörður, and a little over a year ago, she'd written a much-lauded exposé of sex crimes involving players from the national men's soccer team. The journalists' association had awarded it Investigative Story of the Year. Soon after, Hlín had moved to Reykjavík for a permanent job. What on earth had she been doing wandering around rural Reykjanes?

'Chasing down a story, presumably, because a smashed camera was found next to her, and she had her camera gear in her bag. A few notes were found in her car. It was parked in the vicinity,' Beta said. 'That's all we know for the time being.'

She continued with a brief update on Olga. Olga claimed to have misremembered the afternoon's and evening's events – she'd gone straight home from her shift at the daycare centre to rest and spent the whole evening there before heading out to the pub.

'I don't believe she's telling the truth,' Hildur said.

'I don't either,' Beta said. 'But she's one of the victims, not a suspect, so we're not going to focus on that anymore.'

The detail continued to vex Hildur. She was less interested in where Olga had been prior to going to the pub than why Olga had lied about it. But Beta was right. Under the circumstances they didn't have the resources to dedicate any more time to looking into any individual victim's account. They had to devote their energies to more critical issues, such as links between the victims.

'By the way, did Olga know any of the other victims?' Hildur asked.

Beta answered in the negative. 'She didn't admit to knowing any of them. They all say the same thing. The hit-and-run in Selfoss said he knew the veterinarian because they worked together. But apparently the others had never even heard of each other.'

Hildur pondered. If animal welfare activities were the link between the victims, the victims didn't want anyone to know. That meant there could be something about those activities that wouldn't stand the light of day.

Beta said she'd been thinking the same thing. 'I'll talk to Hlín as soon as the doctor gives the go-ahead. As a journalist, she might know something crucial to the investigation.'

Hildur said she'd continue looking into links among the victims and phone right away if she found anything. She ended the call and climbed the stairs to the station. She flicked on the lights and sat down at her desk. The next order of business was calling a professor of folklore at the University of Iceland. Maybe there were details related to the Yule Lad song they hadn't even considered yet.

Chapter 35

Rovaniemi, December 2021

There was one parking spot on Valtakatu Street, near the courthouse in Rovaniemi. After killing the engine, Jakob glanced at himself in the rearview mirror. He looked pale. The heat had been blasting on high, but he was cold.

He couldn't remember ever having been so nervous. Not even when he and Lena had argued over custody of Matias at the district court in Oslo. He'd felt like an underdog throughout the entire judicial process in Norway. He understood Norwegian pretty well, but the vocabulary of the legal system had been unfamiliar to him. Despite the presence of an interpreter, he'd felt like an outsider. He'd been a translation behind everyone else the whole time.

Now he had the home turf advantage. It was Lena's turn to have to communicate through an interpreter. He'd be speaking his native language and automatically understand everything.

Walrus-moustached attorney-at-law Joonas Pirinen was standing in the agreed spot outside the Lapland district court. Jakob had only met Joonas face to face twice, the first time when Pirinen picked him up from the airport in Rovaniemi. During their second meeting, Jakob and Pirinen had gone through the upcoming hearing in a conference room at Jakob's hotel. The lawyer had explained how the day would unfold and prepared Jakob for the judge's and opposing attorney's cross-examination. The practice session had instilled Jakob with confidence. He was nervous, but he believed he could do this. He might even beat Lena.

Jakob locked his car and started walking toward Pirinen. The solicitor had agreed to take on the case, despite his one-man law firm being located hours away in central Finland. Jakob was grateful. He'd found a lot of praise for Pirinen in online discussion forums. Those who'd been through custody battles saw him as an upstanding guy with a keen eye who frequently got what he asked for, because he knew how to ask for the right things. Pirinen had explained to Jakob why he shouldn't start asking for custody right now. They'd get the visits in order first, and a little later they could try to change the custody arrangements. It was better to eat the cake one slice at a time instead of trying to gobble down the whole thing at once.

It was cold in Rovaniemi. The temperature had dropped to –30° Celsius during the night. The cold instantly bit at Jakob's earlobes. He'd left his beanie in his hotel room.

'Did you get any sleep?' Pirinen asked, extending a hand. They quickly shook hands and stepped in through the courthouse's glass doors.

'I dozed off for a few hours after midnight,' Jakob replied, unzipping his coat. He realised his hands were still shaking.

Pirinen eyed his client tenderly and gave him a pat on the shoulder. 'This will be over soon. I'll handle everything. All you have to do is sit there quietly and answer calmly when someone asks you a question, just like we practised.'

Jakob was at peace. Pirinen knew what he was doing. Jakob had to trust in that.

The day's hearings were posted on a printout pinned to the bulletin board. The courthouse in Oslo had had big screens, and Jakob could still remember their cold blue glow. He leaned in to scan the list. The printout showed the case's docket number and abbreviations, the names of the parties involved, and the information that this was a custody and parental visitation rights hearing.

Jakob pulled himself up to his full height and started off after Pirinen. On the way to the courtroom, he nearly bumped into a bald police officer standing in the corridor. Jakob cursed his slow reflexes and mumbled a quick apology.

He stepped into the courtroom, where he and Pirinen were shown to a table. The bespectacled court reporter, a woman verging on middle age, was already in her seat and greeted them with a nod. Jakob coughed and took a sip of his water to moisten his dry throat.

Lena walked in with her interpreter and her stout attorney, Lotta Lahtinen. Jakob hadn't found a single newspaper article on Lahtinen or her cases. That had been good news. This time Lena hadn't been able to afford a star lawyer.

Out of his peripheral vision, Jakob could see Lena staring intently at him, but he consciously avoided looking in her direction. He focused on the judge's desk and wished the terrible day would come to an end as fast as possible. Jakob noticed two policemen standing at the right edge of the courtroom.

'What are they doing here?' Jakob whispered to Pirinen.

Pirinen replied that Lena's attorney had arranged for police to secure the proceedings. She'd claimed to be afraid of Jakob.

'She's trying everything,' Pirinen said, giving Jakob an encouraging pat on the shoulder. 'Don't let it get to you.'

Jakob was livid, but he maintained a poker face. It was a public hearing, so even Santa Claus could show up to observe the proceedings.

A little before ten, the judge stepped in, and the room collectively rose to its feet. The corners of the judge's mouth were turned down, and his overgrown monobrow gave him a permanently cross appearance.

Pirinen had told Jakob the judge's harsh demeanour was deceiving. Antti Keinänen had a reputation as a fair man. He preferred to take his time considering and deliberating the various aspects of any case as opposed to arriving at a hasty judgement.

After introductions, the judge nodded in approval and glanced at his papers. 'So the plaintiff is seeking a change to the visitation rights.'

Pirinen had also explained to Jakob what would happen over the course of the day. First the judge would listen to both parties and ask questions. Then in all likelihood he'd ask the child protection authorities to conduct an assessment of conditions in the home and issue a temporary judgement in about a week's time. The temporary judgement would lay out how visits would take place until the final decision was reached during the trial in the spring. The processes were intolerably slow.

'So what are the plaintiff's demands?' the judge growled, turning from his papers to Pirinen.

Pirinen rose to his feet and addressed the judge politely. He explained that his client wanted the visitation rights established by the Norwegian courts to be honoured. That meant a videocall once a week at the agreed time as well as two-hour face-to-face meetings on four consecutive days every two months under the supervision of the child protection authorities.

Pirinen glanced at his client, then across the aisle at Lena, and continued: 'In addition . . . when the visitation rights were established, Matias was in daycare. Now he's in school and has holidays determined by the school year calendar. My client would like for holidays to be taken into account when establishing visitation rights so Matias could visit his father in Iceland for three weeks every summer and five days every other Christmas and Easter vacation.'

The interpreter sitting on Lena's other side translated Pirinen's words into Norwegian. Jakob saw Lena shake her head and exhale between her painted lips in apparent frustration.

Pirinen ignored Lena's theatrics and continued: 'My client is prepared to pick up his child for the flight to Iceland and travel back with him as well as cover all travel expenses.'

Jakob didn't want to argue over money: the less there was to negotiate, the better.

Barrister-at-law Lotta Lahtinen stood to address the judge and curtly stated: 'My client opposes all new demands.'

The judge lowered the documents to his desk, set his pen down next to the documents, and leaned forward slightly in his chair. 'I see. So the parties aren't on the same page, so to speak.'

A moment of absolute silence followed. The court reporter sat stony-faced at her computer, fingers at the keyboard, ready to record every word uttered in the courtroom.

'The plaintiff has presented his demands and justifications for them. I'd like to hear why the other party opposes his demands.'

Lena's attorney stood and addressed the judge. 'Your honour. The plaintiff's inappropriate conduct toward his former spouse and his child are in conflict with the child's welfare. My client was awarded full custody by the District Court of Oslo, and the father has not honoured all scheduled monitored visits. Based on years of experience, my client feels more visits could put her child at risk.'

Jakob had the impulse to pop up and let the lawyer have it, but he knew it would be wisest to hold his tongue until asked to speak.

Lahtinen pulled a stack of papers from her satchel and showed them to the judge. 'My client has compiled here a list of all occasions on which the plaintiff has attempted to sabotage the visitation rights established by the District Court of Oslo. Among other things, he has shown up on my client's doorstep without permission multiple times, frightening the child. The plaintiff has not honoured physicians' statements indicating illness prevented Matias from participating in a scheduled visit. The plaintiff has repeatedly demonstrated he is more interested in his visitation rights than he is in the child's health.'

Jakob could barely contain himself as he listened to Lahtinen's lies. On nearly every occasion he and Matias were supposed to meet in the presence of a social worker, Lena had insisted Matias was sick and unable to come. Jakob had seen with his own eyes occasions on which a supposedly feverish Matias was outside playing happily with Lena or going to the shops with her. Jakob was irritated he hadn't taken photographs. They might have helped his case now.

Once Lahtinen had detailed five examples of Jakob's purported poor conduct in conjunction with the visits, the judge gestured for her to stop.

'I get the point. How does the plaintiff respond to these allegations?'

Jonas's attorney Pirinen denied all allegations. He went through the document Jakob had prepared listing every instance Lena had cancelled a scheduled videocall or planned face-to-face visit in Oslo, claiming Matias had fallen ill.

'Your honour. This list contains five sheets of cancelled visits over the last two years alone. I'm no doctor, but as the father of schoolchildren myself, I can't help but be surprised by how often Matias is sick and somehow always on certain specific days.'

The judge shot Pirinen a sharp warning look. Pirinen apologetically raised his palms in surrender.

The judge addressed his next question to Lena. 'Do you feel Matias is sick a lot? Does he have any serious illnesses that ought to be considered when scheduling the visits?'

The interpreter translated the question, and Lena replied quickly.

'Just ordinary colds. Matias catches things easily, and there was always something going around at daycare and now school. But no, he's not seriously ill,' the interpreter translated.

Lena's solicitor assured the judge Lena had a doctor's statement for every time Matias was sick.

The conversation swung back and forth for a good hour. Both barristers examined their client and the opposing party. Sometimes the judge posed brief clarifying questions and jotted down notes for himself. The court reporter's keyboard tapped steadily in the background. Jakob did his best to keep up, but it was hard. He felt woozy.

Jakob saw day finally begin to break outside the window. The sky had faded from black to pale blue, and the soft bluish light would last at least a few hours.

The judge took off his reading glasses and looked at each of the individuals sitting in the room in turn. He let out a deep sigh and began speaking very slowly, giving careful thought to each word.

'Based on what I've heard today, I understand the child knows his father and, under the circumstances, the two of them have a good relationship. The father would like to see his child more often and feels that the scheduled visits have not taken place as determined in the original agreement.'

Lena's solicitor raised her forefinger and was on the verge of saying something, but the judge gently waved her to silence. He wanted to continue.

'Matias has frequently been ill when scheduled to have a visit with his father. Children get sick sometimes, and there are doctor's statements confirming the illnesses.'

Jakob saw a self-confident smile flash across Lena's suntanned face. The fine lines at her eyes deepened as the corners of her mouth turned upward.

'I must admit, I don't quite grasp how it's not in the child's best interests to spend more time with his father, as the plaintiff has requested. I'd like to hear more from the opposing party on this specific issue,' the judge said, nodding lightly in Lena's direction.

Lena's solicitor whispered something to Lena, and she stood. Her interpreter translated her Norwegian statements into Finnish.

'Your honour. My former spouse and the father of my child works as a police officer in his current country of residence. He does not have a criminal record. He appears to be a calm, rational person.'

Lena held a brief pause. She pushed up the sleeves of her sweater and pulled herself up to her full height. The white sweater set off her tanned arms, and the thin gold-coloured bangles tinkled at her wrists like an angel chime.

The sound set off a stabbing pain at Jakob's temples. The faint throbbing he'd felt at the back of his head that morning had spread into a full-on headache.

Lena paused every few sentences so the interpreter could translate. Her rhythm was carefully considered. Jakob felt worse and worse. His stomach was roiling. He looked over where Lena stood talking and felt his win slipping away, his strong cards being ripped from his hands. Lena was carrying out some scheme she'd cooked up in advance. That he was sure of. He saw it in her deliberate phrasing and her overly formal tone.

'I know this is hard to believe, but Jakob has a dark side. He has difficulty dealing with conflict. He'll withdraw into himself for long periods, then suddenly explode. I'm afraid he'll snap when my child is with him. That's why I oppose increasing the frequency of visits and any overnight visits at all when no social worker is present.'

The judge listened intently to Lena, and Jakob noticed his face growing tighter with every sentence. Apparently, Lena noticed it, too, because she held a brief pause before continuing.

'A few years ago, Jakob threatened me at a playground and tried to hit me. He missed, but Matias saw it happen and was terrified.' Lena looked the judge in the eye. Then she leaned closer to the microphone and added: 'My child has not wanted to return to that playground since.'

Jakob felt the ground beneath his chair give way. The judge's expression changed. The frustration had evaporated and been replaced by a look of concern.

'Did this matter arise during the earlier proceedings?'

Lena shook her head. 'We didn't have proof back then, but now we do. There was an eyewitness.'

Lena's solicitor handed the judge some documents. The furrows in his forehead deepened as he perused them.

Jakob couldn't sit still. Lena had gone too far. The anger inside him boiled over, and he leaped to his feet so forcefully that his wooden chair fell to the floor. Pirinen tried to calm him, but it was no use.

The judge banged his gavel against his desk and told Jakob to sit down.

'It's lies, it's all lies! I'm not a violent person. That woman has planned this all down to the last move.' As if to underscore his words, Jakob leaned both fists on the table and knuckle-punched it a couple of times. He was getting tongue-tied: 'You can't believe her lies! She, she . . .'

The judge banged his gavel again. The police officers observing from the side of the room had risen to their feet, but the judge gestured for them to sit back down.

'There is no shouting in my courtroom. Please sit down,' he barked. He punctuated his words with a third gavel bang, Pirinen stood, righted the toppled chair, and took Jakob by the shoulders. He half-forced his client into his chair and asked him to calm down. Pirinen turned toward the judge with an apologetic smile and begged pardon for his client's conduct. Then he glanced at the policemen and nodded; things were under control.

Jakob clenched his fists and dug his nails into his palms until they hurt. The pain calmed him. He felt his breathing grow shallower and his forehead break out in a cold sweat.

Before he buried his face in his hands, he caught a glimpse of Lena. Her brows were raised mournfully. The smile had vanished from her face, and her lips were pinched in a straight line. Her eyes were glistening. At a quick glance, one might have thought she was incredibly sad. But Jakob knew better. He knew it was all just an act.

Chapter 36

The stern-faced judge lifted his glasses to his forehead and looked both parties sharply in the eye.

'Twenty-minute recess for coffee,' he announced. Then he lowered his glasses and returned his attention to the papers before him. The court reporter rose, nodded at the judge, and strode from the room.

Jakob stared at the courtroom floor, clammy fingers loosely interlinked. Pirinen had just stroked his arm gently a couple of times and urged him to breathe, as if to remind Jakob what they'd discussed while preparing for the hearing. Allowing himself to get provoked was a nonstarter, and Jakob knew it. He knew if he raised his voice in court and started causing a commotion, he'd lost.

Drops of sweat rolled down his palms. The slippery wooden chair felt uncomfortable against his pelvis. The courtroom was brightly lit, and one of the ceiling lamps flickered distractingly. Since the disruption, Jakob had withdrawn into his shell and forced himself into a position he wouldn't emerge from until it was time to exit the room.

The anger was coursing through his veins with too much force. He saw himself stand, walk slowly over to Lena, grab her by the shoulders and shake her back and forth like a rag doll. But he'd dedicated a lot of time to making sure he wouldn't lose his temper. He meditated, he knitted, he tried to focus on remaining calm.

Jakob knew the moment he showed anger he'd be weak and Lena would be strong. At their most brutal, custody and visiting right hearings were a zero-result game. There was only one winner in the courtroom: the one whose demands the judge agreed to.

Jakob had thought he'd succeeded in patching all the weak spots inside himself and preventing Lena's attacks, but he'd been wrong. Once again, Lena had broken him.

Jakob could vividly remember back through the years to the custody trial at the courthouse in Oslo. Lena had pulled out an ancient clip from her mobile phone that showed Jakob losing his temper. It felt awful, letting her whack him in the face with the same hockey stick again today.

Jakob emerged from his reverie. Chairs were clattering around him. Out of the corner of his eye, he saw Lena and her solicitor had risen to their feet. The two women exchanged a few words as they made their way toward the door, heads angled toward each other. They were speaking so softly that Jakob couldn't hear what they were saying. The police were staring at him from their seats next to the wall.

Jakob couldn't help it. His eyes wandered over to Lena. Her back was as straight as it had been the day they'd met. The impression was of a soldier determined to carry out a duty that had been assigned to her. There was no doubt as to the nature of Lena's duty. She wanted to crush Jakob, and he still didn't completely understand why.

Once the initial infatuation had passed, Jakob had started watching what he said. Lena had never been in the wrong. Ultimately, everything took place on Lena's terms. Regina was the card Lena threw down anytime they fought. It felt unfair, because Lena had been bossing Jakob around long before he was driven to seek comfort again from Regina. Jakob had been in the wrong, he knew that. But how long was he supposed to keep paying for it? Lena always managed to scheme herself into a position where she appeared the innocent victim while her opponents seemed violent or otherwise unreliable. At the beginning of the relationship, Lena had told him stories about difficult ex-boyfriends who'd treated her poorly and caused her distress. She'd sobbed about her bad luck with men. Jakob had believed it hook, line and sinker and done everything in his power to protect and please Lena. What an idiot.

'I'm going to have a cigarette and get some fresh air. I want you to take a little break, too, get up and stretch your legs,' Pirinen said, giving Jakob an encouraging pat on the back. 'We'll be continuing soon.'

Jakob sighed. He had a bottle of sparkling water in the backpack under his chair. He unstoppered the bottle but did it too fast, and the contents spurted into his lap. *Goddammit!* He took a couple of tissues from the box on the table and tried to dry the table so his solicitor's papers wouldn't get wet. Jakob tossed the sopping tissues into the wastepaper basket next to the wall and set out to look for the men's room. He might be able to dry his shirt with the hand-dryer.

There was a unisex bathroom off the corridor. Jakob pulled open the door and strode to the far end of the sizable sink area. The hand-dryer was the latest model, the kind that started up when you put your hands in. He looked around to make sure no one was watching and stripped off his shirt. He slipped the wet garment into the hand-dryer and started drying it.

A moment later, he sensed movement behind him. One of the stall doors opened, and suddenly Lena was there standing next to him.

If she was flustered by Jakob's presence, she was good at hiding it.

'No need to get undressed for me,' she said with a smile as she started thoroughly washing her hands. She took her time spreading the soap, staring at Jakob through the mirror the whole time. Once the soap had made its way between every finger and into every cuticle, Lena turned on the water and rinsed her hands with exaggerated slowness. She shook off the biggest drops, then stepped over next to Jakob and thrust her hands into the same dryer as Jakob's shirt.

The fan was loud, but Lena leaned so close to Jakob's ear that it was impossible for him not to hear. 'You're a little unstable. Just drop it. You already lost.'

Jakob had succeeded in crumpling his courtroom rage into a little ball, but now he could feel it unravelling again. His fists clenched and his pulse rose as he shouted:

'You're sick. You need help.'

Lena looked at him, then burst out laughing and pointed at the mirror. She spoke with exaggerated softness but loudly enough for Jakob to hear. 'Oh, I'm the one who's sick? Look in that mirror there, and you'll see who's sick. And I'm going to make sure Matias never has to suffer because of you ever again.'

That was it. Jakob couldn't take any more. He flung his shirt to the floor, clenched his right fist, and swung. Lena dodged the blow and winked at him.

'So close,' she whispered, then turned and exited the bathroom, hips swaying.

Jakob felt himself exploding inside, and then his rage erupted: 'I wish you were dead!'

Jakob's shout echoed against the tile floor and walls, and then everything grew very still. He could hear his frantic heartbeats, sense his shallow breathing. He turned on the tap and twisted it to cold. He splashed his face with icy water and tried to let his breath steady and calm himself.

And then one of the stall doors behind him opened, and the bespectacled court reporter emerged. She stared at Jakob, eyes wide, and quickly slipped out without washing her hands.

Chapter 37

Ísafjörður, December 2021

Hildur drummed the desktop with her palms. Her computer had automatically launched an operational update and was taking forever to start up. A moment before, Beta had called again with the latest on Hlín. Hlín's body temperature had only been 32° Celsius when she was found. That was incredibly low. *That's a hypothermia-level reading*, Hildur reflected. When body temperature dropped below 25° Celsius, the heart and respiratory system stopped functioning. The medics who'd arrived at the scene had said the full-length down parka Hlín had been wearing had presumably saved her life. She'd been in bad shape but was already doing a little better.

Hildur was burning with curiosity; she wanted to know what her journalist friend had been up to in Reykjanes. The only things out on the windy peninsula aside from a few villages were a luxury spa and the airport. No one wandered out there by accident.

Hildur's screen turned blue, capturing her attention. *Update Complete*, hallelujah! Hildur quickly logged in and opened her email. During the call, Beta had mentioned the camera found in Hlín's possession. The lens had been shattered and the frame smashed to bits, apparently with the frying pan. The perp had removed the memory card.

The Reykjavík police had been by Hlín's workplace and been granted her employer's permission to search Hlín's workstation.

The editor-in-chief had explained photographs were stored not only on the memory card but also instantly uploaded to the newspaper's cloud servers. Beta had received the photo folder a moment ago and had sent it to Hildur.

There's not much here as far as I can tell, but maybe you'll see something I didn't. B.

Hildur opened the zip file, arranged the contents on her desktop in chronological order, and opened them. There were about fifty pictures, and according to the metadata they'd all been taken on the same day. If the camera had GPS, it hadn't been on, because Hildur didn't find any location data. On the other hand, it wasn't hard to guess the location based on the images and where Hlín had been found. Hildur opened a map app and zoomed in on the Reykjanes peninsula. According to Beta, Hlín had been found at the north-west part of the peninsula, between the villages of Garður and Sandgerði. It was summer in the map's street view and it was winter in real life, but the surface forms were the same. Deserted and empty.

Hildur began reviewing the images. The first photographs were of a large pasture with horses in it. There were at least fifty horses, some clearly small in size. *Who breeds horses this time of year?* she wondered as she zoomed in for a closer look. A row of round hay bales wrapped in plastic stood outside the paddock. Hay from the bales had blown around, as the plastic was torn at several places. It seemed so thin there was no way the hay had been cut the previous summer.

The next images were taken at closer proximity. The metadata indicated they'd been shot using a 70–200-millimetre lens.

Hildur made out a figure in dark clothing among the horses. The figure was wearing full-body coveralls, the kind people wore ice fishing. In the countryside, the coveralls were a practical choice for outdoor work. They protected one from the wind and kept one warm.

Hildur rolled her sore shoulders in both directions a couple of times, then refocused her gaze on the screen. The next photos showed someone leading a horse across the pasture. Hildur zoomed in on the figure walking in front of the horse, but couldn't see the face, because the head was turned away from the camera. Judging by the size of the typical Icelandic horse, the person was about 175–180 centimetres tall. They were of average build, and Hildur couldn't say anything about the hair, because the hood had been pulled up over the head. Three video files captured the person in coveralls leading the horse. Hildur couldn't tell for sure, but she was pretty sure the person had a limp.

The last ten pictures had been taken of some sort of wooden stall standing in the pasture. The horse's lead had been tightly tied to the wall of the stall. Hildur was disgusted to see pain in the horse's dark eyes. They looked nervously up and to the side, and she could see their whites. Aside from its round belly, the horse was thin and in poor shape. Horses that spent all year outside were often long-haired and shaggy, but this one looked different. Its coat was lifeless and dull. Big clumps of hair were missing at the neck and flanks. Hildur couldn't exactly see what the person in coveralls was doing, but she saw a hose or tube hanging next to the animal and some sort of canister at the person's feet. There was a grey pickup truck on the far side of the pasture, but as it was parked perpendicularly to the shot, the licence plate wasn't visible.

Hildur left the images on the screen and opened a text file Beta had scanned. It was a sheet from the notebook found in the back seat of Hlín's car. There wasn't much there, mostly individual words. Hlín surely had more notes related to the story, but they hadn't turned up yet.

Mares' blood – buyers?
L says much more blood is sold than official statistics indicate.
Amounts?
Who sells it?
Locations
Transport . . .

After taking another look at all the photos Beta had sent, Hildur quietly considered what she'd seen. Hlín had stumbled on an interesting story. Someone was selling the blood of gestating mares, and there was something shady about the enterprise, because Hlín was investigating. How long had Hlín had her eyes on the mares' blood business? Who had tipped her off?

Hildur had heard about mares' blood farms. Everyone who lived in the countryside knew about them. There were over eighty thousand horses in Iceland, and not all of them were used for riding or raised to be sold abroad. A large number went feral and just ate hay in the pastures. Blood and urine were collected from gestating mares for the hormones they contained. The raw materials were sent to biotechnology and pharmaceutical companies.

Hildur brought up the website of an Icelandic biotechnology company. The site featured gorgeous shots of Icelandic horses and stunning mountain vistas. The company said it sold ethically sourced mares' blood. A blog post on the site emphasised the trade in blood was closely monitored. The blood was drawn by veterinarians. Only a certain amount was taken every year and never in winter, so owners who allowed collection wouldn't breed their horses mid-winter to stimulate hormone production. But judging by the photographs and notes Hlín had taken, she was onto something much bigger. At the very least, animal welfare laws had been broken. And if there was a black-market trade in mares' blood, financial crimes were also involved. Money lured folks to go to where the threshold was low, where mares were tied up and whips flicked.

Hildur stared at the photo of the pained horse and thought. Hlín had been assaulted by the Yule Lad killer. All the other victims had a connection to animal welfare. Someone was trying to eliminate risks that put the illegal blood trade in jeopardy.

Hildur meant to spend the rest of the day on the Yule Lads. The professor of folklore had told Hildur about the origins of the Yule Lad legend and recommended a couple of books. She pulled on her coat and set out for the library. The solid white edifice, one of the most beautiful buildings in town, was Ísafjörður's former hospital. When the hospital moved to new, more modern premises a few hundred metres away, the building had been renovated into a library and museum. Hildur climbed the stairs and stepped in through the double doors.

The friendly librarian was delighted by Hildur's request for assistance. 'Everyone asks Google these days. It's nice to still be needed,' she chuckled, before asking Hildur to wait a moment. She said she'd be right back.

Hildur remembered the Yule Lad songs and stories from her childhood. But she didn't know anything else about the legends. Maybe the perp was trying to say something by referencing the Yule Lads? She meant to find out.

The librarian returned with three books. 'Here's Jóhannes Bjarni's little book *Christmas is Coming*, written in the 1930s. I imagine you're familiar with it.'

Hildur recognised the slim volume; it had a drawing of a candle on the cover. The book contained Christmas songs and rhymes. The best-known rhyme was the long Yule Lad poem, which had solidified the names of the thirteen Yule Lads in the popular imagination.

The librarian smiled as she handed two other books across the desk. 'These two might be of more interest. The first one is about the history of Christmas in Iceland, and the one on the bottom is about mountain giants.'

Hildur retreated to the reading nook with the books. First she read Jóhannes's Christmas poems. They reminded her of childhood. Even though the mood at home had occasionally been oddly formal, she only had good memories of the holiday. Mum had cooked and baked; Dad had shovelled snow and built a snowman in the yard. On Christmas Eve, Hildur had played late into the night with her little sisters. Those had been wonderful moments. When had Hildur last been around children at Christmas? She couldn't remember. Hopefully, Jakob would get to spend more time with his son after the hearing. Hopefully Matias would be able to spend Christmas in Iceland sometime. As a matter of fact, Jakob had told Hildur that if he ever had Matias for Christmas, he and Guðrún would invite Hildur to spend the holiday with them too. That had been a nice gesture on Jakob's part.

The stories of Icelandic Yule celebrations from pagan times to the present day made for a fascinating read. Christmas had once been a celebration of light, and preparations had included cleaning and washing. The last week of the year was often called the crazy week, because those who owed money worked hard to pay off their debts by year's end. The Yule Lads became part of Christmas celebrations in the 1600s, the Christmas shoes on the windowsills not until the 1950s.

Hildur read the passage on the Yule Lads closely. The Yule Lads were first mentioned in the folk poetry of the 1600s. They were young, scary-looking lads, cannibals and half-trolls. They lived in dark caves far off in the mountains and couldn't tolerate daylight. That was why they usually only ventured out in the winter, when there was no sun. The Yule Lads wore black so they could move around without being noticed. They sowed fear by harassing people and eating them.

Hildur lowered the book to her lap and looked out the window. The crowns of the trees that rose behind the nursing home were swaying. The wind had picked up.

Hildur thought about the crimes she was investigating. It was clear that whoever was committing the assaults and homicides was familiar with the details of the Yule Lad poems. The Yule Lads threatened people who behaved poorly. The perpetrator of the recent crimes threatened animal welfare activists. The objective was to create an atmosphere of fear; the murderer-slash-assailant was putting on a show of strength. The Yule Lads lived in a secret place in the mountains, from where they descended among humans. The murderer had a lair somewhere, too, but where?

Chapter 38

Car park, December 2021

Whoever was in the passenger seat got to control the radio volume. She didn't understand what the DJs were saying, but they were playing good music. She'd always loved the Swedish band Ace of Base. 'All that She Wants' was her favourite song. A woman who lived alone woke up early and dreamed of sunbathing. She'd meet men, but by the next morning she'd gather up her belongings and vanish.

'I like you, but your taste in music is awful,' the driver said, pulling into a small car park. She stuck out her tongue at him and cranked the volume in protest.

Amused, the driver shook his head and killed the engine but left the battery on so the radio would stay on.

'How sweet of you,' the woman said, stroking the driver's stubbled cheek.

She'd wanted to join him for the supermarket run, since their plan to decorate their new home for Christmas had been pushed back a day due to their child's floorball practice.

'This won't take long, will it?' she asked. It was almost seven.

The driver shook his head and said he just had to pick up an envelope. 'We'll have time to make it to the store afterward.'

'What are we doing in this dark car park?' she asked.

The driver said he was missing an important document.

'It was nice of him to offer to bring it here so I can finish the presentation tonight. We'll be able to review it at the management team meeting first thing in the morning,' he added, impatiently tapping the steering wheel.

A moment later, there was movement at the passenger window. A figure in dark clothing knocked on the glass. The driver unlocked the window, and it started sliding down.

When it was open, a blazing light suddenly filled the vehicle. The person outside was wearing a powerful headlamp. The driver said something and raised his hands to his eyes to keep from being blinded. The light was so close to the woman's face that she had to close her eyes. She didn't fully understand what was happening, but clearly something was wrong. The figure had appeared out of nowhere. The last thought to cross her mind was about her little boy.

Who's going to pick him up from floorball practice?

The shot echoed in her ear. She was too terrified to open her eyes, but she could feel the driver collapse into a heap at her side. One second passed, and another shot rang out.

Ace of Base was still playing on the radio.

Chapter 39

Ísafjörður, December 2021

Hildur felt incredibly tired. The walk back from the library to the station wasn't a long one. She popped into the grocery store and bought a baguette for lunch. She skipped over the salami version; images of the suffering horses had been etched too vividly onto her consciousness. What the hell was going on at these out-of-the-way horse farms?

The empty office looked unwelcoming. If only Jakob were here. Work was more fun when she had company. Hildur realised she missed her friend with a surprising intensity, even though he'd only been gone a few days. She reached for her phone and selected Jakob from the list of outgoing calls. The result was the same as last time. A clinical automated voice told her the number was unavailable.

Damn it, Hildur cursed under her breath. She flung the phone to her desk, and it bounced over to Jakob's side. Hildur rose and walked to the window. She opened the ventilation flap and let the cold air stream in. The breeze stirred the papers on her desk.

Hildur focused her thoughts on the perp. The violent acts had taken place within a short time span and in different locations. The perp or perps must have planned their assaults carefully – especially since a different form of violence had been selected for each victim. The assailant had been familiar with the victims' habits.

Hildur jotted down some notes on a piece of paper. Olga was a regular at the local pub. Felix's cross-fit sessions always took place at the same time on the same day. According to the forensic pathologist's report, Luka had died of a drug overdose. His body had shown no signs of assault, let alone stab or gunshot wounds, so it was possible he was dead before the perp arrived at the scene and the perp had merely hung him in the fish pen. The woman whose head had been bashed against the door had been victimised at home – all the perp had had to do was follow her or wait for her in the entryway. The man found in Selfoss with a package of hot dogs had been near his residence.

Hundreds of Icelanders worked in various roles related to animal welfare. The perp's malice seemed to have targeted too haphazardly. There were countless volunteer animal welfare activists. Why had these specific individuals been selected? It couldn't be chance, since each incident involved details that would have required forethought.

Whoever was guilty must have known where the victims would be and when they'd be there. The perp would have had to procure roofies, tie the body to the wall of the fish pen, and know the route the young veterinarian took when walking home from cross-fit. The perp had gone through a lot of trouble, and that didn't add up to the victims being random.

Hildur opened a new browser tab and logged into Facebook. Her profile was almost empty. She didn't even use her real name. Her account was for investigative purposes only.

When two Icelanders who didn't know each other met, the first thing they did was figure out how they actually did know each other. Since everyone was related, if distantly so, a connection always existed. *Who are your people?* was an ordinary conversation starter. One of the most useful functions of Facebook was the information it provided about friends. Unless the Facebook user had restricted access to their friends list, one click revealed it. Surprisingly few users went through the trouble of changing their profile's privacy settings. *Which is lucky*, Hildur thought to herself as she consulted her notes and entered Olga Ragnarsdóttir's information into the search field. The social media accounts of Olga and her fellow victims had already been reviewed, but there was one thing Hildur wanted to check.

Olga's dreadlocks were clearly identifiable, which made it easy to pick the right Olga Ragnarsdóttir from the list. Hildur opened Olga's profile in a new tab, then entered Luka's name in the search field. She did the same for each victim. After a few clicks, she felt the energy start flowing through her veins. A few of the victims were Facebook friends. Not all, but a few. That was a good sign.

So some of the victims were connected via Facebook, despite their blanket denials they knew each other. Did people approve people they'd never met as Facebook friends? Hildur wasn't sure she was up on social media etiquette. *That's a subject I should spend some time looking into someday*, she reflected.

Of the victims, Luka had been the most active on Facebook. He'd posted images of everything from meals to horses. Hildur started reviewing his status backward from the present moment, tracing his updates for months. She came across a breakfast photo that wasn't the typical bowl of granola, but a beautifully arranged plate of fruit. According to the caption, the photo had been taken at the Hilton hotel in Reykjavík in September. No one else was visible in the picture, but Olga, Felix and a few other names Hildur didn't recognise had been tagged.

A chill ran up Hildur's spine. She walked over to close the window and returned to her computer, sitting in a shoulderstraining hunch. She needed to look up the unfamiliar names tagged in the photo. Her fingers tapped at the keyboard faster and faster.

Two of those tagged in the fruit-plate photo had hidden their information from strangers, but she learned more by googling them.

She slammed her palm down on the desk so hard a pencil bounced to the floor. That was it! All those tagged in the photo were somehow involved with animals or animal welfare. Every single one. Without taking her eyes off the screen, Hildur retrieved the pencil. The names tagged in the photo popped up in an article on an animal rights demonstration. An older woman who'd been tagged appeared on the contact page for a refuge for homeless cats in Reykjavík.

Hildur googled the name of the hotel and the September date.

'Holy moly,' she muttered when she saw the search results. She reached for her phone. She was ashamed that she hadn't had the sense to conduct the search before. Her thoughts had been so firmly fixated on the Yule Lads. A moment later, she heard rustling and Beta's voice from her phone's speaker.

'I know who's still in danger,' she said.

Hildur explained she'd found a closer link between the victims on social media. All the people mentioned in the case file had attended the September dinner at the Hilton hotel in Reykjavík. The event had been sponsored by a big gaming company that regularly donated money to local animal welfare organisations.

'It has something to do with their social responsibility programme,' Hildur said. 'The company sponsors a dinner every year and invites animal welfare activists to hobnob with top management. Every single one of our victims was at that dinner. That can't be a coincidence.'

'Including Hlín?' Beta asked.

Hildur tapped at her computer for a moment. 'No,' she said in disappointment. 'She's not listed. But . . . but I don't think she uses her real identity on social media.'

Even if they didn't follow the latest developments in journalism or regularly read the news, everyone in Iceland knew who Hlín Jónsdóttir was. Hlín, the first-class journalist, had written so many stories for various media outlets over the past year.

'Hopefully we'll be able to talk to Hlín soon,' Beta said. She asked Hildur to send her the list of names so she could arrange for patrols to keep an eye on all those who'd attended the dinner. 'I'll say we're running some secret undercover operation they aren't allowed to discuss for security reasons,' she added.

The police didn't want news on their work ending up in the media unless doing so was of benefit in an investigation. This information wouldn't even be shared internally except on a strict need-to-know basis. Panic and chaos were the last thing anyone needed.

Hildur could already see the headlines in the country's only tabloid.

SERIAL KILLER LURKS IN THE SHADOWS, POLICE POWERLESS.

NIGHTMARE BEFORE CHRISTMAS FOR ANIMAL LOVERS.

All the police somehow involved in the case were aware of the assaults, but Hildur, Beta and Tumi were the only three aware of the links between the victims. Even Jónas didn't know about them. *Nor is there any reason for him to yet*, Hildur said to herself. Luckily her boss was still out of the country.

A few small stories about the assaults had appeared in the press, but nothing major. Hildur took time every day to browse through the topics in the main discussion forums. There hadn't been much chatter about the incidents there either. Homicides were widely publicised, but assaults were so ordinary they didn't pique the public interest or generate clicks for the media outlets' websites. A lot had been written about the deaths, but the newspapers hadn't connected the two cases.

In the first place, the death of the foreigner seemed less deserving of column space than that of the Icelander. No stories about Luka had appeared after the first couple of days. There would have been more, no doubt, if someone on the force had leaked the detail about the meat hooks. Now the death had just been publicised as a body found in the sea, and that was for the best. Almost nothing was told about the background of the foreign victim, nor were his Icelandic colleagues or friends interviewed. But by now everyone knew where the athlete lived, as well as his educational background and global cross-fit reputation and the names and jobs of his best friends.

'Have you interrogated Ívar yet?' Hildur asked.

Among the postcards Ívar had addressed to Tinna, Hildur had found one sent from Reykjavík in mid-September, a few days before the dinner attended by the animal welfare activists. Although the date on the postmark wasn't an exact match for the date of the dinner, Hildur reported this discovery to Beta. It was evidence Ívar had been in Reykjavík around the same time.

Hildur listed her questions: 'I wonder if he was at the dinner. And if so, why?'

'Ívar texted that he'd come to Reykjavík tomorrow,' Beta said. 'Tumi and I will question him. Then we'll know more.'

This was good news, but it did nothing to dispel Hildur's unease.

Beta said she had to run to her next appointment; the weekly meeting of narcotics investigators was about to begin. She and Hildur promised to keep each updated on developments.

Hildur started putting together a detailed list for Beta including the names of those who'd attended the dinner and their contact information. She'd almost finished when her phone rang.

Maybe that's Beta or Tumi with good news, Hildur thought to herself as she groped for her phone and answered without looking at it: 'Hello.'

For a moment all she could hear was a loud crackling. Hildur moved the phone further from her ear and gave her name.

'It's Jakob.' Jakob's voice sounded strange. He seemed panicked. 'Could you come here?'

'Come where?'

Hildur could feel Jakob's panic spreading to her. The line was bad. She pressed the phone firmly to her ear and plugged her other ear with her free forefinger so she could hear.

'Guðrún and I have been trying to get in touch with you for days. What's going on?'

'The hearing's over, and it went . . . it was a disaster. And now . . .' Jakob's voice cracked.

Hildur jumped up in agitation and crossed over to the window again. It was so dark she could barely make out the snow-brightened mountains. The moon was somewhere far off beyond a thick mass of clouds.

'Hildur, I didn't do it. Seriously, I didn't.'

Christmas lights were shining outside the window. Some residents had put up flashing plastic reindeer and glowing Santa

Clauses. Tacky. Hildur shook the pointless thoughts from her mind. She knew people could focus on strange details when they were panicking.

'I'm suspected of the murder of Lena and her husband. Could you come here? I need help, and you're the only one I trust.'

Chapter 40

Helsinki–Kolari, December 2021

Hildur woke to the lurch. She fumbled around the niche next to her head, where she'd plugged in her phone for the night. She cracked her eyes and glanced at the screen: ten past six in the morning, so just 4 a.m. in Iceland. The time difference weighed on her temples, but from experience she knew she wouldn't be falling back asleep. She stretched under the blue blanket and readied herself to get up. A few ankle-rolls in either direction. Curl the toes, then spread them, back and forth a few times. She sat up on her bunk and stretched the soles of her feet and the small muscles in them, against the floor. Now she was ready for the day.

The train compartment was compact. There wasn't room for much on the floor other than her feet and the winter boots she'd left by the door. Her backpack was on the upper bunk; her purse hung from a hook next to her parka. Since the pandemic, individual berths were no longer sold in sleeping cars. Solo travellers had a whole compartment to themselves. The orange, brown and blue décor made for a pleasant trip back to the 1970s.

Hildur cracked the curtain. It was so early that it was still completely dark outside. By her estimation, it wouldn't be light for another few hours, sometime around eleven. Evidently, the train had stopped in some larger city. A blue illuminated sign on the platform indicated they'd pulled into Oulu. *Oulu.* Hildur tried saying the short name. It felt impossible to pronounce. *Oyly.*

She still had a few hours before they reached the end of the line, Kolari.

When she'd set out the previous day, Hildur had called Jónas to let him know she'd be working remotely for a couple of days. She hadn't given any specifics as to where she was planning on working and Jónas hadn't asked. He'd been rushing off to some meeting and in a hurry to get off the phone. Hildur had a lot of unused overtime, but she hadn't dared suggest taking it now. Not now that Jakob was gone too. As recompense, she'd promised to man the station for the week after Christmas, including New Year's Day, so Jónas could have it off. Hildur knew she'd come to regret her promise, but she'd deal with that when the time came. A few days' absence from investigating the spree of violence against animal welfare activists was the source of most of her stress. On the other hand, Beta and Tumi would have no trouble keeping things moving without her. The important thing had been getting to Finland as fast as possible.

Hildur brushed her teeth in the sleeping compartment's tiny sink, then slipped out into the cramped toilet in the corridor. She shook her head at the woman looking at her in the bathroom mirror. What on earth was she doing? She'd lied to her boss, left an investigation unfinished, and jumped on a train to solve a double murder in a place she'd never been and knew no one. The situation was strange, undeniably so, but no other alternative had been conceivable. Jakob had sounded so frantic and helpless on the phone.

Hildur wasn't close to many people. All she really had aside from Tinna and Björk was Jakob. He was not just her first friend, he was her only friend. Hildur's lack of companionship didn't really bother her. Although she was often alone, she rarely felt lonely. But she'd never had the sort of connection she had with Jakob with anyone else.

When she got back to her sleeping compartment, Hildur dressed quickly. Wool underwear, padded trousers, a heavy-weight fleece top, and thick wool socks. Finland was a completely foreign place to her. Before her hurried departure, she'd googled winter conditions in northern Finland and concluded the thicker the layers, the better. In Lapland the temperature could drop to as low as forty below. That had sounded brutal.

Hildur didn't have a whole lot of information about the case yet. Jakob's call had been brief. His former wife Lena and her current husband Filip had been found shot in their car in the car park of some out-of-the-way café. Two days before, Jakob had raged in the district courthouse in Rovaniemi and threatened Lena. In addition, someone had seen Jakob around the time of the murder, stumbling around the car park where the bodies were later found. Hildur had to admit things didn't look very promising.

Jakob was being questioned today. His attorney had told him to plan on spending the entire day at the station. The earliest Hildur could see him would be late that night. But she had no intention of twiddling her thumbs until then, so she'd made some preparations.

She'd looked up the phone number for the Kolari police station online. A calm male voice had answered and listened without interrupting as Hildur explained her reason for calling. Then the voice had sighed deeply and apologetically and said he was very familiar with the sad case. The policeman had introduced himself as Simo Saari. He and Jakob had been classmates at the police academy in Tampere. Simo had been surprised by the call and the news that Jakob had requested help from Hildur, but had nevertheless said he'd be happy to meet with her.

So. It felt unbelievable to Hildur. No one knew the entire truth about anyone, not even those closest to them. Hildur thought she knew Jakob well. The two of them had instantly trusted each other and become fast friends. A natural connection had formed between them. Besides, Hildur had always thought of herself as someone who could read people well. She was easily able to establish connections during interrogations and felt like she was pretty good at predicting people's thoughts and behaviour accordingly.

On the other hand, everybody had sides no one else ever saw.

Chapter 41

Reykjavík, December 2021

Beta seated herself at Tumi's side. They almost always positioned themselves this way during questioning, with the person being interrogated sitting back to the wall and the police closer to the door.

Across the table, sixty-six-year-old mechanical engineer Ívar Finnsson was chewing his left thumbnail. His grey dress shirt was worn at the sleeves, and the top button was missing. When Beta reached out to Ívar, he'd been on assignment in East Iceland. A part had required replacing in the HVAC system of the country's newest aluminium smelting plant. He'd come in for questioning as soon as he'd finished the job. Beta had recited the formalities from memory and started up the video camera. Tumi's strength was in the field, with people. The burly man with sideburns inspired trust in both adults and adolescents. As usual, Tumi would handle the majority of the talking today. Beta would take notes and observe.

Once the names of those present were recorded, Ívar was told he was being questioned in connection with a string of violent acts that had occurred around the country over the past few weeks. As Tumi recounted the general nature of the crimes, Ívar's face paled.

Tumi asked Ívar to describe his work.

Ívar leaned forward. He seemed cooperative, but the answer didn't come right away. He was on the verge of saying something, then stopped himself. His nervous shifting made a nasty squeak as the metal chair leg scraped the floor. 'Uhhhhh . . . I mmmmain . . . tttttain . . .'

He took a sip from his plastic cup and lowered both palms to the table.

Beta looked up from her laptop and eyed Ívar. 'Is everything OK?'

Ívar closed his eyes and nodded. '. . . the equipment at aluminium smelting plants.'

Beta noticed Tumi's probing gaze as he assessed the older man, a thoughtful look on his face. 'You've had your own machine maintenance company for a couple of decades now. Which smelting plants do you service?'

Ívar was still having a hard time getting the words out. A long, breathy vowel emerged from his throat but didn't lead to anything. Ívar used his finger to draw a flattish circle on the tabletop: a rough map of Iceland.

Tumi gave him an assist: 'All the smelting plants in the country?'

Ívar nodded. Beta knew Tumi was breaking the rules. He shouldn't be coaching the subject with answers. Maybe Tumi knew what he was doing.

'Listen, Ívar, would you like a pen and paper?' Tumi asked.

Ívar nodded in apparent gratitude.

Tumi announced they'd take a short break and gestured for Beta to join him. Beta grabbed her laptop and followed the much taller Tumi out into the corridor.

'He has a serious speech impediment. A stutter. He's clearly eager to talk but can't produce the words.'

'How could you tell?'

Tumi said he'd noticed Ívar's eyes blinking frenetically when he spoke. 'Blinking is one of the most common – what are they called . . . avoidance behaviours. The speaker uses them to try and stop the stuttering.'

Tumi explained his family had had some experience with the disability. His cousin's firstborn had stuttered as a child. Speech therapy had helped.

'But not everyone is able to access therapy, and then the individual suffering from the impediment doesn't necessarily ever get over it. Other problems follow. The person withdraws from contact with others and avoids social situations.'

Beta went to find a pen and some paper so they could continue. After they switched from communicating by speech to writing, the interrogation proceeded more quickly. Tumi asked the questions, Ívar wrote down his responses, and Beta entered his answers into the interrogation record.

A map of Iceland was spread out on the table in front of Ívar. The map noted the location and time of every crime assumed to be part of the spree. When referring to the man assaulted in the town park in Hveragerði and the man found at the fish farm at Ísafjörður, Tumi and Beta spoke of homicides.

'Quite a few of the sites and times correspond with your travels. How do you explain that?'

Ívar looked thoughtful. He studied the locations and dates and considered. Eventually, he wrote down: *I was in Reyðarfjörður a week before those dates in the north and the west. I was there at least three nights. There was a lot of maintenance work to do there.*

One of the country's biggest and most controversial aluminium smelting plants was at Reyðarfjörður, in the Eastfjords.

Beta knew the place well. She'd been a passionate environmental activist in the early 2000s, and she and her boyfriend at the time had demonstrated around the clock at the side of the road leading to the hydroelectric plant construction site. They'd shouted slogans at those entering the site, protesting the aluminium giant and the Icelandic energy company.

Heavy industry always set up shop where energy and other raw materials were the cheapest and the threshold the lowest. Most of Iceland's domestic energy production went to aluminium. The state's energy company had built a huge hydropower plant to serve the aluminium company's needs. Vatnajökull was Europe's largest glacier, and the river that carried its meltwater to the sea had been dammed. The new hydropower and smelting plants had been promised to bring jobs to the emptying countryside, but that hadn't happened in practice. The construction work had been carried out by foreign subcontractors. Beta was still irked by the memories, although well over ten years had passed since the conflict.

In Beta's view, the environmental damage had greatly outweighed any financial benefits from the plant. A reservoir had had to be constructed for the hydropower plant, and the decomposing organic material at its bottom generated greenhouse gases. A lot of plants and animals were displaced or destroyed by the project. The sediment and silt from the glacial rivers exacerbated the project's environmental impacts. The list went on. Whenever the aluminium industry was mentioned, Beta's heart flared up. She thought back to the days when the fire of her passions had simmered inside her. The years she'd spent with environmental activists had been filled with idealistic fervour. She couldn't help but feel some disappointment about the fact those days were behind her now. Mundane concerns had steamrolled her activism. The area around Kàrahnjúkar had been one of Europe's last untouched wilderness areas, and it should have stayed that way.

These days, Beta's kids spent a lot of time with their father, which meant she had more time to herself. Should she volunteer for some environmental organisation again? Maybe she could find some kindred souls there. There wasn't much environmental activism on the force. At least no one spoke of it as an interest in the break room.

Beta felt something knock against her knee. Tumi had nudged her leg under the table and was looking at her quizzically. Darn it, she'd got lost in her memories.

Tumi swept his hand across the northern and western coasts of Iceland as he repeated his question: 'So were you in this area at the times the crimes took place?'

Ívar nodded and wrote: *Yes. You can check from my mileage log.* He gestured at the red notebook he'd brought that now lay on the table. Then he continued writing. *But I didn't go to those places marked on the map.*

Tumi took a stack of postcards from the folder in front of him and spread them out in front of Ívar. The corners of Ívar's mouth tightened, and he leaned forward.

'You sent these postcards to Tinna from many of the places marked on the map. So far the postmark date matches the times six of the crimes were committed. That's quite a lot.'

Tumi intentionally let this statement stand without a follow-up question. Beta could tell her colleague was trying to get Ívar to explain matters in his own words.

Ívar studied the map intently and blew out between his teeth. Then he took the pen and began to write.

It's a coincidence. I travel a lot for work. I have this thing of sending Tinna a postcard from every place I stop. It eases the loneliness, because I know when I visit I'll be able to read them to her out loud. Mailboxes aren't emptied every day in the countryside, and it takes time for the mail to be delivered. I wasn't at the scenes on the dates you're listing.

The light tapping reverberated from the walls of the spartan interrogation room. Beta felt a fleeting envy of Hildur's aunt. Tinna had met someone who sent her confessions of love from every corner of the country.

Ívar continued writing: *Except once. The only place that's an exact match between my travel dates and the dates you have listed is Hveragerði. I was there that day, but I spent the whole day at the therapy centre there, in speech and occupational therapy. From morning to evening. It will be easy to verify.*

Tumi and Beta exchanged glances. Beta read in Tumi's gaze that they'd formed a mutual understanding: it was highly unlikely the guilty party was sitting across from them. They would, of course, check up on Ívar's claims about the therapy centre.

Beta had the impression Ívar didn't have it in him to assault anyone. Of course, she couldn't put trust too much in the feeling, but other factors argued against his being the perp too. For instance, according to the mileage log, Ívar hadn't been in or near Reykjavík at the time of the front-door assault.

'I used to work in Ísafjörður with Tinna's niece Hildur. I know Tinna,' Beta said, continuing in the same breath: 'Why have you avoided meeting Hildur?'

Ívar's face relaxed and radiated a warmth there had been no sign of a moment ago. He lowered the pen to the paper and leaned back in his chair.

'I-I-I-I d-d-d-don't get nervous t-t-t-talking when I'm alone with Tinna. It's hard for me if there are other people around.'

The unique nature of Tinna and Ívar's relationship put a smile on Beta's face.

But the smile froze when she realised she and Tumi were back to square one in the investigation.

Chapter 42

Kolari, December 2021

The train lurched for the last time. After the fourteen-plus-hour ride, it had reached its destination. Hildur studied the surroundings from the window of her sleeping compartment. A small station, bluish twilight and towering piles of snow.

It's like pulling into the middle of a cream cake, Hildur thought to herself, grabbing her backpack from the top bunk and throwing it over her shoulder.

As soon as the train's doors opened, the dead station yard instantly came to life. People poured out from every exit with luggage and ski bags. The destinations of the few buses parked nearby were hard to make out. *Äkä-käkä-po* . . . Äkäslompolo.

Hildur shook her head. When Jakob had come to Iceland, he'd complained about how unintelligible the road signs were. Things didn't seem any more straightforward here.

She glanced at the clock on the station wall. It said a little after eleven. Simo Saari had suggested he and Hildur have lunch together and said he generally ate around noon.

Hildur tightened the waist strap of her backpack and set out walking toward the police station. The thought of a forty-five-minute stroll sounded more tempting than a taxi ride. After the night spent on the train, she craved fresh air. Besides, she'd get a better sense of the place on foot.

Everywhere she looked she was enveloped in forest. Hildur had the impression that although her feet were moving, it was as if she hadn't advanced through the terrain at all. The road was straight, and the surrounding forest didn't seem to change: just more tall, skinny conifers, branches laden with snow. She caught the occasional glimpse of a lone house between the trees, lights shining in the windows. Then more snowy forest and straight road.

Hildur began to feel the freeze in her fingers. She retracted them from the fingers of her gloves and clenched her fists to get some warmth back into them. She'd be needing thicker gloves.

The snow squeaking underfoot was the only sound Hildur heard. It was eerie. Ísafjörður was small and didn't have a lot of people, but it was never quiet in the fjord. There was always howling, clattering or banging somewhere as the wind snatched up whatever it came across. But here a simple, all-conquering quiet reigned.

The silence was suddenly broken by an approaching vehicle, which slowed as it pulled up alongside her. A curious-looking older man stared shamelessly at Hildur. He didn't open the window, let alone stop. He just stared. Maybe Hildur and her backpack were an unusual sight on the local roads this time of year. No one in Iceland walked anywhere for pleasure either, unless absolutely necessary. Distances of no more than a couple of hundred metres were travelled by car.

The Kolari police station was located in a two-storey brick building. According to her map app, the same complex also housed the library and the town hall.

Hildur knocked the snow from her shoes against the rubber mat and stepped inside. The outdoor silence continued within. Hildur took a few steps forward and listened. She could make out the faint sounds of a radio and fingers tapping on a keyboard. She saw a door that was ajar and knocked on it.

A tall, bald man slightly younger than Hildur was hunched over his computer, talking to himself. Hildur made out the words 'Black & Decker'. She owned a Black & Decker drill too.

'Excuse me . . . or I mean, hello,' Hildur said in English, then introduced herself.

The man sat up straight and shot Hildur a quizzical glance. Then he seemed to recognise her. He rose from his desk and walked over, hand extended.

'Simo Saari. We spoke on the phone. Nice to meet you. Welcome to the north, Hildur.' Sami's handshake was firm. He had a funny way of pronouncing the *u* in her name as a back vowel; Jakob had done the same thing at first. Hildur shook Sami's hand and corrected his pronunciation: *Hildyr*.

'Wow, your hand is cold.'

Hildur explained that she'd walked from the station and was planning on buying herself a warmer pair of gloves at first opportunity.

'I would have picked you up if I'd known you didn't have a car.'

The rental agency didn't have any cars available until four that afternoon. Hildur would pick up her vehicle after four and drive to her hotel. She'd managed to book an inexpensive room near the ski resort, a half-hour drive from Kolari.

'Oh, a little walk isn't going to hurt me.'

'I have no doubt about that,' Simo said with a chuckle, then glanced at his watch. It was coming up to noon, almost time to eat. Simo recommended a lunch place that served decent food.

'We'll take it to go and eat here so we can talk freely. All the county employees eat lunch there. You can't say anything without half of Lapland finding out.'

Hildur smiled. She recognised the phenomenon from back home. Folks liked to talk, and usually the person being talked about knew less about his or her affairs than everyone else.

'What was that Black & Decker thing?' Hildur asked as they strode across the courtyard toward the restaurant.

Simo pulled his beanie tighter over his bald head and said he'd been working on an APB.

'A couple of weeks ago we caught a crew that had been breaking into cabins. During searches of their homes we found property acquired through criminal means and we have no idea who it belongs to. We'll list the items on our website and social media and hope for the best.'

Lunch was fried potatoes and gravy. The side was grated root vegetable salad. Hildur helped herself to some of the orange and yellow gratings to accompany her meat sauce. When they got to the till, Simo offered to pay for their takeaways. Hildur politely accepted and thanked him, although she would have much preferred to pay for herself.

On the way back to the police station, Hildur asked what it was like working in law enforcement in the area. Judging by the view from the train, the place was sparsely populated. Distances had to be long. Simo said a total of twenty or so officers worked all of western Lapland. Most, including the region's lead investigator and three detectives, were seventy kilometres away in Kittilä, which was home to the regional airport and the bustling ski resort of Levi.

Hildur glanced at the map on the wall of Simo's office. The police stations of Muonio, Kilpisjärvi and Enontekiö had been marked with straight pins. *Just like back home*, Hildur thought to herself.

'We're responsible for an area 350 kilometres wide. On weekdays, there's usually only one patrol out and about. So you're spending a lot of time on the road . . . On weekends and during the busiest seasons, when the hordes of tourists arrive, the number of patrols doubles. That means two!' Simo grunted at his joke and led Hildur to the kitchen.

Hildur got the impression Simo enjoyed his work. He spoke warmly about his colleagues. 'I spend most of my time on the job in the car, driving from place to place. You get to know your partners pretty well. It's hundreds of kilometres between villages.'

'But I'm just here temporarily; the future is still to be decided,' he said with a broad smile.

He found forks in the cupboard and moved the newspaper aside to clear space at the table, chatting about the station's affairs the whole time. He was clearly enjoying Hildur's interest in the practices of her foreign colleagues.

Hildur nodded and said all kinds of assignments came up at the little police station in the Westfjords too. 'In October I was shovelling sheep out of a snowdrift.'

A sudden blizzard had caught the local sheep farmers off guard. With the help of the animals' owners, local volunteer rescue teams and firefighters, the police had excavated the sheep, frozen by fear and partially the cold, so they could be moved to safety.

Simo listened to Hildur's stories with reciprocal interest, then stabbed his fork through his last slice of fried potato. They finished their meal, and as they moved on to coffee, Hildur wanted to nudge the conversation toward the matter at hand. Simo seemed like a talkative individual who spoke openly – surprisingly openly at times, in Hildur's view. Maybe he was just trying to make a good impression on his foreign guest.

'You said you knew Jakob from your time at the police academy?'

'Yes, we met in Tampere. But we haven't really kept in touch since,' Simo said. 'Of course, a name that's a little unusual will stick with you.'

He swirled his teaspoon calmly around his coffee mug, then got down to it. 'They say there's proof. Both physical evidence and eyewitnesses.'

Hildur made a mental note of every detail Simo shared. The crime scene had been cordoned off to secure the integrity of the investigation and the evidence. A gun had been found under the victims' vehicle. Wool fibres from outside the car were presently being analysed. Numerous footprints had been taken in the car park, and one pair – according to the technician, one of the freshest – had been made by Jakob's shoes.

'We'll have more detailed information on the fibres later. It will also be a few days before we have the DNA analysis.' Simo took a loud slurp from his mug.

The whole thing struck Hildur as absurd. 'There's no way Jakob could have done it,' she said, mostly to herself.

Simo shrugged. He leaned toward Hildur and lowered his voice. 'We have an eyewitness who saw Jakob at the scene of the murder. It took place in the car park of a trailhead café called *Velhon kota* on the road to Kolari.'

Simo described the little *kota*, an indigenous Lapp tipi of sorts, and explained most of the café's customers arrived by ski or on foot, taking a winter trail from nearby Äkäslompolo – the town where Hildur had booked herself a hotel room. The café was accessible by car, too, and a woman who'd been walking her dog had seen a lone man with a headlamp pacing restlessly across the car park. He'd still been there when she'd driven off.

'The description is a match for Jakob,' Simo said. 'Tall man, red beanie, sweater over his coat, hair in a bun.' Simo underscored his words by balling up his fist at his nape.

A moment later, emergency services had received a call reporting a car in the car park with two bloody corpses in it.

'A local who was out for a walk had noticed a mining company vehicle in the car park. He'd walked over for a closer look, because the company sparks strong feelings around here. That's who discovered the bodies.'

'What about the gun found under the car?'

'Glock 17. The model Finnish police used to use as a service weapon.'

That meant . . . Hildur forced herself to think it didn't mean anything at all. Jakob didn't have a Finnish service weapon. He'd never worked as a police officer in Finland. Besides, the police weren't the only ones to use the make of gun.

Hildur decided to test the ice. 'Is there any way I could get contact information for the person who saw Jakob? If I wanted to ask some questions?'

Simo grinned and pulled a yellow Post-it from his pocket. He appeared to have been waiting for the request.

'With such serious crimes, investigations are handled by the violent crimes unit in Rovaniemi. Some members of the investigative team are in Kittilä, the next town over. We don't have any detectives at the station here in Kolari. My friend at the Kittilä police returned me a favour and gave me the information,' he said, passing her the Post-it. 'But you didn't get this from me.'

Hildur nodded and opened the carefully folded note neatly inscribed with the name *Sari Meri* and a phone number.

Hildur thanked Simo and slipped the note in her pocket. She was off to a start, but she wasn't sure which direction she was headed. She couldn't stop thinking about the gun. Logically speaking, the fact that the murder weapon was a gun used by the police wasn't a significant detail. Reason said it didn't necessarily mean anything, but her intuition balked. Something about the whole thing struck Hildur as off. Or maybe the time difference was just catching up to her.

Chapter 43

The temperature kept dropping. When Hildur picked up the rental car that afternoon, the digital thermometer outside the rental agency had read –25° Celsius. She couldn't remember ever having experienced anything similar. The frigid cold hindered movement. It stiffened limbs and stung the lungs.

Hildur turned on the car radio. The station was playing Christmas songs. She couldn't understand the words of the one on now, but the tune was familiar: she drummed the steering wheel and hummed along to 'Silent Night'.

Hildur had called the eyewitness, Sari Meri, as soon as she stepped out of the Kolari police station. Sari had immediately invited Hildur to afternoon tea.

When Hildur reached Sari's house, she didn't find a doorbell, so she knocked on the window. A moment later, she heard barking in the entryway. A gentle-looking dog was lazily wagging its tail, eyes on the door. Hildur recognised the breed: Finnish Lapphund. The pointy-eared shepherd bore a slight resemblance to pointy-eared Icelandic sheepdogs.

A blonde woman about Hildur's age stepped into the entryway and opened the front door. She was wearing a green sweater and dainty silver flowers in her ears. She seemed friendly enough but avoided eye contact. Her slow movements would have made an unhurried impression if it weren't for her skittish gaze.

When she'd phoned, Hildur hadn't been able to tell Sari she was a police officer, so she'd said she was the suspect's girlfriend and beside herself with worry.

'Thanks for letting me come and see you,' Hildur said, hanging her coat up in the entryway. The dog prancing at her feet got a little scratch.

Sari responded with a discreet, almost imperceptible nod, and turned on her heel. Hildur followed her down a narrow hallway into the kitchen. Banal platitudes graced the room's longest wall. A painting of a sunrise with a caption suggesting love was a matter of will hung above the table.

Supermarket philosophy, three for the price of two, Hildur thought to herself, but she said: 'Do you live alone?'

Sari didn't reply, just smiled. A set of flashing Christmas lights kept time on the kitchen wall. She eventually broke the silence by asking Hildur to sit down. She'd set out fresh-baked rolls and sandwich fillings. 'I don't have visitors often, let alone from as far away as Iceland.'

Hildur took a roll and split it with her thumb. The butter melted against the warm bread.

Sari filled the creamer with whole milk and sat back down at the table. She let out a deep sigh and warily asked: 'So what was it you wanted to talk about?'

Hildur washed down the half-chewed roll in her mouth with some coffee. She tried to frame her words as casually as possible: 'So you saw Jakob, a tall, handsome man, there at the café car park when . . . on the night of that terrible shooting.'

Hildur noticed Sari tense slightly. Her grip on her coffee mug tightened, and her gaze turned inward. The discovery of two bodies in the deserted car park had been major news in the area, and the crime had even crossed the national news threshold. Thinking back to the incident probably wouldn't be easy for anyone.

Hildur had spent the drive coming up with ways of pumping information out of Sari. She'd decided to use the most ordinary tool. People in love did silly things. That was the card she would play.

'See, he and I – well, we've been together for a while now,' Hildur said, speaking more slowly. 'We're deeply in love.' She tried to force a dreamy smile to her face.

She added she knew Jakob well and said what a hard time she was having imagining him committing such a horrific crime. She wanted to understand what had happened.

Hildur saw her chatter wasn't having the hoped-for effect on Sari. Just the opposite: the other woman seemed to be withdrawing even further into herself. The hands wrapped around the coffee mug were trembling now.

'So you came all the way from Iceland for this man?' Sari asked.

Hildur took another roll and smeared a generous dab of butter between the halves. She looked at Sari as sincerely as she could, but the other woman continued to avoid her gaze. 'Yes, I did. We were supposed to get married soon, and . . . and now this.' Hildur explained that she'd proposed to Jakob six months before because he'd never got around to it. 'I mean, I guess a woman can propose just as well as a man, right?' she said, biting into her roll.

Sari indicated concurrence with a nod. 'So the two of you have been together for some time?' She took her eyes off her mug and leaned back in her chair. Then she reached for a slice of sandwich ham and set it on the floor. 'You are so cute! Yes, you are!' she said, addressing her dog as if it were a close friend.

Hildur sat there with her coffee, waiting to exchange a few more words with Sari. But it didn't happen. Sari didn't exactly ask her to leave, but all she seemed to be aware of was the dog gobbling down the ham.

Hildur tried one more time: 'Could you tell me about that evening?'

No reaction. Hildur repeated her question.

'Yes, I know you like going for long walks in the snow,' Sari said, scratching her dog between the ears.

Hildur stood, swept the crumbs to her plate, and set the dishes she'd used on the counter. She leaned against it and folded her arms across her chest. She had a few questions she wanted answers to. 'How did it happen that night? Please tell me, so I can leave.'

It was a few hundred metres from the café to the car park. When Sari had arrived at the car park, she'd seen Jakob. That much Simo the friendly policeman had told Hildur earlier in the day.

'Do you remember what the man was wearing?'

Hildur knew the answer because Simo had told her back at the station. She wanted to hear it from Sari's lips.

Sari spoke without looking at Hildur. 'A red beanie. A white sweater with dots on it. And the same kind of trousers you're wearing. It was dark. He had a headlamp on.'

Hildur recognised the red beanie; it was Jakob's. The sweater sounded familiar too. She glanced at the flexible softshell trousers she was wearing. They were windproof and serviceable in the cold if you wore wool long johns underneath. What on earth had Jakob been doing in the car park? The ski track and pedestrian trail to the village ran closer to the café; Hildur had checked from a map of the area.

'And you didn't see anyone else?'

'He was the only one there. He was pacing back and forth and seemed to be looking for something. It was six forty-five. I don't know what else to tell you.'

Hildur decided to ask something unrelated to the matter at hand. 'Have you always lived around here?'

Sari glanced out the window into the dark front yard. 'I've moved around. I came back a few years ago.'

How did she recognise Jakob? Hildur wondered. 'Did you know the man you saw?'

'Superficially. I lived here when I was younger. I know who Jakob is because he spent a lot of time here as a child and a young man, and everyone here knows everyone else's business.'

'You said this was at 6.45 p.m. How do you know that was the exact time? Did you look at the man first and then check the time or how did that go?'

Sari gave the dog a couple of pats on the head. A faint, clipped laugh escaped her lips. 'I had to pick up a package at the shop before seven. I drove off right after I saw him. I barely made it to the shop; I got there just before seven.'

And with that, Sari started clearing the rest of the dishes from the table. Hildur took this as a sign it was time for her to leave. She thanked Sari profusely for the delicious rolls and made her way to the front door.

Chapter 44

Rural Iceland, December 2021

The sign directed drivers to turn right for short-term parking. The route was familiar. The same roundabouts, the familiar turns, and the last parking spot in the third row at 6 a.m. on pickup day.

I bet I could drive this with my eyes closed if I had to.

Kill the engine, open the door to make sure the vehicle is between the lines.

Of course it was. And, of course, checking was necessary. To minimise risks, it was important to always do things exactly the same way.

Preparation was the best insurance against risks. But one thing had become apparent over the course of a lifetime: nothing was ever guaranteed, and even the most careful preparations couldn't completely eradicate the possibility of surprise.

I was positive I drove to that pasture in Reykjanes without being followed. But clearly I was wrong. Luckily, I saw that movement up by the gate.

Exposure had been incredibly close.

Any disruptions would be most unwelcome; the monthly quotas were hard enough to meet as it was. Nor was there any way to escape the buyers; that was a given. When the previous collector had tried to quit, rumour was they'd been pushed under a milk truck. It wasn't worth finding out whether the story was true.

The nosy visitor had been worth checking out, however.

The poor thing.

The woman's fate hadn't been particularly enviable. But there was no point shedding any tears over that. What good would that do? Not a horsehair's worth.

There were all sorts of people in this world. There were those who thought about themselves, or themselves and their loved ones, and there were those who thought about complete strangers. Everyone focuses on the past, the present, or the future.

I choose to focus on myself and the present. The last thing I want to do is devote any energy to other people or the past.

The woman on the road was in the past.

This moment here in this car park is all that matters.

There was a knock on the window.

As always, the man in the leather coat was on time. He turned over the envelope, and the boot popped open.

'Next time isn't until January second,' the man said.

'I know. Six o'clock, same place.'

Roll up the window. Look in the rearview mirror.

The man removed the two big white coolers filled with bagged blood. What would happen to the blood next was a mystery, and that was as it should be.

It has nothing to do with me or this present moment.

Chapter 45

Äkäslompolo, December 2021

After her visit with Sari Meri, Hildur made her way to the hotel. She left her backpack next to the door and looked around her room. It was small but cozy. She tossed her coat over the back of the chair, kicked off her shoes, and fell stomach-first to the bed.

The reindeer-patterned wool throw on top of the bedspread made her cheek itch. She lay there for a moment, just breathing. Three seconds in, six seconds out. Evidently the rhythm soothed the vagus nerve and reduced stress. But as she inhaled, the hairs from the blanket were sucked into her nostrils. Hildur tore the wool throw out from under her and tried to continue her breathing exercise. It was pointless. Lying still just made her even more restless. She had too many things going through her mind to calm down.

She missed the waves. Being submerged in saltwater granted her a brief respite from onerous thoughts.

Surfing wasn't on the cards right now, but Hildur had another plan. She hauled herself up from the bed, reached into her backpack, and pulled out ski pants, a wool sweater and a lightweight coat. When booking her room, she'd noticed a mention of lit ski tracks on the hotel website. They started directly behind the building and led to the Ylläs network of trails. Hildur had dropped by the ski rental on the way from Sari's to her lodgings.

Fifteen minutes later, Hildur was skied and booted. The desk agent had suggested the three-kilometre track higher up the fell where temperatures were a few degrees warmer than down in the village.

The first two kilometres ran across a flat. The lights rising on either side of the track gave the winter night a yellow tint. There wasn't really anyone else around.

Hildur kicked off. The important thing to remember was to push with the ankle. Her late friend Freysi had constantly reminded her that focusing on the ankle movement helped lengthen one's glide.

Hildur had recently noticed that thinking about Freysi no longer immediately caused an agonising, wound-opening longing. When Freysi was murdered, Hildur had been the one to investigate the causes of his death. The assignment had been one of the most difficult of her law enforcement career, but she'd survived.

As the flat curved up into a long rise, Hildur switched back to a basic skate. She could feel her pulse accelerating. The tightness in her lungs was the same sensation she felt when paddling out to surf. You had to exert effort before you could climb on top of the waves. Skiing followed a similar rhythm: you rose uphill slowly, working your muscles hard. When you hit the descent, you got to enjoy the ecstasy of speed.

The short-branched, narrow-crowned Siberian spruces were so heavily crusted with snow that they looked like candles. Hildur sank into the soft white. The landscape embraced and sustained her. She moved across the surface of the snow almost silently. A wispy cloud slid past the moon, dimming the terrain.

The moon shines, the dead ride.

Hildur felt an unpleasant shiver in her lower spine. Why had that phrase popped into her head? It was from an old Icelandic ghost story, where a recently deceased groom sets out on a steed to fetch his bride to join him in the afterlife. Sitting behind him in the saddle, she sees a hole in the back of her beloved's head. By the time she realises she's riding with death, it's too late . . . There was something macabre about the poem. The dark night, the shining moon, the simultaneous presence of love and death.

Hildur shook off the image and started skiing faster.

Her thoughts turned to Matias. She'd discussed Jakob's son with Simo, the police officer from Kolari. Simo had said the boy had been placed with a local family after Lena was found dead. Matias couldn't be handed over to Jakob because Jakob wasn't his legal guardian. Hildur's heart constricted. She couldn't imagine what Jakob must be going through just now, what Matias had been forced to go through. The boy's lot was surely the hardest. He'd lost his mother and her partner and hadn't even been allowed to see his father.

The lights shook, and more skiers appeared on the track. Yellow ski coats, handknitted wool beanies. Young parents who'd snuck out to ski after the kids went to bed. Amid profound grief, others went on with their lives. Life may have collapsed for one, but for others it continued exactly as it had been.

The three-kilometre track was like a roller coaster. Ascents were followed by descents, speed picked up, speed slowed. Push, kick, push, kick. Every kick propelled her closer to solitude, and just now that felt good.

As Hildur repeated the same pushing motion over and over, a new notion began to take shape in her mind. It wasn't even a fully formed thought yet, just a solitary observation.

Luckily, she'd be seeing Jakob soon and could ask him about it.

Chapter 46

After returning from her skiing jaunt, Hildur conducted a few quick searches online, wrote herself a few notes, pulled on her winter coat, and hurried to a nearby roadside restaurant recommended by the hotel staff.

She scanned the menu. She was starving. Sauteed reindeer sounded interesting.

'How big is the portion?' she asked the young server. He assured her it was big enough to satisfy the heartiest appetite. Hildur ordered it. She was so hungry she didn't want to waste time on starter salads or coin-sized greetings from the chef.

The server took the menu and was just turning toward the kitchen when Hildur stopped him. 'My friend will be here soon. Let's get one for him too.'

'Excellent choice,' the server said with a wink. He disappeared through the revolving kitchen doors. Hildur shook her head and laughed when she realised he was half her age.

A wave of exhaustion was about to crash over her. She sensed it as a growing weight at her shoulders and a budding ache at her temples. Two days of travel, the two-hour time difference, and talking with strangers had taken its toll. It was warm inside the restaurant. The radiator next to the table was giving off heat, and a fire was blazing in the hearth at the back of the dining room.

Hildur heard the bells strung up on the door tinkle. Someone had entered the establishment. She looked over and saw a familiar figure. 'Jakob!'

All the patrons in the dining room turned to see what the commotion was. Jakob's face brightened. He looked delighted. He slipped the red beanie from his head and strode over to the table. He and Hildur embraced.

'I'm so grateful you came,' Jakob said. His voice was quivering as Hildur patted his back.

'Tell me everything.' She urged Jakob to sit and informed him she'd ordered sauteed reindeer for two. Jakob gave her choice the thumbs up.

Then Hildur saw Jakob's joy evaporate. He began massaging his hairline. Hildur could tell he was having a hard time deciding where to begin.

'Tell me about the day of the murder. What exactly happened in that car park? And why were you there?'

Jakob swept his palm across his face and looked straight at Hildur. It was only now she realised how tired he must be. His face was puffy and grey, and he had bags under his eyes.

'Do you know what happened in the courtroom? Have you talked to my solicitor yet?'

Hildur nodded. She'd called the attorney who'd introduced himself as Pirinen from Keflavík airport while waiting for her Helsinki flight.

'I went to the café around six for dinner: pancakes and cloudberry jam and a hard cocoa. I was supposed to meet someone in the car park afterward.'

This caught Hildur's attention.

'I got a text message from an unknown number. The sender didn't give their name, but they said they knew Lena and had evidence I could use against her in court.'

Jakob said the person who sent the message had told him to come to the café car park at a quarter to seven and meet them at the trail leading to Kuertunturi fell. The trailhead was at the edge of the car park. The message sender said they'd be arriving by foot.

'So did you meet?' Hildur asked, glancing toward the kitchen. She was hungry.

Jakob shook his head. 'I hung around for a little while and eventually started up the trail. I thought whoever it was might still be on their way down. The forecast said there was a good chance of seeing the northern lights, and it was a clear, beautiful night. But I didn't see anyone.'

Jakob reached for the water jug, filled his glass, and took a long swig.

'I hadn't even made it a kilometre up the trail when I heard the shots,' he said. 'I hurried back, saw the vehicle, and saw the two bodies through the open passenger window.' He immediately recognised Lena but didn't recognise the man. Jakob had never met Filip face to face. He'd only caught a glimpse of him during a videocall.

'I felt for a pulse and couldn't find one. I saw a handgun partially under the car.'

'There's one thing I don't get,' Hildur said. 'Why did you flee the scene without calling for help?'

Jakob drummed the tabletop. The waxed tablecloth creaked under his hands. 'I realised how it would look to outside eyes. I panicked.'

He left the car park and called a good friend to explain what had happened. 'Luckily, he talked me out of fleeing. He convinced me it would be a mistake. Running wasn't going to solve anything.

And he was right. So I called emergency services, but someone else already had. A police patrol had been sent from Kittilä and forensic investigators had been sent from Rovaniemi.'

The server brought their food to the table and wished them a pleasant meal. The mashed potatoes were steaming, and the crumbled reindeer meat looked delicious with the red lingonberry jam. Hildur took her fork and used her knife to heap it with mashed potatoes topped by some meat. It tasted heavenly. But it was hot; she cooled her mouth by taking a big swig of water.

She then watched with interest as Jakob used his knife to move his mashed potatoes to the edges of the plate and piled his meat in the middle of the starchy ring. 'The mashed potatoes cool faster this way,' he explained.

Hildur asked Jakob about his friend.

'We've known each other as long as I can remember, since we were kids.'

Hildur followed Jakob's example and arranged her potatoes in a ring too. She thought about everything she'd heard. Jakob's version of the evening corroborated Sari's account. He'd been on the scene.

'Did you see a woman in the car park?'

Jakob briskly shook his head. 'I was asked the same thing during the interrogation today. I don't have any memory of seeing a woman. But the car park was pitch dark, and I had a headlamp on, so it's perfectly possible someone saw me without me seeing them.'

'Have you tried calling the number the mysterious text was sent from?'

Hildur immediately regretted her question; of course Jakob had tried.

'I tried sending a text message, too, but it wasn't delivered. Prepaid number.'

Prepaid numbers were a problem in Iceland too. Hildur was frustrated that buyers of prepaid subscriptions didn't have to register anywhere.

'And you told the police about the message?'

Jakob nodded. He'd spent all afternoon being interrogated. He'd told them about the text message and explained that's why he'd been at the scene. But the detective in charge of the interrogation hadn't seemed to give the text message much weight.

'She said I could have arranged with a friend beforehand to have them send it.'

The fibres found near the car and on the victims' shoulders had been matches for Jakob's sweater. This was no surprise; Jakob had felt both victims for a pulse. No fingerprints had been found on the weapon. It would still take some time for DNA results to come in. Jakob's interrogations would continue the following day, and he didn't have permission to leave the area. His passport had been confiscated. Presumably the only reason Jakob hadn't been arrested was because his background lent him some credibility: he was studying to become a police officer and didn't have a criminal record.

'Or because the cells in Kittilä are full,' he added sarcastically.

'Or because they're only doing preliminary questioning. I'm sure they have other suspects too.'

Jakob grunted something and twirled the tip of his fork in his mashed potatoes. He thought for a moment, then looked up at Hildur.

'I know I look guilty. The worst thing is I don't have any idea who could be behind this. I've barely slept for the last two nights. I've been racking my brains trying to think of suspects.'

Jakob said Lena didn't know anyone in the area. The two of them had spent almost no time here when they were together. 'She hadn't even officially started at her new job at the hotel chain.'

Jakob fell silent and filled his mouth with sauteed reindeer. They ate in silence.

Hildur was the first to empty her plate. She gestured for the server to bring her a dessert menu; she still had room for something sweet. Jakob grunted in agreement when Hildur suggested chocolate cake with vanilla ice cream.

'Listen, Jakob,' she said. Something had occurred to her while she was skiing that she hadn't thought of before – which was strange, because it was a ridiculously simple observation. 'You had a motive to kill Lena. And that's why you're only focusing on her now. But maybe we should look at the whole thing from a different perspective.'

The fork in Jakob's hand stopped moving.

Back in the hotel room, Hildur had looked up background information on Lena and Filip. She'd learned Filip had recently been hired as head of corporate social responsibility at the mining company operating nearby. The mine seemed to divide the local population into two camps. That sounded familiar: the aluminium industry caused similar friction in Icelandic communities.

One international newspaper had published an extensive report on mining activities in northern Finland. A few locals had been interviewed for the story. One retired schoolteacher had said something truly chilling: she was sure if a homicide ever took place in the area, it would be motivated by disagreements over the mine. That's how inflamed feelings were. The interviewee's words had stuck in Hildur's mind. She shared them with Jakob, then added: 'What if the murderer was after Filip Jensen?'

Hildur gave Jakob a little time to consider the question.

He shared what he knew of Filip's employer, Arctic Mine. There had been a profitable mine at Kolari until the 1980s. When it shut down, the area began investing in tourism. Hildur had noticed the big groups of tourists, the snowmobile safaris leaving from the hotel, the brightly lit ski slopes. It reminded her of the tourism boom in Iceland: the foreigners lining up for spas, car parks packed with rental cars near stunning waterfalls.

'A company that had been developing a new mine went bankrupt a few years ago,' Jakob said. 'This international conglomerate Arctic Mine bought what was left of it.'

Hildur marvelled at Jakob's local knowledge. He was surprisingly up on the news for someone who hadn't been to the area in years.

'I have a close friend who lives around here, and he's pretty up on all developments. He has reindeer, so the mine is a delicate subject.'

The big landowners were in favour of the mine, and so were most locals. The mine brought jobs to the area and boosted real estate values. The reindeer herders were opposed.

'For them it's about more than just a difference of opinion,' Jakob said. The land was the reindeer herders' bank. The better condition the land was in, the more it produced. Reindeer thrived when food was plentiful. Considering nature meant putting individual concerns aside. One had to think about what was better for future generations. Nature had to be conserved. But mining operations had been granted permits to search for ore in Lapland, even in areas populated by the indigenous Sami.

'Sometimes it seems like it's one individual against a big mining company. And you know how that's going to end.'

Jakob said there were also schisms between the mining and tourism industries. Tourism was dependent on unspoiled nature. 'Tourists don't want to see open-pit mines; they want to see nature in a pristine state,' Jakob said, stressing *pristine*. 'But it's not as if a fell that has been clear cut and its trees replaced with ski lifts is exactly in its natural state, either. And it's not as if the owners of the tourism industry companies have cared a whole lot about reindeer husbandry in the past. But they're remarkably engaged now that their interests are aligned.'

Hildur listened with interest as Jakob continued his tirade on the mining business in Lapland. Multinational companies came in and exploited natural resources. Major corporations sponsored sports halls and children's athletic contests, offered environmental experts high-paying consulting gigs, and tried to influence public opinion. And yet the raw materials for smartphones and electric cars had to come from somewhere.

After concluding his monologue, Jakob suggested they order a beer to go along with their chocolate cake. For the first time that evening, his eyes sparkled with a look suggesting enthusiasm. Hildur took this as a good sign.

It's pretty hard to beat vanilla ice cream melting over oven-fresh chocolate cake, Hildur reflected as she slipped the first bite into her mouth. As she lowered her dessert spoon to the edge of her plate, she said:

'Tomorrow we're going to do some poking around at that mine.'

Chapter 47

Reykjavík, December 2021

Beta felt invigorated. The kids were with their father this week, so she'd decided to take advantage of the free weekday morning and drop in at the dance studio for an extra introductory class to Argentinian tango. The strut and stance had been the easiest to learn. The steps were a different matter. Luckily, she'd more or less mastered the six-step *salida basica*. Beta had been paired with Jóhannes, a recently divorced movie director in his fifties who was as devoted to his new hobby as Beta was. After class, she'd accepted his invitation for breakfast at the art café next door. They'd got along off the dance floor, too, but Beta didn't want to give the matter any more attention.

Take it easy, cowboy, she told herself. *This isn't the time to rush.*

Sure, Jóhannes seemed promising, but work took precedence just now. She had to devote her complete attention to her current investigation or there'd be trouble.

The doctor had informed her that morning that Hlín had recovered sufficiently to talk. Beta had hurried to the hospital straight from breakfast. Hlín had been moved from the ICU to the ward and would remain under observation for a couple more days.

Beta could pick out Hlín all the way from the corridor. She was wearing the same pink hospital pyjamas as the patients surrounding her but instantly stood out. Her angular black glasses accentuated her sharp features as she read the paper on the common room couch.

Upon noticing Beta, Hlín briskly stood and suggested the café downstairs. 'The coffee is better down there.'

The two women took the lift to the first floor and headed to the self-service counter.

'How are you feeling?' Beta asked, taking a juice from the fridge. She'd just finished a substantial breakfast.

'I can't claim to be at my best, but I think I'll be OK. I must admit I don't understand half of what the doctors are saying. Sometimes I just have to take my time reading the treatment record.'

They chose a window table. Before Beta could ask any questions, Hlín answered them.

'I didn't see who knocked me out. Whoever it was came from behind and caught me completely off guard. I don't think there's anywhere near that paddock to hide except those miserable hay bales.'

Beta had been to the scene and noted the same detail. There had been a few big round bales next to the corral. The pasture gate was higher up the slope. From up there, the expansive view reached the full fifty kilometres to Reykjavík in clear weather.

'Hildur and I went through the pictures you took; they were saved on the newspaper's servers before the perp smashed your camera and took the memory card. Do you remember, did the blow come right after you'd taken the pictures and were headed to your car?' Beta asked. As she opened her pineapple juice, she informed Hlín her vehicle had been brought back to Reykjavík. It was now parked in the Hverfisgata police station lot.

Hlín took a moment to think. 'I remember looking through the photos I'd taken. I'd put the camera back in my bag and taken out the mittens I had in there. It was so terribly windy I couldn't imagine not wearing gloves. I think I looked at the photos for about five minutes, tops. After that I started walking back. And that blow, it came . . . pretty fast. I'm sure I hadn't made it very far.'

Hlín's voice didn't so much as quiver as she recounted the chain of events. When Beta told Hlín she'd been found a couple of hundred metres from the corral gate, she just nodded and took a bite of her flatbread sandwich. Beta wondered if Hlín's hard shell was a façade or if her nerves really were so steely. Considering the time that had passed and where Hlín had been discovered, it was more than likely that the perp was the person Hlín had photographed.

'You were working on a story. Can you tell me a little more about that?'

Hlín pinched in her lips tight and shook her head. 'It's a big one. I can't say a word.'

Beta sighed. The most difficult reporters were the investigative journalists who sank their teeth into their stories like hyenas and wouldn't let go, no matter what.

'I understand. But we're talking about a very serious matter. As it turns out, you're not the only victim. Multiple people are involved and at risk. Whatever you can tell us would be a lot of help. I saw some scattered notes on the front seat of your car, so I think I'm more or less on the map. Why are you interested in the mares' blood business?'

Hlín's expression softened. She leaned in toward Beta, and Beta told her that over the last week or so, law enforcement had become aware of five more victims in addition to Hlín. 'Two of them died,' she added emphatically.

Hlín still didn't say anything. Just listened.

Beta continued. 'You'll get your story, but we need the information you have.'

'How can I trust I'll be the one to break the story?' Hlín asked sharply.

Beta considered. Hlín and Hildur were friends. Beta had an inkling where Hlín had got the source material for her explosive exposé on sex crimes and other antisocial behaviours involving the national men's soccer team. Journalists didn't reveal their sources, and Hildur hadn't ever discussed the matter with Beta, but deep down she knew Hildur was the only one who could have leaked the evidence discovered during the police investigation. Besides, Beta had been pleased the men guilty of wrongdoing had been forced to answer for their deeds. It had improved the atmosphere in soccer at every level. Teams had hired nondiscrimination consultants, and all harassment was taken more seriously.

'Hildur was involved in the investigation. You two, um, know each other.'

At the mention of Hildur's name, Hlín's face relaxed even more.

Beta continued: 'I'm going to tell you something no one on the force knows, except me, Hildur and Tumi. We're investigating this crime spree quietly to avoid leaks and any potential panic. We have to catch the perp or perps as fast as possible. Like, yesterday.'

Beta summarised what she knew about the crime spree. The further she got in her account, the more befuddled Hlín grew. 'Did you say Yule Lads killer? That I was supposedly whacked over the head by Stubby from the poem?' She finished her smoked lamb sandwich and wiped her fingers on her napkin. She seemed to be furiously pondering her alternatives. 'Fine. When it's permissible to go public with all this, I get first dibs on the story. Deal?'

Beta nodded.

Hlín began: 'I received an invitation to an animal welfare dinner sponsored by a big gaming company. Most of the guests were activists from an organisation called Animal Lovers of Greater Reykjavík. There were about forty of us in attendance. Apparently, Luka arranged to have me invited because he wanted to talk to me about the trade in the blood of gestating mares.'

Beta said she knew about the dinner for animal welfare activists and that the police had already spoken to all those who'd attended. They were a tight-knit group, and the only thing they'd been willing to speak openly about was their cause.

'No one admitted to knowing each other, and not a single one confessed to having organised any activity against the blood farms. Even though we told them their lives were potentially in danger. Pretty committed bunch.'

Hlín said she'd made the same observation. A few activists had agreed to serve as sources under the condition their names wouldn't be revealed.

'They have source protection,' she said, shooting Beta a sharp look. She then continued in a less combative tone. Animal Lovers of Greater Reykjavík was an association that sold animal-themed cards at Christmastime and donated the money to a refuge in Reykjavík that took in abandoned cats.

'The Christmas card sales are a façade erected by the core group. In reality, the association's inner core tries to intervene in major crimes against animals, which means international contacts with, for instance, a London-based organisation called the Animal Welfare Institution.'

Through these connections, information on illegal blood farms had reached the Icelandic animal welfare activists. None of them had been aware of the scale of the illegal business, Hlín explained, then said what Beta already knew: the blood of gestating mares had been collected in Iceland since the 1970s. The blood contained hormones of value to the pharmaceutical and food industries.

'Legal collection required the close monitoring of mares, appropriate conditions, and the presence of a veterinarian. All that bureaucracy and monitoring slowed the process.'

In Iceland, over 80,000 horses were just standing in pastures, and half of them were mares. There weren't many people, and the pastures were remote, so there weren't really any nosy witnesses to speak of. Collecting blood illegally was easy.

'So there's a demand for large amounts of blood?' Beta asked. It had never occurred to her that the blood of gestating mares could be such a big business it could be of interest to criminals.

'Demand is growing all the time. The official statistics say there are about six thousand blood mares in Iceland. But according to my sources and my own calculations, there are at least three times that number.'

Hormones from gestating mares were administered to production animals so they could have larger litters and produce more meat.

'More and more vegan products are available at supermarkets, but on a global level meat consumption continues to rise.'

Hlín had done an incredible amount of background research. She told Beta about an Icelandic company that specialised in selling the blood to the food industry. The company made a profit of about four million euros a year.

Sure, that's a lot of money, Beta thought to herself, *but in international crime that's small change.*

'That Icelandic company is just a small part of the big picture. One of its owners is a company registered in Bermuda,' Hlín said. Money acquired by criminal means had been laundered through the Bermudan company. Taxes were being evaded, too, as there was no corporate taxation in Bermuda. Hlín had discovered the corporation's turnover was about 40 million dollars a year.

Beta nearly choked on her juice when she heard the figure. Over ten times the official amount. 'How do you know all this?'

A sly smile crossed Hlín's face. 'I have my contacts. I have all my material stored on secure cloud servers.'

'And 40 million dollars. How is that even possible?'

Hlín's face darkened. 'That's why the animal welfare organisation started looking into the business. The people running the black-market trade got too greedy and began collecting too much blood from too many farms. They thought no one would notice, but all it took was one curious pair of eyes and the whole thing began to unravel.'

Hlín said Luka had noticed mares disappearing from time to time from the farm where he worked. When he'd asked about them, he'd been told in no uncertain terms that it was none of his business.

'A little over a year ago, Luka attached tracking devices, these little clips, to two mares. He found out there was an abandoned pasture a few dozen kilometres away where these gestating mares were gathered and too much of their blood was collected, often violently.' Luka had sniffed out the trade in mares' blood and been shocked by the treatment of the horses.

Hlín explained how the mares were impregnated as often as possible year-round. A gestating mare only secreted the hormone PMSG for a few weeks, generally starting around the fifth week. 'Once the gestation had advanced to the point the hormone was no longer being secreted, the foetuses were aborted so the mares could be impregnated again. If the abortion failed and a foal was born, the foals were taken off to be slaughtered.'

Luka had come to realise what an organised and expansive operation must be behind the trade. He would have never been able to take action on his own, so he'd brought together a group of like-minded souls to help. Once they had enough material, Luka had reached out to Hlín.

'Those animal welfare activists are really committed,' Hlín said. 'They don't admit to knowing each other and don't talk about their fellows' activities. I don't know if you've tried to get them to, but I did. In vain. No one knew anything about anything, allegedly.'

Beta understood what Hlín was referring to. She and Tumi had tried to interview the victims of the attempted assaults, but no one would talk. They viewed the assault they'd suffered as a one-off and their Facebook friendships as a coincidence.

So Luka had been the one to bring the alliance together. Beta suddenly had a flash. 'I'm assuming all this organising wasn't free. How did he pay for everything?'

Hlín shrugged and said she wasn't really sure. 'They presumably got small-scale support from London, but I got the impression from what Luka told me that he was handling the funding himself somehow.'

Beta told Hlín about the drugs found in Luka's stomach and how they'd initially thought his death was somehow linked to the international narcotics trade. As it turned out, Luka had smuggled in drugs to make money for animal welfare work.

After a few seconds, Hlín's hard-boiled expression cracked, and a sad look flickered across her face. 'Luka was funding good intentions with poor choices.'

Hlín laid out the facts seasoned with her opinions, and Beta took notes on everything. When her pen finally stopped, she straightened her back, then sighed deeply and asked Hlín why she hadn't come in to talk to the police earlier.

'If I'd known about these interrelated deaths and assaults . . . of course I would have been in touch.'

Beta understood. Hlín had been working on the story as an investigative journalist and wanted to be able to do so in peace. She, Tumi and Hildur had kept the investigation under wraps just like Hlín. Involving outsiders in an incomplete process was unwise; it could endanger the story or confuse the tracks. They'd all made the same choice.

'I wanted to be one hundred per cent sure about the details. I was this close to discovering the identity of the person collecting the blood,' Hlín said, bringing her thumb and forefinger together.

'Is there anything you can say about that?' Beta asked quickly.

Hlín told Beta about the vehicle at the bottom of the pasture: a grey pickup with a shell over the bed. Likely a Mitsubishi L200. 'I'm not sure what year. I didn't see the licence plate because it was parked perpendicular to the pasture.'

She asked to borrow a pen and a piece of paper from Beta and drew three circles. 'I don't know much about the person in the pasture yet, but I know this company registered in Bermuda is operating behind the Icelandic company.' She jabbed the pen at the upper circle.

She drew lines from Bermuda to the two circles at the bottom. 'It has at least two subsidiaries: this Icelandic one I already mentioned, and a German one. There's an official trade in mares' blood in Germany, and at least the animal welfare movement there believes the same shenanigans are taking place in the shadows of the legal business.'

'And how did you know to go to Reykjanes when you did?'

Hlín laughed and reached for the cotton tote hanging from a chair-back. She took out a cloth handkerchief and blew her nose. 'I'd been driving out there every day for the past two weeks,' she said, folding up the handkerchief and slipping it back in the tote.

Luka had given Hlín the coordinates of several suspicious pastures, but the one in Reykjanes had been closest to Reykjavík, so Hlín had been able to drive out there every day. On the other occasions, all she'd seen were glum horses. 'Those restraint stalls are like little lidless boxes. The horses are led into them, and they don't even have room to move. On the other occasions, I took photos of the restraint boxes and observed the animals, but I didn't see any people.'

'Do you remember the locations of the other blood farms you were told about?' Beta asked.

Hlín shook her head and reached for her tote again. She took out a piece of paper that had been folded over twice. Beta realised it was a map, the free kind tourists found in hotel lobbies and restaurant vestibules.

'I don't remember them by heart, but I have them all marked here. A laminated copy of the original travels with me everywhere I go, and it was still there in the inside pocket of my coat. There's also a copy on the cloud. I asked my nurse to bring me a tourist map and transferred the locations from my map to this,' Hlín said, passing the tourist map to Beta. 'Here.'

Beta unfolded it. She took one glance and immediately felt her heart skip a few beats.

Chapter 48

Kolari, December 2021

The mine's HR director, Mervi Miettinen, pulled the door to the conference room shut with unnecessary force. The resulting gust made the Christmas lights strung inside the window swing into the glass. It was Saturday, but tight schedules meant weekends were also workdays at the mining company.

The mine's offices were surprisingly modest. In the lobby, Hildur had spotted dog-eared posters with illustrated instructions that encouraged children to wash their hands and hang their clothes in the right spots. The single-storey brick building had once housed a daycare centre. The Christmas lights were accompanied by red-and-white checked curtains and white angel decorations. Gingersnaps had been set out on a wooden tray in the middle of the square table. The gingerbread pigs, hearts and stars had been decorated with white sugar cream. Mervi poured coffee into paper cups and nudged the creamer toward her visitor. Hildur dribbled some of the white liquid into her coffee, reached for a gingerbread pig, dunked it in her cup, and took a bite. The soft, coffee-laced gingersnap was tasty.

In order to speak with the mining company's HR director, Hildur had stretched the truth. Jakob was out waiting in the car. Although the present owners were international, the mine employed a lot of locals, and someone might easily recognise him.

Hildur had noticed during her stay that Finns tended to be a little stiffer than Icelanders. All activity was steered by a need for orderliness and planning. Mervi hadn't had a free slot in her schedule until 1 p.m. the following Friday, but Hildur had refused to give in. She'd said she was a friend of Filip's from Norway and would only be in the country for a few days. She'd come to help with practical arrangements, such as transporting the body. Mervi had relented and told Hildur to come by today. Using the transport of the deceased as justification had been Jakob's idea, and it had worked. The employer didn't want the headache of arranging international shipping of a dead body.

'I'm sorry about Filip's death,' Mervi said in fluent English, adopting an empathetic look. 'It's awful.'

Hildur nodded lightly in acknowledgement. She pretended her reticence was due to heartrending grief. Her true motivation for speaking as little as possible was so she wouldn't reveal how thin her knowledge of Filip actually was. She'd read a few news stories featuring or based on interviews with Filip, scanned his LinkedIn profile and other social media channels, but the information available had been scant. Hildur wanted to avoid taking the lead.

So she just sat there in silence, waiting for Mervi's move. Hildur took a second gingersnap and maintained the sorrowful smile on her face.

Mervi glanced at the window. The Christmas lights were reflected in her green-framed glasses. 'Filip had only worked here for a couple of months.'

'Did he leave any personal effects? I could take them and give them to . . .'

Mervi sighed audibly. 'There's nothing. The police came and took everything.'

'Even his computer?' Hildur asked.

A flicker of doubt crossed Mervi's face. She shook her head and said the computer was still in Filip's office. 'It belongs to the company. Keeping personal material on the company's computers is forbidden.'

Hildur understood. For data security reasons, employers often prohibited employees from installing software, and access to social media channels could be restricted. Even so, she was perplexed the police hadn't confiscated Filip's work computer. It might contain something that would prove of use in their investigation. But apparently, belief in Filip's secondary role in the murders and Jakob's presumed guilt was so strong the computer was considered of no importance.

'As soon as the police give permission, his body will be flown to Norway for burial. The insurance company will cover the costs of transporting the casket. I promised Filip's, hmm, family to lend a hand with practical arrangements,' Hildur said.

The bodies of those who died abroad were generally transported home by air. Two caskets were needed. The first was the one in which the body would be buried. That was then placed in a sturdy metal box that protected the body and especially the funeral casket during the flight. Hildur fervently hoped Filip's real family members, if he had any in Norway, hadn't contacted his employer yet. If they had, her tall tale would be exposed. But she didn't notice any signs of suspicion on Mervi's face. Apparently, her story had worked.

'Filip moved here from Norway so fast. We never had a chance to talk properly about his job,' Hildur said, then explained she and Filip had once worked together at a Norwegian oil company. Filip had headed up the company's exports, a crumb of information

Hildur had gleaned from Filip's LinkedIn profile. She said she'd been Filip's assistant. They'd grown close during their years in oil.

'What were Filip's responsibilities here?'

Hildur noticed a sudden change in Mervi's demeanour. The HR director who'd seemed so curious and open shut down in a fraction of a second. Mervi leaned back in her chair and narrowed her eyes. She evaluated the woman sitting across from her and said in an exceedingly calm voice: 'What does that have to do with anything?'

Hildur was caught off guard but did her best to conceal it. She pulled her ponytail over one shoulder and began to fiddle with her hair in supposed nervousness.

'No, I was just thinking . . . Filip and I were pretty close. We'd go for a drink after work regularly. He used to talk about how he hoped to work in the mining industry. I was wondering if he was able to finally realise his dreams . . .'

Hildur left the sentence unfinished and concentrated on staring at the tips of her hair as if this were the first time she'd seen them.

'He handled our international communications. Stakeholder relations, press communications and the like,' Mervi said, then paused.

Hildur was sure Mervi would continue, so she didn't comment.

Mervi lowered her elbows to the table, interlaced her fingers, and rested her chin on her hands. She gave Hildur a penetrating look. 'In recent weeks, he'd been helping the environmental team with permits.'

'Permits?'

Hildur immediately cursed herself. She'd been a touch too enthusiastic and taken the bait the HR director had waved in front of her.

'Listen here, whoever you are,' Mervi said, raising a silencing forefinger as Hildur tried to interrupt. 'Let me tell you something. There are all sorts of people lurking around the mining industry: lobbyists, bureaucrats, militant environmentalists . . . I've developed a pretty good radar. I can spot a bullshitter like you from a mile away. Besides, Filip's family has already been in touch with us.'

Mervi poured herself more coffee from the Thermos pitcher as she continued her tirade. She didn't offer Hildur a second cup. 'I assume you're some environmental activist? Judging by your messy hair. You guys usually have those disgusting, smelly dreadlocks . . .' She turned up her nose and shimmied her shoulders as if shivering in revulsion. She was on a roll. 'So tell me, how did you and Filip know each other?' Mervi asked the question so directly that squirming out of it was impossible.

'We met at the oil company in Oslo—'

Hildur couldn't even finish before Mervi had interrupted her. 'Nonsense.'

But Hildur didn't give up. 'I'm sorry, but I don't understand.'

A knowing smile spread across Mervi's face. She placed her palms on the table and looked at Hildur like a child who's been caught stealing a lollipop.

'I heard some nosy Icelandic woman was in town asking about Jakob. About the man who's been questioned regarding the murders of Lena and Filip. It's not very hard to deduce you're her.'

Dammit. Hildur knew her time with the mining company's HR director was up. Mervi had been one step ahead the whole time, and it was plain from her attitude that she wouldn't be telling Hildur anything of use.

'We're trying to create jobs for the locals and want to be part of the shift to green technologies. You know, raw materials for electric vehicles and IT, for instance. And what do we get? All the environmental fascists in the world who have nothing better to do than hang sheets on flagpoles and amateur actors like you coming in here to waste my time.'

Hildur stood and grabbed a final gingerbread pig from the tray. 'I'll be on my way. Thanks for the coffee.'

Mervi opened her mouth to speak, but Hildur strode from the room, threw on her coat, and crossed the snow-covered lot to her car.

'Total flop,' Hildur informed Jakob, yanking the seatbelt across her chest and fastening it. 'She immediately realised what was going on.'

Jakob tapped the dash with his fingers and nodded at the back seat. 'We have a visitor.'

Hildur started up the engine, then turned around to see a tall man, slightly younger than her in the car. He offered his hand. 'Hi, I'm Esa Lehtinen.'

Hildur accepted the hand and shook it.

'I walked past the room where you were talking with Mervi. The soundproofing is terrible; you can hear everything. I looked out the window and saw an unfamiliar car in the car park and someone sitting at the wheel. I figured it was your ride, so I came out here to wait.' Esa explained he'd worked closely with Filip. 'Mervi's a little special. Pro-mining through and through. She can't stand any criticism.'

Hildur introduced herself and offered her condolences on Filip's passing. 'I mean, he was your colleague.'

Jakob said something in Finnish to Esa. Esa nodded and took a moment to search for the words. 'Filip had been helping me recently with our permit applications. It wasn't his job; he'd been hired as the PR attack dog. We're just incredibly busy; we need all the help we can get.'

Esa described the bureaucracy surrounding environmental permitting as hellish. The tiniest permitting hiccup could cause a project a destructive delay.

'If, say, the emissions from the mining operations are too great or if the mine has other major detrimental effects on the surroundings or nearby inhabitants, the environmental permit won't necessarily be granted. Without an environmental permit, the mine can't begin operations. That couldn't be allowed to happen. I remember how disappointed Filip was when his concerns about waste weren't taken seriously.'

A chill ran up Hildur's spine. She turned up the seat warmer. 'Waste?'

Esa rubbed his palms together and shook his head. 'It's a semi-open secret that all sorts of waste used to be dumped at the site of the former mine, from carboard boxes and pipe-ends to old engines.'

Filip had started looking into it. He'd wanted to know when waste had last been dumped at the illicit site and by whom and whether the environmental crimes had been committed under the mining company that went bankrupt or Arctic Mines.

'There's been talk of illegal dumping for years, and the old mining company had looked into it. But now those documents are nowhere to be found.'

Up in the front seat, Jakob nodded. He remembered having heard rumours about the illicit dump years ago.

'What does the illegal dump have to do with the environmental permit?' Hildur asked.

'Money,' Esa said.

Those behind the big investments wanted their money generating profits as quickly as possible. It was a game that required nerves of steel. There was a big temptation to take the path of least resistance.

'An illicit dump pollutes. It can delay or even prevent the granting of an environmental permit. The mine doesn't want anyone poking around the old waste site so it doesn't start to stink and wreak havoc on the entire project. Filip wouldn't let it be; he kept digging up more information on it.'

'Do you think anyone from the company could have been involved in the crime?'

Esa shook his head and chuckled. 'A publicly traded company makes money, but they wouldn't start killing people.'

Hildur thought about the activists Mervi had spoken of in such disdainful tones. 'What about environmental activists? Are there a lot of radicals in the area?'

'Well, you never know when someone might start thinking it's OK to kill a couple of people to save nature.' The way Esa laughed after saying this suggested he didn't believe in the environmental activist scenario either.

Out of her side mirror, Hildur saw the main doors to the office building open. Mervi, wearing an ankle-length parka, pressed the door shut behind her and strode toward her car. Apparently, senior management had personal parking spaces near the entrance.

'She goes to lunch at the same time every day,' Esa said, stirring in the back seat. 'I don't think I'm going to be of any more use.'

From the passenger seat, Jakob turned to Esa and said: 'Do you know how far Filip got in his research into the waste issue?'

Esa released the door handle, let his head drop back against the headrest, and closed his eyes. He reminded Hildur of the late Steve Jobs. Wire-rimmed glasses, thin lips, short grey stubble.

'Not far, I don't think.'

He hadn't found any internal documentation about the dump. He'd tried to talk to a few old-time employees, but none of them had trusted the new arrival who'd immediately begun digging into the past. Esa wasn't sure if Filip had turned to old newspaper articles, waste transport companies, investigative journalists familiar with the mining industry, or the local police.

'I'm curious as to why you want to tell us all this,' Hildur said.

Esa laughed. 'Because I'm one of those environmental activists Mervi hates. I'm also a geologist. I understand the mining industry. There are a lot of reasons we need to mine more ore. But I want things to be done the right way. Some of these folks want to do things their own way, and that can be dangerous.'

Chapter 49

Äkäslompolo, December 2021

After they left the Arctic Mine offices, Hildur drove Jakob to the police station in Kittilä. The lead investigator had wanted to talk to Jakob again. Hildur and Jakob would be meeting the next morning at the latest.

Hildur took her time getting back to Äkäslompolo. The drive along the scenic route from Kittilä to the small town in the fells along was drop-dead gorgeous. The snow-packed trees stood out white against the pink afternoon sky. At the highest point on the road, she could see many fells at once. The serene, rolling terrain seemed to go on and on, all the way to the horizon.

Hildur wanted a moment to herself. So much had happened over the last few days. She hated standing still when things needed doing. Hildur had a compulsive need to know who'd murdered Lena and Filip and why, what had happened to Rósa, how the investigation was proceeding under Beta and Tumi's supervision, and when Jakob would be returning to Iceland. The uncertainty crackling under her skin was intolerable.

Life would probably be easier if she would just let go of uncertainties. It was hard to imagine a life that was mostly easy and free of cares. Everyone had problems, but for some people they were the scale of a pile of laundry or a child with a cold, things that came and went and faded as the present became the past. Of course she found herself feeling carefree from time to time:

while she was surfing, at the gym, eating, or in bed. *Too bad you can't spend your whole life surfing and screwing.* She laughed at the thought as she pulled up outside the hotel.

The thought of going to her room didn't appeal; she craved fresh air. She set out toward the shopping centre and the lake beyond. She wanted to walk out onto the ice.

Therapy had been suggested to Hildur more than once. Apparently, she might find it useful to process old traumas with some professional. No. She wasn't going to do that again. Hildur had tried therapy a couple of times long ago, and decided it wasn't for her. She'd tried again after finding Björk only to discover it simply increased her burdens. She'd considered reporting this second therapist after said therapist began sharing how she'd experienced a major loss herself when her baby died of SIDS. Hildur knew the therapist had behaved unprofessionally, but she hadn't had the energy to lodge a complaint. The best option had been to simply not return.

The snow squeaked underfoot. She wasn't the only one on the ice, and the sounds of the others' shoes against the snow reached Hildur as a soft whisper. As her fellow strollers drew closer, the whisper transformed into a creak and the creak gradually into a crunch. The sound of the snow under one's own shoes was a faint popping. Hildur walked the paths crisscrossing the Äkäslompolo ice. It was about twenty below, but the cold wasn't bone-chilling. The windless winter day felt almost mild. Hildur wasn't used to that. Back in Ísafjörður, winter was so often a struggle. The snow might gust horizontally for hours. Then the next minute it would rain, turning the streets into skating rinks. The wind was always blowing from some direction. Here winter was present, but calmly, one kind of weather at a time. That made it easier to tolerate somehow.

Everything in Finland felt new. The language, the terrain, the biting cold, the leisurely pace. At least as an adult, her life had been marked by familiarity: she did work that she liked and was good at, had the same pastimes year in year out, and lived in a town she knew and a home she'd settled into over the course of many years. Ought she tear off the old page and start a fresh sheet? Take up some new hobby? Pottery, say, or sewing national costumes?

The night was so bright and the surroundings so dark that the stars twinkled intensely. Hildur sensed her indrawn breath as a tickle in her nose hairs, and her exhaled breath emerged in a vapour that thinned and evaporated in tiny particles that floated off into the atmosphere. The starry sky looked almost the same here as it did back home. Or, at least, Hildur could make out the Big Dipper. She let her gaze roam the heavens. When she found the big U, she was able to pick out the constellation Gemini, which resembled a pair of people holding hands. It wasn't always an easy constellation to make out; it was composed of so many parts. But now she could see it clearly.

You could form all sorts of patterns in the sky when you took a moment to connect the brightly shining dots. Thinking about constellations was a little like the work of a detective. You had to make observations, look carefully at close proximity and from afar, consider how things were connected and spot the pattern. The walk had done her good. And yet the longing lingered and wrapped her in its embrace like an Icelandic fog off the sea. Hildur wanted to feel light for a little while. She remembered a saying about how happiness follows the idiot.

So she turned around and headed toward the shopping centre. She was going to drop by the local pub for a pint or two.

Chapter 50

'*Yksi kalja*,' Hildur said, mimicking the young guy in front of her. Judging by the bartender's amused smile, her first attempt at ordering a pint in Finnish came out more or less right.

Hildur took a sip so the beer wouldn't splash to the counter, then grabbed her pint and pulled a barstool under her behind. The corner of the bar was a good place to sit and observe her fellow patrons.

The establishment's longest wall was filled by three massive screens blaring with some soccer match. Hildur didn't understand a word the Finnish commentator was saying. A surprising number of people were sitting alone, eyes trained on the screen. Cards were being played at one table; a loud conversation was taking place at another. It was only a little past nine, and the mood in the pub was expectant.

Hopefully, the men watching the game were locals. She could ask them about the mine and the dump. Hildur took a sip of her beer and decided to approach one of the men during the next commercial break. Bothering them in the middle of a match would draw the wrong sort of attention.

She knew from experience she'd get the most thorough answers in a pub when she approached people a moment before the game ended, or right after a game the home team won. That's when tongues wagged freely.

Out of her peripheral vision, Hildur noticed a dark, handsome man walk up to the bar, order a pint, and claim the empty stool at her side. He gave her a smile before dipping his upper lip into the glass. Something about his keen gaze caught Hildur's attention. He raised his pint at her in greeting. Hildur ordered another beer and checked the menu in front of her; her stomach was growling. She ordered fries.

While waiting for her food, she reached into her coat pocket and pulled out her phone to go through her text messages. Beta was asking for updates and asked her to say hello to Jakob. Hildur replied to her message and promised to call as soon as a good opportunity arose. She said she hoped to be flying home in a couple of days. She also texted Björk about the cold, the snow and the skiing, and promised to tell her all about the trip once she got home. Hildur noticed the man who'd sat at her side was still staring in her direction. Hildur turned toward him and looked at him quizzically. He didn't turn away.

'I'm just staring. No need to talk.'

Hildur raised an eyebrow. *Well, go ahead and stare then.*

The bartender set the fries and ketchup bottle down on the counter. It was only now Hildur realised how hungry she was. She shoved several fries in her mouth at once and wiped her hands on her trousers.

By now Hildur was tired of the staring contest. She stood, extended a hand, and introduced herself.

'I'm Anton,' the man replied.

Hildur tried to start a conversation about the soccer match, but it didn't seem to spark any reaction in Anton.

'Do you live around here?'

'I do. I'm from a reindeer-herding Sami family and a reindeer herder myself.'

Interesting, Hildur mused. Anton had her full attention. 'Do you have a lot of reindeer?'

Anton laughed loudly and slapped the bar top. He leaned in toward Hildur as if he meant to tell her a secret: 'And how much money do you have in your bank account, ma'am?'

Hildur was thrown, but only briefly. Apparently, asking about the size of one's herd was bad manners. She emptied her pint and ordered another. She shot Anton a look asking if he'd like one too.

'Let's have another, but that means I'm paying. My reindeer run on both sides of the tree. Women don't have to pay around here.'

They chatted for a while, and the topic switched to Anton's fluent English.

'I used to be married to an Englishwoman, but she died.'

Hildur offered her condolences, and Anton accepted with a nod. They clinked glasses and fell silent for a moment.

Then Hildur shared she was from Iceland and had come to Finland to help a friend. 'We have reindeer in Iceland too. But we don't herd them; we hunt them.'

Anton shook his head and asked who this comic sitting next to him was. Hildur explained the reindeer had originally been brought to Iceland from Norway so hunters would have something bigger than birds to shoot. The reindeer hunt lasted a few weeks every autumn, and the permits were chosen by lottery.

Anton laughed loudly: 'You hold a raffle to see who gets to shoot a reindeer?'

Hildur nodded. She scooped up the last of the French fries, shoved them in her mouth, and pushed away the empty plate.

It was halftime, and Finnish oldies started playing from the speakers.

Anton stood and held out his hand. 'Dance with me?'

Hildur replied with a shake of her head. She didn't care for dancing. 'I don't know how.'

'I'll teach you.'

Hildur shook her head again. 'Listen, I'm less interested in dancing and more interested in that mine. Can you tell me anything about it?'

Anton's expression turned wary. He sat back down on his stool, took his pint, and began draining it. 'You don't work there, do you?' he asked from behind his glass.

Hildur shook her head a third time.

Anton slammed his empty glass to the bar top and turned to her. 'Sure, I can tell you. But on one condition.'

Hildur raised an eyebrow to indicate she was listening.

'Come to the forest with me tomorrow to see my reindeer, and I'll tell you everything you want to know. We'll take the snowmobile.'

Hildur gave a little smile. 'There's no way I can make the time. Too much work.'

Anton grunted and proposed they order another. That Hildur had time for. She wanted to hear about Anton's work, and beer lubricated conversation.

Anton said he'd spent all day on his snowmobile, herding reindeer near the village of Hetta. Anton's reindeer travelled in a herd with a few other families' animals. The herding cooperative took turns looking after the reindeer at the winter feeding grounds. In the heart of darkest, coldest winter, the reindeer stuck to a small area, because moving through heavy snow was so taxing. The animals had an easier time getting around in the spring, when the snow hardened, and that's when they roamed around a larger area. In midwinter the work consisted mostly of shepherding and following the reindeer.

'I found a carcass today, killed by a predator,' Anton said, paying the server for the pints. 'I saw three big ravens flying above the treetops. They kept dropping down to the ground, then climbing back into the sky. I drove over on the snowmobile. I knew I'd find a carcass waiting for me.'

Hildur thought about ravens. Back in Iceland, they were the worst enemies of little free-ranging lambs. A lamb that fell on its back couldn't get up on its own. Hildur shared that in Iceland, seeing a raven outside a house often meant death. Or sometimes wisdom. It depended on the situation.

'Óðinn had two black ravens. Thought and Memory. They reported to their master what was happening on earth.'

Anton nodded thoughtfully and took a sip of his beer. He set the glass down on the bar and glanced at Hildur. 'And your namesake is Óðinn's Valkyrie who decided which fallen soldiers would be brought back to life to continue fighting.'

Hildur didn't say anything, just stared at Anton, gobsmacked.

'I've read those old stories about the gods too. I used to study Nordic cultural history purely out of personal interest. My wife wrote a dissertation on the subject; that's what got me interested too. Then she died of cancer. We didn't even have kids. What about you? Is your old man waiting for you at home?'

Hildur wasn't fazed by Anton's directness. She preferred real conversation. Hildur said she didn't have any children and lived alone. 'I prefer it that way.'

'I don't believe it!' Anton exclaimed. 'I can see from three kilometres away you're not happy. Stay here and I'll fix that.'

Hildur shook her head and laughed. She shifted her stool in Anton's direction to make room for people waiting to order. A line had formed at the bar.

'The meaning of life can't be a single emotion like happiness,' she said. 'The point of life is to exist. That's enough for me.'

Anton took a minute to weigh Hildur's words. 'Even so, stay here and be my wife. I have broad shoulders. There's plenty of room for you to exist between them.'

Hildur had just taken a sip of beer. The mouthful went down her windpipe, and she began coughing furiously. Tears welled up in her eyes as she brought up the liquid that had gone down the wrong way. Once she was able to breathe normally again, she glanced at her watch.

'We met a little over an hour ago and you're already proposing to me?'

'Yes. Why wait for tomorrow when you get a good idea? Now is now.'

Anton took a long swig of beer and sank into his own thoughts. He and Hildur sat in silence for a moment. Suddenly, a raucous cry filled the room. Hildur glanced at the televisions. The screens were filled with cheering people. Apparently, the right team had scored. More customers flooded the bar.

Anton repeated his invitation for a wilderness excursion. 'I'll build a fire and make us campfire coffee. I'll melt snow for the water. I'll warm some smoked meat over the flames. Reindeer chops sizzle when they're hot. Now, that's healthy eating. You'd be sitting on a reindeer hide. I bet you've never experienced that before.'

Hildur had to concede Anton knew how to tell a good story. 'It sounds delicious.'

'I can talk to you in Sami if you want.'

Anton's off-the-wall pickup lines put a smile on Hildur's face. She lowered her right hand to the bar to adjust her position. Anton's hand slipped under it first.

Hildur raised her pint and looked at the man who'd materialised in her night: 'Let's finish these and get out of here.'

Chapter 51

Reykjavík, December 2021

Beta and Tumi were sitting in armchairs across from each other. Beta's office was the only place at the station they could meet without attracting attention.

'Are there this many locations?' Tumi asked, bent over the map.

Through her background research, Hlín had discovered over two hundred blood farms around Iceland. The perp they were looking for was targeting animal welfare activists who were in some way involved in trying to hinder the collection of mares' blood.

Tumi massaged his forehead, a look of intense concentration on his face. 'About forty people attended the dinner at the hotel restaurant, but we don't know how many of them were actively involved in the group's operations. There are plenty of animal welfare activists in Iceland, and maybe there are multiple perps too. Hlín was probably cracked over the head by whoever she saw in the pasture with the horses. But the other victims weren't found anywhere near a blood farm. Maybe someone else attacked them.'

Beta was painfully aware of the possibility of multiple assailants. If the investigative team had infinite resources, they could check every blood farm marked on the map. But it was just the two of them. There was no way their time would suffice.

'While you were visiting Hlín, I spoke to the servers who worked the dinner,' Tumi added.

Beta looked at him questioningly. He replied with a shake of the head.

Dammit. Still nothing.

'The waitstaff and the gaming company's senior management have alibis for the times the assaults were committed. None of them have any ties to the Icelandic horse industry,' Tumi said. 'One of the servers goes riding with her old high school friends every summer; that's it for the links to horses.'

The first time she'd seen Hlín's map, Beta had noticed one of the farms belonged to her friend Viðar Viðarsson. So during her drive back to the station, she'd given Viðar a call.

Viðar and Beta had known each other for years. They'd once spent a lot of time together in the East Iceland back country protesting against the aluminium industry. Viðar had since inherited a farm on the southern coast. He'd sold off the sheep and focused on raising horses for meat.

'Viðar was a little mystified by my interest in the mares' blood trade, but he freely admitted he'd sold blood. He said it hadn't been a significant source of income. The procedure was handled by a veterinarian and not much blood was collected. Apparently, the number of rules and regulations mean there's not a whole lot of profit in the business.'

Beta had asked Viðar if he'd heard anything about people who made the rounds of horse farms collecting black-market blood.

'Viðar said he'd heard stories. It's general knowledge some horse owners collect too much and ignore at least some of the rules. He said it didn't really come as a surprise. But he hadn't heard about any mysterious blood collectors.'

Tumi looked up from the map. 'Why didn't it come as a surprise?'

'That's just the way it is on some farms. Some folks who raise animals are pretty lax about following the rules. And monitoring by the authorities is also lax, especially in remote areas.'

Tumi took the map and studied the locations marked on it one more time. He looked agonised. 'Should we head out to the closest farm?'

Beta took a cookie from the package on the table and popped it in her mouth. She shook her head. She had a better idea.

Tumi had rigorously questioned the hotel manager who'd arranged the dinner and the waitstaff who'd worked it. 'But it's possible there were people present at that dinner we don't know anything about yet,' Beta said.

There were always people who lurked in the shadows, hoping to remain unnoticed. They succeeded thanks to those who averted their gaze and pretended not to see. Especially at Christmastime, plenty of folks looked the other way, because no one wanted to spoil the holiday's peaceful mood.

Chapter 52

Beta was in the passenger seat. The fuzzy dice in front of her swung in time to the Volvo's movements. She and Tumi had decided to take Tumi's old, unmarked car – the one he used when driving the streets of Reykjavík looking to help young people who'd run away from foster homes or rehab.

Over these past few days, Beta had noticed how pleasant it was working with Tumi. She had no trouble understanding Hildur's praise for her former colleague. Tumi was an easy-going guy who never seemed pressed for time. He didn't bounce from topic to topic, and she'd never heard the words 'I'm too busy' or 'Hurry!' emerge from his lips. He always had a moment to stop and listen to others' concerns and respond by sharing his views. Beta had to admit Tumi had a unique gift for reading the room. When questioning Ívar, Tumi had quickly noticed the suspect's speech impediment and adapted to it, resulting in a positive outcome.

'Do you have any plans for Christmas?' Beta asked as they passed the Perlan water tanks.

'I'll go to my mum's for dinner on Christmas Eve, but other than that I'll be at work. Christmas is such a damn busy time.'

During the holidays, pastimes were on pause and schools were closed. Life took place within the four walls of the home. If conditions at home were less than ideal, that didn't make for relaxed family time; it made for stress, anxiety and escalating problems.

'Can't someone else cover some shifts so you'd have a few days off during the holiday?'

Tumi guffawed, but it was more of a neutral statement than a disdainful laugh. 'I don't think there's anyone who really does the same work I do. And to be completely honest, I'd rather be at work than at home alone.'

Life was never black and white. It had countless shades of grey; Beta understood that. With time, she'd come to see why her ex-husband had embarked on an affair. He and Beta hadn't been happy together anymore. Óliver had always been practical, a comfort-seeker. He hadn't had the guts to directly propose they divorce; instead, he'd resolved the situation by taking up with someone else. Once Beta discovered the affair, divvying up the silverware had taken place quickly. Yes, the divorce had felt awful, but Beta was more satisfied with her life now than she had been in ages.

When the light turned green, Tumi stepped on the accelerator. His old banger didn't have much juice; newer cars passed them on either side. A glance in the rearview mirror confirmed the right lane was empty. Tumi flicked on his indicator, changed lanes, and at the big intersection at Bústaðavegur curved to the right.

A few days before, Beta had read a comprehensive and fascinating article on problems temporary workers faced at Reykjavík's construction sites. One temp company focused on brokering foreign labour, and its payment irregularities were constant. None of the workers interviewed by the paper had earned even minimum wage for their hours, let alone extra pay for evening and overtime shifts. Serious deficiencies had been discovered in workplace safety too.

None of this was new. There was almost no unemployment in Iceland, and workers were in short supply. Temp companies had sniffed out an opportunity. Icelandic businesses desperately needed labour, and plenty of foreigners were hungry for a shot at a better life and work that would provide a livelihood for their families. People from Romania, Cuba, the Philippines and former Yugoslavian countries came to Iceland in the hope of satisfying that hunger. Bending the rules and neglecting obligations allowed the temp companies to hire quickly, and the biggest beneficiaries were the brokers themselves.

The article had given Beta an idea. She'd called the manager Tumi had spoken to at the hotel restaurant and asked if the hotel ever used temporary workers. After a brief silence, Beta had added she wasn't investigating irregularities in employment. She was conducting a homicide investigation, and she needed the truth. Nothing else was of any concern to her. Eventually, the manager had conceded the hotel hired temp workers as dishwashers and bussers every week, and had done so the week of the dinner too.

She and Tumi were now on their way to the temp company.

'Turn left there. It's the second building on the right,' Beta said.

According to the national register, Women at Work was a three-year-old limited liability company in the human resources industry; in other words, it supplied temporary workers and offered workforce training services. Beta had continued digging. Women at Work focused on predominantly female sectors, which meant a workforce of cleaners, daycare centre substitutes, waitstaff for downtown bars and barbacks. The financial crimes unit had launched an investigation into the company, but it was still in such early stages that no questioning had taken place yet. Beta and Tumi weren't interested in possible tax evasion; they just wanted to know who'd been on the company's payroll the night of the dinner.

Snow had packed up at either side of the sliding doors, preventing them from opening wide enough for Tumi to fit through. He kicked away the snow and used his big hands to pull them open by force. The doors complained loudly as they gave.

When the lift arrived at the third floor, Beta and Tumi stepped directly into the reception area for Women at Work. It was basically an entryway: coat hooks, a small shoe rack, a bathroom door and a low table the size of a shoe box blocking the corridor.

Beta pressed the buzzer, and a moment later, a washed-out woman a little older than Beta appeared in the hallway. Pale carrot-coloured hair hung limply to her shoulders, and her eyes were circled by deep wrinkles and dark bags. She dragged her feet in a weary, worn-out shuffle. Beta assessed the woman's appearance keenly because she knew it corresponded to her own after a long day.

She introduced herself and Tumi, then continued: 'We're investigating a series of serious crimes. We need to ask a few questions about workers your company sent to a specific establishment on a specific night.'

Beta wanted to be as clear as possible regarding the reason for their visit. The sight of police officers either put people on the defensive or made them very cautious. Because the company was already under investigation for financial crimes, Beta was sure the unions and occupational health and safety had already paid visits to the premises. Beta wanted to make it plain she had no interest in issues involving employment laws. She'd be satisfied with the limited information she was looking for.

Beta's direct approach seemed to do the trick. The woman's wariness softened.

'Lilja Finnsdóttir,' she said, shaking hands with the investigators. 'I'm the CEO here.'

Lilja led Beta and Tumi to a conference room and asked: 'So what is this regarding?'

Beta briefly related the facts. The previous autumn, the Hilton hotel in Reykjavík had hosted a dinner honouring animal welfare activists.

'The hotel indicated people sent by your company worked there that night. We need those individuals' information: name, address and other contact details.'

Lilja pulled a pack of gum from her pocket and popped a piece in her mouth. She moved her jaws with a slow relish as she chewed. Her bored expression had been replaced by curiosity.

'OK. I'll get that for you. Wait here,' Lilja said. She nodded at a water jug. 'Help yourselves to water if you're thirsty.'

Beta glanced at the crusty contraption and politely declined.

She and Tumi sat waiting side by side in silence. Tumi took out his mobile phone and went through his messages. Beta knew that youth in trouble, their parents and child protection services had a very low threshold for reaching out to Tumi. He received a constant stream of text messages, WhatsApp messages, Instagram DMs and email at all hours of day and night. He even had a Snapchat account, because he knew young people spent a lot of time on the app. After a few clicks, he locked his phone and slipped it back in his pocket.

'Nice and quiet, no one is trying to get in touch with me. I wonder if this is the calm before the storm . . .'

Just then Lilja returned to the conference room with a stack of papers. 'I printed out all our files for that week. Apparently, it was a quiet week for us, so there isn't a whole lot of information.' She spread the printouts across the table and studied them, one shift list at a time. 'Did you say the Hilton hotel?'

Beta confirmed Lilja had remembered correctly.

'I'm not finding anything here . . .' Lilja started chewing the nail of her left forefinger as her right forefinger dropped down the list line by line.

Beta felt disappointment and frustration wash over her. 'But the hotel said you sent staff there,' she insisted. She was tired.

'Now I remember,' Lilja said, jabbing her finger at the middle of the topmost printout. 'We had people at the Grand Hotel, and it's not far from the Hilton. We'd sent staff to the Grand to wash dishes when we received an urgent call from the Hilton. One of their employees had fallen ill.'

Lilja was visibly excited she'd found the answer to the mystery. It was about a ten-minute walk from the Grand to the Hilton, so it hadn't been a big deal to shift resources around. 'There's an asterisk here next to the worker's name indicating the change. I just didn't notice it.'

'Could we have the name, please?' Beta asked, pulling a ballpoint pen and a National Museum-branded notebook from her bag.

Lilja looked at the paper, then at Beta: 'I don't know her very well. She works a shift for us now and again when she has the time. Apparently, she has a day job, making deliveries around Iceland. But she always takes short-term gigs when she's not driving. Her name is . . . It's Haarde.'

The pen in Beta's hand dropped to the table and rolled from there to the floor. 'Haarde? You mean like the former prime minister?'

Almost everyone in Iceland used a patronymic or matronymic; Haarde was one of the few surnames. The man who'd served as prime minister about fifteen years before was the only Haarde Beta knew of.

A burst of nervous laughter erupted from Lilja's lips. 'Yes, well, I guess you're right. But he's incredibly rich. None of his relatives would be on their feet for hours washing dishes, would they?'

'First name?' Beta asked.

An awkward silence followed. Lilja rubbed her palms together and smiled uncomfortably. 'To be honest, we don't know. We call her the Dishwasher. I do have a phone number if that helps?'

Beta nodded and wrote down the number. They would have to check it as soon as possible. 'Do you know where this Haarde lives?'

Lilja browsed through her smartphone, then glanced at the printouts on the table. Her expression had grown even more apologetic. 'It looks like all we have for her is a phone number. She texts us when she's available to work.'

'Not even a social security number?' Tumi asked.

Lilja shook her head.

'Then how does she get paid?' Beta asked, despite having already guessed the answer.

Lilja squirmed in her seat and swept her reddish hair behind her ears. She seemed to be considering what to say. 'Well, um . . . You're not from the union? And you're not those white-collar police?'

Lilja's games were getting old, and Beta's patience was running thin. 'No. We're not from the financial crimes unit. We just need this woman's information.'

Lilja coughed and looked at Beta, then Tumi. 'We always pay her in cash. We leave an envelope in that mailbox downstairs after the shift. That's how she wants it.'

Chapter 53

Kittilä, December 2021

The grip was firm. Strong fingers held the metal needles and the sweater hanging from them. The loops obeyed the hands' movements. Little effort was required to get them right. About forty centimetres of finished torso hung from the needles. Jakob pulled more of the fluffy yarn from the disc and finished the row. Three, at most four more rows and he could attach the sleeves to the body. Jakob preferred to knit the body to the sleeves using a pair of circular needles if the sleeves were done before he was ready to connect the pieces. He meant to give this sweater to Anton, who spent most of his day working outside. Over the few days Jakob had spent in Finland, he'd noticed Anton always wore the same sweater under his overalls. His friend's old garment was fraying at the waist and had worn through at both elbows.

Jakob had brought the yarn with him from Iceland. It was one of the few things that was cheaper in his new homeland than it was in Finland.

He drew the wooden chair towards the wall to get closer to the heat given off by the radiator. He could hear the water rushing through the heater. The corners of the room were freezing. The aromas of stale coffee and fresh cinnamon rolls wafted from the kitchen. After being questioned, Jakob had parked himself in the station's reception area. He was so drained he didn't trust himself to get behind the wheel right away. His day hadn't gone very well.

Stern-faced detective sergeant Sirkku Sainio and her colleague, whose name Jakob couldn't remember, had interrogated him for almost three hours that morning. During the questioning, the knowledge he might actually be convicted of two homicides had finally crashed into Jakob's consciousness. Sainio had so convincingly listed the factors indicating Jakob's guilt that he would have probably believed her himself if he hadn't known the truth.

The tactical investigators had retrieved his phone data and checked the weather cameras for vehicles at the presumed time the crime took place. Jakob had pulled his rental car into the café car park before six and left a little after seven.

Sainio had also told him the results of the laboratory tests had come in. Jakob's DNA had been found on both Filip's and Lena's skin. This information hadn't come as a surprise to Jakob. He'd tried both bodies for a pulse. But his DNA combined with his footprints, the statement of the eyewitness who saw him in the car park, and the fact that he'd threatened to kill Lena at the courthouse only a couple of days before . . . There were simply too many things he was forced to deny, one after the other. If the combined observations suggested a white raven, it was a white raven. This was a saying Jakob had picked up during his time in Iceland.

At the conclusion of the interrogation, Sainio had informed Jakob this would be their final conversation for the time being. The case would soon advance to a charging decision.

The police had also told Jakob he had to be reachable by them, and he'd promised he would be. And then there was Matias, who'd been placed with a local family. Jakob had been trying to establish a better relationship with his son for years, and so even the detective in charge of the investigation had decided the boy's presence meant Jakob wouldn't skip town.

Jakob believed in the Finnish justice system, but mistakes were made. Innocent people were sent to jail, and guilty people were found innocent. Both were rare, but they happened. What if he was one of the exceptions and found guilty? He felt a stabbing pressure in his heart at the thought of not seeing Guðrún again. He couldn't even think about Matias; it hurt too much. In the worst case, it would be his son's fate to grow from childhood to adulthood in a family of strangers.

Jakob switched out the needles for a longer pair and tried to pull himself together. He had to concentrate on something else to keep his head from exploding with worry. The yarn slid between his fingers as the needles clinked against each other. Loop by loop, faster and faster. Knitting took Jakob somewhere mundane concerns, panic, and angst didn't trouble him. All that existed were the loops, the repetitive movement, and time's safe, steady march.

After a moment, he paused to check his handiwork. Years of manic knitting had made him a master. Smooth and straight. He had almost reached the patterned yoke, the most rewarding part of knitting a sweater.

Jakob decided to sit in the station lobby a little longer and knit until he felt steadier. He didn't know how long that would take, but he wasn't in a hurry.

His molars clenched against each other; his eyes narrowed to slits. They burned with hot tears. The floor blurred, vanished, and was replaced by a quietly shimmering lake. Jakob heard a burble and a faint splash, as if something small had dropped to the bottom. The heaviness had sunk from his temples to his shoulders and arms, but he just kept knitting. One row at a time.

Jakob drew a breath, and at that moment he wished he'd drowned, dropped to the bottom.

He'd threatened to kill Lena, found her dead, lost his son again, and been interrogated for days on suspicion of two homicides. How had his life come to this point? Was it all a consequence of the path he'd stepped on when he met Lena and began living in two parallel realities? He'd done it because he hadn't been able to stand the thought of disappointing anyone important to him. But had that one bad decision established the direction of the rest of his life?

As Jakob was slipping the right needle under the loop on the left one, his grip slipped. A strange thought had occurred to him. He had to talk to Hildur as soon as possible.

Chapter 54

Hildur pulled on the underpants she'd tossed onto the table and dressed quickly. The sports watch at her wrist showed 7 a.m.

Anton was still snoring in her hotel bed, arms wide.

Hildur remembered him having said something offhand the night before about not being in any hurry to get anywhere in the morning. And so she decided to let him sleep. She scrawled out a note and left it on her pillow.

Hey, reindeer herder, I had to head to Kittilä on business.
Thanks for everything ;-)
Have a good one,
H.

A moment later, Hildur was outside, scraping the windows of her rental car. It was so cold her eyeballs felt like ice cubes.

Once the interior of the car warmed up, Hildur took off her beanie and tossed it on the back seat. She gathered her long hair in a coil at her nape and tied off the bun with a rubber band. She flipped down the sun visor and opened the mirror. Her skin was nice and rosy. *Almost glowing*, she thought, smiling to herself.

If you don't look ugly you're not lifting hard enough, Hildur said to herself, flipping shut the mirror. She'd picked up the saying from her onetime weightlifting trainer, Kári. A former soccer player and current powerlifting coach, forty-something Kári felt you were supposed to grimace while you were lifting. Your facial muscles were meant to tense when you exerted effort. It gave an extra boost to your performance.

Hildur tapped at her phone and pressed it to her ear. She was trying the same number for probably the fifteenth time, and so Sirkku Sainio's raspy greeting caught her off guard:

'What the hell is it now?'

Hildur had finally reached the lead investigator at the Kittilä police station. Detective Sergeant Sirkku Sainio hadn't proved a particularly approachable individual. After numerous unanswered calls, voicemails and callback requests, the person in charge of investigating Filip's and Lena's murders had finally answered. Hildur introduced herself in two sentences and asked for fifteen minutes of Sirkku's time.

The detective sergeant loudly slurped some beverage and blurted that no one, not even her lawfully wedded husband, addressed her by her first name. She went by Sainio.

'And I haven't had an extra fifteen minutes since 1975, when my first child was born.'

Sainio then said if Hildur had an urgent need to meet, she could find her at Oula's Gym before lunch. 'Say ten o'clock. Bench presses. I need a spotter. Come if you're not a wuss.'

Sainio's breezy English underscored her curt style. Hildur accepted the invitation and hung up.

She considered the contents of her gym bag, which happened to be in the back seat of her rental. Shorts, T-shirt, wool-blend socks, athletic top, towel, trainers . . . She had everything she needed. A workout would do her good, but the thought of meeting the raspy-voiced Sainio was even more of a motivation than the anticipation of a hard sweat.

Jakob's police academy buddy, Simo Saari, whom Hildur had met upon her arrival in Lapland, had confirmed what Jakob had come to understand during questioning: Sainio saw the double homicide as a cut-and-dried case. And once Sainio had decided to look in a certain direction, turning her head wasn't easy. She never discussed her casework with anyone. Even experienced crime reporters avoided approaching Sainio, because she never commented on ongoing investigations. Apparently, she frightened rookie journalists into silence by being especially rude to them.

A good hour and a service station stop later, Hildur was warming up with a jump rope at Oula's Gym: a hundred single jumps and fifty double jumps. Perfect control of your core was a necessity when the rope travelled under your feet twice during a single jump. After finishing three sets, the blood was moving faster through Hildur's veins and her skin was beaded with sweat. She followed with twenty standing pushups to warm up her chest and shoulder muscles. A quick stretch, and then over to the bench. Hildur had just adjusted the height of the barbell when a woman with a grey bob and a vigorous gait walked toward her, arm extended.

'Sainio.'

Hildur took the hand that was offered, introduced herself, and answered the firm shake. Without further ado, the two women began to work out. They both warmed up with three sets of lightweight presses. First twenty reps with the twenty-kilogram bar, no weights. Hildur added a ten-kilogram weight to either end of the bar. For the next set, fifty kilograms and the reps dropped to ten. When Sainio finished, Hildur pointed at the twenty-kilogram weights:

'More?'

'Yes.'

When the bar's total weight had risen to eighty kilograms, Hildur and Sainio started spotting each other. Hildur laid on the bench and assumed a grip slightly wider than her shoulders. Sainio stood behind her, ready to help if Hildur's strength ebbed.

Hildur planted the soles of her feet on the floor and tensed her shoulder blades for proper support. Then she drew her lungs full of air and pushed the bar till her arms were straight. She let it slowly drop. When the bar touched her chest, Hildur punched it back up. By the fourth rep, the bar wasn't rising very fast. Sainio kept her hands under the bar so she could grab it if Hildur's strength gave out mid-movement. Hildur pinched her eyes shut and focused every ounce of strength on the press. After her arms finally straightened, she let the bar clatter down to the rack. She immediately sat up to ease the pressure that had built up in her head.

'You're not completely useless; I'll give you that,' Sainio said. She reached over to the weight rack for two weights the size of a slice of bread and added a kilogram to either end of the bar.

Hildur found Sainio's attitude amusing but kept it to herself. Sainio seemed to enjoy showing off how strong she was, so why not let her have her fun? Hildur estimated Sainio was approaching retirement age. It was all the same to Hildur how much weight was on the bar; the main thing was it was heavy enough that lifting wasn't easy.

Sainio pulled her bobbed hair out of her face with a thin sweatband and rubbed magnesium into her hands to get a good grip. With Hildur spotting, she did four reps with the eighty-two-kilogram bar. Her face didn't so much as quiver.

A good half hour later, Hildur and Sainio sat in the stretching area, rolling out their upper body muscles.

'As a police officer, I'm sure you understand you're a complete outsider and I shouldn't say a single word to you about the investigation.'

Hildur conceded this. She shifted the roller under her arm to massage the area between her ribs and armpit. Working the area hurt like hell, in other words was incredibly necessary.

'Jakob is my friend. We've worked together for two years. I can't believe he's guilty of two homicides. I assume you have other lines of investigation too?'

'Guess how many times I've heard that. "I never would have thought . . ."' Sainio chuckled, then launched into an example of a surprising case from the year before.

A woman had stabbed her husband to death at the dinner table. Evidently, none of those who knew her well could imagine her rising up against her husband and killing him while they were slurping down beef soup.

'The guy had been beating her for years, and then she just snapped in the middle of dinner.'

The family's fourteen children had been sitting at the table. The two who'd reached legal adulthood had testified in court as to their mother's guilt. Her fingerprints had been found on the knife, and her husband's blood had been found on her clothes.

'It was an unusually clear-cut case, but even so a lot of people were convinced to the end that the killer had been an outsider.'

Hildur shifted to a sitting position and started stretching her hamstrings. 'Sure, but this is a little different. Unless I've completely misunderstood, there was no eyewitness to the crime.'

'Different and different,' Sainio said, then noted there was a stack of evidence against 'the southerner' – a term indicating Jakob wasn't a local. 'On top of everything else, he won't answer most of my questions during interrogation!' Sainio snorted, adding she'd now told Hildur too much.

'Is there anything I could do to help?' Hildur asked. 'In an unofficial capacity, of course. I know I don't have any authority here.'

Sainio grunted and rose from her roller to sit cross-legged: 'Sure. Slip the perp's name and the evidence into an envelope with my name on it and deliver the envelope to me at the Kittilä police station.'

Although Hildur didn't respond to the jibe, she silently decided Sainio would be getting a white envelope delivered directly to the Kittilä police station.

Sainio turned her attention to her triceps and looked Hildur dead in the eye: 'I agreed to meet with you because I want to ask about Jakob. It sounds like you know him well.'

Hildur nodded but didn't speak. She continued stretching her upper body as she listened to Sainio open up. A double murder was a serious crime. There were currently no other suspects. According to Sainio, she had a big stack of open cases on her desk, and she wasn't about to start turning over stones for fun.

'Tell me about Jakob. What kind of guy is he, in your mind? Knits like a lunatic and doesn't talk much. Have you ever seen him lose his temper?'

Hildur shook her head. It was easy for her to express how peaceful Jakob was, because she'd never seen him enraged. Not once. 'He's reliable and calm. Doesn't lose his temper, even in difficult situations. And he doesn't care about official working hours if he wants to get to the bottom of something.'

Hildur paused. She was wondering if she ought to tell Sainio about the sisters she'd lost as a child. 'My sisters disappeared in the 1990s, but Jakob was the one who knew to look at my family for the answers. It's largely thanks to him we solved the mystery, or at least part of it.'

A curious look sparked in Sainio's eyes. She pushed herself into a sitting position and looked down at her palms. She began picking at the skin around her fingernails. 'That fits.'

Hildur crossed her legs beneath her and straightened her back. 'Fits what?'

Sainio exhaled through her tightly pinched lips. 'You're not from around here, but you're really damn nosy. Have you heard what happened at the lake in Äkäslompolo when Jakob was a child?'

Hildur shook her head. She had no idea what Sainio was talking about.

'You ought to know.' And with that, Sainio launched into the story. Not all locals were familiar with it, because many had moved to the area since. But those who worked in law enforcement still remembered the incident, as the case remained unsolved.

'A grade-school boy drowned. He'd come down to the local lake with two older boys. The three of them had been seen riding their bikes along the village road an hour before the accident.'

The way Sainio emphasised the word 'accident' sent shivers running up Hildur's spine. Sainio said that to this day, no one knew how the youngest boy had ended up under the surface, because the other two boys had never revealed anything.

Their reticence had been initially suspected as resulting from shock.

'I talked to them in the presence of a social worker. It was one of my first cases as a police officer. The boys didn't say anything, and I couldn't pressure them, because they were children. But as I studied them, I got the sense they'd agreed beforehand not to talk.'

Sainio rubbed her wrists and trained her small, almond-shaped eyes on Hildur. If a person clammed up when faced with a difficult topic, in Sainio's world that meant they had something to hide.

'And one of them refused to talk about it again today.'

Hildur felt the floor beneath her fall away.

'I'm sure you understand why Jakob's silence doesn't look very good from our perspective,' Sainio said.

Things, faces and events flashed past Hildur's eyes in a single, fast-moving filmstrip. She tried to take it all in. Then she opened her eyes and looked at Sainio, who was standing in front of her, hands on her hips.

'You said there were two older boys at the lake.'

Sainio nodded. 'Jakob and his good friend Anton. The child who drowned was Anton's younger cousin Mikael.'

Hildur maintained a neutral expression, but her insides were crackling. Could it be a coincidence? *Anton.* Hildur couldn't even follow the thought to its conclusion. Her post-workout relaxation had evaporated.

Sainio pulled off the sweatband and let her straight, severe bob fall in her face. She placed her hands on her hips and raised her chin as if to punctuate her defiant stance:

'I intend to apply to the district court in Rovaniemi for permission to detain Jakob. He can sit in a cell for the remainder of the preliminary investigation. Those damned boys weren't caught for their mischief when they were kids, but I'm nailing one of them now. I'm going to do everything in my power to ensure he doesn't get off scot-free this time. What happened back then can't be allowed to happen again.'

Chapter 55

Reykjavík, December 2021

Beta and Tumi were eating kebabs in her office, considering their next steps. Tumi was going to go through all capped-bed grey Mitsubishi L200 pickups registered in Iceland. Hlín had seen one near the pasture at Reykjanes.

As soon as they'd got back in the car, Beta had looked up the information connected to Haarde's phone number. No dice; the mysterious dishwasher had a prepaid subscription. When Beta had tried to call, the phone had been off. None of these things had surprised her. Haarde requested her pay for legitimate work under the table and was involved in activities suspected to be criminal in nature. The temp company's CEO had said Haarde spoke fluent Icelandic, so the chances of her being an undocumented immigrant were slim.

Beta had also done some more digging into the German company Hlín had mentioned. It was Pferd Technologie, 'Horse Technology'. Beta had assigned the task of researching the company to a subordinate, and he'd promised to put something together for her at the first opportunity. It was possible there was something in the company's background that would aid them in their investigation.

During the drive, Beta had also called the officers who'd been assigned to check on the homes of the animal welfare-linked individuals who'd attended the dinner. None of the patrols had reported suspicious characters or surveillance vehicles near any of the homes or anything else out of the ordinary. That felt odd, because there were more Yule Lads to go. If the assailant had left the Christmas poem unfinished, why had they done so? Had something happened to the perp?

'Listen, Tumi,' Beta said, after forking the last of her kebab into her mouth. 'Something about the crimes' MOs is bothering me.'

Tumi wiped the kebab sauce from the corners of his mouth, crumpled up his napkin, and dropped it in his Styrofoam to-go box.

'I get the motive, because the animal welfare activists are trying to expose the criminal's mares' blood business.' Beta grabbed the bottle of disinfectant from the windowsill and cleaned her hands with the mint-scented solution. 'But MOs cribbed from old Yule Lad stories aren't a good fit for the motive. Some fictional serial killer might do something like that. But if the goal is securing financial interests . . . Why all the fooling around with hot dogs and meat hooks?'

Tumi listened attentively and nodded in agreement with Beta's conclusions. He straightened his long legs under the coffee table, then interlaced his fingers behind his head and stretched.

'I agree; it's weird.' He added he hoped he'd get a chance to ask the suspect these very questions as soon as possible.

Beta dropped her disposable gloves in the wastebasket and walked over to her desk. She raised it to standing height and turned on her computer. The most recent email in her inbox was exactly what she'd expected, a report on the German company. Beta clicked on the message and downloaded the attachment.

As a legal entity, Pferd Technologie was a general partnership, a *Gesellschaft bürgerlichen Rechts*, or *GbR*. She skipped over the next rows, because she was familiar with Germany's various types of legal entities. Beta used to comb through German companies as a financial crimes investigator, so she knew a general partnership was a tricky corporate form. No capital was required to set one up; a simple written agreement sufficed. It could also be hard uncovering much information on a general partnership. At least two parties were required for their establishment, but those parties could be anyone at all: private individuals, cooperatives, associations, or even foreign entities. It was often difficult to determine the parties pulling the strings, and that was the case in this instance as well. Beta's subordinate had discovered Pferd Technologie was owned by two companies owned by other companies and so on and so forth.

Damn. Beta smacked the stack of folders on her desk. There wasn't enough time to sift through all the information on Pferd Technologie, even if every financial crime investigator in Iceland were assigned to the case.

Beta returned her attention to the report. She shifted her weight to the other foot as she browsed through the document. *Nice work*, she thought to herself. Economist Mats Ákason, who'd joined her unit six months before, had proved worth his weight in gold when it came to tracing corporate ownership and investigating streams of money. Mats had found a blurb about the company on the website of *Bændablaðið*, an Icelandic newspaper popular in rural areas.

'Hey, listen to this,' Beta called out to Tumi, then began reading the story cited in Mats's report. It was several years old.

'*A campground that has fallen on hard times finally has new owners. Scout troops from the Reykjavík area built the campground on the shores of Hvalfjörður in the 1980s. The site was meant to serve all Icelandic scouts . . .*' Beta skipped a section of text, '*. . . extensive moisture damage . . . the scout troops didn't have the funds to make the necessary repairs . . . The campground has been for sale for several years.*'

Beta read faster and reached the most significant passage, which Mats had underlined.

'*According to the Icelandic Boy and Girl Scout Association, the buyer is a German tour company that intends to renovate the site and turn it into a rural hotel for package tourists. Tour companies have been acquiring real estate at an accelerating pace to ensure sufficient lodging capacity for their customers. Representatives of the purchasing party had no comment on the deal. According to the deed of sale, the buyer is a German company, Pferd Technologie.*'

Tumi had walked over next to Beta and was reading the screen over her shoulder. 'Well, goddamn. Where is this campground?'

Beta's fingers danced across the keyboard. Ákason had included the address in the report, and Beta entered it into the map software. The map opened full-screen, and Beta pointed her pen at the fjord's southern shore. 'There, about ten kilometres toward the base of the fjord from the new junction.'

She glanced at Tumi.

'We need backup,' Tumi said, rubbing his forehead. 'We don't know what we'll find waiting for us there. We can't go out there alone.'

Beta was on the verge of calling her superior when there was a knock at the door. Svana, a law student in her early twenties who worked part time as an assistant in their unit, opened the door and remained at the threshold. She begged pardon for the interruption.

'Reception sent over a visitor. She'd come him asking for Hildur or Jakob. They told her to come here.'

Beta frowned. Someone at reception must have remembered she used to be Hildur and Jakob's boss.

'She seems harmless. Some horse girl, at least judging by the smell,' Svana whispered, waving a well-groomed hand under her nose. Her long nails had been painted with a pearly polish.

Beta thanked Svana and asked her to show the visitor in. Svana turned to say something to the person standing behind her and opened the door wider.

A young woman in riding trousers and a worn green oilcloth coat tentatively stepped into Beta's office. Beta noticed the horsey smell too. The young woman's leather ankle boots were popular with equestrians.

The visitor started speaking quickly: 'I work at Sel farm up north. I came to the city today to run some errands and decided to stop by while I was in town, because I remembered something. I tried to call Hildur and Jakob, but no one picked up at the numbers they gave me. I figured since there are so few police officers here in Iceland maybe someone here would know who I should talk to.'

Beta introduced herself and Tumi. She said the two of them were investigating Luka's case with Hildur and Jakob. Then she shook hands with the young woman. 'And your name is . . .?'

The young woman's hand felt cold. She blushed and picked at the holes in the sleeve of her coat.

'Oh, I'm sorry. I'm Lisa Weber. I work at the farm where Luka used to work. The owners are still in Spain on their winter vacation. Hildur and Jakob came by to talk to me. After they left, I remembered something that's been bothering me. Maybe it doesn't matter, but I remembered how Hildur said even tiny details can sometimes be really important. So that's why I thought maybe it's better to tell someone.'

She spoke so fast that Beta had a hard time keeping up with her English.

'Shall we sit down? It's nicer to talk without rushing,' Beta said, indicating the sofa set. Tumi gathered up the investigative documents from the table and closed his laptop.

Lisa sat near the edge of the sofa cushion and fiddled with her hair, which was damp from the wet, windy winter weather. She told Beta and Tumi the same things she'd told Hildur and Jakob before.

'Luka and I counted the horses every night. One night one of them was missing.'

Lisa said Luka had called the farm's owners. They'd been on vacation in Italy just then. Apparently, they hadn't been at all concerned. They were sure their staff had counted incorrectly, because the fence was undamaged. There was no way a horse could just disappear from the pasture.

'They told us to stop worrying over nothing,' Weber said. 'They travel a lot. Luka and I basically ran the place in the winter.'

'Did the missing horse ever turn up?'

Lisa nodded. 'A few evenings later, the horse was back in the pasture. The weird thing was this happened a few times, and it was a different horse every time. First the horse disappeared, and within three weeks it was in the pasture again.'

Lisa explained how a few days before he left for his trip abroad, Luka had brought one of the horses inside. 'I wasn't sure why, but Luka seemed to know what he was doing. He just said it was for the best and I should keep an eye on the horse to make sure it wasn't taken anywhere.'

'Where would it have been taken?' Beta asked.

Lisa spread her arms. 'I have no idea. I wondered the same thing, but that's all Luka said.'

Beta remembered blood was collected exclusively from gestating mares. 'The horses that went missing were all pregnant mares, right?'

Lisa nodded and looked at Beta in bewilderment. 'How did you know?'

Beta gave a noncommittal answer. She had no intention of sharing the details of an ongoing investigation.

'I didn't do anything wrong by keeping that horse inside, did I?' Lisa's voice rose toward the end of her sentence. She sounded as if she were about to burst into tears.

'You haven't done anything wrong; just the opposite. It's a good thing you came to talk to us,' Tumi said slowly. He glanced at Beta. 'Is there anything else about those incidents you described? Anything you remember? Did Luka say anything that stuck out in your mind, for instance?'

Lisa reached into the pocket of the coat she'd folded and laid next to her, took out a tissue, and dabbed the corners of her eyes. She stared at the table and didn't immediately reply. Then she looked at Tumi.

'The first time we realised one of the horses was missing, the farrier came to the farm. There was something really odd about it. The farrier had a gear bag but not one of those aprons farriers wear,' Lisa said, drawing a rectangular figure on her thighs.

Beta knew the apron served as safety equipment. Almost all farriers wore them, because the apron protected the legs from sharp tools and nail punctures.

'And the farrier didn't seem to know anything about shoeing horses. I asked if the horses would be getting calks, too, because it was winter, but the farrier didn't even seem to understand what I was asking. They just muttered something and went outside to the horses.'

Lisa said that wasn't the only time the farrier had come by the farm. The last time was a few days after Luka brought the horse inside.

'When the farrier saw the horse in the stall and me sweeping the floor, they whirled around, hurried back to the truck, and drove off. It was like something freaked them out.'

Beta noticed Tumi tapping the floor with his foot.

'What did the farrier look like?' Tumi asked.

'I didn't get a good look. She always maintained a little distance. At the time I thought she was really paranoid about Covid.'

'Did you say "she"?' Tumi asked.

'Yes,' Lisa said, then turned to Beta. 'A little younger than you, I think. The skin on half of her face looked weird. I think it was burned. I've seen it back home before on people who work at the industrial laundry.'

Lisa had asked the farm's owners about the farrier, but according to them there was nothing strange about the incident. Apparently, there were several farriers in the area, and they made the rounds of the local farms according to their own schedules.

'There's one more thing I remember,' Lisa said, pulling herself up to her full height. 'The farrier had a grey pickup. One of those with a covered bed.'

Chapter 56

Äkäslompolo, December 2021

Being surrounded by the snow-blanketed forest was like being enveloped in cotton.

Hildur and Jakob had set out skiing together, and the empty ski track was a good place to chat. Hildur had a lot of questions for Jakob. She decided on a cautious approach.

'How did the interrogations go yesterday?' she asked, then leaned forward and picked up the pace.

'They kept on asking the same things over and over. Why did I do it, where did I get the gun, and so on,' Jakob answered feebly, using the back of his hand to wipe away a bead of frozen sweat from the side of his nose.

'I met with Sainio this morning,' Hildur said.

Jakob looked at her in surprise. 'I didn't think she ever discussed ongoing investigations.'

'She wanted to ask me about you.'

Out of her peripheral vision, Hildur saw Jakob's face tighten. She had to find out more. 'Why didn't you tell me this wasn't the first time you'd had dealings with her?'

The question elicited a gasp from Jakob.

'She told me about the lake, Anton, and Anton's cousin.'

Hildur was irritated. She'd travelled all the way to a foreign country to help a friend, only to find out that friend was keeping things from her.

Jakob still didn't answer. Just kept skiing. They hadn't come across anyone headed in the opposite direction. Apparently, Christmas vacation hadn't started yet. No doubt the small town in the fells would undergo an utter transformation when vacationers from the south swarmed to Lapland to enjoy some cross-country or downhill skiing. Or so the server in the train's restaurant car had told Hildur.

Hildur stopped. She stuck her pole out in front of Jakob so he'd be forced to stop, too, then turned to him and shouted: 'What the hell, Jakob? Either you tell me everything now or keep it to yourself forever. If you keep it to yourself, I'll take the next flight home. Think carefully about which you want!'

Hildur held Jakob's gaze for a couple more seconds, then kicked off and skied ahead as fast as her skis would carry her. She emerged from the trees a moment later and saw a descent up ahead. It was a steep hill. Hildur planted her poles and pushed off, dropped into a deep squat, and shifted the weight off the ball of her foot, which made her go even faster. She picked up speed, the whine of her skis filled her ears. The air whooshed in her ears, and the cold froze the tears on her cheeks into icy droplets.

Her momentum carried her all the way to the hut where they'd planned on taking a break. The log cabin looked inviting and warm against the frigid landscape. Smoke rose vertically from the chimney.

Hildur took off her skis and leaned them and her poles against the ski rack. Jakob came up behind her and did the same.

'I'm sorry.' Jakob didn't immediately continue, but his body language spoke of surrender. He stroked his skis and looked at Hildur. 'Anton and I had a deal that we'd never talk about that day at the lake. I can't break that promise. But believe me, Hildur, we didn't do it on purpose. We tried to find him—'

Jakob swallowed down the rest of the sentence. He couldn't continue.

'At the time I didn't understand . . . what could happen. We were playing and things got out of hand. I'll tell you the whole story someday. But I can't yet. Believe me.'

Hildur saw the panic and angst on Jakob's face. He looked lost and incredibly sad. Something about the emotion felt profoundly familiar. She knew from experience that she had a hard time forming attachments with anyone who hadn't known grief.

Things were quiet at the cabin too. Before they went in, Hildur stopped at the wooden sign outside. It advertised a reindeer soup lunch that included bread, juice and coffee.

Hildur felt her stomach growl. Lunch didn't sound bad, even though it was only eleven o'clock. *If I get hungry later, I can always eat again*, she decided, as she and Jakob entered the dim cabin. The door squeaked as it opened. A white dog ran over to them and sniffed their legs, begging to be scratched. They petted it for a moment, and then a woman wiping down the long table whistled for the dog to return to her. A big hearth stood in the middle of the room, with drying hooks and racks set up around it. They hung up their sweat-dampened mittens and hats. The fire was crackling. The aromas of coffee and baking filled the air.

Hildur and Jakob took their lunch trays to a table behind the hearth. Jakob spooned some of the steaming soup and blew on it to cool it before putting it in his mouth.

Looks like we're not going to be talking about the lake again today, Hildur thought to herself. 'How far did we ski?' she asked.

Jakob glanced at his watch: 'From the hotel car park where we started, a little over an hour. It'll only take forty-five minutes to get back. It's mostly downhill.'

The woman who ran the café added wood to the fire. The logs caught light within seconds and blazed up. Hildur felt herself getting stuck on something Jakob had just said. She stared at the burning wood and swirled her spoon around her soup. The thought was taking shape in her mind. Suddenly, she caught hold of it: *time*.

'The woman at the car park. She said she saw you at a quarter to seven, then drove to the supermarket to pick up a package. The postal desk there closes at seven. She said she had to hurry. You know the area better; you tell me. How long does it take to drive from the car park to the store?'

Jakob considered. 'In winter conditions, maybe five minutes.'

Hildur took a bite of buttered rye bread. She didn't wait until her mouth was empty to continue: 'So not fifteen minutes?'

'On a moped maybe, but not in a car.'

Hildur thought. If it was no more than a five-minute trip, why on earth had Sari spoken about a fifteen-minute drive? Jakob had been at the car park at around a quarter to seven. He remembered it that way too. He'd glanced at his watch as he walked from the café to the car park.

Something wasn't adding up. What would Sari get out of claiming to have been driving to the supermarket when, based on timing, she could have still been at the car park? Hildur would have to check what time the package was picked up, and she meant to do that next.

'Listen, there was something I couldn't stop thinking about after the interrogation yesterday,' Jakob said. 'How did you know to talk to that eyewitness?'

'Your old classmate from the police academy wanted to help. He gave me her contact information.'

Jakob frowned. The furrows on his face aged him years. 'Old classmate? What was his name?'

'Simo Saari. From the police station at Kolari. I went straight from the train to meet him.'

'I don't get it,' Jakob said.

Hildur retrieved her hat and gloves from where they'd been drying in front of the fire. She looked quizzically at Jakob as she handed him his.

'I've never even heard of the guy.'

Chapter 57

Hildur had retraced the drive Sari said she'd made the night of the shooting, starting from the car park and ending at the supermarket, and even though she drove under the speed limit the whole way, it only took five minutes. At the post office service desk, Hildur had pretended to be a friend of Sari's from her exchange-student days. She'd said she'd sent her friend a package.

'I'm on my way to visit her now. I was just curious if she'd already come in to pick it up.'

The young woman behind the counter reached for a blue folder next to the register and opened it. 'Let me check.'

She ran her finger down the rows looking for the right entry. She must have been new. She seemed a little unsure of herself and tried to make up for it with overly attentive service. 'I need to know what delivery company you used. Which one was it?'

Hildur strained her memory. Sari had mentioned DHL.

'DHL.'

'Then it's not here. We only handle packages for the postal service, bus deliveries, Postnord and Schenker. A lot of people have asked about DHL, but at least at the moment it's not a service we offer.'

Hildur thanked the smiling young woman for the information. She hurried to her car and drove straight to Sari's home.

Snow began falling steadily in small, tight flakes. The motion of the car transformed them into fine white lines. Hildur's high beams were the only source of light in the dark landscape. She was used to driving in winter conditions, even challenging ones, but the unfamiliar terrain and the dense snowpack on the road made her cautious.

She had to know why Sari had lied.

When Hildur pulled into Sari's unlit drive, she saw lights on inside. Sari was home. Hildur had noticed people in Finland didn't leave the lights on when they weren't. Apparently, electricity was expensive.

When Sari came to the door, it was plain from the look on her face that Hildur wasn't a welcome visitor. The last time, Hildur hadn't paid much attention to the entryway décor, but now she let her gaze circle the room. An orange plastic lamp hung from the ceiling. The weak light given off by its incandescent bulb was absorbed by the dark wooden walls. A woman's winter coat hung from the coat rack, along with dog leashes and dog show rosettes in various colours. Dozens of photographs hung on the walls, and when Hildur took a closer look, she saw a dog appeared in every one. A dog on the beach in summer, a dog in the snow outside a house, a dog on an obstacle course, a dog eating. In one of the photos, a dog with a colourful ball in its mouth was looking at the photographer, challenging them to play. A blue sign in the background said JYVÄSKYLÄ.

'Did you live there?' Hildur asked, pointing at the photo.

'For a few years,' Sari said at little more than a whisper. 'Then I moved to Helsinki and eventually back here, where I grew up.'

A local newspaper was open on the low table in the entryway. Hildur couldn't read the text, of course, but she could see the story was about a hotel opening and mentioned the hotel's manager, Lena.

'What does the headline say?' Hildur asked.

Sari glanced indifferently at the newspaper: '*My husband and son are looking forward to moving here*.'

Hildur took the paper and eyed the photos. They were of a happy-looking couple leaning against each other with fells in the background. Hildur folded up the newspaper and set it back down on the table. The address printed on the back of the paper caught her attention.

'So it's not your subscription?' Hildur asked, trying to sound casual. Sari lived in Kittilä. According to the address label, the paper was delivered to Kolari. Hildur made a note of the name on the sticker.

'My friend lent it to me. He gets the paper at work.'

Hildur was sure Sari wouldn't react well to pressure. She decided to proceed gently.

'The package you picked up from the store at 7 p.m. on the night of the murder: it was sent by courier? The supermarket doesn't handle DHL deliveries,' Hildur said calmly. She remained standing next to the door to indicate she didn't mean to stay long. 'And it doesn't take fifteen minutes to drive from the café to the supermarket,' she added softly.

Sari pulled away from Hildur and backed up a few steps. When she ran into the wall, she stopped and leaned against it. She started tugging at the hem of her sweater and glanced at her dog again. But she didn't say anything, so Hildur continued.

'I just drove that trip. It took six minutes, and I was driving an unfamiliar route cautiously. I think you'd make it in less time.'

Sari began sliding down the wall. It looked like she was expecting the wall behind her to open and swallow her up. When she reached a squat, she wrapped one arm around her dog and started petting it. She whispered something in the dog's ear; Hildur couldn't hear what.

'Why didn't you tell the truth?'

Sari glanced at Hildur from behind her dog. The look in her eyes sent a shiver up Hildur's spine.

Hildur couldn't help that she had a hard time looking Sari in the face. The last time they'd met, they'd sat at the kitchen table eating freshly baked rolls. Sari had consistently avoided her gaze then. Now Hildur got the sense she was seeing two different people at once. Although it was dim in the entryway, she could clearly make out the jitter in Sari's eyes.

'Because what I saw was the truth.'

Hildur pounced: 'And what did you see?'

Sari tightened her grip on the dog. Hildur knew she couldn't force the other woman to talk. She couldn't take her in for questioning. There was nothing she could do. She shrugged. She wrote her phone number on a receipt she found in her pocket and set it on a stool in the entryway. Then she encouraged Sari to call if she wanted to talk more later.

Hildur opened the door, and just as she was stepping into the icy air, she heard a low roar behind her. She stopped and turned her head.

Sari was still squatting against the wall, dog at her side. 'Stay away from that man. Break off your engagement. Leave him. He'll make your life a misery. The man in the car park was Jakob, and he could have easily shot those two people. He's lied before, many times.'

'Lied to whom?'

'To me! We were together for almost twenty years, and the way he left me was incredibly cruel.'

Sari's shell was cracking. Hildur was sure Sari was ready to talk if Hildur offered a little encouragement. And so she adopted an empathetic expression and said she'd be happy to listen if Sari wanted to tell her what happened.

'Jakob came to Helsinki on a business trip. We fell in love again. He promised me the world, but when he got back to Norway, he abruptly cut off contact. Deleted his social media, changed his phone number, didn't answer my emails. He vanished from my life without a trace.'

Sari's voice had hardened. By the last sentence, she was practically shouting. Then she lowered her gaze and petted her dog in long, slow strokes, as if seeking to be soothed by the animal.

'I found out he had a family in Norway and had just been using me.' Sari explained that a year or two after Jakob disappeared, she'd caught a glimpse of him between the shelves at the supermarket in Äkäslompolo. He'd been with a woman and a small child.

'There was his new woman, putting yoghurt in the shopping cart. Jakob was holding the boy. He looked just like his father.' Sari pressed her elbows together and made a swaying motion with her arms.

When she saw Jakob, she'd had a panic attack. She'd run out of the store and tripped when her trainers came untied. 'I fell outside the supermarket and momentarily lost consciousness. Luckily, an old friend was just loading his shopping into his car. He helped me to my feet and took me home. That was the worst drive of my life.'

Sari stared defiantly at Hildur.

'Up until then, I'd thought what Jakob did as a boy was the only bad thing he'd ever done. But I was wrong. Not only is he cruel, he's also a damned coward. That child was a toddler.

A two-year-old! Jakob had had a new family for at least three years and hadn't said a word to me about it. He just disappeared and deserted me.'

An icy, metallic tone had entered Sari's voice. The words clanked as she uttered them. Hildur was horrified. The voice was one of cold hatred: 'Jakob hated Lena as much as I hate Jakob. Jakob was in the car park the night of the murder, and I know it. That's what I saw.'

Chapter 58

Hvalfjörður, December 2021

Tumi and Beta had been sitting in the cold car for almost two hours now. They'd parked behind the sole building in habitable condition at the Hvalfjörður campground to make sure they wouldn't be seen from the road. Anyone who showed up would drive onto the property before they spotted Beta and Tumi. The road leading down to the campground was too narrow for a quick U-turn and a getaway.

Southern Iceland had been drenched with rain and sleet for the past few days, but there had been no sign of snow. Beta tried to dig back to memories of white Christmases in Reykjavík, but no luck. The images of Reykjavík Christmases weren't of peaceful snowfall, but of darkness, rain and strong wind.

Only a few of the orangey outdoor lights were on. Almost half the property was hidden in darkness. Beta had decided to use the gloom to her advantage in the stakeout. Two police Škoda Octavias were parked behind her. Just to be safe, she and Tumi had asked for reinforcements.

A couple of ravens flapped back and forth across the property, but there were no other signs of life. Tumi was still reviewing the list of Icelanders who had a Mitsubishi L200 pickup registered under their name.

'How's it going?' Beta asked, plucking biscuit crumbs from the front of her coat.

'Really damn slow,' Tumi said without looking up from the laptop. 'Most of them are registered to companies.'

Beta sighed. The names of the companies' owners would have to be looked up in a different registry, and that would take time.

Beta had been in touch with the CEO of Women at Work and learned Haarde the dishwasher had headed to a short gig in Selfoss a little before noon. A local restaurant there had needed someone to step in for a busser who'd called in sick. Christmas lunches were an important source of income for Icelandic restaurants.

Tumi pushed back his seat and stretched his legs. The hours in the cramped car must have been pretty uncomfortable for such a tall guy.

'Hey, look,' Tumi said, nodding toward the road. A pair of headlights was approaching through the darkness. But their wait wasn't rewarded yet; the car drove past. The CEO of Women at Work had guessed Haarde would be back in Reykjavík around four. But Hellisheiði, the mountain road that ran between Reykjavík and the towns east of the highlands, had just been closed due to a local snowstorm. Traffic had been redirected to the narrow coastal road that circled the mountain but added over an hour to the trip.

Beta glanced at the car's digital clock. It showed four thirty.

A quarter of an hour later, Beta saw another pair of headlights approaching. The lights slowed. The vehicle was turning into the drive.

Beta nudged Tumi in the ribs. 'Now!'

A grey pickup glided slowly down the narrow road to the property and headed toward a storage building with big double doors. Beta and Tumi had checked to make sure the doors had to be manually unlocked with a key; the driver would have to get out of the car to open them.

'Come on, come on,' Beta said impatiently, patting the steering wheel with her mittened hands.

She knew the patrol officers had things under control. As soon as the driver stepped out of the car, she would be apprehended. Beta and Tumi would monitor things from a distance.

The seconds passed. After a brief lull, a freezing rain had begun to fall again. The sleet plopping against the windscreen hindered visibility, but Beta didn't want to start up the engine. The driver might hear and flee. It was unlikely she would get far; the pickup looked so old its fastest miles were long past. But a pursuit on a slushy road didn't sound appealing.

Beta took the binoculars and peered through the water sliding down the windscreen. The driver's door of the grey pickup opened, and a figure in a long coat sprang from the driver's seat to the pavement. A big hood had been drawn over the head, making it impossible to see the face from a distance. The truck's licence plate was clearly visible now, and Beta recited the number to Tumi.

The figure took a small object from its pocket. Beta interpreted it as a key. The lock was at eye level in the wall to the right of the door. The two patrol cars that had been waiting behind Beta started up their engines and sped over. They only had to cross a couple of hundred metres, but under the circumstances, even a few seconds could make a difference. The Škodas surrounded the pickup in such a way that for all practical purposes the driver was trapped.

'Bingo!' Tumi cried.

Beta kept her eyes on the figure who'd climbed from the pickup as she listened to Tumi.

'The vehicle is registered to Björk Holm!'

Beta shot Tumi a quick look. What was he talking about?

'Hildur's sister!'

Björk's name was a gut punch. Beta would have to process that later. Now she had to focus on the arrest. Beta started up the car and turned on her windscreen wipers.

Both police patrols stepped out of their cars. One pair held back as the other two calmly walked toward the driver and said something. Judging by the driver's body language, she was surprised.

The driver replied to the approaching officers, raised her hand to her mouth, and squatted, head hunched over her knees. The arrest took place quickly and calmly. As the police led the woman to the car, Beta caught a glimpse of her face and was startled by what she saw. The skin on one side was covered in rough scar tissue. It looked stiff. Her damaged face was impossible to read.

'That's not Björk,' Beta said. She lowered the binoculars and glanced over at Tumi.

'That means that she lent the car . . .' Tumi said, and gasped.

'Good God . . .' Beta began, lowering the binoculars to her lap. The answers had come in a flash: why there was no information on the mysterious dishwasher in the register, why Hildur wasn't allowed to ask any questions about Rósa, why Björk was the only one who knew anything about Rósa. Beta completed her colleague's sentence.

'. . . that's Hildur's other sister, Rósa Holm.'

Chapter 59

Äkäslompolo, December 2021

Hildur accelerated to eighty on the straight. She had to see Jakob as soon as possible. There wasn't any traffic, and there weren't any roadside cameras either, so she decided to step on it and overshoot the speed limit a little. Snow-covered forest rose in the distance; the bare crowns of fells gleamed beyond. A thick layer of snow lay over the trees, sheltering them from the wind. The soft cold kept things in place. The sky hanging above the scene glowed with a blue winter light.

The second visit with Sari Meri had provided a critical twist. Sari had behaved strangely. One minute she seemed rational, and the next her stories had reached toward the unknown. Hildur also had to speak with Sainio as soon as possible, but the lead investigator wasn't answering and hadn't returned Hildur's call despite Hildur's voicemail request to do so.

Sari's place was a long way from everything. The road ran through the wilderness. Trees upon trees, then they finally ended and the landscape opened up. Hildur found herself thinking of home. Vistas were always expansive there.

Hildur suddenly spotted movement at the forest's edge. She slowed and pulled over for a closer look. A few dozen reindeer were loosely clustered in the white terrain. They stared at her vehicle inquisitively. Their gaze was both mild and disinterested. They may not have been in control of their lives, but they still lived wild, in a natural state. Free and captive at the same time. The moment was somehow extraordinary.

The sound of her ring tone jerked Hildur back to the present moment. She glanced at the phone vibrating on the passenger seat. She was happy to see the name flashing on the screen.

'Hey, Beta! How are things?' Hildur hadn't thought about Beta and Tumi since morning. She'd planned on calling them after she'd spoken with Jakob.

Hildur didn't immediately hear anything at the other end. She repeated her question. When Beta finally answered, she didn't sound like herself.

'Where are you right now?'

Hildur said she was sitting in her rental car, looking at reindeer.

'Good. So you're not driving?'

What is she getting at? Hildur wondered. 'Judging by the sign, I'm at a bus stop.'

'There's something you need to know. I'll get straight to the point.'

Hildur sensed she was about to learn something unpleasant. She killed the engine and closed her eyes, tried to focus on her breathing. A slow, deep breath in, an even slower one out. She realised she was afraid.

'The temp who worked at the restaurant the night of the hotel dinner and the individual Hlín photographed in the pasture. It's the same person.'

'How did you get on their trail?' Hildur asked quickly. She didn't give Beta time to respond. The questions came rapid-fire, one after the other: 'Who is it? Did they act alone? Are any international organisations connected? Did the Viking Squad help with the arrest?'

The Viking Squad was the specially trained armed unit of the Icelandic police that handled dangerous arrests and situations where parties were suspected of being armed.

Beta cut off the flood of questions. 'Hildur, I need you to listen. You can't participate in the investigation any longer.'

Hildur felt a heavy lump form in her throat. She felt like she'd taken a bigger bite of an apple than intended and hadn't chewed it properly before swallowing.

'Damn it. I was really hoping to tell you this face to face,' Beta said. 'Try to stay strong.'

Hildur urged her to continue.

'Hildur, it's your sister Rósa. Rósa Holm. Everything points at her having been in Iceland for a long time.'

It took a moment for Hildur to process what Beta was saying. She had to get out in the fresh air, feel the wind against her body, the cold from head to toe. Otherwise, she'd black out. Hildur lifted her legs out of the car, actually used her hands to hoist them out of the vehicle and set them on the ground. Her right hand reached for the top of the open door to pull herself up and out. Phone still in her left, she leaned her full weight against the car.

Beta said something about a farrier, Germans and a campground. The details didn't fall into place; they ricocheted randomly inside her head.

Is this what it feels like to have your world lurch out of place?

'Can you repeat what you just said? I . . . I had to get out of the car.'

Beta said they'd found a campground that was presumed deserted at the shores of the Hvalfjörður. Connecting the dots led to their being prepared when 'Haarde', who lived at the campground, had arrived.

'The name Haarde is a fabrication, naturally,' Beta said.

Hildur drew a breath. She was trying to arrange the multitude of questions spinning through in her mind into some sort of logical order. 'How do you know it's Rósa?'

Beta sighed deeply. 'The pickup she drives is registered to Björk.'

Hildur felt a stabbing pain in her forehead. She had no idea Björk had two vehicles.

'The vehicle alone doesn't prove anything, of course.' Beta spoke slowly, as if to ensure Hildur had time to digest what she was hearing. 'I requested a photograph of her from the Faroes. The official photograph is old, but it's clearly her. Besides . . .'

Beta paused.

'It doesn't have anything to do with this, but you'd see it right away later. One side of her face is somehow scarred. But the other side looks exactly like you.'

Hildur held her phone to her ear. She felt the freezing air sting her face and slither under her shirt. She was so cold she was shivering but she couldn't get back in the car yet. She folded over, torso to thighs, to protect herself.

'I have to come back,' Hildur whispered into the phone.

Beta disagreed. There was no rush. 'We'll start questioning her tomorrow. I'm calling you because someone might leak the story to the media. I wanted you to hear everything from me first, unofficially.'

Hildur was at a loss. She thanked Beta for the call, hung up, and tossed the phone onto the sweater in the passenger seat.

She ought to be with her sisters now, but Jakob needed her help too. Where should she go from here? What should she do next? Which way should she turn? She wasn't sure.

Hildur stood next to her car and looked in the side mirror. She saw her reflection there, and the familiar sight alarmed her. Just now the way she looked didn't correspond to how she felt. Her breath passed through her like a gust blowing across a barren field. She was like a gutted fish. Empty on the inside. And alone.

She pondered. There wasn't anyone here who could decide for her. No one was going to be able to tell her anything. No one but her knew the answer.

She squatted and scooped up some snow, then used it to scrub her tear-swollen face. She dried her face on her sleeve, climbed into the car, and started it up. She would drive to her destination and do what she could. Sometimes you had to struggle to get to a place of peace. That was what she would do. Despite her uncertainty about the direction, she had to keep soldiering on.

Chapter 60

Jakob ended the call. He set the sweater aside and entered a few lines of text into the document. He'd been sitting at his computer for over an hour, connected to his phone via handsfree. He'd paid for a day at the coworking space above the supermarket. The coworking space had a soundproofed phone booth, which was a more convenient place to make private calls than a cold car or outside. His family's old cabin wasn't winterproofed, and he was tired of staring at the walls of his now-too-familiar hotel room. He needed peace and quiet, and he didn't have time to waste. Hildur had just called him and reported she was on her way to Äkäslompolo. She had to make the last flight out that evening, and they had a few things to clear up before that.

Jakob and Hildur had decided they'd come up with a list of Finnish parties who stood to benefit significantly from the mine. After reading dozens of pages of PDF files and making countless calls to municipal bureaucrats, he'd determined the land parcels corresponding to the mine and the owners of those parcels. Luckily, customer service at the land registry maintained by the National Land Survey of Finland would email you the names of parcel owners more or less immediately. Nothing about the list had struck Jakob as unusual. Most of the land was owned by the municipality. Other landowners included the parish, the local wilderness hiking association, and a nature conservation association from the neighbouring municipality. It had been over a decade since the conservation association's last entry in the registry maintained by the Patent and Registry Administration, and its social media channels hadn't been active for years. There were about a dozen private landowners.

Jakob had also gone through a list of local construction companies, but they were all small-time operators – so small they couldn't play a very significant role in the mine's massive construction projects. The big infrastructure and mine construction would be handled by companies from elsewhere.

Jakob reached for his needles and focused on his knitting. Another row or two and the sweater would be long enough. He pondered as the yarn slid through his fingers. Who but the landowners and construction companies would benefit from the mine's arrival in the municipality? Local entrepreneurs, moving companies . . . and property owners, of course!

He looked up the nearest chimney sweeping company and reached for his phone. The name of the company was Pulju Electricity and Chimney Sweeping, and it was located in the centre of Kolari.

Jakob could have put together a list of the owners of local homes and apartments the official way, but that would have taken too long. No one was more informed as to who owned properties than those who sold them services every year. Homes had to have their chimneys swept regularly, and all residential and commercial buildings required the services of electricians.

His call was answered after a few rings.

'Is this Pulju?' Jakob asked, before introducing himself.

Pulju curtly replied: 'Ya.' He added a few more words a moment later. 'I'm in a hell of a hurry. If you're selling something or want me to answer to some damn survey where I have to rate things on a scale from one to five, you might as well hang up.'

Jakob assured Pulju he wasn't selling anything. 'I'm calling because you know something that matters to me. This won't take long.'

Pulju switched back to his policy of the fewer words, the better. 'Aha.'

'You do chimney sweeping and electrical work in the area. Who owns the most real estate around here? I mean, aside from the municipality?'

There was a weary sigh at the other end of the line. 'Can't you get that information from the government registries?'

'Sure,' Jakob said. 'But that takes time, and I don't have any.'

For a moment it had sounded like Pulju was about to hang up. But apparently, he'd appreciated Jakob's directness, because he continued: 'There's a huge number of people who own one property, a home or cabin, and I don't remember their names.'

Jakob assured him that wasn't necessary. He was only interested in the biggest owners.

Jakob heard Pulju smack his lips. 'Only the biggest ones, huh? Polar Holiday Homes Holding owns almost a third of the newest cabins. It's a big company, registered in the Netherlands, if I remember right. By the way, they never pay their invoices on time, the bums. The parish owns real estate, too, and so do a few unions.'

Jakob silently crossed out the alternatives. Unions and parishes didn't own real estate for profit-making purposes. The Dutch holding company sounded too far away. They surely owned real estate around the world.

'Then there's that new company . . . It's just a couple of years old, as I recall. It bought a bunch of rowhouses and small apartment buildings in a short period. And land.'

This caught Jakob's interest. The plans for the mine had taken a big leap ahead last year, when Arctic Mines had assumed operational responsibility.

'It's called Handsome Homes. At least they pay their invoices on time. They also brag they've bought so much land more homes are going to be popping up.'

Pulju firmly added he absolutely had to get back to work. He still had the electrical panels of ten new cabins to inspect today.

Jakob thanked Pulju and hung up. He brought up the free database on company registered information and searched the database for Handsome Homes. When he saw the name of the chair of the board of directors in the search results, a string of curse words spilled from his lips. The almost-finished sweater fell to the floor as Jakob sprang to his feet and rushed out.

Chapter 61

Hildur felt like having a cold beer, but she was driving. She ordered a coffee and French fries and took the corner table that seemed the quietest, as far as possible from the hockey match being shown on the television. Jakob had looked into local land ownership and summarised the results for her over the phone. Everything had fallen into place. It looked like she'd be able to catch the evening flight to Helsinki and continue on to Iceland in the morning.

Hildur folded up the newspaper that was on the table, set it aside, and lowered her elbows to the tabletop. The first reaction had been disappointment. She'd considered herself a good judge of character. Was she losing her touch? She was used to seeing through people, irrespective of whether they were telling the truth. It wasn't simply an ability to read body language. For instance, everyone versed in body language knew a person often shifted their gaze to the left or blinked a lot when they were lying. Of course she paid attention to such things, too, but for her exposing a bullshitter was more a matter of instinct. She could sense if the person she was talking to wasn't on her side, was teetering somewhere between hiding something and lying outright. She'd imagined she'd could easily tell fibbers from truth tellers. But this time she'd been seriously mistaken. He'd just seemed so nice. Too nice. Paid for her food, paid for her drinks, demonstrated interest in what she said. Goddammit, she was pissed off.

The pub's front door opened, and Jakob stepped in. He raised a finger at the bartender and mimicked pouring a pint, then walked over to Hildur.

'How are you?' he asked, giving Hildur a manly pat on the back.

She'd already updated him on the latest news from Iceland.

'I'm keeping it together. But I don't want to talk about it right now.'

Jakob nodded and took a seat. Jakob was easy to get along with. When you came to an agreement, it held. She'd made a promise to not ask him any more questions about what had happened at the lake, and she'd kept it. In return, Jakob had promised to not ask about the latest twists in the criminal investigation in Iceland. They would talk it out when the time was right. Now they had more acute concerns to deal with.

'Quick briefing, then you'll bring it home, right?' Jakob said.

Hildur nodded. The server brought Jakob a pint of lager and placed a basket of fries and a bottle of ketchup in front of Hildur. Hildur took the bottle, squirted a stream of ketchup over the fries, and dug in.

'I printed out all the documents,' Jakob said, pulling a plastic folder from his bag.

Hildur didn't even try to read the Finnish-language papers. Browsing the passages Jakob had highlighted in fluorescent orange was all she needed. One detail jumped out at her, but she let Jakob talk first.

The company's primary business was real estate. Handsome Homes had purchased dozens of houses and apartments over the last two years as well as significant land holdings further from the skiing and tourism centres for dirt-cheap prices.

'It was a smart plan to try and get rich, but the risk of failure was just too high.'

Handsome Homes had bought the residential properties with borrowed money, apparently, in the hope that construction would begin on the mines. That, in turn, would lead to a cash-fuelled race for homes and land. The company could rent housing to the incoming construction workforce and the mine's future employees at a high price. Either that, or his plan had been to buy, hold and flip.

'If the prices of real estate and land had risen significantly, his profits from this many homes would have been in the millions of euros,' Jakob said. 'A lot of people in the neighbouring municipality made a lot of money back in the day through smart land deals, and he tried to repeat the performance here.'

Jakob took a sip of his beer and wiped his foam moustache on his sleeve. 'Now the company is having trouble keeping up with its mortgage payments. Costs have gone up, and interest rates are rising too. If the mine doesn't come, he's going to be really screwed. He might not be able to handle the interest payments on the loans.'

We're this close to solving this, Hildur thought to herself.

She closed the folder. She'd be delivering it soon.

But time was passing, and she had to get going. She fished the last of the French fries from the basket and shoved them in her mouth. Her coffee had gone cold long ago, but it still did the job as a chaser. Hildur had decided to grab the bull by the horns.

'Listen, Jakob. I went back and spoke to the eyewitness who'd seen you at the scene of the murders. She holds a grudge against you.'

Jakob's expression sharpened, and a question flashed across his face.

'You cheated on Lena with her, then dumped her in a really ugly way. I'm talking about Sari Meri.'

Jakob didn't immediately reply. He seemed to know what she was talking about, but the look on his face was one of genuine confusion. 'Sari Meri? I've never heard of her. My ex-girlfriend's name is Regina. Are you saying this woman, this Sari Meri, is behind all this?'

Jakob's shoulders slumped. He looked as if he'd just lost something. He shifted restlessly in his seat.

The two of them sat in silence. Hildur had decided to wait until Jakob spoke.

'Regina was my long-term girlfriend. She suffered from serious depression, and eventually it got to be too much for me. I couldn't get close to her anymore. I fell in love with Lena, but I couldn't tell Regina. And then Lena . . . She was so insanely jealous I couldn't tell her the truth about Regina. It was a terrible time. I've never had as much anxiety as I did then.'

Hildur raised her hand, cutting off his monologue. 'I'm not judging you. But that woman told me she's your former girlfriend and she hates you.'

The front door suddenly opened behind Jakob, interrupting their conversation. Hildur recognised the newcomer immediately. He walked over to their table and chose the seat at her side. The man and Jakob greeted each other warmly.

'This is my friend Anton.'

Anton extended a hand and introduced himself using his full name: 'Anton Aikio, reindeer herder.'

Hildur buttoned the top button of her coat collar and pulled on her wool beanie. Then she shook Anton's hand. 'Nice to meet you. Hildur Rúnarsdóttir. Detective from Ísafjörður. And I'm just heading back.'

Anton held on to her hand too long, but Jakob didn't seem to notice.

'Have we met before?' Anton asked, a big smile on his face. 'You look familiar.'

'It's possible,' Hildur answered drily, as she put two and two together.

She was annoyed Anton had played stupid that night at the pub. Of course he'd realised who she was, because Jakob would have told his best friend that his Icelandic coworker was coming to help him. Hildur decided to not give the matter any more weight. She had to get going if she wanted to make it to Kittilä in time for the Helsinki flight.

Anton laughed. It was happy laughter, and his eyes were laughing too. Eventually he let go of Hildur's hand and drew his chair closer to the table.

He directed his next words at Jakob. Apparently, he'd just popped in and would be continuing on his way soon. Jakob raised an eyebrow and reached for his pint.

'My cousin just called,' Anton said. 'She was saying all kinds of crazy things, that Jakob's finally going to get what he deserves and she and Mikael will get justice.'

Jakob's face went pale and his grip on the pint tightened. 'Wait. Regina's full name is Sari Regina Nieminen. She's been called Regina since she was little. I thought she lived in Helsinki—'

Anton cut him off. 'She took her grandmother's last name when she moved back a few years ago. At the time she said she wanted to start a new life. Bought a dog and got into agility competitions. Obstacle courses, stuff like that.'

Jakob lowered his pint to the table and directed his words primarily at himself: 'So your cousin's back in the picture.'

Chapter 62

A little over an hour later, Hildur pulled up outside the police station in Kittilä. She hurried in through the front doors of the white brick building. She had to be at the airport in an hour. The timing was tight, but she'd make it. Hildur strode down the corridor. The details Jakob and Anton had revealed had sharpened the image that had formed in her mind over the course of the day. Hildur felt agitated but energised. Too many things were floating around in her working memory, and the clock was ticking. Hildur tried to use a slow breathing technique to activate her parasympathetic nervous system, but it didn't take. Aunt Tinna had listened to an audiobook on the effects of an active vagus nerve on stress and mental state and had shared the technique with Hildur. Hildur had listened to Tinna's explanations out of courtesy, but the truth was the topic hadn't really spoken to her. It was hard to slow her breathing when she was stressed. The best stress management was completing tasks that needed completing.

Just then, she heard Sirkku Sainio's voice. The detective sergeant had spotted Hildur through her open office door. 'You again, Icelander.'

Sainio peered over her glasses at Hildur, who had stopped in the doorway. The detective sergeant was casually dressed in cargo pants and a red and yellow sweater.

Hildur said she wanted to talk, and Sainio didn't stop her. Hildur stepped into the office, which looked surprisingly like her own. The desk was overflowing with papers, folders and books. The heaps of documents continued on the floor.

Without being invited to, Hildur sat in the only free chair in the room. She leaned forward and looked at Sainio. 'I know this isn't my investigation. But I have information it would be good for you to know.'

Sainio took off her glasses, opened the glasses case on the desk, took out a cloth, and began carefully wiping her lenses. The whole time, she stared at Hildur like a teacher disciplining a disruptive student. 'You're right: this really is none of your business. Not a stitch of it. This isn't some witch hunt. We've reviewed many scenarios.'

Hildur noticed the flipchart behind Sainio. She stood, walked over, and grabbed the marker. 'Give me ten minutes,' she said. 'After that I'll get out of your hair. I promise.'

Sainio swivelled her chair around and rolled her eyes, but seemed to give in.

Hildur drew the café car park where the two bodies had been found. She added a nearby fell and two paths to the sketch.

'The eyewitness saw Jakob here at a quarter to seven on the night in question,' Hildur said, stabbing the paper with the marker. 'I don't know whether the autopsy is complete yet, but I bet the findings will support the eyewitness account of the time of death. I'm sure you've gone through Filip's and Lena's call data? Lena has a small child. She probably made some calls about him after school.'

Sainio tapped her fingers against her knee. Hildur could tell she'd piqued the detective sergeant's interest. 'Wait a minute. How did you know the time of day?'

'I visited said eyewitness. Twice. Sari Meri saw Jakob at the scene, but she didn't see the shooting. She didn't even see Lena and Filip's vehicle arrive.'

Sainio was on the verge of saying something, but Hildur jumped in first. She quickly shared everything she knew about the case up to that point. At the gym, Sainio had told her about the fibre samples, the footprints that matched Jakob's shoes, and Jakob's fingerprints on the seatbelt pulled across Lena's torso. The gun had been abandoned under the car, and there weren't any fingerprints on it. Gunshot residue samples hadn't been taken in time, because Jakob hadn't been brought in for questioning until the following morning. GSR didn't have much sticking power; traces typically vanished from a shooter's hands within hours.

'Jakob was there in that car park. Someone had lured him there with a text message.' Hildur paused: a moment of calm before the storm. 'You're probably wondering how I knew to talk to Sari Meri, who told me about her.'

Sainio stared at Hildur without replying.

'The overly friendly police officer Simo Saari, who works at the station in Kolari.'

Sainio immediately interjected: 'Very part time; no more than a few shifts a week. He hasn't worked for us much lately. He's had some challenges in his personal life. Picks up shifts here and there.'

Hildur wrote *Police Officer in Kolari* on the flipchart and tapped the words with the tip of the marker. 'Sari Meri offered herself as an eyewitness, didn't she?'

Hildur studied Sainio's face but couldn't read anything there. The detective sergeant's expression was so blank that Hildur suspected her nose hairs had frozen.

'Sari was invited to the car park at a quarter to seven. She'd been told all she had to do was show up, remember what she saw, and note the time.'

Hildur had realised Sari had made a ten-minute mistake. She'd been caught in a lie when she said she'd hurried off to fetch her package. The truth was she saw Jakob at the scene and left before the shooting took place.

'That café car park was really buzzing the night of the shooting,' Hildur said. 'Their donuts must be something else.'

Sainio had pulled a pencil from the pen stand and was twirling it in her fingers 'What exactly are you driving at?'

'Officer Saari misled the police and used this so-called eyewitness to do so. The gun found under the car, the Glock 17. That's a police service weapon, isn't it?'

Hildur was surprised to get a clear answer from Sainio. 'These days the Finnish police use Walther pistols. The Glocks are gradually being replaced, but there are still some out there.'

Hildur nodded. 'I can't prove it, but I'm pretty sure the gun is Simo's.'

Sainio exploded. She stood and slammed down the pencil so hard it bounced across the piles of papers on the desk before rolling to the floor. 'You have some nerve, coming in here with these fabrications!'

Hildur raised both palms and asked Sainio to calm down. 'There's more. After I finish you can throw me out yourself, if you want.' Hildur tapped the toe of her shoe against the floor. 'None of you have revealed the identity of the eyewitness to Jakob?'

Sainio snorted. 'Of course not!'

Hildur understood. A suspect couldn't be allowed to interfere in an investigation. The witness's name would eventually be public knowledge. It would appear in the preliminary investigation report, unless keeping it confidential was necessary to protect the witness or their loved ones or if the maximum sentence for the crime under investigation exceeded seven years. Jakob would have learned Sari's identity from the report once it was completed. But it would have been better for everyone if he'd been able to see the name immediately.

'Sari Regina Meri is Jakob's former girlfriend from years ago. She began a new life after discovering Jakob was involved with someone else at the same time. She changed her last name and began using her legal first name.'

Hildur told Sainio about the difficult end to Jakob and Regina's relationship and Jakob's cheating. 'Regina is the little sister of the Mikael who drowned in the lake,' Hildur added.

Sainio gave a slight nod. She must have known. After all, she'd looked into Mikael's family when investigating his drowning.

'Are you claiming Jakob is suffering from some nice-guy syndrome, and as a result of that two people are dead?' There was no amusement in Sainio's laugh.

Hildur ignored the reaction and let out a deep sigh. 'Sari assumed her testimony would put Jakob in jail. She wanted to get revenge.'

'Giving false testimony is known as perjury,' Sainio snapped.

Hildur didn't see the point in arguing over trivialities. She settled for a nod.

'You hinted something about Simo's weapon a moment ago. What sleeve did you pull that card out of?'

Hildur wrote four letters on the flipchart: S, L, F and J.

'Did you know your colleague Simo owns a company called Handsome Homes?' Without waiting for an answer, she explained what she knew about the company that had invested major sums in real estate.

She pointed at the F. The mining company's new, inquisitive VP of social responsibility had become aware of potential problems of the mine having once served as an unofficial dump. Filip had contacted the police to ask if a criminal complaint had ever been lodged over the illicit waste, or if the illegal site had ever been investigated.

'My guess, and Jakob's, too, is that when Filip contacted the Kolari police station to ask about the old investigation into the dump, the officer who took the call was our friend Simo. I'm sure you can confirm who was on duty from your system.'

Hildur remembered what Jakob had said about the county council: 'Simo also sits on a council committee with several individuals who work at the mine. He could have heard about Filip's questions there too.'

Sainio stared doubtfully at Hildur's drawing but didn't comment.

Hildur continued. 'Simo isn't from here, but he's lived here a long time. He knew Sari.'

The address label on the newspaper at Sari's home had read Handsome Homes. Simo had given Sari the paper.

Hildur underlined the S and explained how the heartbroken Sari had shared her life story with Simo years before, including the role Jakob had played. Filip's snooping looked like it might delay the opening of the mine, which would have been a catastrophe for Simo, who'd probably borrowed the money for Handsome Homes's real estate transactions. Simo had read the article in the local paper about Lena and Filip and realised the connection to Jakob. Sari had indicated that Simo had also been aware of Jakob's custody battle.

'People were gossiping about it. Simo knew about the hearing and volunteered when a request was submitted for two officers to provide security. Apparently, he'd hoped he'd see or hear something that would be of use to him. And his wish came true.'

Hildur circled the letters L and J. 'Simo put two and two together and decided to take action. He came up with a plan that would rid him of the guy who was putting the brakes on the mine. Filip's wife Lena had to disappear with him. Jakob was made out to be the killer, because Sari had a motive for revenge too.'

When she reached the end of her speech, Hildur drew a breath. She looked first at her illustration and then at Sainio.

Sainio seemed to hesitate, then reached down to pick up the pencil that had fallen to the floor. 'The motive for the double murder feels a little clumsy.'

Hildur capped the marker and placed it in the tray. People did stupid things sometimes.

'Mine money is big money to a little guy. Once greed wraps its tentacles around you, it won't let go. Simo wanted to get rich.'

'Dammit dammit dammit,' Sainio finally said with sigh.

Hildur lowered a white envelope to Sainio's desk. 'I'm sure everything I've said will be easy to confirm by bringing in Simo and Sari for questioning. Just to be sure, I prepared a summary of my suspicions. Delivered in a white envelope, as promised.'

Sainio put on her glasses, took the envelope, opened it, and began browsing through the documents.

'I don't think you'll be requiring my presence here any longer.'

As Hildur walked out of the office, she glanced at the clock on the wall. She'd still make her flight.

Chapter 63

The departures hall was packed: families, groups of young people, solo business travellers carrying laptop bags. Ski bags and wheeled suitcases occasionally ended up on collision courses and crashed into each other. Alternating whiffs of sweat and perfume wafted past. The Christmas lights in the terminal's windows gave off a soft light. The illuminated advertisements on the walls depicted various iterations of snowy terrain, log cabins and red-cheeked, white-bearded Santa Clauses with their reindeer.

Hildur returned the car keys to the rental agency's desk, then went to the self-service kiosk to get her boarding pass and luggage tag. The backpack weighed heavily on her back. The kiosk requested the reservation number and asked the standard baggage questions. After it was satisfied, it printed out the necessary documents.

Hildur was just attaching the long, skinny tag to the handle of her backpack when she felt a hand on her wrist. She instinctively grabbed the assailant's arm with her right hand and twisted. Nearby travellers' heads swivelled around when they heard the resulting howl.

'Anton, what on earth?' Hildur let go of Anton but didn't apologise.

'Damn, you're fast,' Anton said, rubbing his wrist. His face broke out in the now-familiar lopsided grin. His lips curled a little higher on the left as his left eyelid drooped.

'Why do you go around scaring people like that?' Hildur asked, hoisting her backpack onto the self-service baggage belt.

Anton grabbed the bag so the belt wouldn't carry it off. Sighs of frustration erupted behind them. The line wasn't moving.

'I'm sorry I didn't tell you I knew who you were. I thought maybe you had some rule against getting involved with the friend of friend.'

Anton kept holding the backpack with one hand as he explained he'd come to Kittilä to do some shopping after leaving the pub. 'Stay a little longer.'

Hildur removed Anton's hand from the backpack and let the reader scan the bar code on the luggage tag. The backpack started gliding down the belt.

'I do have one rule,' Hildur said, reaching for the shoulder bag at her feet. 'I never hold up a line.'

She and Anton moved aside, and Anton stepped in toward Hildur. Any closer, and his pupils would have touched hers.

'Marry me.'

Hildur burst out laughing. She was laughing so hard she bent over double. 'We've met twice. And you've proposed twice.'

Anton's left eye narrowed to a slit as his smile broadened. 'And there won't be a third time.' Then his face grew serious.

Hildur nodded. Not a bad-looking guy and a lot of fun. His face was sincere, his body language calm. Anton felt timeless. A solitary adventurer who whistled as he traversed the wilderness on his snowmobile. She found him intriguing, of course she did.

'I'm sure you know the two things you should never do,' Hildur said, after her laughter died.

Anton turned aside and started laughing in turn. 'You remember that stupid saying.'

Hildur remembered everything Anton had told her. 'Never take a reindeer from the north or a wife from the south. In the end, they both always go back.'

Anton walked at Hildur's side to the security check. 'At least stay a little longer. You and I can get to know each other better. We'll go have a look at those reindeer.'

'I can't.'

Anton stopped. He looked calm and determined. Then he firmly hugged her farewell and wished her safe travels.

Hildur made her way to the gate. She passed a café and a little shop selling leather bags. There was a quiet spot next to the wall. Hildur lowered herself to the wooden seat and leaned against the tall backrest.

She didn't want to think. A moment without words. No talking, no listening.

Two children were building a tower at the play area near the gate. The older one was stacking some wooden rings. The younger child's demeanour spoke of frustration: the older child was stacking the rings in the wrong order. He'd put the smallest ring at the bottom and the next smallest on top of it. The younger child said something to the older one, and the older one replied. Judging by the body language, the disagreement wasn't escalating. The smaller child waited for the older one to put the last ring in place. Then she grabbed the completed tower in both hands and flipped it over, so the fattest ring was against the tabletop. The little one beamed in satisfaction. All was as it should be.

Hildur started. It had felt nice, sitting on the wooden chair and letting her mind wander. And then the realisation popped into her head. A few days before, she'd departed on a journey and left the unfinished drama behind. And while travelling, she'd found something to take home with her.

Now she knew what had happened back in Iceland.

Chapter 64

Reykjavík, December 2021

Beta glanced at the woman sitting across the table from her. She was having a hard time looking at Rósa Holm. And it wasn't because of Rósa's damaged skin. Beta had seen that before: a face burned by acid, injuries resulting from fires and assaults. The harder thing was seeing the physical similarity between Rósa and her sister. It was too obvious. Hildur and Rósa had the same build. Broad shouldered and big handed. Thick, dark hair, a keen, direct gaze, a straight nose and a firm jaw. Beta felt as if her colleague were sitting in the interrogation room with her.

Hildur had just arrived in Iceland. She'd called as soon as the plane landed and said she'd be coming directly to the police station on Hverfisgata.

Beta glanced at the clock on the wall. They wouldn't wait for Hildur, because she wouldn't be able to participate in the interrogation or even observe it through the one-way mirror anyway. As a police officer, Beta couldn't share the tiniest shred of what she learned during questioning with Hildur. Things had been rocky enough at the Metropolitan Reykjavík police department as it was. Internal investigations and changes in job descriptions had introduced a wariness to the organisation. Those elbowing their way up the ranks were waiting with bated breath for someone higher on the ladder to make a mistake, stumble or be transferred. Beta counted on Rósa's public defender Hilmar

Valgeirsson to keep Hildur informed as to updates on the case. That was allowed.

Hilmar was one of the public defenders regularly assigned to suspects who didn't have legal representation of their own. The childless Hilmar could usually answer the call when it came. He was always at work, home or the gym. His nickname at the station was 'the cab driver'. When you called, he showed up.

The subdued-seeming Rósa was at her solicitor's side, near one corner of the square table. She looked small next to the massive bulk of the former freestyle wrestler. Tumi sat across from them at Beta's side.

Tumi led the interrogation; Beta kept the minutes. The personal information and mandatory formalities went smoothly. Rósa gave her real name, stated she was a Danish citizen, and said she had a Faroe Islands passport. Then Tumi told Rósa what she was suspected of. She firmly denied guilt.

'I have no idea what you're talking about.'

Tumi listed the assaults that had taken place in Iceland over the past few weeks and the homicides where the victims had links to the animal welfare group.

'All the victims were aware of the trade in mares' blood.'

At the mention of mares' blood, Rósa stirred.

Tumi coughed drily and continued: 'Were you at Eyjafjörður on the fourth of December?'

Rósa glanced at her lawyer, who nodded. 'Yes.'

'At the Snæfellsnes peninsula on December eighth? Were you in the village of Grundarfjörður on the evening of that date?'

Rósa conceded again. She said she'd spent a few hours in the village. Had filled up her vehicle at the service station there, among other things.

'Why were you there?'

Hilmar and Rósa exchanged glances. The two of them had spoken privately that morning. Beta was sure Hilmar already knew how Rósa would answer.

'I work with horses. You know that already. I have no reason to lie about it, because there's nothing illegal about what I do. Collecting blood from mares is legal if you follow the rules. If you don't, you're guilty of wrongdoing. But I'm not suspected of violating animal welfare laws, so . . .'

Rósa left the sentence hanging. She swept back the hair that had fallen to her shoulders. Her voice was steady. She spoke clearly and consistently, sat upright and waited for the following question. The look in her eyes wasn't defiant or irritated. Just the opposite; it was genuinely quizzical. She took a sip of water from the plastic cup on the table in front of her. The rim of the cup crumpled in her grip.

'Hveragerði on the tenth of December. Where were you then?'

Rósa reached for the white plastic cup again and drained it. 'I was working for two days in the vicinity of Rangárvallasýsla. I spent the next day returning to Reykjavík. The drive took longer than normal due to the Hellisheiði blizzard,' she said, defiantly eyeing first Tumi and then Beta. 'Why are you asking these questions?'

Tumi spread his arms in a gesture of surrender. Then he leaned forward and began speaking in a calm, steady voice as if talking to a friend. The assault outside the bar in Snæfellsnes, victim's hair burned. The front-door assault in Reykjavík. The hit-and-run in Selfoss. The fatal assault with a baseball bat in Hveragerði. The man who lived in Eyjafjörður and ended up fish food in the Westfjords.

Tumi scratched his head with his left forefinger, as if thinking hard. 'Look. See, you were present in all the locations these crimes took place. A wooden baseball bat was found in your home and has been sent off for analysis. A coil of yellow rope was discovered there too. It looks exactly like the rope used to tie up the victim found in the fish pen. Your vehicle is being combed by forensics as we speak.' Tumi paused and glanced at the notes in front of him. 'And pictures of the Yule Lads were found on the wall of your cabin.'

Tumi continued, explaining the pictures were of the exact same Yule Lads whose stories Rósa had brought to life through her horrific crimes. His voice had constricted. There was no longer any sign of the chatty tone. 'Thanks to your sick games, two people are dead and several have been seriously injured. I think you're looking at a lengthy sentence.'

Rósa stopped twirling the crumpled cup in her hand and lowered it to the table. 'Yule Lads? Now I understand even less what's going on.'

Tumi started telling her about Sausage Swiper, Meat Hook and Door Slammer.

Rósa cut him off with a wave of her hand. 'I remember the stories. It's not like you can forget your childhood.' There was a mocking aggression in her voice. 'Would you like to hear why my face looks like this? I can see you staring at it the whole time. You're probably wondering what on earth happened to that poor woman. You've seen the child protection services reports, I assume? I'm guessing you didn't find the answer there.'

Beta continued writing. The massive Hilmar looked lost at Rósa's side. He whispered something to Rósa, but she didn't listen. Rósa shifted her chair further from him, until she was sitting at the very edge of the table.

'It was an ordinary late-winter day. Not that the time of year really matters, because it was always the same,' Rósa began. She explained how her mother, then corrected herself and said Hulda, was often away for long periods. No one knew where. People would see her walking around the island. Weeks could pass without Hulda speaking to the children or anyone else. 'She just got lost in her own world,' Rósa said.

'It was Björk's birthday. We didn't go to school, because the school taxi drivers were on strike. Björk asked for her favourite meal. Deep-fried cod. Hulda wasn't home, so I took a pot from the cupboard . . .'

Rósa had filleted the fish, dipped the fillets in egg, then patted both sides in flour seasoned with black pepper and salt.

Beta was surprised by the level of detail Rósa still remembered.

Björk had sat at the table doing crafts and admiring her big sister's kitchen skills. Rósa had hoped she'd know how to prepare the fish correctly. When the oil was hot enough, Rósa had dropped the breaded fish into the oil with a slotted spoon.

Beta listen closely to every word as she recorded Rósa's story. The late-winter day came to life in Rósa's telling. Beta could see the two little girls in the kitchen, smell the sweet odour of frying fish.

Rósa had flipped the fish over in the hot oil, then lifted them out onto a big porcelain plate lined with paper towels.

'Björk was so excited about the meal,' Rósa said.

Then there was a pause.

Rósa looked out the window. Her gaze had carried her somewhere far from the interrogation room. Rósa explained she'd lifted the pot of oil off the stove to cool next to the open window. She'd forgotten to straighten the kitchen rug that morning after cleaning up. Her foot caught on the edge of the rug, and the pot's contents flew all over her.

'This is just the visible part,' Rósa said, turning the damaged side of her face toward Tumi and Beta. 'The rest is under my clothes.'

Silence fell over the room. Neither Tumi nor Beta spoke. Rósa stared steadily at them. Hilmar poured himself a cup of water from the glass pitcher.

Rósa broke the silence. 'What else do you want to know?'

Tumi coughed again and looked down at his notes. 'Do you admit you were at these places at these times?' He pushed a sheet of paper across the table, leaving it between Hilmar and Rósa.

Rósa eyed the list row by row and admitted to having been at those places at those times.

'Why go through all this trouble?' Tumi asked.

Rósa just stared at the piece of paper.

Tumi repeated the question.

Rósa's body stiffened. She slammed her palm down on the table. The crumpled plastic cup rolled to the floor. She raised her voice: 'I didn't do anything to those people!'

Hilmar touched Rósa's arm and leaned in to whisper something in her ear. Rósa closed her eyes and nodded. She didn't say anything. During the silence, Hilmar poured himself more water and took a slow sip.

Tumi let his gaze rest on the opposite wall and adjusted his position. Then he repeated the facts calmly and one at a time. Beta continued writing and reflected how strange this all was.

'I think this is what happened,' Tumi said, launching into a monologue.

Tumi guessed Rósa saw Hildur as guilty for what had happened to her and Björk as children. That's why she hadn't wanted to have any contact with her sister and had chosen Hildur's hometown as the starting point for her campaign of threats and fear.

'That man who died of a drug overdose: you planted him at the fish farm, didn't you?'

Rósa simply shook her head.

'The fact that young children were taken from the home they knew, brought to a foreign country, and left there among strangers, was horrible. It caused a trauma.' Tumi said colleagues had helped him recover child protection services records, police reports, and teachers' notes from Rósa's years in the Faroes.

Learning problems, an eating disorder, inexplicable bruises on both children, violent behaviour in school, running away on multiple occasions . . . It had made for hard reading. Child protection services hadn't really done much on the sisters' behalf. Hulda had probably tried her best as a foster mother, but her best hadn't been good enough.

'What happened to you two as children wasn't your fault,' Tumi said, attempting to make eye contact with Rósa.

Rósa shot Tumi a quick glance, then lowered her gaze back to the table. Her shoulders rose and fell in time to her breathing. The movement put Beta in mind of a boat riding the waves.

'It wasn't your fault. Or Hildur's. She didn't choose to stay behind. She was a victim of circumstance, just like you. Adults made bad decisions.'

Rósa started picking at her cuticles. Beta noted the weathered skin at her knuckles, the rough hands used to outside work.

'You all have it so good you don't even realise it. You have jobs, cars and homes, right?' Rósa said. 'I have to slave away outdoors every day and do things I don't even want to do. But I don't have a choice. This is the only job that pays enough for me to keep a roof over my head, eat and pay off old debts.'

'What debts? Tumi asked.

Rósa said she had no intention of revealing that.

Tumi glanced at Rósa's foot, which was sticking out from under the table. 'You avoid putting weight on that foot. What's wrong with it?'

'Osteoarthritis in the knee. I'm saving up for that, too; I still can't afford a private operation,' Rósa said, then laconically added: 'And I'm going to fix this face of mine first.'

Tumi told Rósa of the eyewitness who'd seen her at the bar in Grundarfjörður. An individual who favoured one foot was seen in the company of the victim shortly before the crime took place.

Rósa nodded warily and stopped picking at her skin. She wrapped her arms around herself as if she were cold. 'Yes. I was there,' she confessed.

Beta saw Hilmar start. He was an experienced solicitor. But apparently this piece of information had caught him off guard, and he hadn't been able to conceal his surprise.

'Yes, I was at the bar that night. I went and had a beer after a long day on the road. I stood at a table at the back of the bar.'

Hilmar whispered something in Rósa's ear and suggested a short break in the interrogation. But Rósa declined; she wanted to continue.

'But I wasn't the only one there. I didn't go there alone,' Rosa said. Every time she spoke, she turned the healthy side of her face toward whoever she was talking to. Beta wasn't sure if it was a learned behaviour or coincidence.

Rósa said she'd almost never travelled alone for work. She'd been alone the day before, but that had been an exception. Whenever possible, she liked to have company with her in the car. The changing terrain was nicer to experience with someone else. Rósa said she'd had company that evening when she'd been sent to bus tables at the dinner for the animal welfare activists too.

'So who was with you, then?'

Rósa shifted her weight off her chair and nudged the chair up to the table again.

'We were taken away from here as children. Now that I have to criss-cross this island for work, it feels like a second chance to get to know my real home.'

Beta kept writing, eyes glued to the screen. She felt like tapping out Rósa's answer then and there, because she knew what Rósa was about to say. Hildur had told Beta the same thing that morning on the phone, but Beta hadn't believed her. No, even though Hildur was sure about her hunch. The timing matched. Björk had driven to Hildur's place in the Westfjords around the same time Luka's body had been discovered in the sea. When Hildur visited Björk, Björk had just arrived home, supposedly from a work gig. Hlín had been assaulted on the job that morning. Björk had constantly asked Hildur detailed questions about her profession. But it hadn't been out of curiosity; she'd been gathering information.

Hildur had understood. The protected had become the protector.

Rósa lowered her hands to the table and calmly said: 'Björk. She's always gone every place with me.'

Chapter 65

Keflavík International Airport, March 2022

The snow had melted from the lava fields. The volcanic expanse that went on for kilometres pulsed in murky shades, craggy and grey. Most of what was visible from the car's windows was black rock void of any plant life. Away at the horizon, a few volcanos rose from the terrain.

'How are you doing?' Rósa asked, lighting a cigarette. Hildur unrolled Brenda's front windows. She couldn't stand cigarette smoke in her vehicle. Hildur had come to notice over the past few months that there was no point asking Rósa to not smoke. She wouldn't listen. The grass skirt of the hula dancer on the dash flew up to her ears as the wind blasted through her namesake Land Cruiser.

'Well enough, I guess,' she shouted over the rush of the wind.

The afternoon news broadcast was blaring from the radio. The news anchor reported on climbing inflation and pressure on the Central Bank to raise interest rates. Hildur turned off the radio. The Helsinki flight would be landing in fifteen minutes. Jakob was returning to Iceland, and Hildur was driving to the airport to pick him up. Work had prevented Guðrún from joining, but she'd be waiting when Jakob and Hildur arrived in Ísafjörður that evening.

Simo Saari had been convicted of two murders and sentenced to life in prison. Jakob had followed the trial and communicated the main developments to his colleagues in Iceland. Sari Meri had changed her statement and avoided perjury charges. In addition to her testimony, the murder weapon had been a key piece of evidence against Simo Saari. He'd only meant to kill Filip, who'd been lured to the car park with the promise of documents about the illicit dumping at the mine, but as Lena had happened to be in the car, he'd killed them both.

When Jakob had called the day before yesterday and confirmed his return to Iceland, Hildur had jumped for joy. Jumping for joy wasn't something she realised she was capable of. The news had felt especially nice, as the year had got off to a heavy start. Björk had been arrested and jailed on suspicion of perpetrating the 'horse vampire' crime spree. That was the term the media used to refer to the case. The case had served up an incredibly juicy story for journalists. Mentions of Rósa and her involvement had made it into in-depth articles about the trade in mares' blood. Hildur had got her share of publicity too. Stories that touched on the relationship between the three sisters had wired the imaginations of editors whose staffs churned out online news to completely new frequencies.

TRAGIC FAMILY SAGA FROM THE WESTFJORDS: ONE DETECTIVE, TWO CRIMINALS AND PARENTS WHO DIED YOUNG.

Hildur had taken sick leave during the most intense news cycles. She'd packed her surfboard and toured the Westfjords' bays, seeking comfort in the sea. When the worst of the media storm had ebbed, she'd returned to work. She and Rósa visited Björk every couple of weeks, sometimes more often. Considering the circumstances, Björk seemed to be managing well. But Hildur couldn't help worrying about her sister.

Another good piece of new year's news had been Jónas's resignation. The Icelandic embassy in Washington had offered him project-based work doing PR for the country. Jónas had accepted the job. Of course. Jónas loved being attached to the embassy. The mere mention of it elicited respect and admiration among listeners. The job of chief of police for the Westfjords was open again. Not a single application had been received. Beta had urged Hildur to apply. But before Hildur gave it any thought, she'd decided to take all the overtime she'd accumulated. She was going to fly to Hawaii for three weeks of surfing. Anton had promised to join her for the vacation. The thought made Hildur smile. Life couldn't permanently consist solely of surfing and screwing, but maybe it could for a little while.

Hildur rolled up the windows. 'I still haven't decided whether to apply for that position,' she said, glancing in the side mirror. Some loser in a sports car was riding her tail. She was driving eighty-five kilometres an hour in a ninety kilometre an hour zone. Hildur huffed in frustration and stepped on the accelerator.

'I'd apply, if I were you. You'll make more money.'

'Money isn't everything,' Hildur began, then immediately softened her message. She suspected Rósa was having financial problems. She hadn't spoken openly about her circumstances yet, just told Hildur she was managing. 'What I mean is, I don't want to take responsibility for other people. I just want to do my work, and that's it.'

Rósa took a little freezer bag from her pocket and dropped her cigarette butt in it. 'I get it. That's why I like my job. I get to work alone and set my own hours.'

Hildur didn't reply. She didn't want to rock the boat by talking about things that would annoy Rósa, so she just nodded encouragingly. Rósa was still making the rounds of horse farms, collecting blood. She claimed to be working exclusively for an

Icelandic company that developed hormone medications. The company had invited journalists to visit its horse farms in an effort to transparently show interested parties the proper way to collect blood. It also wanted to show how well the animals were treated. The company had insisted the horses wouldn't suffer; a local anesthetic was used and only a small amount of blood was collected. Veterinarians always performed the procedure. Blood was only taken from horses used to being handled by humans, not from half-wild outdoor animals who panicked around people. Surveillance cameras and investing in the beasts' welfare. *What, they're not offering the horses the services of masseurs?* Hildur had thought to herself. To her ears, the corporate messaging had sounded too calculated. The slogans had definitely been penned by some PR wizard. But maybe they were telling the truth. Who knew?

'Should we go visit Björk again next week?' Hildur asked as she steered Brenda into the roundabout. They were almost at the airport.

'Sounds good. Meet at the petrol station?'

Hildur nodded. Visiting hours started at five in the evening. She would fly from the fjords to Reykjavík and rent a car. They'd developed a tradition of having a coffee at a little service station just outside the Reykjavík suburbs. It was a little over half an hour's drive from the service station to Litla-Hraun, the prison where Björk was being held.

'Do you think Björk will be convicted?' Rósa asked softly, looking out the passenger window.

Hildur was pretty sure she would be, but she still couldn't say so out loud. 'I don't want to guess. We'll know soon enough. I think the decision will be handed down before Easter.'

Björk had confessed to everything. Luka had been dead when she'd found him. She said she'd come to scare him, but when she got to the farm, he'd been lying on the ground outside the stable. Björk said she'd put his body in the boot of her car and driven to Ísafjörður, which she'd been planning on visiting the following day. Björk had claimed in court that hanging the body in the fish pen had just been an off-the-wall whim. When it came to the veterinarian in Hveragerði, Björk had denied murdering him. She'd only meant to hurt him, not kill him. The judge would decide how Björk would be sentenced for her deeds.

It seemed like a clear-cut case, but just as with the accusations made against Jakob, there was something about the whole thing that bothered Hildur. The charges felt unbelievable. Amid the consternation and grief, Hildur had – and it had come as a surprise to herself as well – felt a pride of sorts in her little sister. Björk had helped Rósa, and from the Faroes, no less. She'd arranged a vehicle and phone for her sister, as well as everything else requiring identification. Björk had offered Rósa a wing to shelter under while she lived her unconventional life. After Björk had moved to Iceland, the sisters had been in frequent contact.

Hildur veered out of the roundabout at the third exit. The airport was just a couple of kilometres away now. Low-flying jets appeared in the sky. The flights from European cities landed at about this time.

Rósa reached into her pocket for her cigarettes again.

'Can you wait till we're there?' Hildur asked in frustration.

Rósa shook her head and pulled a smoke from the pack. 'You should try losing your temper. It might do you some good. I don't know if you've noticed, but you can be wound pretty tight sometimes. If you don't ever lose your temper, you're going to explode someday, and it's going to be ugly,' Rósa said, placing the cigarette between her lips.

'Don't light that,' Hildur said more loudly.

Rósa pulled her lighter from her pocket and struck a light while looking directly at Hildur. 'Try harder. It's not going to kill you.'

'Damn it, stop fucking smoking in my car!' Hildur roared, beating her steering wheel in a rage. 'Stop it, stop it, stop it!' Luckily the road was straight, and she maintained control of Brenda.

A silence descended over the vehicle. It sounded light.

Rósa put the lighter back in her pocket and the cigarette back in the pack. 'That was a decent start,' she said, smiling broadly. The strangeness of the moment provoked Hildur to laughter too.

According to the screens hanging from the ceiling, the flight from Helsinki had landed ten minutes ago. The first of the luggage was circling the carousel.

Hildur found a spot next to a pillar to wait. Rósa had gone off in search of coffee. The minutes seemed to drag. Hildur shifted her weight to her other foot. Twice already she'd thought she'd caught a glimpse of Jakob, but both times it had been some other guy wearing a sweater. Then the sliding doors opened. Jakob's hair was pulled back in a neat bun, and his beard was trimmed. He was wearing a grey sweater. He looked better than he had in ages. He was pushing a fully loaded baggage cart with one hand. His other hand was holding the hand of a little boy in a bright green parka.

Something about the sight was so moving that Hildur had to hide behind the pillar for a moment. This was the second time she was meeting Jakob at the airport. A few years ago, she'd driven to the airport in Ísafjörður to pick up a lost-looking knitter. It was happening again, except now she knew the man. Back then they'd both been alone. Now they weren't.

The district court in Rovaniemi had just handed down their decision: Jakob had sole custody. Matias had been allowed to move to Iceland with his father.

Jakob let go of the baggage cart and waved. When he got close enough, he grabbed Hildur's shoulder and squeezed. Rósa stood off to the side, watching them. She smiled as she introduced herself. Then she handed one of the three coffee cups to Jakob and offered to push the baggage cart.

Once they were in the car, Hildur took off her gloves, glanced at Jakob, then focused her gaze on the lava field behind him and the roiling sea beyond. A jet emerged from the mass of silver-grey clouds as it made its descent. New people were arriving on the island again. New people, new opportunities for catastrophe, happiness, or something completely ordinary.

Neither of them spoke. No words were needed. Life was good at that moment, and they both relished it.

For the most part, life was relatively uneventful. But when the continents shifted, many things changed at once. Even then, you had to focus on one thing at a time. They had a long drive home to the Westfjords ahead of them. Everything else would have to wait.

Once Jakob had buckled his seatbelt, his phone pinged, signalling an incoming text message. He pulled the phone from his pocket, and as he read the message alarm spread across his face.

Hildur was about to ask what was wrong, but just then Matias pointed at the low-flying jet outside the window and laughed. The distress evaporated from Jakob's face. Hildur decided to let her questions about the message drop; she'd ask Jakob about it later. Because for the first time in a long time, she felt incredibly light. Just now, everything was as it should be.

Epilogue

Baden, Germany, June 2022

The sun was beating down. The little restaurant was in the middle of the wine region, only a few kilometres from the French border. The picturesque patio gave onto a view of nearly vertical slopes where grape vines climbed stubbornly toward the baking sun. Baden was one of the warmest areas in the country. The sun shone more here than anywhere else in Germany.

A man, about fifty, had informally rolled up the sleeves of his white dress shirt past his elbows. The discreet silver Rolex looked stylish against his tanned wrist. Rolex Man poured a drop of pale red wine into a glass and handed it to a woman in a white sundress.

'Spätburgunder.'

The silver bracelets at her wrist clinked as she raised the glass to her lips. She nodded in approval.

'My wife is a better judge of wine than I am,' Rolex Man explained, filling four glasses. 'She always tastes for us.'

'Spätburgunder is our Pinot Noir. Pale, light and acidic,' his wife said, raising her glass to her lips. 'A superb but difficult wine that not everyone is capable of appreciating.'

Árni and María raised their glasses to their lips. Neither understood much, if anything, about wine, but they both loved new experiences. Over the past few years, they'd had the chance to go on all sorts of adventures: snorkelling in Fiji, hiking in the Alps, hang-gliding in the Maldives. They only returned to Iceland in the summer, and their stays there had grown shorter and shorter over the years. The staff handled the farm and the company. That gave them time to focus on all sorts of other things, now that they were wealthy enough to live off their investments.

Árni studied the contents of the plate before him. The selection of charcuterie and cheeses ordered to accompany the wine interested him more than the details of how the wine was made.

'A third of all German Spätburgunder is grown in Baden. The varietal's first vines were planted in this area back in the 800s. That was about the time people in your part of the world were preserving your food in urea, no?'

Árni laughed and popped a slice of sausage in his mouth. The cultural one-upmanship practised by their Central European friends was a familiar schtick. It went in one ear and out the other. The four of them were conducting business, and things would go more smoothly if he didn't allow stupid jokes to get under his skin.

Árni wiped his greasy fingers on a napkin, took a long sip of the light red wine, and looked seriously at Rolex Man. 'Shall we continue where we left off?'

Rolex Man and his wife exchanged a quick glance across the table. The time for small talk had passed.

'Of course. The meat industry is growing by leaps and bounds. Our Chinese partner has hinted at significant opportunities,' Rolex Man said, his finger drawing a circle on the white tablecloth. Árni wasn't sure what the circle was supposed to represent, but he didn't want to interrupt his associate.

Meat production was a growing business, especially in Asia. Operations were increasing in size, and their systems were being optimised. The Chinese needed massive amounts of hormone products for pig farms.

'Demand exceeds supply many times over. We can raise prices significantly and still sell everything you can collect.'

Árni and María nodded in satisfaction.

Rolex Man's wife interjected. Her raspy, dramatic voice was a match for her striking appearance.

'Blood farms are becoming a billion-euro business. The veterinary pharmaceutical giants rely on the raw material. It can only be collected from horses, and that's one thing you have plenty of. A cool climate, healthy stock, and a high level of hygiene guarantee the product's superiority.'

Árni and María exchanged smiles. Their future looked bright. People could claim what they wanted, but for them economic success brought peace of mind.

'Has the dust from that newspaper article settled yet?' Rolex Man asked, pouring himself and Árni more wine. The women still had some in their glasses.

The sun had slid out from behind a shadow. María put on her sunglasses, dabbed on some sunscreen lip balm, and smacked her lips together: 'Yes. It's old news.'

Hlín Jónsdóttir had published an article about Iceland's blood farms earlier that spring, and the story had caused a huge scandal. It had been cited in the international media countless times too. The Icelandic public had been infuriated by the poor treatment of animals, and the tourism companies were seething, because the stories had landed a huge blow on Iceland's image. The authorities had promised more monitoring, and the possibility of stricter laws had been flashed in Parliament.

The outrage had lasted the usual three weeks. Then, as typical in Iceland, a new scandal had come along, and older matters were forgotten.

'Look, Icelanders are like horses,' María continued with a cloying smile. 'When the weather's bad, we turn our backsides to the wind and wait. After the storm has passed, we forget all about it and frolic, enjoying the fine weather.'

Rolex Man and his wife laughed heartily, and the wife leaned forward, directing her words at María: 'It was a good idea to include those Yule Lad stories. They temporarily derailed the investigation, which gave us more time to get our own strike teams in order.'

'María is as sharp as a butcher's knife,' Árni said, briefly stroking his wife's bare arm. Then he turned to the Germans, a serious look on his face: 'Do we have to find a replacement for our friend with the burned face? She was so damn good. Our network's most efficient bloodsucker to date.'

'Of course we'll keep her,' Rolex Man said. He knew for a fact Rósa didn't want to stop. 'That girl owes so much money that she'll be happy to continue working for us. And now that the general public is convinced animal welfare issues are back on track, she has all the room she needs to manoeuvre. The media never publish two big stories back to back on the same topic.'

'It's a good thing Rósa called us from Sel to let us know Luka had caught on to gestating mares vanishing,' Árni said.

María nodded: 'In addition to being far too nosy, he was also far too self-righteous.'

Árni and María had decided to frighten Luka into silence. When the person hired to do it had arrived at Sel farm, Luka was found semi-conscious outside the stables. The contact information for all those in Luka's circle of animal rights activists had been found in Luka's phone, along with chats revealing who was aware of what had been going on at the horse farms and how much they knew.

Árni guffawed. 'It was like a fairy-tale ending.'

They took a moment to admire the view from the terrace. The sky was blue with no hint of clouds. The grape vines stirred in the gentle breeze. A bird sang somewhere.

Rolex Man's wife broke the silence. 'Does she think her sister was behind everything?' she asked in a lowered voice, almost a whisper.

There was only one other party at the restaurant, and they were seated so far away there was no way they could hear. But you could never play it too safe.

María nodded. 'That's what's so ingenious about the scheme. They both think the other one committed the assaults. They'll protect each other to the end. They want to do good, but everything they've done has led to misery. They don't understand that too much protection is harmful. The cop sister is looking after them both. And we have eyes on all three of them.'

Rolex Man drained his glass and spread his arms victoriously over his head. His tone was good-natured now: 'Let them do what they will, for their misfortune is our good fortune.'

Árni chuckled, took the bottle, and poured more of the blood-red wine. Then he raised his glass and proposed a toast:

'To the protectors among us.'

A Note from the Author

The Shadow of the Northern Lights is dedicated to my mother. She died of breast cancer the week I started writing this book and a month before the previous book in the *Hildur* series, *The Grave in the Ice*, was published in Finland. While in this world, she never learned what happened to Rósa and Björk. But maybe she has her ways of finding out after the fact. Mothers always have aces up their sleeve.

Although Hildur could be my friend, she's a work of fiction. Most of the locations mentioned in *The Shadow of the Northern Lights* are actual places in Iceland and Finland, but the events and characters are inventions.

Regarding the characters' names: In Iceland, patronymics and matronymics are generally used instead of traditional surnames. In this system, a child's surname is based on the mother's or father's first name. Because Hildur's father's name was Rúnar, Hildur's surname is Rúnarsdóttir, 'Rúnar's daughter'. When it comes to the residents of northern Finland, I didn't attempt to come up with local surnames.

Mares' blood has been collected and sold in Iceland for decades. Although violations of animal welfare have been associated with the trade in recent years, I want to stress the reported abuses are nowhere near the magnitude depicted in *The Shadow of the Northern Lights*.

Any possible similarities between the book and reality are happenstance. But that's what life is like: haphazard, wonderful, and sometimes horrific. We bounce between places and collide with each other. Sometimes those collisions have fatal consequences. Sometimes nothing happens. Sometimes we just have to take a chance and hope for the best.

Acknowledgements

My warm and sincere thanks to all those helpful individuals who supported me during the writing process. Thank you, Ingibjörg Elín Magnúsdóttir and Aldís Hilmarsdóttir, for patiently answering my questions about policework in Iceland. Thank you, Antte Lauhamaa, for explaining the day-to-day of policing in Lapland, and thank you, Sami Isoniemi, for telling me about your experiences as a Finnish policeman in Iceland and Finland. Thank you, attorney Jyrki Kuusivaara, for your expertise in international custody cases. Thank you, reindeer herder Jenni Kaaretkoski, for sharing your observations on reindeer herding and other matters. Thank you, Pirita Näkkäläjärvi, for reviewing the sections of text related to Sami culture. Thanks to those numerous parties in Helsinki, Äkäslompolo, Kittilä, and Iceland who have answered my questions about any manner of topics, from the razing of Lapland to mining and Icelandic yarn. A warm thanks to my Instagram followers as well, for helping me with questions about Finnish Lapphunds and Norwegian pronunciation.

Thanks to my office-mate at the coworking space Kohta in Äkäslompolo. Thank you to my coworking space friend in Iceland, knitwear designer Sigríður Sif Gylfadóttir, for helping me with details related to knitting – and helping Jakob create a sweater out of double Plötulopi yarn for his friend! It turned out beautifully.

If any mistakes have made their way into the book, they are naturally mine.

Thanks to my publishing house, WSOY. A particular thanks to publisher Anna-Riikka Carlson for your enthusiasm about the *Hildur* series and giving it a chance! My rock-solid, gold-hearted executive editor Hanna Pudas – you're the best! On top of everything else, I'd like to thank you for your local knowledge of Äkäslompolo and Kolari and the shared moments there. Thank you for proofreading, Irene Vehanen. A thanks to my fellow Satu, Satu Sirkiä, for the fantastic marketing and communications work on the *Hildur* series and for looking after my well-being. You have been an irreplaceable support in every way over these past few years. I'd also like to thank CEO Timo Julkunen, marketing and communications director Reetta Miettinen, and the sales team, especially Laura Lyytinen. A warm thanks to Harri Mäki. You – and of course all those books – make every visit to WSOY's KIRJA! bookstore an event.

Thank you to Eleonoora Kirk, my literary agent at Bonnier Rights Finland, for helping to bring the *Hildur* series to an international readership.

Thank you, Lippo Luukkonen, for the legal assistance.

A thanks to the City Theater of Turku and especially Mikko Kouki, Satu Rasila, Anne Rautiainen and Börkur Jónsson, for adapting *Hildur* for the stage.

And a huge thanks to the team at Take Two, the production company developing the *Hildur* television series, especially Eero Hietala, Lasse Koskinen, Sara Nordberg, and Matti Laine, as well as the gang at Sagafilm.

I'm thrilled to see what's going to happen next in Hildur's world.

Thank you loved ones, friends, and above all my family Björgvin, Saga, and Sæla, and my sisters Suvi and Sini. You're the ones I entered this world with, brought into this world, and happened upon here in this world, and I'm eternally grateful.

Satu Rämö
Ísafjörður, September 2023